This book should be returned to any branch of the
Lancashire County Library on or before the date

01-05-15

2 7 OCT 2016

definitely one to watch. Get this book. You will not be
disappointed'   Darynda Jones

By Leigh Evans

The Trouble with Fate
The Thing About Wolves
The Problem with Promises
The Danger of Destiny

For Wild Bill Evans
Ever loved. Ever missed.

Now. . .

Dear Cordelia,

Forgive the crap handwriting. Trowbridge's head is on my lap, which makes letter writing complicated. Don't worry—he's not wounded; he's just taking a short nap. Ever the Alpha, he's claimed my leg, declaring it a preferable pillow to the stone floor. The latter is hard and unforgiving, and in that way it's rather like Merenwyn.

Yes, we made it to the Fae realm.

Big surprise, huh? Last you saw of me, I was walking into the hotel on my way to meet the wolf council. My prospects didn't look good and I wouldn't have bet my last stash of chocolate that Trowbridge and I would have got out of that kangaroo trial. But we did. We proved our innocence to St. Silas and the other members of the council, and Whitlock died.

I killed him myself, Cordelia.

Told you I would.

Anyhow, the end result is that the Ontario wolf pack is no longer in hot water with the council. I don't know if you care about that, but if Creemore is home to you, you can go back to it.

I'm smiling right now because I'm imagining you reading this.

Your face is screwed up into a diva scowl, and if there was a thought bubble over your head it would read: "Who gives a damn about Creemore? What the hell are you doing in Merenwyn?"

I didn't have much of a choice. The council wanted the Safe Passage sealed, and the Fae, with the key to it, dead. I was told to track down the Gatekeeper, kill her, and close the portal forever.

Unspoken in those orders was, "And don't come back."

Trowbridge told me not to go.

He was there at the Peach Pit, handcuffed to the fence surrounding the mini-train enclosure. Though no one actually came out and said it, it was very much a case of "do what we say or your mate gets it."

When St. Silas told me to take the jump, Trowbridge said that we shouldn't. That we should just take our final bows right then and there. He was really pissed with the NAW.

Plus, he knew what was waiting here.

But I had to take the leap.

I did it partially because I was completely convinced that there could be no happily ever after for any of us until the Old Mage's Book of Spells was turned to ash. That thing is a recipe book for bad magic, and it has fallen into the worst hands. Every spell that the old wizard ever conceived, every conjure that he ever produced, every exploration in ele-

mentary magic that he ever made—the details are all there, written in ink by his hand. And now the old man's protégé has begun to read it.

Evil will come your way when the Black Mage reads that last page.

It will come for all.

Tonight, no matter what happens, I've got to see that part of our epic quest through to the end, or little of this makes sense. I have to put a match to the book, see the flames dance, watch its pages burn.

I have to.

Goddess, I wish I was home. Even if it was just to receive a tongue-lashing from you. You're angry, right now, aren't you? Your mouth is a tight line; your shoulders are stiff—you never lose your posture even when you're ready to blow.

Okay, Cordelia: you're right. I also crossed the gates between the two realms to rescue my twin. Before you start cursing me from here to Creemore, remember: I made the original bargain with the Old Mage.

I *set everything in motion.* I'm the person who said, "Why, yes, Old Mage, thank you for asking me to be your nalera. I accept!"

It should be me sharing my body with the old guy. Not my brother.

And before you point out that Lexi was already a wolf-killing drug addict who amounted to a waste of space, you need to understand that when I jumped I believed him to be salvageable. And that I was running on guilt, because I'd briefly experienced being a wizard's nalera.

How do I explain what being a nalera means to someone who hasn't lived it?

Imagine that you wake up blind. After a few seconds of blinking in total darkness, you realize you're posed on a bed of satin wearing your best dress and those tap-taps *that woke you are the sounds of someone hammering in your coffin nails. When you work your throat to summon up a scream nothing comes out. When you tell yourself to move—to hammer on that coffin lid for some help—you can't. You're fully aware, you're mentally struggling, but for all your angst and agony your efforts to free yourself amount to squat.*

That's what sharing your soul with a powerful mage feels like.

You are his bitch. The legs to his will. You do what he says when he tells you to do it. And you have no place to hide because you're sharing your mind with your master. He's inside you. Seeing everything.

I thought I couldn't leave Lexi in that claustrophobic hell.

You're probably muttering, "Yes, you bloody well can. And you should let him take care of the book."

As always, you're right.

But I won't.

As I stood at the portal to Merenwyn, making a decision between certain death and maybe death, I didn't fully understand why I couldn't trust Lexi to burn the encyclopedia of magic on his own. I was more fixated on the fact that I needed to get here, as soon as possible, because if Lexi saw three sunrises in Merenwyn the soul merge would become permanent.

Now, I understand those instincts were there, telling me I must jump, but there's just not enough paper left to explain them to you. And perhaps it's our story: Trowbridge's and mine. Lexi's too . . .

Since I've been in Merenwyn, I've seen the evi-

dence to support the notion that those wards the Old Mage placed over his pages are degrading, flaking away faster than that cheap nail polish you bought and moaned about for a solid week back in the summer. Believe me when I tell you that the old man's apprentice, the Black Mage, has been thumbing his way through the book and that I'm pretty sure he's close to the end of it.

I know what's written on the last page now.

A little late—it's starting to look like we might not win this fight ahead of us.

Which is why I ripped this honking big map out of its frame and penned this long-assed letter on the back of it. If I feel death coming, I'm going to try to get to Threall before I take my last gasp. There I'll put this paper into Mad-one's hands and I'll fill her brain with as many memories as I have of you, so that she'll recognize you when she finds your tree.

Yes, that may take some time, but time passes differently in this realm. Trust me, she'll have the time.

I think you have a soul-bearing tree in Threall. You are a Were, which makes you a descendent of a Merenwyn wolf. And I firmly believe that whether a person is a Fae, a wolf, or a mutt, they have soul in Threall.

I have to believe it.

Mad-one might not be able to harm a mage directly, but she's been dancing to their tune for a very long time and she wants to be free of them. If I fail, I think she'll help you.

If you get this map, you'll know that Trowbridge and I aren't going to be able to fix this. Bad things are coming your way. You have two choices: try to hide or come after the mage. If you decide to come, bring your courage and perfume, as many vials of

iron shavings as you can carry, and this map. Don't
bring Anu with you.
    I never said thank you.
    I should have.
    Also, I never said how I felt about you.

Love,
Hedi

Before...

Chapter One

I've made a few quiet and unsettling personal discoveries.

Sad fact: I've always thought I was a nature lover. Partially because I like flowers and butterflies and the scent of woods—spruce, maple, pine, earth, bark—invariably gives me the warm fuzzies.

Guess what? I'm not Hedi, the tree hugger.

After a while, no matter its girth or its magnificence, a tree is a tree. And a gorge fades from an awe-inspiring visual to a thing placed there with the sole intent of frustrating the shit out of you.

Other things this city dweller has placed high on the hate list during her first day in Merenwyn: almost invisible flying bugs that make a peculiar humming noise as they zoom in for a snack of my Fae-sweet blood; heat rashes in sensitive places; prickers that try to pierce my baby-soft soles.

Believe it or not, I'm starting to miss Creemore.

And cars. Those I *really* miss.

You see? This is the problem with epic quests. No matter what's on the list, the damn things seem to come with gritty realities that just drain all the epic out of them. For instance, the necessity of wrapping my shoe-deprived feet with the sleeves torn from my mate's sweatshirt because Trowbridge and I traversed the Safe Passage into the Fae world without any travel preparations—my shoes, a box of matches, an industrial-sized bottle of DEET, a case of PowerBars, a roll of toilet paper—or, for that matter, any discussion.

There'd been no time for it.

I'd vaulted through the Fae portal first, all hell-bent on rescuing my twin, Lexi, and the world. Since then, I've had a few hours to think about that leap. And I've asked myself—was that a piece of heroism or what?

Unfortunately, the answer is "hell no."

My hop, skip, and jump into Merenwyn was 80 percent guilt fueled

I left my brother bearing the burden of my own mistake: being the Old Mage's nalera was no walk in the park. Plus there was the whole save-the-world issue. Foul magic dripping through the portals and polluting everything that is good and fine and untouched in my home world.

People will get hurt. Like Cordelia, my mom-that-isn't, and Anu, my niece.

I can't have that either.

But here's the element of doubt. Would I have been struck by the pressing need to protect the innocent if the goons with the guns hadn't been giving me the buh-byes? After all, St. Silas had made it impossible for me to *not* take that step.

Turns out, I'm not heroic at all.

Sad, no?

On the other hand, Robson Trowbridge came to Merenwyn because he's heroic and he loves me. Any doubt I had on the subject of my mate's devotion was wiped out the instant I'd recognized the cacophony coming from the portal for what it was—the metallic shriek of a chain-link fence scoring the passage walls as it was dragged willy-nilly into the land of the Fae.

St. Silas, one of the big woofs of the werewolves' Great Council back in our world, had handcuffed my mate to such a fence. The asshole should have cuffed the Alpha of Creemore to a Chevy. My Trowbridge simply brought a six-foot panel of chain link with him, as well as a fence post, a set of handcuffs, his scent, and—not to overwork the phrase— his love.

Trowbridge loves me.

I turned my head slightly to regard my beloved. After enveloping me in a breath-defying hug that had quickly evolved into a truly memorable and searing kiss, my lover had divested himself of the handcuffs. Then, he'd taken care of what was left of the fence by rolling it into an untidy cylinder, which he'd stashed behind a handy outcrop of rock. After that, he'd performed a quick scent test of the air and a squint-eyed examination of the forest below. Finally, he'd turned to look at me. For four long seconds he'd stared at me, his expression inscrutable, but in the end he'd swallowed down whatever sermon he'd entertained delivering and all he'd said was, "Ready?"

I'd smiled back and said, "Born ready."

Though his mouth had tightened, he'd never thrown that back at me, not once, during the last few hours.

Now my Trowbridge lay supine on his flat stomach beside me, propped up on his elbows, his eyes narrowed on the scene below. As visual feasts go, what he was frowning at was the ultimate photo op—literally a landscape of improbable beauty. Two thick wedges of old forest framed the green valley. Diamonds of light glinted from the winding blue river, and the tops of the grasses on its banks swayed. Add to this perfection the requisite background of wooded hills rolling to oblivion and beyond—

Goddess, Merenwyn would have given Ansel Adams a chubby.

Yeah, yeah, yeah. Not a tree hugger, remember?

Let's go back to talking about Trowbridge.

Normally, I'm all about the splendor of his face: eyes that were as blue as the Mediterranean, cheekbones that could cut glass, a lower lip that could be hard or tender. But at the moment, he was scowling again, so I allowed my eyes to rove over and my nose to enjoy the other totally Trowbridge delights. Like his body and the totally appealing scent of his sweat.

Mine.

If I blurred my eyes a bit, he was naked Trowbridge. Which, by any personal measure, is a better thing than a paper bag filled to bursting with Cherry Blossoms, Kit Kats, Skittles, and chocolate fudge.

My mate had come through the gates wearing the clothing he'd been given before his trial in front of the council: a pair of jeans that were too large and a sweatshirt that was too small. That's it, except for the fence. Nobody had coughed up a T-shirt for the doomed Alpha of Creemore. Also—and this was crucial—nobody had thoughtfully tossed him a pair of tighty whities either, because he was wearing his jeans commando.

I knew this because I'd been watching his back all morning, enjoying the "now you see it, now you don't" scenery as those jeans tried to shuck themselves off his narrow hips, then biting my lips every time he'd jerk them back up again with a hiss of annoyance that I found inexpressibly endearing.

One man's pain, another woman's gain.

When he'd gone down on his belly to case out the valley, those faded jeans had already been sailing at very low mast. Now they rode so low, I could see the dimples at the base of his spine and the upper swell of his tight ass cheeks.

And the small of his back.

I'd become fixated on that patch of skin. I wanted to tramp-stamp it with the words "Hedi's property." I wanted to lick it and stroke it, and press my cheek to it so I could absorb his heat, and breathe in his scent—woods, salt, sex, and yum. I'd do all those things right now except my bone-liquefying exhaustion had placed all lustful thoughts into a holding pattern.

Later.

That's when I'd satisfy my need to claim that patch of skin. If one didn't dwell overlong on the sub-goal list, I had lots of "laters" in my future, during which I could explore every slope, plane, swell, and groove of his body. *He's mine.* I exhaled, glorifying in the awesomeness of him and me, and my breath bounced back, slightly sour and definitely metallic.

Yup. Later.

Right now, we were trekking to the rendezvous point—a place named Daniel's Rock—where Trowbridge and I were supposed to meet Lexi. Though time differences between this realm and the other are vast, we had lots of time.

We were early.

I mean, really early. I don't know precisely how early, because one Earth hour is the rough equivalent of eighteen Merenwyn hours and that is a bitch to figure out without a calculator and piece of paper.

But Trowbridge and I had crossed far earlier than instructed. Which meant we were way ahead of schedule and at this moment Lexi was betwixt worlds, still going through the unenviable process of having his addiction torn from him.

I tried to imagine what it felt like for my brother. Waking and realizing that you're trapped inside a fog-filled portal passage. Slowly recognizing that you're a prisoner—you can't go forward to Merenwyn, and you can't go back to

Creemore. And worse, your transit plans are hostage to your own addiction. There'd be no freedom until such time as *a mage*—and Lexi has no fondness for them—pronounced you clean of your cravings for sun potion.

It would suck balls.

It had to be worse than being stuck in LaGuardia for an indefinite layover, your only company the walls, the clock, and an evangelist preacher.

Goddess, Hedi, when you screw up, you screw up.

I cleared my dry throat and nodded toward the river. "This looks like a good place."

"Uh-huh." Trowbridge scratched his nose, then looked up at the mid-day sun with a scowl. The thin wedge of maple he'd fashioned into a homespun toothpick gave another bob. He'd given me my own stick to chew earlier. Apparently, they keep the hunger pains at bay. Mine had fallen out of my back pocket when I squatted behind some bushes. No way was I putting that back in my mouth.

I pushed the tall grass aside to get another look at the river below. Its banks were pebbled, the center of its span an undeniably *traversable* froth of water.

Finally.

I closed my eyes and rested my forehead on the crook on my arm. No more tramping along the escarpment, trying to exude resolute calm while inwardly being piddle-pants scared about the very real possibility of toppling into the River of Penance's churning water below. No more—

"My gut's not happy," he said.

Neither was mine. It kept squeezing, making clear its expectations that I should hustle and find a honey hive or five for its satisfaction. The handful of berries we'd nibbled on a couple of hours ago were naught but a faint memory.

Don't think about food.

"No," he repeated thoughtfully, "it's not happy at all."

I worked up a reply for that.

Normally, I'm quick with the quip and observation. I'd started our journey through the Fae realm leaking exclamations—*"the sky's so blue, Trowbridge!"*—but my general enthusiasm had naturally ebbed as the realities of being in Merenwyn had worn in.

We needed to cross the River of Penance. Because the two places high on my must-see destination list were on the *other* side of it and because its deafening roar had battered my right eardrum all morning. It had been nothing but rapids and waterfalls.

Finally, it had shut up and calmed the hell down.

I was done with the River of Penance and all its frickin' tributaries.

Done.

Merry slid down the inside crease of my elbow, snaring her feet in my tangled hair. I slit my eyes open and watched her through my lashes. She landed near my nose in a tiny puff of dust, then stalked along the inside of my curved arm.

My best friend was a sentient being, enchanted and imprisoned inside an amulet that hung from the chain I wore around my neck. She was an Asrai, like Ralph, the amulet that Trowbridge wore. "Merry and Ralph are hungry. We should feed them," I said, pointedly adding, "when we get to the *other* side."

"Mmmph," my darling man said.

With frayed patience, I carefully scratched around an insect bite. "Tell me again why we didn't cross the river where the Gatekeeper did."

I'd hated parting from her trail. Without the Gatekeeper, we were stuck in the land of the sneaky biting midges, because I didn't know the sequence of words and secret hand gestures to reopen the Safe Passage. The portal had closed itself while Trowbridge was occupied hiding the crumpled chain-link fencing. I'd tried to stop it from sealing, but the stone I'd quickly rolled into the doorway had been crushed into pea gravel.

The only plus? I hadn't followed up on my first instinct of shoving my foot into the doorway.

Ralph unwound two long golden strands from his setting and re-formed them into two long legs. He pushed himself upright, his bright blue stone winking with a self-satisfied light, then trotted to the end of his chain, so that he could take a gander at the old River of Penance. The line of grasses edging the outlook obscured his view so he hopped onto Trowbridge's forearm and started to prance upward.

Smack.

My guy swatted Ralph off like he was annoying ant. Indignantly, the Royal Amulet righted himself, then whipped out two more strands of gold, presumably to fashion them into something sharp and pointy with which he could demonstrate his outrage.

Trowbridge's lip lifted enough to expose his teeth and the chew stick clamped between them.

And just like that, the fight went out of Ralph. He lowered his pincers, and he stood down, save for the little blip of insolent white light bleating from his jewel.

My mate removed his toothpick and said softly, "When you travel with an Alpha, you don't get in his line of vision. Ever. You watch, you listen, you try to be helpful, and if you want your Alpha not to leave you swinging over the gorge you make an extra effort to stay still so that your chain's not sawing away at the back of his neck. But most of all, you keep your shiny ass out of his line of vision. Got that, Ralphie?"

Point taken. Ralph picked up the slack in his chain and sidled out of the Son of Lukynae's sight line.

"Who's the big bad wolf?" I murmured with only a little bit of sarcasm. "Now, returning of the question of why we ditched the Gatekeeper, your answer is . . ."

"If we followed her across the river, we'd be walking right into the Fae's hands. We've got time. It's smarter to play it safe."

True. We'd journeyed into this world a day earlier than anticipated, so we were ahead of the game, considering there was a time limit on my epic quest. Time considerations only became crucial once Lexi finished his passage between the two realms. If the old man's soul wasn't wrenched from Lexi's by my twin's third sunset in Merenwyn, their soul merge became permanent.

Don't think about it. Just do one thing at time.
Get to Daniel's Rock.

Though, you see, there it was—another tiny crack in the mental image I'd held of what Trowbridge, aka the Son of Lukynae, Hero Alpha of the Raha'ells, would be like in Merenwyn. I'd figured he'd be impatient. Feral. Violence simmering, glinting eyes showing hints of his undomesticated masculinity, musk so strong that it made me damp.

He wasn't.

He was . . . pragmatic. Calculating. And mostly, very damn quiet.

Huh.

I listened to the sound of the water running over the river's rocks. It was clean and fresh, a cheery chortle versus an outraged thunder. Merry's chain tightened, signaling she was on the move again. I could feel the pinch of her little vine-tipped feet as she minced down my arm for a better view of the valley.

Why was Trowbridge balking now? For the first time in a couple of hours, we were on a section of cliff that had great handholds. We could make it down to the valley below without loss of limb and life. And even more important, the freakin' River of Penance had worn out some of its anger. Sure, it was moving fast, but we could ford it. And even if we lost our footing, the other side could be reached in a few determined strokes—after all, the river didn't look *that* wide.

I kept my eyes closed, careful not to look at him. "Is this because you're afraid of water?"

"I'm not afraid of water."

"I'm a great swimmer," I told him. "If you lose your footing, I'll tow you."

"That's. Not. Going. To. Happen."

"So *it is* about you drowning."

"You do remember that I'm an Alpha, right?" I heard Trowbridge murmur mildly. "And that I'm used to—"

"Ordering people about like a puppet master." The sun was pleasant on my back.

"Choosing the correct path for my pack." He shifted, releasing a thread of scent that slid along my arm in an invisible caress. "People used to jump when I spoke."

"Not. Going. To. Happen." My empty stomach rumbled.

Trowbridge's head swiveled, his blue eyes narrowing on me. "Where's your chew stick?" he demanded.

"It was bitter."

"Chewing it will make your belly hurt less."

"I'm not hungry." But my words came out sharper than I meant—*he loves me*—and so I softened my tone. "I'm tired. That's all."

He chewed on his toothpick for a thoughtful moment, his gaze roving over me. His eyes missed nothing. My bundled feet, my sweaty hairline, the pulse at my throat, the sunburn that made even smiling hurt.

The shuttered look in his eyes hurt me. Because I couldn't shake the thought that he understood something I didn't and instinct told me that I wasn't ready to ask what it was. After a beat, he turned his head to study the scene again. "Something feels wrong down there, Tink," he said. "And I can't put my finger on it."

Crap. That was different. Merry scuttled for a more secure perch as I went up on my elbows. "What am I looking for?"

"Not sure," he said, his head swiveling. "But it's too quiet."

I scanned the valley. The river was blue; the firs were green; the forests on the other side of the river stretched for eternity and beyond. I tucked my hair behind my pointed Fae ears and concentrated, trying to listen over the sound of the river rushing over the rocks.

He was right.

Missing were the ambient forest noises. The *tweet-tweet-tweet* of the cardinals having the last word about who's the prettiest; the rustle of leaves as squirrels moved along the wood's arterial highway of thick tree boughs searching for nuts and other delights.

I shot a glance at Trowbridge. His chin was tucked in, his focus intent: a wolf tracking sound that still eluded my Fae ears. "Something has spooked the wildlife."

I went back to studying the terrain. Nothing, nothing—

Something.

At least five miles north of us, a flicker of unexpected light. Very tiny, very brief. As small as a speck of glitter. What was that? A trick of light? The sun reflecting off a weapon? I focused on that spot, willing for the flash to happen again. And it did, not a second later, except this time it was an elf-sized fistful of flickers, clustered over the distant notched treetops. I leaned forward, my own eyes slitting.

"Trowbridge," I said, pointing to far-off trees. "Do you see it?"

He squinted, then gave his head a rough, impatient shake. "Show me."

"Look northeast and concentrate on the tops of that stand of firs. You have to really focus to see it. Look for a blurred sheen over the horizon. And—there! See those tiny flashes?" My finger outlined its shape. The almost translucent haze was moving fast, heading in what looked like a zigzag pattern. "What *is* that?"

"Some short of Fae shit," he said under his breath.

"Have you ever seen it before?"

Grimly he shook his head.

I watched it for a while. "It reminds me of that alien movie with Arnie."

"Huh?"

The scar on my wrist was aching faintly. "You know, when Arnie's staring at the trees and he realizes that there's something off?"

"*Predator*?" He twisted to stare at me. "We're in Merenwyn where we're at the top of the wanted list and you're thinking of some old Schwarzenegger flick?"

"If the sun wasn't reflecting off its glittery bits, I'm not sure if we'd have seen that thing. At first glance it's more of a pixilation than anything else. A blurring of the defined edges. It moves fast. What do you think it is?"

"There are no aliens running around Merenwyn, Tink. There's just a lot of Fae shit." Abruptly Trowbridge rose to his feet in a fluid motion of muscle and grace.

"You realize that I find the term 'Fae shit' vaguely insulting, right?" My fingers went to the pointed peak of my ear. I'm half Fae *and* half Were.

Trowbridge began pacing. Six steps in one direction, hands jammed in back pockets, a turn, then six steps back to me. A short but energetic circuit.

Kind of mesmerizing, really.

All those muscles, all that grace.

I rolled on my side, planted an elbow, and propped my

head on my palm to watch him. He was either thinking or worrying. Whatever the distinction, my mate was walking and just watching him made my feet hurt. Despite the swaddling insulation of Trowbridge's socks and two layers of fleece jersey, they were sore. Fully washable 60 percent cotton does not measure well against shoe leather.

I cleared my throat. "Are we crossing the river here or not?"

"Fucking jeans," he said, yanking them upward again.

That would be a no. "I can't see how a tiny bunch of sparkles in the sky—"

"Listening to my instincts has kept me alive over here."

I rolled to sit and stared at the vista on the other side of a river whose rightful name should be Frustration, not Penance. "We're not going to get to Daniel's Rock tonight, are we?" My voice was small.

"Not until I understand what's going on down in the valley."

I drew my knees up and leaned my chin on them. "Can I see the rock from here?"

His knees brushed mine as he sank to his haunches beside me. "No, but you can see the Two Sisters. Daniel's Rock is right behind them."

"What sisters?"

"See those two hills?" he asked, lifting an arm to point across the river.

I twisted my head slightly, searching for two rounded humps that could be potential siblings, and came up empty. He glanced at me, then muttered out of the side of his mouth, "You need to look farther east."

East?

Oh, my word. The twin peaks—and they were *peaks,* not hills—were decidedly east if one was thinking of foot power. But hadn't I noticed those two snow-topped dames a couple of hours ago? If so, we'd been performing a long, lazy loop around them all freakin' afternoon. My gaze flicked to his. "How much of a detour did we take today?"

"It was worth it," he said, lowering his arm. "Everything on the other side of the river is Fae territory. The area's populated with farms. We can't pass as one of them. I haven't got the ears, and we haven't got the right clothing."

But I was an excellent thief. I could have raided someone's clothesline. "And what's this territory?"

"All the land on this side of the river belongs to my pa—" He stopped himself, mid-word.

He didn't have to finish it. I knew he was going to say "pack."

"This is Raha'ell territory?"

"Yeah."

Oh. Joy.

You would think that the two of us would have had some sort of discussion about the Raha'ells before this. But we hadn't. Our landing in this realm had been abrupt and on the heels of near disaster. Since then, we'd been on the move and it hadn't come up.

Okay, I'll own to not being terribly keen about opening a topic that touched on the fact that I had sent my lover to Merenwyn for nine numbing years. A lesser man wouldn't have survived exile to a realm that hunts wolves. However, my Trowbridge had thrived, discovering unsuspected leadership qualities as the Alpha of the Raha'ells. Under his tutelage, the dissident pack's guerilla warfare tactics had sharpened and their war on the ruling Fae had evolved from a fringe irritation to a real threat.

It was a given that Trowbridge would rise to the top of the Fae's wanted list. Eventually, he was captured and brought to the Spectacle grounds, a prison within the Fae castle that serves as a theater of death for those with wolf blood. Executions are scheduled for full moons and well attended by the Fae. After all, it's a fine spectacle for those in the stands—gladiator games played without any weapons. Death was inevitable for a wolf; the only thing left to chance and self-will was the length of time it took to die. I'll be forever grateful that Lexi kidnapped Trowbridge and led him out of those killing grounds.

But it had looked bad.

It had appeared that the Son of Lukynae had turned his back on his people.

Trowbridge squeezed my arms, then stood.

"What will happen if we run into them?" I asked. Would the Raha'ells tear him apart limb by limb? Feast on his internal organs? Use his head to play soccer?

Goddess, my imagination is too vivid.

For a long time, he said nothing. "A cowardly Alpha who turned his back on his people—there's no coming back from that. They'd go to town on me and they'd have every right to do it."

"You're not a coward. You were under Lexi's compulsion spell. You would never have—"

"Left some of my pack to die at the Spectacle? Walked right out of that hellhole with my pack's worst enemy? That's what I did. Doesn't really matter why I did it."

Note to self: see a Raha'ell, run like hell. "What are our chances of encountering them?"

"I know their hunting grounds. I know which trails they take, and where they choose to camp down for the night. We've stayed clear of those areas and the wind's been in our favor. As long as we stick close to the river, we should be all right."

I hate the word "should."

"I doubt we have anything to worry about," I heard him say.

Not a fan of the word "doubt" either.

He walked away, turning his back to me to meditate on

the land behind us. We'd been following the edge of what had to be a very long escarpment. Behind us were mountains. Big ones. A long range of the type that adventure seekers flock to. Take Everest, K2, Mount Ranier, and Mont Blanc and throw in some of their craggy cousins.

"What are you thinking?" I asked, hoping it didn't involve scaling K2.

He turned back to study me. Rubbing a hand over his bristled hair, he shook his head at my jersey-wrapped feet. "Jesus, I wish we had shoes for you."

"You're not wearing any."

"I'm—"

"Used to this place."

"I was going to say that my feet are like leather." He walked back to me and sank into another squat. Two large, warm paws reached to cup my jaw again. Blue eyes surveyed mine. I read approval and respect. Love and worry. "We'll take a rest here." My mouth opened to issue the usual lie about being "perfectly all right," and he said, "We both need it, sweetheart."

"I can take whatever's coming, Trowbridge," I said, and found, to my surprise, that I meant it.

His expression grew tender and he shook his head. "When are you going to stop calling me Trowbridge?"

"The day I find a better name for you."

He grinned, and he was Robbie Trowbridge again. The guy who played a guitar and had long hair, instead of this buzz cut that I couldn't reconcile myself to. I studied him, taking in the gaunt beauty of his face. Then I finally said what I should have said several hours ago. "Thank you for following me back to this realm, mate."

His thumb stroked my bottom lip.

"Open," he said, tilting my jaw upward.

My tense smile softened into my Lolita come-hither. My lids lowered and my mouth parted, ready for his kiss. But instead of lips that could be either hard or warm, I felt the intrusion of a stick of wood that tasted like Trowbridge and bitter bark sliding into my mouth.

I opened my eyes.

Blue ones gleamed at me. "Chew, sweetheart. It will keep the hunger away."

Chapter Two

Trowbridge, being wolf, likes to cuddle. And caress. Bottom line, with me he's inexplicably tactile. It's startling and wonderful and odd. Having spent a hug-deprived youth, I was having to relearn being held. Most of the time, I delighted in it. But here, in the spot he'd found us under a tree, I couldn't find a comfortable position in his arms. It was still daylight—the sun was bright and hot—and even though my body was beyond tired, my mind was busy.

Despite his suggestion, I couldn't catch forty winks on the drop of a dime.

My brain was too busy concocting a nightmare situation where I ran into a Fae or a Raha'ell and Trowbridge was unable to communicate on my behalf, being (a) suddenly mute or (b) amnesic, and/or (c) feverish and unable to do anything other than sing the entire chorus of "Baby Don't Leave Me" in falsetto.

Up in Threall—a mist-shrouded place where the souls of the Fae hung from ancient trees like beautiful balls of light—I spoke the language. Hell, in *that* realm Fae bon mots just flowed from my tongue. There I was the Dorothy Parker of the Fae. But in the land of the Fae—the one place where speaking and understanding the language might prove near indispensable—I was disturbingly unilingual.

What does one say to a person who may or may not wish to kill you and/or your mate?

"Stop squirming," said Trowbridge.

"I'm not."

His chin scraped my temple. "Relax. I'm the wolf. Keen eyes and nose. If anything creeps up on us, I'll know long before it gets close."

A branch snapped deep in the woods.

His arms tightened. "It's nothing."

"I hate not knowing where I am." My sense of direction had been screwed by our long detour. "Can you draw me a map? Show me where we are and where we have to go?"

"You're going to get yourself riled up more."

"Map."

He allowed himself a man-sigh. "Sit up."

I leaned forward, and he uncoiled himself with his customary grace. Trowbridge walked a few feet into the woods and came out carrying a stick. He knelt on one knee to clean the ground of pine needles and sticks. Then, my mate drew a single curved line, an artistic effort that could be interpreted as a half-moon lying on its side after a quart of tequila.

"What's that?" I asked.

"That's the river we've been following. We started about here"—he tapped the far right of the line—"and now we're here." The end of the stick moved along the curve all the way to the left. He filled in the interior curve of the shape with light hash marks. "All this is Fae land."

"Just as an FYI—if we ever have treasure to bury, I'm drawing the map. There's no scale; there's no north and south."

He etched the letter *N* at the top of the drawing. "Always the critic."

"You'd get too full of yourself if I didn't pull you down a notch. You being so beautiful and studly and all that."

" 'Studly'? Is that a word?"

"It *is* in my dictionary." I jerked my chin at his map. "Keep going, Picasso."

Grime had embedded itself into his calloused knuckles. With a wry grin, he leaned forward and drew an *x* in the middle of the Fae territory. "Daniel's Rock."

I scooped up one of the twigs he'd ejected from his drawing area and used it to make two smaller *x*'s to the left of it. "The Two Sisters."

"Very good." He sketched an elongated circle.

I stared at the oval he'd drawn. "That's the castle? Are you telling me that we landed in Merenwyn just south of the freakin' castle? We've been moving away from it all this time?"

"Told you. It was necessary." He frowned at his map, then scratched out his first castle effort and redrew the shape a little north of where he'd made it. "That's better."

"That's so annoying," I said. "If the water had run a little slower, we could have crossed the river and been there hours ago. How did the Gatekeeper ford it?"

"There's a rope bridge to the east of where we landed."

"There's a rope bridge?" I repeated slowly.

"Better this way," he grunted. "No one would expect us to come at the rock from this direction."

"You're expecting trouble," I said quietly.

He used the side of his hand to erase the map. "I always expect trouble. Right now, we have to focus on getting to Daniel's Rock. There's a lot of hoops to jump through before we start worrying about storming the castle."

Storming the castle? I was thinking we'd be "sneaking" into the castle.

He stretched, working the kinks out of his neck. "Rule of the road," he said. "Rest when you can; hydrate when you can. I say we rest for a bit. You're exhausted, Tink."

"I'm not." My empty stomach was keeping me awake.

"We'll take a break. After the Fae shit moves off, I'll find some more berries."

Oh, goodie.

"Then we'll put in a few more miles before the sun sets." He moved back to his former position, spine braced on the back of an ancient tree, arms open, legs splayed wide for me. "Come here."

"I can't nap during the day." But I could cuddle. Yes, I could do that. I moved into the space he'd created for me. "Move, Ralph," I told the amulet resting on my mate's chest.

Still miffed, Ralph didn't. Trowbridge hooked his chain with his forefinger, then tossed Ralph over his shoulder. I leaned back, telling myself to relax. Merry settled into the space between my boobs.

"Shhh," Trowbridge breathed in my ear. His fingers began working into the knot between my shoulders. His scent curled around me, another set of arms, and licked away my tension.

It was comforting.

I'll still never sleep.

It was my last conscious thought before I slipped into the land of Nod.

Beneath my ear, his abdomen muscles suddenly tensed. "Hedi."

Shhhh.

My dreamworld had never been so sweet. I was sitting in my chair in the Trowbridge kitchen about to dig into the bowl brimming with Grade A maple syrup. The room smelled of Were and happiness, for it was jam-packed with my family, all of them clustered tightly around the round oak table. Everything was right; everything was as it should be. Trowbridge held my free hand. Merry supped from a spoon of honey while Cordelia ruled court from the kitchen sink. Harry leaned against the tall cabinet, still wise and alive. Biggs was there; my affection for him was unpolluted by the knowledge of what he'd done.

My family was complete.

Because Lexi sat opposite me, sandwiched between Anu and Biggs; his bowler hat hung from the back of his chair's spindled top. How long had it been since I'd seen my twin grin so freely? *Look at him; he's the guy he would have grown up to be, if the Fae hadn't—*

"Hedi." Trowbridge said more urgently.

The dream shattered and with it the sense of rightness. I woke to the distinct flavor of danger.

It was in my nose—Trowbridge's scent was spiked with sour stress. And it was flaring at my breast—Merry was hotter than a potato taken straight out of the oven. I bolted upright, curling my body into a comma so she could swing free. Sweet heavens, she was so hot, I was surprised she didn't leave a smoke trail. Not only was she telegraphing distress with her heat, but she was also broadcasting it with light. The heart of her golden amber was suffused with a dull red glow, the hue of a coal that had been sparked to life.

"What's wrong?" My fingers curled on his thighs.

"Horses," muttered Trowbridge.

My gut tightened into a hard knot. In Merenwyn, the Fae ride and wolves run.

He pushed me forward. "Keep low and shadow me."

Merry ratcheted up her chain as we did a low sprint toward the overlook. Five feet from the edge, Trowbridge caught my arm, urging me to drop to my knees. I did and followed his belly crawl to the overhang.

My breath whistled through my teeth as I scanned the scene below.

For the life of me, at first it all looked the same as before—a rippling ribbon of water, two swaths of woods—but as I studied the valley the scar on my wrist began throbbing and the single tooth indent left from the bite took on a greenish tinge. The dental imprint was a lasting memento of an encounter with a cornered kid. Somehow, the boy's magic has attached itself to the wound, and now I had a built-in sorcery sensor. I don't know why the scar glows when I'm near a spell, or a ward, or a mage, but it's turned into a handy warning system.

I leaned forward, lifting myself higher on my elbows, in an effort to see better. *Magic's near.*

Trowbridge's arm swept out, pinning me hard to the ground.

"I told you to stay low," he growled into my ear.

"I need to see."

"There's nothing to see yet." But he lifted his heavy arm, letting it slide down my back to rest at my hip. He pulled me closer to his body, then parted the grasses wider so that I could peer through the hole he'd made in the line of scrub edging the overlook.

"What direction am I looking in?" I whispered.

"Watch the east side of the river."

Goddess, if we'd used the Shallow Crossing when I'd wanted to we would have walked right into a Fae hunting party. And we'd be either captured and dead or simply dead. The whole epic journey would have been over before it had really got off the ground.

"They're close," murmured Trowbridge.

Wolf ears. I could hear little over the Penance's murmur. A bee droned by and I didn't even blink. I kept my eyes on that strip of land, my anticipation rising. I hadn't seen a full-blooded Fae since Lou.

But when the Fae finally appeared, my first reaction was: *So?* Change out their clothing, cover up their pointy ears with a Maple Leaf toque, and you had your basic Canadian. And also, not to make too much of the point, but it was two men, not the squad that Trowbridge had anticipated.

They emerged from the trees on the river's bank. Both were astride totally unremarkable horses. One carried a sword; the other had a bow slung over his shoulder. The bow carrier was a tracker wearing fawn-colored leathers; his eyes were downcast, searching the ground, while the guy in the bottle blue uniform seemed to be content to be sitting pretty in his saddle.

Just two riders, stopping by a river.

A "meh" reaction, quickly squashed, because I was leaning the length of me against the length of Trowbridge and my body felt the abrupt change in Trowbridge's when he shifted from battle-ready tension to statue stiffness.

I turned my head.

My mate's eyes were slit, the faint lines fanning from them tense slashes. He was focused on the scene below, but I sensed he wasn't seeing it. His face had the stark quality of a man revisiting a brutal memory.

I touched his hand. "Trowbridge?"

His fingers fisted. "The tracker's name is Qae."

It was how Trowbridge said the name—as if it were a gutter curse—that told me what I needed to know. Somewhere, somehow, Qae had hurt my mate. I focused on the tracker, committing his features to memory. Medium height. Shorn brown hair. Wide face. Nothing overly distinctive about any of that; he could be easily missed in a crowd.

Qae dismounted. He led his horse to water, then walked along the edge of the bank. The man was light on his feet, and he walked with calculation as if he was as much aware of his own tracks as the ones he was following. It was his tell, and I knew if ever our paths crossed I'd recognize him by his gait.

You're dead, I told him silently. *If I meet you in a blind alley, Qae, my magic will be cinched around your throat before you can let out a surprised squawk.*

The tracker toed the ground briefly and then turned to say something to the other Fae. In response, horse-guy stood up on his stirrups and twisted to look back behind himself.

"What's he looking for?" I whispered.

"Probably the rest of the company."

The horseman resumed his seat. And for an uncomfortable stretch that probably amounted to less than ten seconds but felt like ten hours, nothing much happened. A small brown ant followed the spine of a piece of grass, reaching the tip, then turning and going back down again. Trowbridge breathed loudly through his nose and held me too tightly. My right boob registered a squish protest. My wolf created gaseous hell in my lower gut.

I was afraid.

Of Trowbridge's reaction to the tracker, of not knowing what was going to happen.

Meanwhile, Qae and company appeared to be waiting. The cavalryman pulled out a linen-wrapped packet and proceeded to eat from the contents. Que squatted to inspect his horse's fetlock. Just as my heart was starting to reregulate itself, the scout wheeled around sharply in our general direction, his buttock resting on his heel.

Crap.

"Don't. Move," Trowbridge breathed into my ear.

Really, really hard not to. My body was telling me it was flight or fight time, and there was no doubt which option my feet preferred.

The tracker's gaze slowly swept the woods on either side

of the river, before he rose to his feet to gather his horse's reins. His focus turned to the long ridge of the gorge that Trowbridge and I had followed all afternoon.

A methodical man, Qae started to scan from left to right. A bonus for us, as we were slightly to the right of the long, curved overlook. With acute care, Trowbridge slowly closed the peephole he'd made in the grasses, allowing them to feather back together.

My man's gaze flicked to mine. His eyes were flat and cold, not a flicker of Alpha light in them. "If I tell you to run, you do that, got it? You don't look back. You head up the mountain."

"What do you mean, don't look back?"

An answer that will forever remain a mystery, for that's when the cavalryman wearing the bottle blue jacket called out to Qae. The tracker turned around. His companion gestured to the northwest sky.

I inhaled sharply.

Skimming along the wood's ragged tree line was a milky haze. It was similar to the fistful of sparkles we'd seen earlier but far larger. And unlike the earlier specter, this thing knew where it was going—it poured over the top of the woods, a low, thin, undulating blanket of fog, heading straight toward the horseman and the river.

A cloud of ill will.

Don't ask me why my instincts attributed that to the rolling mist. It was actually a strangely beautiful thing. Almost alive, the color of bleached bone, rippling with movement and depth. The afternoon sun was strong and bright, and its rays caught the shimmering particles suspended inside its wavering shape, turning them pink, and purple, and plum.

Qae observed its progress with no visible emotion—a marked contrast to his companion, who followed the glimmering miasma's approach with the anticipation of a guy sitting in the third-base stands watching a strike turn into a fly ball.

Gonna-get-it, gonna-get-it was written all over the cavalryman.

My Fae was a hard knot bothering my sternum. "Elemental magic," I heard her say quite clearly. "You must flee, sister."

No shit, Sherlock.

Qae caught up his horse's reins and threw himself up on the saddle. He tipped up his jaw to the other man, who nodded and put away his confection. In unison, they turned their mounts around and melted back into the forest from which they'd emerged.

"They're going?" I asked, confused.

"No," Trowbridge said, his tone hard, "they're waiting."

"For the other Fae?"

His face taut, he shook his head. His gaze flew from Qae's hiding place to the cloud now streaming at breakneck speed toward the river. He twisted on his hip, tilting back his head. His nostrils flared as he inhaled long through his nose, and then—I swear I didn't think it was possible—his body got harder and tighter.

His hand slid off my hip.

"Trowbridge?" I asked him as he started to rise to his knees.

I think for a moment he'd forgotten I was there beside him. But at the sound of my voice he froze, his arm braced.

His eyes turned toward mine. His face was drawn in stark lines. At that moment, I didn't understand his expression; there was too much mileage between us for me to comprehend. I understood only the most obvious—his anger and frustration—before he shoved his feelings into lockdown.

There were more emotions, balanced on top of each other like a shaky Jenga tower. But that is all that I understood at the time, for I was awash in my own responses. Mainly, shock and gut-wrenching disbelief as I watched the Son of Lukynae slowly sink back to his belly. He breathed out and parted the grass again.

"Trowbridge?"

I waited for him to turn to me. He didn't. When I reached a tentative hand toward him, he leaned away from my touch.

I withdrew. "Tell me what's going down."

A muscle moved in his jaw; then he jerked a nod to the cloud. "It's a fucking ambush; that's what's going down."

The thing in the sky had covered much ground in the short seconds it had taken for him to rise and sink back to his belly, and now the inherent malignancy I'd sensed on first sight of it was palpable. The haze was no longer milky; it was a dead bone gray fog, spitting sparks of purple and red. In gleeful pursuit, it frothed over the forest's canopy, boiling around the tall spires of the firs in its haste to bring down its quarry.

Horrible and frightening. "Why is it changing?" I asked myself.

"Don't know," Trowbridge grunted. "But it's driving them right into the Fae's hands."

I didn't have to ask whom he meant by "them."

Who runs while others ride?

I lifted my nose to the catch the breeze, testing the sweet Merenwynian air for confirmation. I got woods, and Fae magic, and the pungent, fox-astringent scent of Trowbridge's stress, and then . . .

"Wolves," I said.

"Not just wolves." Dry despair in his whisper. "The Raha'ells."

My breath caught when the Raha'ells came hurtling out of the woods. There were people—that's how I saw them at first. Not as feared warriors who might wish to kill my mate. Not even as wolves in human form. I just saw them as people.

Women, children, youths. Twenty or more people running for their lives.

I leaned forward, my fist going to my mouth.

The fastest runner of Trowbridge's old pack was very young, not a teen, but a boy. Ropes of hair streamed behind him as he burst through the trees at top speed. He was armed with a bow, and a quiver of arrows that bounced on the small of his back as he ran.

Merry tightened at my throat, her heat flaring.

Hot on his heels came a woman with hair the color of sunset. She sprinted with a bow gripped in one hand, the other tightly cupped under the round bottom of the child she balanced on her hip. The woman shot a hurried glance upward at the cloud spitting sparks, then sped up, tearing across that field for the shallow crossing, legs pumping.

"We have to warn them," I said, starting to rise.

He shoved me down hard, his hand splayed on my back. "Stay low!"

"We can't just watch this! We have to do something." I pushed his arm away and surged to my knees. "They're nothing but kids and women; we have—"

He threw himself on top of me.

"Let me go!" I bucked under him.

"Stop it!" he hissed in my ear. "These are Raha'ells! They'll smell the horses soon and they'll cut back into the forest. My warriors will be in the rear of the retreat. It's our way." His thighs were weights on mine, his arms steel brackets, his jaw a hard pressure on my neck. "My pack knows these woods better than I know Creemore."

My gut dropped at his use of the possessive pronoun.

It plunged further when a moment later the tail of the Raha'ells came crashing through the undergrowth. Contrary to Trowbridge's words, they were no brawny warriors bringing up the rear, and the pack did not as one veer off into the woods again. Instead, they ran for the river and certain ambush.

"Jesus, where are they?" Trowbridge's tone was raw as flayed skin. "Where are my warriors?"

Dead, I thought in sudden instinct.

I huddled into myself, my lover's weight a stone upon my back.

Alone, unburdened by children or loyalties, I suspect most of the women could have easily outpaced the menaces behind them. But it was apparent that for Trowbridge's old pack there was no such thing as every woman for herself.

Nobody outran the kids.

Those little wolves who could sprint on their own were doing so. But on either side, they were flanked by mature female warriors. Behind them, more women, shouting encouragement and threats. Their words were spoken in a tongue foreign to me, but I understood them. "Don't look behind you. Don't look up at that cloud. Hurry. Run."

Pinned beneath Trowbridge's taut body, I could taste the sour spike of his scent on my tongue and feel the suppressed violence cording his muscles. His growing anguish only added to my own swelling sense of claustrophobia.

I was deeply angry with him. For protecting me when he should have been protecting them. For not being the fearless, brave guy I'd thought he was. For proving himself to be a smart man instead of a heedless one.

I wanted a hero.

And I wanted him off of me.

Because I was going to be forced to watch and bear witness and doing so was going to be a very bad thing. It was going to push me across some threshold that up to that minute I hadn't known existed. And I knew in my guts that I wasn't ready for it. My life in Creemore had been piss-poor preparation for whatever I was going to see.

I could hear the drumming of their horses' hooves getting closer.

Any second now . . .

The Fae erupted from the forest.

The full visual impact of a cavalry charge can twist your bowels. Anyone in the path of that incoming of violence would have to be either an idiot or a very brave woman not to scatter in the face of it—it's a wave of death pouring toward you.

If I live to be ninety, I'll never forget the spine-chilling calls those riders made as they thundered across the field—mocking hoots that sharpened into high yips as they bore down on the pack.

"Fuck, fuck, fuck," said Trowbridge, turning the swearword into an obscene prayer. A few of the mounted men carried spears, but most carried cavalry swords; the latter being long, thin, and slightly curved.

No one can be "born ready" for this world.

I need to go home.

The bulk of the Raha'ells running from the horsemen had reached the Penance before the horsemen had covered half the clearing. As the women waded across it, they held their children high and leaned forward against the current's pull. I scanned the trees on the opposite bank. I could see no sign of the archers who I knew waited on the other—the *safe*—side of the river.

I started silently praying, *Don't kill them. Please don't kill them.*

For those on the run, it must have felt like a moment of false reprieve before the axe's fall, because just short of the water their pursuers reined in their mounts sharply and came to a wheeling stop.

The last to enter the river was an old man who ran with a jerking two-step that set his grizzled dreads dancing. As he splashed into River of Penance, he turned to look behind him.

I saw relief spread across his face.

He thought the horses weren't going to follow them across the river.

He was right.

He lived with the hope of freedom for another four or five staggering feet before the archers stepped out from the opposite bank's tree line.

"Don't kill them," I repeated. My lips moved against clenched fist, and my breath bounced back to me. It was warm and scentless for we Fae have no scent.

Inside me, my wolf began moaning.

Down in the river, there was much wheeling in dismay and aborted dodges. Two women started splashing downstream, but a rider cut off their retreat, herding them back into the center of the shallow crossing. I had my own instant of false hope then: for a second, I let myself believe that it was going to be a bloodless capture, a comfort that was swiftly shattered when the fleet-footed youth who'd led the rush into the plain raised his weapon.

His bow was taunt, his arrow pinched between his fingers.

"There's too many of them, Varens," I heard Trowbridge's despairing whisper.

Oh, Goddess, don't make me watch this. Don't make my mate see this.

The boy let loose his arrow.

His aim was off. His missile grazed the Royal Guardsman's horse high on the shoulder. As the animal reared, front hooves flashing, back legs dancing, Varens scrambled to pull another arrow from his quiver.

Not fast enough.

A javelin whistled through the air.

What followed—the boy wavering, then falling in slow motion to his knees, the cavalryman nosing his horse to his victim intent on spear retrieval, all of that—played out in a dreadful slow motion for me.

A woman let out a keening cry.

The youth fell sideways, the long spear still sticking out of his mid-section.

And with that, I stopped feeling. With a paid observer's detachment, I noted important details, which later I'd replay in an endless loop. Like how quickly the current pulled the ribbon of red down the river and the fact that Trowbridge's back had arched as if that spear had gone through his gut and spine, not the boy's.

This was the Fae? I thought numbly. *These were my mother's people? Oh, sweet heavens . . . my people?*

Suddenly the old man lurched sideways. He threw himself at the leg of a rider, grappling to unseat him. The Fae cut him down with two slashes of his blade.

The other riders surged inward, squeezing the people into a tighter knot. An arrow whizzed harmlessly through the air, blades flashed, and another body dropped facedown in the water.

It was going to be a massacre.

I pressed my fist so hard against my mouth I tasted copper.

The low cloud hovering over the scene let out an earth-shaking rumble. It was an unnatural noise, too deep for a thunder roll, too loud for a storm clap. One of those children let out a terrified shriek.

And damn me if that cloud didn't respond.

It let loose another hellish grumble.

The young ones started crying en masse then, and with

each sob and terrified cry the murky nebula visibly swelled and darkened, seemingly gaining nourishment from the anguish within each terrified howl.

One of the Fae shouted something, at which a few of the Raha'ells dropped their weapons. But some held on to them, their gaze moving to the redheaded woman.

She stood tall, a toddler on her hip.

Her free hand held her bow.

The lead horseman shouted again. His meaning was clear, for he jerked his head at her weapon. She stared him down. Red-faced, he shouted another order, this time shorter and more compact. The redhead turned her hip slightly, so that the child who rode it wasn't in direct line of his fury.

"Drop it, Ophelia," whispered Trowbridge. "Don't be stupid. Drop it."

Then, a lone rider emerged from the dark woods.

"Fuck," said Trowbridge.

I knew the man on the chestnut stallion, though I'd only seen him though borrowed dreams and nightmares of my own making. And each time he'd filled me with enough fear and rage to justify murder.

In real life, the Black Mage was all about discrete menace. His clothing was all shades of black, from deepest ebony to pearl gray. His boots were glossy, his jacket tight against his body. His hair was a long sheet of straight dark silk.

He rode well, sitting in the saddle as if born to it.

Arrogance set in the downward curl of his lip; the mage urged his mount into the water. His horse fussily picked its way through the pebbles, tail lifted.

"He'll kill them," I murmured with awful certainty.

I felt Trowbridge's jaw flex. I didn't think he'd answer, but he did. "No," he said flatly. "He'll want them for the Spectacle. We still have a chance to free them."

The self-titled wizard made his way to the rider whose horse had been injured by Varens's arrow. The skittish mount wasn't buying any of his rider's efforts to soothe him. He was hock deep in a busy river, and he had a cloud over his head and the scent of blood and predators stinging his nostrils.

"Wild-eyed" did not even come close to describing that horse.

Mouth pulled down, the Black Mage studied the blood oozing from the shallow gash on the wounded creature's shoulder. The mage removed his riding glove with short, tugging jerks. Then, leaning sideways in his saddle, he placed his hand flat on the quivering animal's injury.

He began to talk, his tone a soft croon.

It took the Black Mage all of eight seconds to heal the wound.

Once finished, the mage bestowed upon the animal a few comforting strokes, then straightened in his own saddle. He spoke to the rider, deliberately raising his voice so that all could hear him. I didn't know what he was saying—the language barrier prevented me from following—but Trowbridge sucked in a hard breath at his words.

"What did he say?" I whispered.

My mate didn't answer.

The mage's words had vastly cheered the rider of the injured horse. He handed his reins to another and splashed his way to Varens's body. There he unsheathed his knife, then sank to a crouch beside the corpse.

I wanted to close my eyes. I couldn't.

I had to see.

The cavalryman lifted his arm high, poised to bring it down in a strike. He held the blade in a grip better meant for hammering than for scalping.

Sweet heavens, he's taking the boy's teeth.

I whimpered in horror and Trowbridge's arms tightened around me painfully.

Once finished with his gruesome task, the Royal Guardsman straightened, pocketing his tokens with a satisfied grin. He cast a question to his mage, whose response was a languid wave in the general direction of the rapids. The rider put a boot to the boy's body and pushed him in the swifter-moving current.

I closed my eyes.

A droplet of warm water splashed on my cheek and dribbled to the seam of my mouth. I licked it away and tasted the salt of Trowbridge's tear.

And I forgave him.

For not being my white knight on the white horse and for being rational in the face of danger, instead of recklessly courageous. For crying silently as he held me in a punishing grip.

I nudged his hand. He wrapped his fingers hard over mine.

The River of Penance accepted the Fae token and carried Varens downstream. With stunned disbelief, I watched that boy's progress over rocks until he was carried around the bend of the water. Then, I looked down to Trowbridge's hand, tightened so rigidly into a fist around mine that the veins on the back of it stood out in angry relief.

One of the archers began yelling at the group, repeating the same phrase.

"What is he saying?" I asked.

Trowbridge's voice was rough. " 'Drop your weapons.' "

The redhead appeared to be deliberating the wisdom of doing so. And to me, it seemed that as long as she held up the rest would too.

"Let it go, Ophelia," Trowbridge said. "Be smart. I'll find you. I'll find all of you."

The Black Mage cocked his head at the redhead and clicked his teeth, and within a splash or two he and horse were a monument of arrogance parked a hair's breadth away from the redhead's arrow.

Flickers of reflected red light dappled his face.

He studied the woman for a long, long moment. Then, without breaking eye contact, he pointed upward to the cloud seething overhead. Lazily, he sketched a wide circle with his finger. Immediately the dark mass started to turn—its movement sluggish at first, though it gained momentum with each circuit.

When the cloud swirled like a whirlpool in search of a likely sinkhole, a nubbin appeared at the bottom of a mass. This button sprouted a tail, which in turn became a directionless thread of twisting wind.

The Black Mage turned his hand palm up.

A rumble of thunder, a protest of magic being condensed and compressed, then the whole twisting funnel streaked downward like one of the archer's arrows. It landed square on the center of the wizard's palm.

Was it showmanship? Or did the magic need to lick his life lines and test the shallow depth of his heart line? The twister of wind danced upon the mage's skin for four long seconds.

Then he flicked his head and the entire cloud of magic and thunder simply poured itself downward, like oil poured through a funnel, to disappear into the wizard's open hand.

A cruel smile tweaked his mouth.

He made a fist, then nudged his horse forward toward the woman who'd dared to defy him. She stumbled backward until she and her toddler stood perilously close to the foot of the rapids. She could go no farther, though she kept her arrow primed on the mage, who smiled down at her from his mount.

Cool as ice, the Black Mage leaned sideways in his saddle. He stretched to hold his fist—the one that had swallowed that terrible cloud—over the head of her child.

The boy looked up and wailed.

The redhead's resistance snapped. The Raha'ell woman turned her bow horizontal, and with defeat weighing her shoulders, she dropped it. A moment later, the rest of the Rha'ells followed suit.

The Black Mage threw back his head and laughed.

Then he opened his fist.

It was empty.

Chapter Three

The Black Mage departed soon after, leaving the tiresome duty of prisoner patrol to those lesser beings.

It took some time for the guardsmen to rope the captured Raha'ells together—a perplexing problem when there were so many staggered heights—and took longer still for the Fae to retrieve their gruesome bounty from the dead. But eventually, the place of the Raha'ell ambush was empty, except for the floating detritus of forfeited bows and arrows.

When the sounds of the forest resumed, Trowbridge rolled off me. We didn't look at each other. We did not speak. There was too much to say but no useful words to fit the complicated emotions stirred. I'd lost some faith in Trowbridge and found most of it again, but I'd never see him quite the same way. But then again, I suspected I'd never see anything in quite the same light again.

It's not every day you witness a genocide in process.

That's what it had been, even if my brain had difficulty accepting it.

I want to go home.

We waded into the River of Penance. The first body was the old man's. His mouth was bloodied and open, his missing

canine teeth an affront. My mate bent over him. Trowbridge murmured something—his tone too low for me to
catch it—then closed the man's eyes.

He left the old man's body where it was, then turned
for the next.

A few feet farther downstream, a woman's body lay
lodged in some bulrushes. Trowbridge didn't reach out to
touch her as he had the first body. Instead, he squatted on
the backs of his heels, arms resting on his thighs, his shuttered gaze fixed on the quill embroidery work on her quiver
of arrows.

Girding himself, I thought.

Who was she to him? A friend? Or worse—a lover?
Oh, please not that.

Sickness washed over me as I crouched beside him.

The dead woman's dreads were long and the river's current strong. Undulating ropes of hair streamed over her
face, offering brief glimpses of a cheek, a nose, a sharp
chin, and a defaced mouth. The angle of her head was
wrong; I thought her neck might be broken.

The words were wrenched out of me. "Why do they take
the teeth as trophies?"

"To sell them." His tone was flat, all emotion leached
from it. "Most of the Fae shoot blanks. Owning a wolf's
canine is supposed to make them potent."

I wanted to touch him but didn't because he was holding himself so rigidly, the thought came to me that he'd
splinter apart on contact.

Trowbridge said in a low voice, "It doesn't add up. If they
had to travel into the Faelands, why weren't these women
and children escorted? They're the most vulnerable members of my pack. The most precious . . ."

He lifted his shoulders, and his heated scent swirled
around us.

I'd never asked how many people he'd left behind. I

hadn't wanted to know because then we'd be talking about individuals, not a collective group known as the Raha'ells. And if I asked about his Merenwyn pack, Trowbridge might mention a special person—a friend who became a brother—and I would feel his grief and that would feed my guilt.

That's not all, is it, Hedi?

Okay, here was the bigger fear: that there would be a name he might gloss over, a hole in the story that would pinprick my feminine intuition. I'm selfish and possessive, and I can't bear the thought of him loving anyone else but me.

I stared at the dead woman.

Don't be the girl who took my place.

I'd sent Trowbridge to this realm to heal, and by my Creemore calendar it had taken him six months to get better and find a way home. What I hadn't understood was how much faster time passes in the Fae world. A single Earth day is the rough equivalent to eighteen in Merenwyn. While I'd morosely witnessed the passage of three seasons in Ontario, Trowbridge had lived through *nine* winters in Merenwyn.

That's a long time to live with a cold bed.

My mouth was dry. "How many Raha'ells did you leave behind?"

"Fifty-four. Almost fifty-five. Johnet was pregnant." He rubbed his hands over his scalp, shaking his head in a mixture of disbelief and anger. "Where were my warriors?"

I thought of the redhead standing in the river, her bow primed. And of the dead woman by our knees who'd died clutching an arrow. "They were here," I said quietly. "Every woman and child stood their ground."

He lifted his head to stare blankly at the riverbank.

Don't cry again, Trowbridge. I'll break into pieces if you do.

But when he turned to look at me, his eyes were dry and flat of light. "Yes, they were," he said, reaching forward.

He parted the woman's dreads.

"Who was she?" I asked, my heart thudding in my chest.

"Saranna. She's—she was—Gerrick's mate."

Relief swept through me and then a well-deserved flush of shame.

Killing Saranna was two for one for the Faes, I thought bitterly. If one mates goes, the other follows. It was a double heaping of sorrow for the Alpha of the Raha'ells.

Trowbridge thumbed the deceased young woman's eyes closed with exquisite tenderness, then brushed his thumb sideways across her forehead.

A ritual?

"May your soul find its way to the hunting ground." Gently, he cupped her jaw, then rotated her head until it was more or less realigned. "That's the best I can do for you, Saranna," he whispered, his thumb stroking her cheek. "Happy hunting."

He sat back on his heels.

"We can stop to bury them," I offered quietly.

Trowbridge inhaled, then shook his head. "Can't." He reached to slide the dead woman's quiver off her shoulder.

"Why?"

His tone hardened. "Because Qae's nearby." Water sheeted as Trowbridge rose to his feet. He emptied the quiver of a quart of water, then slung it over his shoulder. He snagged a bow caught in the bulrushes and ran his hand along its dripping wooden curve.

"Cracked," he said viciously, dropping it back into the Penance.

"Trowbridge, I'm sorry. It's—"

"Save it," he bit out.

"Don't." My tone matched his for hardness. "Don't let

the foulness of what happened here become a wedge between you and me. I know you're sad and angry but—"

"I'm not sad," he ground out. "Maybe later I'll be sad, but right now I have to find a bow that wasn't made for a kid or a woman and a place to spend the night. And I don't want to talk, okay? Not about the ambush, not about a fucking cloud that disappeared into that bastard's fucking palm. Not. Right. Now."

The back of his corded neck was slick with sweat.

Okay, I thought.

But Trowbridge spun around to glare at me. "The cloud is new, okay? *New!* The Black Mage never had power like that before. My people were chased by hounds and hunters, not some Fae magic shit that ran them to the ground."

"He's gained some power he didn't have before."

"Before I left, he was a cruel bastard, but now he's a magic-strong cruel bastard. He never had power like that! If he had, he would have used it. Which means—"

"He's picked up a few more spells," I finished for him, "and the wards the Old Mage placed over the Book of Spells are degrading."

My mate's tone turned stiff and accusing, "You told me that the wards would hold as long as the Old Mage's soul lived."

"That's what I understood," I replied carefully.

"Well, surprise, surprise, he—"

"Lied."

"Will you stop finishing my sentences?" he asked in a savage voice.

My chest tightened.

Did he blame me? Did he think that I set this all in play? I swung away from him, the need to put some space between us urgent. *I didn't cause this. It's not my fault the Old Mage lied.* I spotted another bow farther downstream that had been snagged by the long spar of a felled cedar that jutted into the river. I picked my way toward it, my cloth-bound feet sliding on the algae-slick rocks.

I could feel Trowbridge's gaze on my back.

"Be careful," he finally called. "Don't go out of sight."

Don't talk to me.

I slogged through the water, edging very slowly along the spine of the log to stretch for the bow. Were the people who stole teeth and got their jollies out of terrifying children *my* people?

There had to be some good Fae. My mother had been a good Fae.

I was thinking about Mom and her smile, and her kindness, and the way she'd made water dance when I saw the boy's leg.

For a second I didn't recognize it for what it was. It gleamed, pale as the underbelly of a silvered fish, under the water's rippling surface. Even as my mind was saying, *Don't look,* my gaze traveled, slowly absorbing things not easily accepted—that the pale limb was attached to a body and the body had a terrible belly wound. Impossible not to add details that I knew would live in my memory forever. Varens's small clawed fingers were dug into the splintered wood. Little fragments of wet cedar clung to the half-moons of his nails.

And then, this—oh sweet heavens, the final horror— that Varens's eyes are open and aware.

"Trowbridge!"

Trowbridge started when he saw me, supporting the boy's head, cradling it so that the water didn't stream into Varens's partially opened mouth.

"He's alive!" I cried as Trowbridge hurried to me.

"Varens," Trowbridge muttered, slipping an arm under the wounded Raha'ell. His gaze slid to the gaping gut wound, and the hope I'd seen briefly light up his face died.

The boy's eyes lifted heavily. He murmured a name—it sounded like Luke.

"Shhh," Trowbridge soothed, gathering up the boy. He lifted Varens tenderly and, with the strength of a grieving father, carried him to the bank. There Trowbridge sank awkwardly to the grass, the wounded youth cradled in his arms.

Shivering, I followed.

"What can we do?" I asked.

Trowbridge grimly wagged his head.

Nothing.

I reached for the boy's lax hand, barely suppressing a gasp when his fingers tightened around mine with a strength both weak and tenacious.

Oh sweet heavens. Never had I felt so helpless.

Merry lengthened her chain and slid down its links until she reached the swell of my breast. There she paused to delicately withdraw two vines from the complicated nest of gold that surrounded her amber stone.

"Can he be healed?" I whispered to her.

She used one vine to prop herself in order to better see the boy who lay so trustingly in Trowbridge's arms. The other she thinned until all the bristling edges of her ivy leaves were flattened and the arm of gold was smooth. With the gravity of a doctor placing a stethoscope on a terminal patient's chest, she rested the end of her vine on the boy's pulse.

After a moment or two, she gave her medical opinion. From her amber belly came a throb of light. Yellow-brown.

No.

Mournful and final.

Varens's nostrils flared and he murmured something—a string of upward notes that clearly finished with the name Lukynae.

Trowbridge flinched.

"What did he say?" I whispered.

My mate's jaw hardened. "That no Fae could hold the Son of Lukynae forever. That he knew that I'd find a way to escape. That I'd come to lead them again." He stroked the kid's cheek, then leaned to whisper something into the boy's ears.

Varens let out a mewl.

Merry moved, letting gravity pull her pendant to the bottom curve of the chain I wore around my neck. Despondently she wove her arm back into the nest surrounding her amber, then she gave a shudder, and her setting tightened into an intricate, protective knot.

Whatever Trowbridge had said had dismayed her greatly.

"She's upset," I said.

"I told Varens that I was going to bring him home as soon as he answers some questions." The Son of Lukynae raised his eyes to meet mine. "I have to know what happened to the rest of the pack. Why this group left the camp without any escort." His tone was flat. "Shit's gone down. I need to know what."

Why was he staring at me so fixedly?

"The Raha'ells believe that their souls cannot go to the hunting ground without my blessing." His gaze never left mine. "If I had a heart, I'd let him go easily."

You have a heart. It's breaking right now underneath all that stoicism.

"We need to know," I said, my voice low.

What followed was a back-and-forth, a gentle interrogation conducted by a sorrowful Alpha and a dying boy. Trowbridge translated for me where he could.

"Why did they leave base camp?" Trowbridge asked Valens.

The boy started shivering and his scent turned musk tinged with fright. "Because of the terror of the sky," he told Trowbridge. It had found the Raha'ells' hidden home and chased them down to the lower lands.

"When did it first appear?" Trowbridge prodded.

Ten days ago.

A comet spun in my mate's eyes. "Where was the rest of the pack?" he probed.

Varens wasn't sure; they'd split into three groups the night before last.

Trowbridge shook his head at that, clearly dismayed. "Why?" he asked.

Because they'd soon realized that the cloud found them more easily when they were in a large group. The Raha'ells reasoned the best thing to do would be to split up. Hope that that three groups would be harder to find.

"Why was Varens's group traveling without any warriors to protect them?"

Here the boy began crying again. Soundless tears that leaked from the corners of his eyes. They'd needed food, and their warriors had left them to hunt. But last night, they'd heard screams and howls south of their camp. And a woman in their party had died soon after.

Trowbridge asked one last question. The young warrior's strength was clearly ebbing, and my mate had to bend low, his ear hovering over the boy's mouth, to listen to his reply. Trowbridge straightened very slowly, his tortured gaze moving to the sun.

I would like to say that Varens died between one soft sigh and another.

That didn't happen.

Even after Trowbridge said the blessing.

Five agonizing minutes later—during which I wanted to cover my ears and close my eyes to his gasps—Varens died. With shaking fingers, Trowbridge closed the dead boy's eyes. "May your soul find its way to the hunting ground," he repeated, his voice a terrible benediction.

* * *

The Son of Lukynae carried Varens's body to the base of a very old tree. He sank down onto his knees and removed the boy's laced-up moccasins with efficiency tempered with respect. These he placed beside his hip; then, with stoic care, he arranged Varens's hair so that the long dark dreads were neatly over the boy's shoulders.

Trowbridge remained kneeling, his head bowed.

I gave him some privacy, going to the river to rinse my hands. I swished them and watched the current carry the traces of red downstream.

When I turned back, Trowbridge was straightening, shoes in hand. I dried my hands on my jeans as I walked to him.

Trowbridge held out the moccasins. "Put these on."

"No," I said automatically. "I can't wear those."

"They're the only ones that will fit your feet." He went down on one knee and tapped my calf. "The squeamish die fast in Merenwyn."

Averting my gaze from Varens's body, I reached for the tree beside me to balance myself, then extended my sopping, jersey-swaddled foot. Swiftly Trowbridge rolled up my jean leg and began unpicking the sodden knot. He worked the two ends loose, exposing my foot.

I hadn't seen it in a couple of hours. It was dead white and wrinkled. Except for the crimson line where a stone had nicked me on my instep.

Hurriedly Trowbridge slid Varens's moccasin onto my foot. He pulled the laces taut, then crossed the ends of the leather over each other and made a quick knot. Though the shoe was wet and clammy, it fit as sweetly as Cinderella's glass slipper. My toes curled into the indents left by the last owner.

"Next one," Trowbridge said.

I shifted my balance so that he could attack my other

makeshift shoe. It's amazing how well he used his hands considering the damage to them. I watched in dull admiration as they nimbly worked the jersey's knot loose.

When he'd returned to me, after his sojourn in this realm, I'd thought him rendered down to bone and muscle. I was wrong on that. You can get thinner, given the right combination of ungodly stress, limited rations, and no sleep.

I touched his neck.

His back went absolutely rigid. Matter of fact, every muscle visible to my eyes—from biceps to that patch of skin above the sagging jeans—tensed.

"You did what you had to," I said.

"I know." He stripped away the wet rags and quickly slid the other moccasin over my foot. "You feeling brave?" he asked.

I nodded. "Why?"

"Because Qae's going to come after us."

I twisted around to stare at the woods. "You said he didn't know we were here."

"He knew something wasn't right. Either he caught my scent—"

"Is he a wolf?"

"Half," Trowbridge muttered. "Could have been just his instinct. That's what makes him so hard to shake—he uses all his senses. The bastard dogged my trail for three solid days."

"How did you lose him?"

"I didn't. He was the tracker that led your brother's hunting party to me."

Lexi, performing a portion of his employment duties as the Black Mage's general dogsbody and all-round bad guy, had hunted my mate and brought him to the Spectacle. They'd hurt him along the way—either my brother or the tracker—because my mate had been dragged into the arena, his back flayed, his head lolling.

I'd never asked Lexi who was responsible for that, nor had I inquired of Trowbridge.

I couldn't.

The truth could kill everything. It could render everything impossible to mend.

"Trowbridge." That's all I could get out—his name. Two syllables, one soft, one broken. He didn't look up, probably not wanting me to read the hate in his eyes. So, I sealed my mouth and watched his hands move. Saw the way his knuckle-less pinkie stood out as he tied the knot. Noted the white scars and the odd callus on his thumb. He made a final knot and it took that long to figure out what I should say.

"I love you," I said helplessly.

"Hold on to that thought," he said, "because I'm going to push you hard." He rose and turned me to face to mountains in the northwest. "We're leaving the river and going up."

Was that snow on K2's peak?

My feet. My *fucking* feet.

"Horses can't follow us up there. If you can get a Fae to dismount, you can level the playing ground," he said. "You're going to hate me, sweetheart. It's a hard climb."

"Hard climb," I said. "Check."

"But if we can get high enough, there are caves halfway up, and running water. We can rest."

There's always water in Merenwyn. And hills. And mountains. And forests.

And now, apparently, trackers.

Chapter Four

Legs like lead. Each ragged breath dragon fire scorching my windpipe. Trowbridge's fist a bruising manacle, hauling me up every time I lost my footing.

And trust me, I kept stumbling.

Insights.

There can be no worse plight than knowing that you're being pursued by relentless trackers. No lousier realization than the fact that your escape would be determined by how quickly you could sprint.

Bullshit.

There's worse. You don't really hit the bottom of the emotional well until you have realized the aforementioned and had a chance to start reflecting on how well your natural abilities were going to meet the challenge. Yeah, that's the bad part. When you start thinking that you're not strong enough. You're not fast enough. You're not going to outrun a horse or two hunters determined to track a wolf and a woman who may or may not be a wolf.

Predictably—because *nothing* went right whenever Trowbridge and I embarked on an escape plan—within three-quarters of an hour of our K2 summit challenge our progress was shadowed from above by our very own Peacock-Trowbridge hellhound.

The cloud had been a small, distant milky shimmer when we first noticed it an hour ago. Now it was the same color as Toronto's dirty pigeons and, for a mini-cloud, somewhat corpulent. Pursuing prey seemed to make the thing grow fatter, not leaner. It hadn't as yet emitted a rumble. That was a plus.

On the negative side, Qae and the guy wearing the bottle blue jacket were following it and, therefore, us.

I was slowing Trowbridge down. I knew I was, but I couldn't go any faster. I'd run the last twenty minutes with a hand clamped over my side. My bruised feet weren't fleet; they were unforgivably clumsy. Even wearing Varens's moccasins.

Horses against people on foot. It wasn't fair.

Qae and uniform-guy were gaining on us. I hadn't heard or seen them yet, but Trowbridge's ears were keener than mine and, though my mate had restrained himself from progress reports, his body language spoke volumes.

We were being hunted.

Trowbridge stopped suddenly and I almost lumbered into his back. Hand to the fire in my side, I panted while he studied the terrain above us. We'd left the woods behind us a few minutes ago. Now it was mostly outcrops—jagged rocks chiseled by hungry winds—leading upward to K2's peak. Scrubby growth that may or may not serve as handholds.

Goddess, how am I going to climb that? My legs are quivering.

It would be a long, slow crawl.

"Well, here's a bonus," I rasped between pants. "They'll have to dismount, right? Qae's going to have to hoof it like us. We can use that, right?"

Trowbridge's hand tightened on my wrist, but he didn't respond.

By now, I'd figured out that silence from my guy meant he was thinking something he'd rather not tell me. So I tried to put myself in his shoes, turning to look at what he was staring at—K2's incline.

No . . . "staring" or "looking" was the wrong verb. He wasn't looking—his gaze was an odd combination of calculation and resignation—as much as he was seeing. Yes, *that* was it. He was *seeing* that climb exactly like I had, not a second ago, despite the bravado I'd just spewed.

And what he was seeing was one hill too many.

For Jill to get up that hill, Jack was going to do most of the work, literally hauling her up it. And while he yanked, tugged, dragged, or carried his Jill, his back would be presented to the bad guys. Hers too. Both spines amounting to twin bull's-eyes, wonderfully convenient to the trackers who would follow us.

Que had a bow.

I sagged. My gaze jerked from K2's to Trowbridge's. "How far can arrows fly?"

Again, I read his blue eyes, too easily. *Damn, damn, damn.* I pulled my wrist from his grip and breathed into my fist. Three pants. Four. My gaze slid from K2 to a lichen-covered stone and the succulent that grew in its shadow. The plant had starry white flowers.

Enough, Hedi. Enough.

My lower lip trembled against my thumb joint. I pressed against it, bruising it into submission, then dropped my hand.

"You go on without me," I told him.

"No."

"You're faster; you're stronger. You not injured; you can lose him this time." I wouldn't look at Trowbridge—the flower had a yellow center the color of the sun—but I could smell him. His scent was sharp, spiced with anger and adrenaline. "I'll find a place to hide. Qae's tracking your scent, not mine. I have no scent."

"You smell like me now."

And then I started to babble. "I'll find water and rinse your scent off. You go. You keep going; you get higher to a place where no Fae would dare climb. You find a cave. You hunker down. Then you wait. We'll both wait. And then you come and find me. You'll find me, and we'll both be okay. And then we'll—"

"I'll carry you."

I lifted my eyes to his. "Don't be an idiot, Trowbridge. And don't turn me into one either."

His mouth tightened because I'd said the truth and we both knew it and, really, what's there to say once the facts have been laid on the table? Except a long and complicated good-bye, and I didn't want to do that.

I'd only just got him back.

I stared at the white starry-centered flower and kept my head down, thinking that I'd won the argument, even though he hadn't moved. I was sure I had, even though winning felt like a loss. "Start moving," I muttered.

I'd hide somewhere, and then later, not too much later, I'd start wondering if I did right or wrong.

I can't let Qae get his hands on Trowbridge again. And if my mate's set on protecting me rather than than saving his own hide . . . No . . .

Trowbridge isn't going to carry me up this hill.

Not this Jill.

So, I'd wait somewhere—I'm good at hiding—until Trowbridge showed up with a cocky grin and Qae's scalp or a strange wave of numbing fatigue slid over me. And if the latter happened, I'd know I'd failed. I'd accept the downside of being mated to a wolf. I'd welcome the slowing of my heart.

Life without Trowbridge.

Been there. Done that.

"Go on," I told him harshly. "You're wasting my time. I've got to find a place to hide."

You see, that's the difference between him and me. I leap and babble; he glowers and thinks. Trowbridge had been doing some rapid calculations of his own while I was working things through. His reply was non-verbal. He caught my wrist again.

"Keep up," he growled, dragging me into another stumbling run.

It was a direction change. We were no longer on a dogged, despairing slog upward but were deviating to the right of the mountainside, where the slope eased downward before meeting a wall of rock.

He was taking us on a parallel line away from our pursuers. Where the hell were we going? If I weren't so winded, I'd have asked.

We hurtled down the slope, following the wall of rock's seams and fissures, until we came to a hidden opening. How Trowbridge knew it was there I do not know. But he knew of its location, because he skidded to stop—braking by slapping a hand on the wall of rock—then he pushed me into what looked like a crevice but wasn't. It was a dark tunnel, not wider than two and a half feet, smelling of moss and moisture. He followed me inside, turning sideways so that his broad body could fit.

"Go, babe," he said, pushing me with his shoulder.

Sound battered my ears. It took me a second to recognize it for what it was, the *shhh-shush* of running water. My breath, still coming out hard, was almost lost over its drumming beat. Ahead, down that narrow tube of rock, I saw light—brilliant and white. Two more shuffling steps, then my eyes adjusted to the dimness and I knew I wasn't seeing white light at the end of the short tunnel but the white froth of a waterfall.

Trowbridge pushed me all the way to the end and then to the left. He gripped my arm as we shuffled along a ledge that hung over a big drop.

I'd visited Niagara Falls. Most Ontarians have, at one point or another. We've all paid too much for parking and joined the throngs walking toward the lookout. And like every other tourist, we politely—oh, all right, not that politely—waited our turn at the wall, then stood there for about three and half minutes before we realized that waterfalls are basically one-trick ponies. A waterfall don't really change, you know? It's not like the current changes direction. Water rolls off the lip and thunders to the basin below.

That's what it does.

Mind you, this was no Niagara. It was a gushing shower in comparison and the drop insignificant in contrast, but standing there, so close to that rushing stream's plummet . . . hearing its roar in my ears . . . being embraced by its natural wonder . . . it was like talking to my Maker. I could feel its water on my lips, slaking my terrible thirst. I could see the sky—so freakin' blue. I could enjoy the soaring tips of trees of the forest below. I stood surveying my Goddess's kingdom, my bare toes curling inside the boy's moccasins.

If this was the last picture, it was a good one.

Trowbridge's grip tightened on my elbow as I leaned out to look down.

Goddess, I hate heights.

Mountain-cold, the falls plummeted perhaps fifteen feet, then sheeted over a huge and slimed boulder, then plunged again—this drop another twenty feet or more—into water that was darker and probably deeper. From there, it cascaded over two easier drops, merging into a funnel of water that ran all the way down the River of Penance.

What if we tried to jump?

If we cleared the boulder, the next drop would be unpleasant but probably not deadly. As for the rest after that . . . I chewed my lip. It would be a series of bruising plummets. But it was all moot. We'd need a running start and a jet-fueled springboard to propel us far enough out that we'd clear that first boulder.

Trowbridge must have come to the same decision. He scowled at the rock wall on the other side of the falls. "That magic you got," he shouted to me, "can it stretch that far?"

What was that? A distance of forty feet? Had I ever asked my magic to thin itself that far?

No choice. It was time to test her Gumby qualities. I gave my Fae talent a nudge. She surged upward, sending a flush up my body, and coursed down my right arm—liquid heat—to simmer at my nail tips. I stretched my arm back and cast out, and she spun from me, a cord of magic that thinned as it shot over the chasm.

Trowbridge wrapped his arms around my waist, clasping his hands over my belly.

Bliss—that is how my Fae felt upon release. As if Merenwyn's magic perfume air was a taste memory long forgotten and now it was here, on her tongue and mine, and the delight of its sugared appeal was goosefleshing happiness.

"I am free," I heard her hiss.

No, you are not. You are always part of me. And we're in trouble. Reach for the wall.

I'd never seen my magic stretch into such a fine filament of green fire. My gut hollowed out and my wolf moaned as she unspooled.

Thin, thinner, thinnest.

Come on.

But a girl, even one who's only a voice in my mind and magic in my blood, can only stretch herself so far. My serpent broke apart into individual particles of mayhem and magic, a mere half yard from the rock face.

Green sparkles danced in the mist.

Directionless.

"To me," I called.

She streamed back, gaining form and shape. Her nose nuzzled my swollen fingers. A flare of pain as she slid back inside me.

Bowing my head, I dropped my weighted hands to Trowbridge's.

"No-go?" he said.

"No."

He gave me a reassuring squeeze. Then he pushed me back against the damp wall and leaned out on the thin ledge to look upward. He scanned the cliff face, his eyes narrowed. Without any warning, he jammed his hand into a tight crevasse in the wet wall, planted his left foot, and twisted, swinging his body out over the void. I shot forward and snagged his jeans as his chest hit the rock face with a hard thud.

He tried to be the pathfinder.

He truly did.

I heard him claw at the rock and saw shale shower down, felt his body stretch until it shook, but finally he swore and eased himself back onto the rock ledge beside me.

"It's no good!" he shouted over the noise of the water. "We can't do it!"

"Then, we'll make our stand here," I told him, turning to face the entrance of the tunnel. "They'll never see my magic coming."

At that declaration of war, my magic flamed once more. "Yes," she sighed. "We shall fight to the death."

Hard hands caught my shoulders and spun me to face

my mate. His gaze scorched me, then he leaned close—
warm, mine, love—and shouted in my ear, "This water
runs into the River of Penance! It's a rough ride, but it's
survivable. Once you get to the river, you should be golden.
You let it carry you all the way down to the shallow crossing. You get to Daniel's Rock. You remember the Two
Sisters?"

"Of course I do, but—"

"You keep a lock on those two. There's a trail between
them. You take that and it will lead you right to the rock.
You get yourself there and—"

"What are you talking about?"

"There's a way out of this." He pivoted us back so that
we were facing the void. His arms wrapped around my
waist. "Lean back and look up, sweetheart."

Water droplets beaded my cheeks as I tipped my head
back to gaze upward. And there it was: a freakin' tree.
Stunted and twisted. Seeming to grow out of a crevasse
some fifteen feet above and to the right. Its trunk was
hooked. Its roots were invisible.

"You toss a line of your magic up there!" shouted Trowbridge. "Loop it around the tree trunk. Then I'll pull you
back and give you a good push. You'll swing out just like
Tarzan. You let go and drop into the deep water."

I looked down. If I let go at the wrong time, we'd land
on the boulder. And one of us—likely Trowbridge because
his legs were longer—would break their femur or whatever.
Or maybe, I'd crack my head open or break my spine. And
then we'd lie there, gradually fading as the water leached
the warmth out of us.

Though that's only if I let go at the wrong time.

I wouldn't.

"You're light and I'm great with Frisbees. You'll fly. It
will work," he said. Then he repeated it, with the fervor of
a man filled with more hope than belief, "It will work."

Wait a minute. He's not talking about us *flying like Tarzan. He means me.* I shrugged out of his embrace. "I'm not going without you. My magic can hold the both of us. Just because it broke—"

"The tree can't hold our weight."

"It will," I said stubbornly.

"For once just listen to me without arguing." He snagged my arms again. His cheekbones were flushed with color. "I can lead them away from you. By the time they think to look for you, you'll be long gone. If I can get up that mountain there's a place where I can even the odds. And if I can't get there . . . I'm the Son of Lukynae. If Qae catches me, he's not going to kill me. He's going to bring me back to the castle."

Trowbridge was going to sacrifice himself for me? "No!" I shouted. "You are not Hawkeye and I'm not what's-her-name. We're not doing this!"

"What the fuck are you talking about?"

"The Last of the Mohicans!"

"This is not a fucking movie!" he yelled.

"And I'm not doing it!" I screamed.

"They'll find you and they'll hurt you!" he shouted back, giving me a shake. "They'll hurt you in front of me. And they'll keep doing it until I'm begging for them to kill you. Do you want it to go like that? I don't. You were talking about chances . . . then I say let's bring them on. You trust me. You let me swing you into that pool. Then you go find your brother. Get that fucking Book of Spells and turn it to ash."

"Qae will capture you. You won't have time to get away."

"I have a chance, which is more than I had last time. Tink, we can do some good here."

"I don't want to do good anymore."

His gaze scorched me. "I know, sweetheart. But you will." Face set like stone, he removed Ralph and eased his chain over my head and then lifted my hair so that the links of gold lay close to my neck. "Just in case," Trowbridge told me. "I don't want the Black Mage to have the Royal Amulet."

No, no, no.

"Come with me," I pleaded once more. "We'll both fly like Tarzan."

"Told you. I can't swim."

"I don't want to do this without you."

He silently nodded, his thumb dragging along my trembling lower lip. "I'll always find you. You got that?"

My throat hurt.

"I got that," I whispered.

He kissed my forehead, his lips warming the furrows there. He pulled back to look at me, his eyes traveling over my features. Then, his hard hands clamped either side of my jaw and he slanted his mouth across mine.

It was an angry kiss.

But it was a promise too.

Then he turned me to face the void. He wrapped his arms around my waist and bumped his hip against mine to urge me forward until my toes were hanging over the void.

I leaned out again and raised my hand.

"Attach," I said.

Magic-mine streaked skyward. She twisted herself around the tree's gnarled base. Once. Twice. I gave her a tug. Shale coursed down. The cedar tilted, canting toward the drop, then held. I was putting my trust in a taproot.

Seemed to be a theme.

I swallowed and manufactured a smile. "Swing me, big boy."

"Hold your breath, sweetheart," he said into my ear. "And don't scream when you fall. I don't want Qae to hear you go."

And then he did exactly what he said he would. He played Frisbee with me.

I swung out.

Air, tree blurring, rocks, rocks.

And I let go.

I did not scream. I just fell, for what felt like forever. And then I hit—the surface of the big pool, not the boulder, the water soft and airy bubbles—and I slipped under the churning water. So cold that I wanted to gasp and cry.

I was the sock; the pool was the old-style washing machine. Upside, downside, and all-round side, it tumbled me.

Until finally it spat me out.

He'd asked me to let the current carry me—I had. Once my head broke the surface, I was flotsam, and I'd not cried out as I'd plummeted twice more, nor sobbed as my body was ground over rock beds and was pummeled against stone walls. I'd let the river tributary carry me away until I couldn't stand being taken any farther from him; then I'd pulled myself out of the water.

Wearily. Jerkily.

Someone was making small little noises—broken breathy *heh-heh-hehs*.

Me.

I found a bush big enough to qualify as cover. I ducked under it and crouched on the backs of my heels. Then shivering, I wrapped my arms around myself and looked way up. I couldn't see the falls over the trees above me, but if I leaned back I could see the place where we'd stood, and the mountain, and the outcrop of boulders and ridges or rock that Trowbridge had chosen over the long fall.

And I could see the cloud. A traveling smear of dark purple glitter and glints, tracking something that was already moving quickly toward the craggy cliffs.

Maybe that's when the animal within me started to take

over, though I didn't realize it then. I shuddered at the cloud and the dark, and then I turned to do what he'd told me to do—because every other action made a mockery of my choice and his—and I made tracks.

I ran, trying not to make a noise, trying not to cry. Trying not to stumble.

I ran in the opposite direction from the cloud.

I ran, thinking that's what I needed to do.

Fool.

You can't outrun your destiny.

Chapter Five

So, I ran, blind, my emotional pain blurring everything into a collage of thick tree trunks, undefined knee-high vegetation, and low-hanging branches.

I didn't the feel the heavy weight of Merry and Ralph bouncing on my chest, nor was I conscious of the nicks and bruises I was accumulating to the bottoms of my feet. I just kept going, crashing through the old forest, destination momentarily forgotten.

Grief mixed with burgeoning fear is a powerful jet fuel, but as propellants go it burns fast. Within ten minutes of plunging into the dark forest I hit empty, and shortly after that my lungs and leg muscles advised me they'd gone as far as they meant to.

I staggered to a stop, bracing my hands on my knees for a dry-heave session. My head spun sickly. The edges of my vision darkened, then drew inward, gathering up all the light to turn the world around me dark.

No, no, no.

Must keep going.

I sank to my knees, still thinking, *No.* And then I was sliding to one hip, and falling in slow motion to the ground.

I moaned when my head met earth. The back of my skull was acutely tender.

I shouldn't lie here, I thought. *I need to keep moving . . .*

"Wake. Up."

The words were said in two distinct sound bites. The voice was feminine, the vowels elongated. The sound of it didn't stir any glad feelings. I started to drift away from the irritation.

"Wake up, Hedi of Creemore," she said again, her tone harsh enough to strip paint.

My eyes shot open.

I saw fog, wet and thick as the proverbial pea soup. Though, as opposed to a bowl of the green stuff, this substance was bluish-gray in hue and sweetly fragrant. Also unlike the soup, this myst was chilled. Its dampness sliced right through me.

I inhaled again. It smelled like Threall.

But . . .

As a rule, when I soul-traveled to the realm of the sleeping Fae I woke up facedown in a small stump-rutted field, my head turned toward a long row of hawthorns. That didn't mean I couldn't wake up as I was—lying at the base of a fir tree, curled on my side, one arm around my aching head—but still, if this was Threall something had definitely changed. I'd never seen the myst this thick, nor had I come to consciousness resting on a bed of dried pine needles.

I frowned. "Mad-one?"

"You must refrain from sleeping. Or you will fail in that which you promised, and all will be for naught."

I bolted up into a sitting position, and a stab of pain lanced through the back of my head. The urge to faint was there again. I fought against it, but for two ticks the only thing keeping me semi-upright was the ballast of my ass.

"Do not go to sleep again!"

"I'm not going to!" However, performing a less than graceful swoon was entirely possible. Geez, what had I done to my head? My fingers probed the curve of my skull. There was a lump back behind my ear the size of an ostrich egg.

I remembered the washing machine and a sudden bloom of pain during the spin cycle.

Her voice came from my right. "What is an ostrich?"

"A bird with very long legs, and enormous eyes." *Goddess, how long had I been out? Five minutes? Five hours?* I couldn't tell with all this blue fog surrounding me. *Time is important.* Trowbridge was on the run. I needed to find a place where I could search the sky for the cloud. I put a leg under my butt and braced a hand to push myself to my feet.

"Trowbridge is being hunted," I muttered, managing to get to one knee. "And I have to meet him at Daniel's Rock. I need to . . ." *get up,* I finished silently.

"Yes. You must gather your resources and move again."

"Mmmm," I said, blinking hard.

"I am curious of this ostrich."

I felt a familiar push inside my brain. Fae can speak through thought-pictures—simple images without any meme dialogue to punch up the irony. A mental nudge, such as the one she'd just aimed at me, signaled either an incoming image or a request for a visual.

But it was a case of too late, too little. Trading thought-pictures was for family and dear friends, and her mental push was the equivalent of a stranger opening our door, then saying, "Knock, knock," as they wandered down the front hall, heading toward our kitchen.

Huh.

I looked at her through slit eyes. "I didn't say that bit about the ostrich egg out loud."

"No, you thought it."

Oh crap. I could feel her in my head. Sitting there, all comfortable, taking a look around. "What are you doing?" I gave her a violent mental shove out of my private thoughts. "Are you touching me?" I whipped around to look behind and groaned at the resulting stabbing skull pain. When the pulse of ouch subsided, I spoke through gritted teeth. "Aren't there rules about mystwalkers messing with other mystwalkers?"

"There are no rules," she said dryly. "Naught but the ones made by mages."

The sensation of sharing my brain subsided but didn't necessarily go away. Kind of like when a wave hits the shore, pulls back, and leaves a film of wet bubbling on the sand.

She was still there.

One hand clamped over my ostrich egg, I turned on my knee, peering this way and that, trying to locate her in all that blue myst. "Where are you hiding?" I shouted.

"I am here." The hem of her blue gown materialized to my right.

I tipped my head to look up at her and found that hurt too much, so I grabbed a handful of velvet and jerked her down to my level. "Oof," she yelped. The fog swirled as she stumbled into an ungainly ass-plant. Then, the myst settled, enveloping her once again, except for her bent knee and her silk slipper.

Toes really can be stiff with outrage.

I heard her draw in a shaky breath, which she expelled in a long whistle of incredulity. "You touched me."

"Said the pot to the kettle. And technically, I touched your skirt, not you."

"You are endlessly provoking."

Yes. I was. I leaned forward and blew. The fog parted, revealing her heart-shaped face. Heavy-lidded eyes, a long nose, country club written all over her. Expression set in her usual disdainful scowl. If she ever smiled, the Myst-walker of Threall would be a knockout.

"You want to tell me what's with all the myst?" I drew a lazy circle in the air to illustrate my question, and ghostly tendrils of smoke eddied around my fingers. "And why did you call me to Threall? Because I don't have time to—"

"I did not call you and you are not in Threall."

"Well, let's do a checklist: there's blue myst, and—oh yes—you. You're sitting so close, I could touch you again"—I faked her out with a taunting finger—"and you never leave Threall." She couldn't. Like me, Mad-one had been born with the rare ability to mystwalk, which meant she could separate her soul from her body and travel to the secret realm.

At night the tops of Threall's trees glowed with the golden light of thousands of soul-balls, which hung like ripe fruit from their boughs. Mad-one referred to the trees as citadels and the single soul that hung from each citadel as a cyreath. I just called them fucking beautiful. The sight of all those lights stirred my twin mystwalker inclinations: the instincts to protect and to own. It's the last attribute that gave us dream-walkers problems: we become possessive of that we protect.

Think dog with a really good bone.

And that's how you end up more than a trifle mad, marooned in a shadow realm that you no longer wanted to be in. You're pulled by instincts to stay, and you forget how to go home.

"Stop thinking of me," she chided. "And embrace the truth. You are not in Threall."

Beneath my fingers, I could feel the pulpy swelling of the enormous bruise. She might have a point—I always wake up in Threall without a scratch, no matter what indignities my body suffered before I traveled to the realm. My hand slid down the back of my neck, moving to the front of me. My shirt was muddy. I peeled it up to inspect my ribs. There was a graze down the left side that continued right under my wet waistband.

Huh.

I looked upward, searching for a soul-light in the boughs above, but I couldn't find one. Not a single glowing golden glow.

"Okay. I'm not in Threall," I said slowly. I thought about that for a moment. Then, with a swallow, I asked, "Am I dead?"

"No."

I drooped with relief. "But you're here. With me."

"It is but an illusion. Like the myst." She moved her hand from left to right as if she were wiping a window clear of dew. The smoke curled away, vanishing into the undergrowth. I saw the forest around us; I saw her weariness; I saw the ferns I'd crushed before I'd fallen.

"How?"

"In Threall, my palm rests upon the spine of your tree. I tried to speak to you through thought alone, but of course you were resistant to my attempts. You need to see. To touch. To examine. Thus, my illusion."

"So, you're touching my citadel, right now? Up in Threall?" *Oh, ew.* She was sucking up my experiences like a kid with a straw and a soda. "Well, thanks for stopping by, but it's time for you to go."

Mad-one's gaze roamed. "It has been a league and more since I've seen this forest."

"Yup. Time to go."

She made no move. Her eyes were uncharacteristically wide. If I wanted to I could count the tiny flecks of brown in her blue eyes.

She wasn't going anywhere.

"So you're not really here?" At her absent nod, I reached over to touch her skirt. The velvet nap rolled under my fingers. "That's a really good illusion. You want to fill me in as to why you stopped by for a visit?"

She picked up a handful of pine needles. "When the light of your cryeath dimmed, I knew you were hurt, perhaps badly. I checked on you."

She'd been watching over me in Threall, I thought, eyeing her as she lifted the handful of fragrant pine to her nose. She sniffed it delicately, and an expression of fleeting bliss softened the set line of her jaw. *Damn, damn, damn.*

"Thank you," I said awkwardly.

"Once I did, I discovered that you were unharmed."

"I've got an ostrich egg growing on the back of my head."

"And that you were sleeping."

"Ever heard of the word 'concussion'?"

She lifted her shoulders. "Does it matter if you were asleep or rendered unable to stay awake? More alarming is the fact that your soul was traveling to my realm." She bent her neck to study the dried needles in her palm. Her expression hardened back into her usual setting. With a head toss, she flung them into the ferns. "You must not return to my realm until such time as you are ready to complete your promise to me."

"I wasn't planning on penciling in a jaunt to—"

"You must not falter. You must not fail. I cannot help you—do you not understand? I can only watch the light change inside your cyreath; I can only touch the bark of your citadel and sip from your experiences." Frustration sharpened her tone. "Why do you let your attention falter? Why can your focus not stay fixed to the problem? You move from distraction to distraction, threat to threat! Do you not comprehend what rests on your shoulders? It is not just your fate or mine! It is the future of all those we choose to protect. And it is lives of those we love." She thumped her chest with her clenched fist. "I love, Hedi of Creemore, and your dallying is threatening the man I love."

"Dallying? How dare you! Do you know how many miles Trowbridge and I have covered? How long it's been since I slept?"

She shook her head. "I don't care. Simeon has protected my body in Merenwyn this age and longer, and I will protect him to my last breath. You must stay firm to your course! Fail and I will destroy you! I will tear the skin of your cyreath with my teeth and laugh as the wind carries your soul to oblivion."

I cocked my head to study her. Her eyes snapping, her face alive. Animation had set fire to her cold beauty, making her almost appear mortal. "You can't," I said quietly. "My life is connected to Lexi's and his to the Old Mage. He won't let you."

I shared my citadel with my twin. Two trunks, one long taproot. Our futures were tied together. If I died, he died. And if that happened, the Old Mage was shit out of luck, for his soul had no place to call home. Thus, the old geezer would allow no bodily harm to me or my cyreath. It was that simple.

She knew it was an empty threat, but I guess that's all she had to use. Now she folded her arms over her chest hard enough to plump her breasts and took in a shuddering breath.

I watched a tide of red crawl across her cheeks.

Embarrassed for her, I scraped some of the sludge off the front of my tee with my nails. The scent of the drying paste oddly comforted me. Was I concussed or what? Grimly, I wiped the pads of my fingers clean.

"I love too, Mad-one, and my mate is missing. A hunter is following him, and I don't know where he is. I can only follow his progress by a cloud, and now I can't even do that.

I can't see the sky. I'm deep in a forest, and I think I'm lost."

"You are not lost."

"Feels like it."

Without turning, she pointed behind her. "Head in that direction. The forest will thin and soon you should be able search the sky for the sun." She let out a bleak sigh. "Night is drawing nigh in Merenwyn. You will need to find a safe place to spend it. One with walls if possible. And you must not sleep, nor leave your place of sanctuary."

"I've got a concussion. Don't suppose you have any wake-up juice to lend me?"

She leaned over to gently touch the swollen lump behind my ear. I felt a burst of heat, a flush of happiness, and then my head cleared.

She sat back.

Cautiously, I checked my skull. No egg. No pain. I was healed. "I didn't know you could heal me." I tucked that information away, thinking it would be handy to have a medic on call.

"I cannot heal you again, Hedi of Creemore. I have used what I keep for myself, and now I am vulnerable." I watched her gaze grow unfocused. "But your cyreath is shining again."

"Can you see Lexi's light? Is it brighter than before?" *He should be almost through his healing. If good health shone, then . . .*

And with that thought, she shut down.

Fear coursed through me. "Mad-one? What's happening with Lexi?" At her small negative headshake, I reached for her arm. It tensed under my grip. "Let me in, Mad-one. Let me see what you're seeing."

"You do not wish to see this."

"What's wrong with Lexi? Didn't the healing take? Is

he still addicted? Is he fighting the mage?" She didn't answer. I pushed harder. "Tell me! Is he okay?"

"You must hasten. Time is but one of your enemies."

"Not till you tell me what's wrong with Lexi."

"He is not unwell," she said. "But you must not dally. You must reach Daniel's Rock as quickly as you can."

"I'm supposed to have plenty of time," I said, totally confused. "I'm way ahead of schedule. Trowbridge and I weren't supposed to cross the portal for another day. I know that time is all screwed up between the two realms, but by the Old Mage's reckoning I am *early*. How is getting to Daniel's Rock a day before I need to going to help Lexi?"

"Time is melting, Hedi of Creemore. You must hurry."

"No, no, no. That's not good enough. You've got to tell me why I have to hurry. You have to tell me exactly what's happening up there, or I swear to God, I'll come up there to see for myself."

"No!" She shook off my arm. "Do not come to my realm when you are weak and unprepared. For he is here, and he is there. He is everywhere."

"What the fuck are you talking about?"

"There are worse things than death, Hedi of Creemore. Do not squander our one last chance! Come only when you are ready to battle." Her head turned sharply as if she heard something that I could not. "I must leave," she whispered.

Myst started swirling around her.

"You're not leaving me with these questions." I lunged, searching for her in the fog.

Her voice was a thread of caution. "Your clothing is wet, and there is no sun in this part of the forest. You must quit this portion of the woods. You must find the sun again, then shelter for the night. Daniel's Rock is to the east. Do not sleep. At first light head for the rock."

"Who's everywhere?" I shouted. "Are you talking about the Old Mage?"

I again lunged through the fog, searching for her. I felt velvet and clung to it. "At least tell me that Trowbridge is okay," I pleaded as the fabric thinned under my touch. I tried to hold on to her. I really did. But between one breath and another, I lost her. "Goddess curse you, Madone." Heart pounding, I sat back on my heels.

"That has already been done," came her faint reply.

The fog thinned to vapor, then melted into the forest.

Chapter Six

ONE WRETCHED HOUR LATER

"Seriously?" I whispered to my amulet-friends. "Seriously?"

Ralph didn't comment, having turned moody once Merry disengaged herself from his embrace to move higher on my neck. As for my dearest buddy, if she could swallow I think I would have heard a big gulp. But she couldn't, so all Merry did was pull another vine out of her nest of gold and touch my sunburned cheek.

Softly. Kind of a distracted pat, pat.

Once I'd brushed off the pine needles, I'd hauled ass, steadfastly heading in the direction that Mad-one had pointed to. Soon enough, I'd come out into a section of the woods less densely populated. I found the sun—*oh shit, that low?*—and picked up my pace. As long as I kept my back to the yellow ball in the sky, I figured I was trotting loosely east. But I'd been moving in that direction for what felt like a long time and a few minutes ago the sun had slid behind a stand of trees.

Since the forest is old and its growth exceptionally tall, I thought I had an hour before true sunset. But still, I knew, with cold clarity, what I had to do. I definitely had to stop walking. Find a dry hollow. Then cover myself up with pine boughs, or mulch, or some other body-insulating shit, to keep myself warm through the night.

Exposure can make you sleepy. Exposure can kill you. I knew this because I'd watched *Survival Stories*.

I also knew how easy it was to get messed up if you had no fixed point of reference. Once darkness fell, I might start walking in circles. That's a tip I picked up while watching the episode about the elderly couple whose GPS had sent them straight to hell. When they'd tried to turn their Ford Focus around on a logging road's narrow track, they'd gone into the ditch. Husband had left to get help. Wife had stayed in the vehicle.

Hubby walked in circles until he died. Wife semi-starved but was found clinging to life a few weeks later. Clearly, that last tale is a honking big point in favor of staying put until the sunrise. There was one huge problem with that line of thought. If I stopped walking, I couldn't maintain the conceit that I was heading toward something—"*you get to that rock and I promise I'll meet you.*"

Staying put also meant waiting for things to find me.

Like sleep.

Or wolves. Or Fae with arrows.

And sitting gives you too much time to think. About Mad-one's admonitions. About "him" being everywhere. About things I couldn't handle.

But mostly about him.

Trowbridge is fast. Strong and smart.

He'll outrun Qae this time.

So, I'd kept walking longer than I might. Because if I chose inaction over action I was courting the very real possibility that the fear roiling in my gut might overwhelm me. And then what would happen? Would I panic and resume the mindless-running routine?

Possibly.

I was on the edge of another meltdown. My skin felt tight; my hands kept shaking. The only way I'd kept from toppling over was to keep replaying every conversation I'd ever had with Trowbridge. Yeah, it was all there in my memory, stored away on a surprisingly short tape. From our first hello in that motel that had reeked of hard liquor and old sex to his most recent good-bye. He'd given me some good survival tips—sprinkled treasures in our talks. They were there, if I focused on them.

We really hadn't spent that much time together. And yet he was part of my soul. Which was why, whenever I came to the end of the tape and found myself back at the water-fall speech again, I hit fast-forward as fast I could.

Tears are useless.

They change nothing.

Besides, I don't believe brave girls cry. Maybe they do if they're contemplating the amputation of their arm or something equally dire, but they wouldn't dissolve into a boo-hoo session because they're frightened. Or lost and thirsty. No. People with courage get on with it. They chew a maple stick to keep from getting hungry. They keep their eyes open for any source of water that could ease the burn in their throat. They keep moving even if their souls are bleeding and the bottoms of their feet are shredded.

They try to see the forest beyond the trees.

Which is why I was twenty feet off the ground, with both arms wrapped in a death grip around a maple tree. I'd made a sweaty effort to get the big picture.

Goddess. What did I do to piss off Karma?

Why here? Why now?

Isn't it enough?

I'd been looking for the right tree for a while. It had to be on a rise with a bough low enough for me to catch and swing myself up onto (*check*), it had to be healthy because

Merry and Ralph needed feeding (*double-f'ing-check*), and it had to have good strong branches so that I could squirm my way high enough to see the lay of the land (*triple-fuckety-fuck-fuck-check*).

Fortune smiled on me.

Before the gray light turned into no light, I found my maple. I climbed it to the point where my courage said, *That's good enough.* And then, my amulets and I had embraced the big picture.

To which I can say, "Shit."

From our perch, we could see the Two Sisters, and yes, clearly my orienting skills needed fine-tuning. Either the hills had moved or I'd veered off course several degrees south.

No matter. Tomorrow, we could, and would, cover the ground.

But tonight . . . *oh sweet heavens* . . . I wiped my cheek dry on my shoulder and Merry stroked my face again in wordless comfort.

Sometimes during daylight, it's possible to see both the sun and the moon in the same sky. I used to wonder how that could be—the moon was a nighttime creature, no?—until I found a book in Bob the blind bookseller's second-hand store that explained it. The author went into more detail than I wanted, but eventually I understood that it's a trick of reflected light.

So, there you go. Sometimes you can see both.

At least you can on Earth, viewed from a fairy pond in Creemore. I don't know what or how science explains the phenomenon in this realm. Perhaps the same laws apply; perhaps they don't. Doesn't change the fact that I could see both the sun and the moon.

Merenwyn's moon was low. She seemed more white than silver. But her outline was solid enough.

Damn, damn, damn.

My wolf trembled inside me, anxious for her treat.

Tonight's moon would be a full one—she was round as an uncut wheel of cheddar cheese. She'd sing to the wolves of Merenwyn this evening.

Well, at least I wouldn't have to worry about falling asleep.

If a person's life is flattened so there are no peaks or dips, it would basically be one thick line on an otherwise blank canvas, bisected here and there by slashes to indicate points of interest.

The early years of my life had three distinct events: Hedi was born; Hedi lost her family; Hedi found Lou. Then we had a long uninterrupted line unmarred by any activity because nothing much happened. Which, by the way, is exactly what happens in a person's life when they wait for something to happen.

But six and a half months ago, Hedi stole into Trowbridge's room. She inhaled his scent and her inner-bitch moaned. And from that point, her time line grew jagged. Now, if you were a clinical scientist, you might eye those wins and losses—Hedi claims, Hedi kills, Hedi screws up—without any appreciation for emotional growth. On the other hand, if you were a florist, you'd be rubbing your hands in glee, because the tight little bulb that was me was poised to go into full bloom.

For crap's sake, I'd been moving toward meeting my wolf ever since my first orgasm with Trowbridge. My inner-bitch's presence had progressed from a mild salivation issue whenever I passed a deli to an entity I'd struggled with tooth and nail. Every time I'd come close to letting her go, I'd pulled back, frightened that her presence would diminish the Fae in me.

However, my inner-wolf had claws too. And she wanted out.

I was exhausted. My defenses were down. In this flat-earth world, there was no physical interference to mute the moon's voice. No electrical cables buried underground. No cell-phone towers. No satellites. However well I blocked my Fae pointed ears with my fingers, I'd still hear the moon's siren song.

I could plug my hearing. Or, for the first time in my life, I could open my ears and listen.

Fae have no scent. But wolves do.

Come find me, Trowbridge.

The bleeding sun that had briefly rimmed the trees had disappeared, and the wash of gray that had stolen the color from the shadows had deepened.

I shivered, though I was not cold.

Once I'd made the decision not to fight my transformation, I'd moved fast. From my treetop, I'd scanned the area for a safe place to change into my wolf. The pickings had been slim, and the spot I'd chosen for the event was elected chiefly because it was close and offered some shelter. It wasn't so much of a cave as an overhang of rock, which was open on three sides. It smelled ripe with musk. That excited me.

All scents did. Every breath I took through my nose was a sensual feast.

I blew on my fingers. Payback pain hadn't found my hands and I was becoming increasingly convinced it never would. Maybe that's why Fae in this world use magic so easily and dismiss its effects so readily. There are no consequences for using it.

"On or off?" I asked Merry, my tone clipped and hurried.

With a deliberation to match my own, she tightened her chain until she sat near the base of my throat.

"You planning to choke me? I'm pretty sure"—I paused to shudder—"that my wolf's neck is thicker than mine."

Faster than I could blink, she zip-lined down to my mid-chest, where she gave a throb of orange. Then, with equal speed, she ratcheted herself back to her former position.

"Got it," I said. "You'll go with the flow."

Tears burned my eyes.

Stop it. They are useless.

My skin crawled. The base of my spine ached.

There remained the problem of Ralph. At the best of times, he was an unhappy passenger, prone to peevishness. While I was in mortal form I could deal with his nonsense, but all bets were off when I wore fur. I'd been around wolves enough to know they didn't tamp down on minor irritations. They dealt with them. Immediately and, in most cases, with little thought to the future. Unless Ralph was in the mood to cooperate with my wolf, things could go foul very fast.

"What about you, Ralph?" I tested. "You with me or without me?"

With stilted distaste, he unwound three strands from his Celtic knot. Two of them became thin legs; the third became an arm. He gripped his chain, kind of like a woman grabbing the edge of her dress's train, and walked up the slope of my breast until he'd reached my shoulder. There he gave his chain an upward jerk—a very clear indication that he wanted "Off" with a capital *O*.

Typical.

I removed him and placed him in the corner, near the wall. "Stay," I said, knowing that the ungrateful sod planned to bail on me as soon as I had a tail. That was not going to happen. He was not going to ditch Merry or me. I turned, searching for something heavy, and immediately spied a rock about the size of a bowling ball. Just sitting there.

Waiting to be pressed into service. How providential. Grunting, I rolled it to where Ralph glowered. I flitted briefly with the idea of flattening him with it, but in the end I simply rolled its weight onto his chain.

He gave me an indignant flash of light.

"Make yourself comfortable, chum," I told him, hoping he'd figure out that meant "stay put, asshole."

Clothing next.

I caught the hem of my shirt and lifted it over my head. Another shiver racked me. I gritted my chattering teeth waiting for it to pass, then took time to fold my shirt and place it by my feet. My jeans followed. Denim is slow to dry; they were still faintly damp from my swan dive off the waterfall and they put up a fight to stay where they were. It took effort to yank them off my hips and more work to shimmy them down my legs.

Given their clamminess, it was absurd to fold them too, but I did it anyhow. My jeans and shirt were talismans to a life I wanted to go back to.

I turned my back from Ralph to remove my bra. My fingers felt thick, and I had the violent urge to rip the thing off, instead of taking time to unhook it. *Breathe. Just breathe.* Two deep inhales steadied me. Methodically, hook by freakin' hook, I removed my bra. Again, I folded it neatly, cup inside cup, and placed it on the thin stack of my clothing.

Cold air beaded my nipples.

I was naked; I was anxious. A virgin about to be deflowered.

My Fae was utterly still. I could sense her watching my wolf and me. I could intuit her fascination warring with her jealousy. She did not want me to join my wolf. She did not wish to be minimized. Not here, in *her* realm.

But she could not squash my growing moon-lust.

Here's what I'd never understood when I'd stood among

the Creemore pack and watched them staring at the moon with the gap-jawed lust of the class nerd poleaxed by the hypnotic bounce of a cheerleader's breasts—that bitch in the sky is a beautiful singer.

So foolish me for being deaf to her. Every time I'd stood there, vaguely superior with my less than superior thoughts, they'd been listening to this—

No words, no chorus, no melody line.

Just pure beauty. A lyrical call, sweet and high. Full of movement—up a scale, down a scale. Each dip, a feather stroke of solace to unbearable pressure at the base of my spine; each rise, a tug inside me.

I pressed my shaking hands against my skull and paced.

I wanted it to go on forever. I wanted it to stop. I wanted it to get louder until I couldn't think anymore, until the fear inside me, and the fright and the uncertainties and the—

"Oh Goddess!" I howled as the first stab of agony skewered me.

I fell to my knees.

I thought I knew pain. Thought I knew every word for it, every nuance to it.

I knew nothing.

Don't scream. They might find you if you do.

Shaking like a woman with a fever, I rolled on my side, stretching for the pile of neatly folded clothing. I hooked my jeans, dragged them to me. Another spasm. Another stab. Moaning, I stuffed the pant leg into my mouth and bit down on it.

Let it be fast.

Escape. That's all I wanted. Escape from the bite, the gnawing teeth, the chew, the stinking stretch, the blood, the awful, horrible split second when I knew I was poised to go, that I couldn't hold on any longer, that being here—human, grunting, legs kicking, back breaking—had to be worse than hovering on the brink of the threshold.

I toppled, mentally at least.

And went there. To where my transformation would kill me—*Goddess, just let me die*—or it all stopped.

Alive. Free. Hungry.

Who's that?

Free.

Who's free?

Hungry. Thirsty.

Geez. That's my wolf talking. I can understand her. Wow, that's so—oh, look at that, I can hear me too. That's so weird. I'm talking to myself, and I can hear—

Hungry.

Both freaking conversations. My internal one and hers. Does Trowbridge think like himself when he's got a tail?

Food.

Hey . . . I'm pacing . . . Son of a bitch! . . . I'm pacing on four legs. Goddess, I'm furry! Sweet heavens, I did it! I am wolf. Did I pass out? I must have. How long have I been pacing around my pile of clothing?

Alive.

Yes, you are. We both are. Well, slap me on my furry rump and call me stupid. I haven't lost me. I've just merged me and she. And look at the bonuses. I feel so light on my feet. And powerful. Gad, I'm so powerful. I'm not short and round. I'm not the spaz who never got picked for school yard dodgeball . . . This is amazing. I am balance; I am muscle; I am strength. I am . . .

A girl with a really long tongue.

Geez Louise, I'm such a fur ball. What color is that? Black? I'm a black wolf? Huh. I always thought I'd be a gray wolf. Black, eh? It's kind of a rich ebony, though, isn't it? Oh, what's this? I have a silver-tipped ruff? That's an upgrade, isn't? Damn, I really won the wolf lottery. I've got deliciously pretty fur. Take that, League of Extraordinary Bitches. I am—

Hungry.

Okay, I'm a hungry wolf, that's what I am. With silver-tipped fur.

Prey. Fox. Fox. Fox.

Yes, it does stink of fox in here.

Run.

No. Not safe. We have to stay here. We can't wander.

Hungry.

Geez. My nose is command central. Inhales are explosions of knowledge, emotion, response, thought—

Prey.

Okay, enough about the fox. I know its lingering stink is hugely annoying to our sensitive nose—an itch we need to take care of—but the fox hasn't been here in a long time. It had its kits; it ate a rodent or two. Even the scent of its pee is old. Ignore it . . .

Fox.

Hey! I said, "Ignore it."

Oh shit, I'm squatting. I'm peeing on the pee.

Hunt.

No, we'll go back into the den area. We'll just pace and pee over everything that bugs us, okay? Got plenty of pee.

Hunt.

No. We'll stay here. Geez, what's that movement? Squirrel? Oh shit—

My wolf took off, and this time I got to experience what it feels like to sit as a passenger, hanging on to the seat belt, hoping doofus in the driver seat doesn't steer us into trouble.

Hell-on-wheels fun, that's what it is.

Being a ride-along is a whole lot of good times.

The faster she ran, the more her joy flooded into me.

And the longer she ran, the less I feared. Because wolves don't care jack about what's up ahead. They're all about the moment. They live in the now, not the back there or up ahead. That mind-set had to suck if you were a sixty-pound Chow Chow stuck in a two-room city condo, but it was beyond wonderful if you a were a wolf in the wild.

The chase. The sheer joy of hunting.

Somehow in the running and hunting, the union between my wolf and Hedi self changed. A new form of soul merge. I didn't fight, or swim against the current of her needs. For the moment I let her be—let her run, let her think, let her lead us over hill and dale—while I floated on her emotions.

We lost that prey, which as it turned out was not a squirrel but a chipmunk that very sensibly went down a hole. A few moments later, we picked up another trail. It was faded, forty-eight hours or older, possibly that of a female porcupine. Not particularly tasty. Whatever. We set off in pursuit for no other reason than the sheer inexpressible pleasure of running free.

I had a body, a perfect instrument of balance and grace, and I enjoyed using it. As a mortal, I'd never been able to so much as jog to the kitchen before without being aware of my weight, of the heavy bounce of my breasts, of my feet slapping on the hardwood floors. But this was so much different. I knew my paws must have touched the ground.

I *knew* I didn't fly.

Physically impossible, right? And yet running as a wolf was a very similar sensory experience to those times in Threall when I effortlessly skimmed the air above the ground, a bird without wings, a mortal without the fetters of gravity holding me earthbound.

Also? Nothing beat lupine concentration.

That's the second thing that hooked my fascination. A

wolf intent on hunt thought of little else, and let's be honest. Mortal-me had the attention of a gnat.

Make no mistake. It was strangely addictive to be so single-mindedly focused. When you poured everything you had into one single activity, all the other crap was silenced.

No questions.

No anxiety.

No wandering down paths of needless speculation. I found the utter purity of unwavering commitment to be cleansing. I clung to that single-mindedness, diving deep into her mind-set, because the alternative was pacing under an overhang of rock. Glancing at the sky. Wondering where he was . . . No, not where, but if.

If he was still safe.

I sank deep inside her, and I let her carry me. We pursued the scent of the porcupine, snout to ground, tail fat with excitement. We ran; we veered; we crisscrossed our own path.

That is, until our prey found a tree.

And then, oh man, what I'd have done for a pair of opposable thumbs.

Enough; eighteen times around a tree does not make the porcupine fall from it. Once I recognized that, my joyous lupine moment deflated. What the hell was I doing? I shoved her out of the control seat and, with a heavy sigh, sat down, prepared to bring her to heel.

We'd covered an amazing amount of ground in that short spree and she and I were tired and very thirsty by the time we'd backtracked to the point where I could see the outcrop of rock again.

For the record, a thirsty wolf is far thirstier than a dry-parched mortal. I could smell water, and its scent struck me as sweeter than the honey the farmer's market used to sell. I made a short detour, seeking to slake the ache in my throat. I found running water. Shallow, not very wide. Another one of Merenwyn's freaking rivers or, more likely, another annoying tributary that led to the River of Penance.

I hoped it was the latter. I could still visualize the map Trowbridge had drawn me. Once I got back to the overhang where I'd left Ralph, I'd perform a recon and use the river as a reference.

I padded into the stream, then unhinged my jaw and let my tongue unroll.

Oh yes.

I lapped, and lapped, and lapped. As a method of drinking, the furry version was messy and a lot of work, but it felt far better than downing a glass of juice. Maybe it was all those taste nodules. Maybe it's because of my lupine one-thing-at-a-time absorption in the task.

The water's surface was a wavering mirror.

Well, hello, beautiful.

My wolf had nice ears.

We heard a rumble and we lifted our head to gaze at the sky. It was clear. The moon baleful, the stars bright dots of light around it.

Another low grumble of distant thunder.

My left ear pivoted.

There. In the northeast. Together, my wolf and I searched the night sky again, cringing when it was lit up by a jagged flash of lightning in the distant northwest.

A single thundercloud, a personal hellhound.

Trowbridge.

We paced; we watched; we listened. The thunder rumbled eight more times, but there were no more strikes beyond that single abbreviated fork of electricity, issued from a single small storm cloud that hovered low over the distant hills.

Finally, the cloud began to move again. We watched it until we could see it no more.

The need to howl was deep inside me. I kept it smothered. I kept it leashed.

But how I wanted to howl.

The path of the least resistance is a well-trod one. That's one of those sayings you frequently stumble over. Either in essays preaching moral turpitude or in one of those entertainment magazines that are trying to be sly as they dispassionately detail a starlet's slow slide to a dismal future.

Anyhow, the cliché is worn but true.

I was dog tired. And worried about the storm cloud, and Trowbridge, and the day ahead of me. My mortal anxiety provoked a terrible hunger. For food. For my mate. For warmth. For my mother-that-wasn't, for Harry, for Anu, for Biggs . . . for people I knew but didn't even like.

I was filled with the need to be connected with something living, even if it wasn't my species. I nosed the ground. A large animal—a deer from the scent of it—had left a trail. The scent of it made my salivary glands flood.

I followed the tracks, ever so often glancing upward to make sure that I wasn't getting too off course from my intended destination.

It happened where the path narrowed to thread itself between two trees.

There was a click.

My ears heard it—*What was that?* Then before my brain could catch up to what I was hearing there was a snap.

Excruciating pressure on my hind leg.

Oh Goddess, what's got me?

Around ankle—paw—leg—what was it? The closed jaw of metal teeth.

Get it off!

Chapter Seven

Ugly. Black. Metal. *Thing.*

Teeth biting me. Metal mouth closed on my hind leg. Long chain attached to the thing. Staked somewhere. Couldn't see where.

Trapped.

My wolf's panic flooded me. And whatever slender control I owned over her feral nature broke. I was all animal, beyond reasoning, a senseless crazed beast who didn't understand that it was a Fae-made device that had me caught in its teeth.

To my wolf it was a thing. A terrible *thing.*

In frantic fear, we thrashed and rolled, heedless to the injuries we were adding in our desperate attempt to flee the jaws biting down on us. A horrible repetition of action began: lunge, yelp, nip, chew.

Freedom. Fight. Live. Run.

Bad thing.

Bite.

My gums grew bloody. Caught in the cycle of reaction, time elongated and all mortal means of measuring it disappeared. My wolf fought; I endured, unable to wrestle control from her until her flight response receded into a dumb, blind resignation.

Exhaustion wore it out.

And finally, the moment came when I eased my wolf aside and took ownership of our body. Sides heaving, we lay on our side whimpering, our tortured leg pulled back behind us. I lifted my heavy head and assessed the device with mortal eyes, for a long sick moment.

Goddess.

And thus began the list of wants.

I wanted fingers and opposable thumbs; for my tongue's sensory buds to be free of the copper taste; for my memory to be cleansed of the sight of my lacerated flesh.

I wanted to go back in time, to before the click and before the snick. To before Mad-one's visit and her warnings about last chances.

I wanted my wolf's innate healing process to kick in. Why wasn't my flesh making an effort to knit back over like it should? Because it wasn't showing any sign of regeneration at all. Not even on the outside margins of the wound.

How badly injured is a wolf when her body forgets how to heal itself?

More "wants."

I wanted to tear at the pale throat of the monstrous Fae who'd planted the metal trap so carefully. To feast on the guts of the person who'd dug the hole, and buried the trap, and staked the end of it to the tree. To chew on the bones of the unseen enemy who'd trapped me with this steel-toothed device.

But most of all, I wished that the pain—pulsing, living, biting—would stop.

Just. Stop.

The moon had moved from the middle of my horizon

to a few degrees left. How long before I was found? How long did I have to live through this?

What if no one ever came?

A ripple of fear raised my fur into hackles.

I'd used my Goddess's name a lot in my life. I'd raised it as shorthand for disbelief (*Goddess, spare me the sight of another human*) and I'd wasted her goodwill on stupid stuff (*Goddess, don't make me fat for eating this Kit Kat*).

But now I really hoped that she could hear me.

For I knew that I had to wait.

And endure.

At the very least, until it was morning, when I had hands again, not paws that were useful for digging but lousy for grasping things. The trees around me blurred. *Don't go to Threall.* I placed my muzzle upon my front paw. Inhaled the scent of bruised sweet peas and churned-up earth.

One last desperate quiet plea was quietly added before I passed out.

Goddess, I need you.

Please stay with me through the night.

You see, that's when my luck started changing. Though I didn't know it then. But really, few of us do sense a change in opportunity when we're at the bottom of a very dark pit looking upward at the sunlight, do we? We just see the light and wish we could be teleported to it. We spend so much time longing for a new situation other than misery and hopelessness that we're insensible to the moment someone scoops us up with gentle hands and lifts us higher.

But believe me. My luck had changed and my Goddess had heard me.

For I lost consciousness.

And that was a very good thing, for it gave my Goddess time to work things out with Karma.

* * *

I came to slowly. Automatically I moved slightly, hoping to ease the ache, and hot sensation corkscrewed through me, streaking upward from the fire that encircled my ankle.

"You don't do things by half, do you, Hell?" I heard my twin murmur through my fog of pain.

Lexi?

A shudder of dread. Had I fallen asleep? Had I gone to Threall? I opened my wolf eyes. Saw nothing beyond me but the earth I'd churned up with my claws, and the fragments of broken bark, and the water that I wanted but could not have.

"You're hurt. Tell me what's happened," said my brother's voice. "Where are you?"

I'm here.

"I don't know where 'here' is. Open your eyes again so I can see through them." A hand stroked my fur, from my thick ruff to my rear flank. "Please, Hell. Show me what you see."

I lifted my heavy lupine head and looked around me. There was no fog, no smoke, no mystwalker, no twin. Lexi was not by my flank. Not by the top of the narrow trail. Not by the ribbon of water. He was *not* there.

And there was nothing to see. Except my wolf's mangled leg stretched behind me, and bits of fur and other stuff I didn't want to look at.

"God's teeth," said my brother, shock sharpening his tone. "She's caught in a trap."

Get it off me.

My fur ruffled as phantom fingers moved down the tendons of my leg. "It's bad." His voice sounded terrible. Anger cutting into it. "She's done a lot of damage. She'll never get out of this on her own."

Who was Lexi talking to?

Is Mad-one there?

I waited, ears pricked forward. Maybe Mad-one had more healing. Maybe she could come visit me and place her hand on my paw and I wouldn't hurt so much. I waited a long time for an answer. Too long. My head grew weary of the effort of holding it high. I let it droop to my front paw. There was no one here, except me, and the trap. No people. No friends.

Alone.

"You're not alone," he told me, his tone rough. "We are *all* here."

All? I repeated the word inside my head, knowing it was important. The reasoning part of me was dulled; my brain circled around the word "all" like a wolf examining something that smelled bad.

"Don't think so hard," said Lexi.

And then I felt it—the gentle push of his mind against mine, the knock-knock he used to send me before we exchanged a thought-picture.

Yes. I sighed, gratefully abandoning the task of thinking.

I opened my mind and felt him slip in. Warmth. Twinship—two vessels on the same current of emotion and thought.

I was not alone.

Then I felt an interior tug, one I'd never encountered before. Followed by the oddest stretching sensation, as if my twin had caught the tailing length of my pain and he was pulling it out of me and bringing along with it the awful memories of this night, and the night before that, and even beyond that, back to the dreary life between the night of his abduction and the day I found Trowbridge.

If only briefly, my twin emptied me of some of the awful, and, in return, he sent me an image. A thought-picture—of us, the summer before he was taken. A towheaded boy and a brown-haired girl sitting on a boulder, set by the edge of a pond. Dirty knees, sunburned cheeks.

I sent him back another image. Of the trail from the Creemore fairy pond that leads up to the Trowbridge ridge. Then, on the heels of that, another of the house that could have been made into a home.

I want Trowbridge. The thought was a cry.

The answer came after a long pause, during which my hopes climbed to pitiful heights and my little wolfish heart thudded hard. Eventually, my brother said quietly, "We can't, shrimp. We can't send him."

Why not? I howled in frustration.

"Mad-one doesn't know where to find his soul in Threall."

Mad-one's there?

"I'm talking through her."

That didn't make much sense to my lupine brain. I let out a whine of frustration and chewed at my paw. A moment later I received a hazy image of Mad-one's hands pressed upon the spines of both trees.

Tell her to come. I need her to touch my leg. It hurts.

"She can't, Hell."

Then you come. Come and get me out of this. I want to be free.

"I can't make it there in time, shrimp." His tone was quiet, but remorse weighted every word. Thick as a raw steak and twice as bloody. "I'll see you soon. Just rest. We're sending someone to help you."

No. I'm going to come to you. I won't hurt in Threall.

"No! You must remain where you are. Help is on its way. It won't be long."

How. Long?

"A few hours."

If he'd said "thirty minutes," I'd have cringed. But hours . . . oh sweet heavens . . . hours. All those fears and whimpers I'd kept on lockdown broke free. *I can't do it. I can't last that long. I'm so scared, Lexi. I don't know where I am—*

"But I do. You just have to wait. Then I'll see you at Daniel's Rock."

I don't know how to find my way there! I don't know the land. I don't speak the language—how can I find my way if I can't speak the language? And I don't know these people—oh, Lexi, what they've done to the wolves—

"Shrimp, you know the language." Another stroke of an unseen hand. "You spoke it in Threall. You just need to remember it."

I can't—

"I'll help you remember it. I have magic . . . it will help."

Shivering, I leaned into the phantom's cool caress.

"She's in pain," I heard Lexi say in a low voice. "Give me more magic, Mage; give me . . ."

Don't make bargains with the wily old goat. He's tainted, Lexi. His magic will be bad for you. Just stay here with me until help comes.

He wasn't listening. Ever headstrong, he kept talking to the mage.

"Give me more magic!" Lexi shouted. "I don't give a shit what it costs. You do this, Mage . . . Don't tell me I'm not ready. I've been in this hell long enough. Don't stand in my way—Yes! I'm guilty of a lot of things. Don't lecture me now, Mage! Stars, I have not asked for much, but you will give me this. Give me the magic to take her pain."

Lexi. Don't. You don't want this pain.

"It's going to be okay," he said quickly. "You're going to feel good soon; I promise."

Don't do it.

But had he ever listened to me? The pain . . . it had been a weighted blanket that I couldn't remove. Suddenly I felt it lift, and now my legs could move without hurt and the air could circulate and the dreadful cloying heat of that horse blanket was gone . . . It was gone . . . It was gone . . .

"Don't cry." The pacing of his words was strange, as if he was talking between deep inhales.

I'm not. Wolves don't cry.

He didn't answer. Not for a long time. And then I felt his hand again, resting on the side of my fur. It trembled. And I did something that I didn't understand but felt compelled to do anyhow.

I lifted my bloodstained snout to the moon and howled.

I woke to dulled sensation, half-aware of birds chirping and the vague distraction of other sundry "let's greet the morning" forest sounds. I ached unbearably, both inside and out.

I knew myself to be alone.

And likely, I'd spent the night in solitude. For I was still here: near enough for the water's scent to torture my throat, completely unable to slake my own thirst.

Lexi's voice had been a hallucination, born of my loneliness and pain. I'd wanted to believe that my brother would rescue me like he had when were kids and playing Knights of the Round Table. I'd pleaded with my Goddess not to leave me to suffer alone. And when no one came, I'd created a piece of fiction to comfort myself.

Depression swelled.

I was still stuck in the trap. And now, smelling my own blood, I was utterly convinced that the conversation I'd held with my brother had been completely conducted in my own head. I'd needed him, so I'd presented myself with a facsimile. Not a walking-talking illusion such as Mad-one had presented me, mind you. Just a kindly voice to comfort myself.

It had promised me everything I wanted. Help on the way, a certificate of language proficiency, and of course the much-needed pain relief. The only thing my fantasy bro hadn't volunteered to do was spring the damn trap himself.

Wake up and smell the blood, Hedi. You're still here, still thirsty, hind leg still caught in the trap's metal teeth. Victim to the squeezing pressure of its jaws . . .

Wait a minute.

I drew in a breath, listening hard to my body.

Son of a bitch. I wasn't in agony anymore. Instead of shrieking about unendurable pain, my body nattered about being uncomfortable. It whined about the continued squeeze of the trap, it moaned how my back, my rump, and my shoulders were aching with cold, and it topped off its list of complaints with a mention of my punishingly dry throat.

Unbelievable.

I slit my eyes open a fraction. Through the veil of my wet hair, I saw my own hand—very mortal and dirty—curled in a half fist. The lower trunk of the tree beside me had most of its bark clawed off. Little hunks littered the ground, as well as what looked like a canine's nail. I looked beyond that and saw the ribbon of the river. Early-morning mist scudded over it.

I was "me" again.

The sun had risen while I slumbered, and I had gone through the metamorphosis of wolf to mortal without waking. I had two arms again. Fingers that curled and would be soon put to work. A very human and distressingly dry tongue that was busy exploring the inside of a mouth and rejoicing over the fact that it was filled with teeth, not a canine's pointed fangs.

Me, me, me.

Was I still caught in the trap? My leg felt heavy and hot but not . . . I moved my leg slightly and cringed when I heard the metal monster grating sickeningly on my anklebone. *Goddess.* I couldn't feel my foot or my ankle. Everything right up to my knee was numb. *Shit, shit, shit.* How long could a foot last without blood moving through it?

What if my foot had already turned black? I squeezed my eyes shut again in dismay. I knew I had to check, but knowing that your body has suffered grievous injury and seeing it in gritty detail are two completely different things. One's intellectual; the other's emotional.

Open your eyes, I told myself. *You've got to look.*

But I don't want to look.

You're stronger than you think you are, I reminded myself. *And besides, you've got magic. She can spring us out of this trap.*

Now there's a plan.

I felt for magic-mine and found her, brooding in my gut. I gave her a mental poke and told her to rise. She curled into a tighter ball of "don't want to."

Seriously? Was she sulking that she'd been the odd girl out while my wolf and I had bonded? That was beyond ridiculous. The only time she tolerated being girl-to-the-power-of-three was when she sensed the possibility of mayhem and murder.

Enough. She can murder the trap.

I gave her another tap, this one firmer. Grudgingly, she entered my bloodstream. My chilled body heated as her magic coursed through my veins, spreading upward. Past my heart, past my shoulders, down my arms. To each one of my cold, clawed fingers.

I felt stronger.

All right, I thought. *I'll count to three. Then, my magic and me will pry apart the teeth, and following some requisite screaming we'll be free. Ready to hobble to Daniel's Rock.*

We can do this.

Yup, I was feeling pretty damn optimistic when a young

man spoke up and nearly scared the crap out of me. "I tell
you the dead woman's wearing an amulet."

"She's not dead," replied a woman.

"Near enough."

Shit.

Cautiously, I eased my lids open a fraction. I saw my arm,
plump and white, but no sign of the speakers. Which meant
the squabbling duo had to be behind me. My spine crawled
at the thought of them observing all parts of my naked vulnerability. I wanted to clench my thighs, but if I did that
I'd lose the whole element of surprise.

I willed my body to lay lax as a *Penthouse* babe's while
I figured out who they were.

Were they Fae or Were? Foe or friend?

I inhaled lightly through my nostrils and found no scent,
except for horse. Fear rose a notch; who rode while others
ran? The Fae.

"It does not matter if she's alive or dead. Find something to pry open the trap." The woman's enunciation was
refined, her tone dismissive.

Holy crap. I could understand her perfectly. She was
speaking in Merenwynian and I could understand every
single plummy word. Hell's bells, I could even detect the
gaping difference in class between the two of them. She
was top-drawer; he was not.

My skin prickled.

Lexi had said he'd take my agony and I was painless.
He'd promised to bestow upon me the gift of language and
I was following their conversation as easily as listening to
the radio.

Ergo, Lexi *had* visited me last night.

He'd also promised to send help. Were these Fae the
help? They sounded more like body-looters.

The young male's tone ripened with disgust. "Who'd

waste precious gold on a wolf's choke restraint? Besides, I told you—I saw an amulet."

Yep. Looters.

"I see no pendant."

"I didn't say 'pendant,' now, did I, *Mis-tress*?" The young male broke the salutation into two long syllables of poorly suppressed irritation. "I said 'amulet,' and you cannot see it because it *moved*. It scuttled under her hair."

The woman drew in a shocked breath. "You forget your place, mutt. I am—"

"The Fae who doesn't know how to get back to her own castle. You don't know these woods, do you? Not like you know the ones you nip off to in the middle of the night."

"You are insolent," she said in a low voice.

"Aye, and proud of it." The male walked into my sight line and I was treated to a quick view of rough clothing and a hank of medium brown hair and incredibly grimy feet. Had he ever worn shoes? His feet were so soiled the dirt looked part of him.

He held a burlap sack, tied with a piece of rough twine, which he placed down with distinct care. He bent to pick up a stick.

Hit me with it and it will be the last thing you do, I thought.

My eyes strained to follow him through my downcast lashes as he moved around me again. My Fae swelled at my fingertips. My ankle might be held immobile between a trap's teeth, but now that I was in my mortal shell I was not helpless anymore.

I had magic.

"Your kind are always dreaming of the found treasure," dismissed the woman. "It's likely a wolf collar, and if not that, it's but a chain with a trinket on the end of it. Wolves don't wear amulets."

"The Son of Lukynae did. I saw him when they brought

him to Wryal's. He wore one and they couldn't get the bleeding thing off him." He drew in some air sharply through his nose; then he clicked his teeth. "She doesn't carry the scent of the Raha'ells or even a Kuskador, even if with my own eyes I can see the bits of fur from her change." His tone turned flat. "She's a mutt like me."

The male walked past me again, the stick in his grip tapping a tuneless beat against the side of his leg. "But I don't recognize her," he said thoughtfully. "And I know all of my own kind."

"You don't need to," the woman dismissed. "Help me open the trap. Once it's off her leg, we can leave." I heard a creak of saddle leather and the slide-thump of a person dismounting. Leaves shivered as she tied her mount's bridle to a tree.

"Who is she, then?" Feigned nonchalance in his tone, caution marked by the tension of his naked toes. "What does she mean to you?"

"I will stand for no more of your questions, Mouse."

Mouse? How do you live down a name like that?

With bravado, it seemed.

"We're not in the castle anymore, Mistress," he said, sinking into a crouch before me. "And you hired me to lead you back to it." He balanced himself on the backs of his heels. "You know what the Royal Court would say if I brought them an amulet?" The stick dangled from his grip. " 'Are you hungry, mutt? Here is a joint of beef. Are you tired, mutt? Here is a soft, warm bed.' "

I don't think so, buddy.

Merry, who'd been so silent and still, stealthily unfurled two arms of ivy. I allowed some of my Fae essence to stream from my fingers.

The woman huffed. "More likely they'd say, 'Let's torture the insolent mutt.' "

"Indeed?" He rose to his feet. "Well then, perhaps it's best if we leave the lass here."

"You will help me," she spat, low and mean.

"I can leave you flat, Mistress," he said very softly. "I could leave you here and none would be the wiser."

"Help me free her and I'll pay you double."

"You've paid me nothing so far beyond a promise of riches," he said dryly. "Before I set her free, you'll tell me the truth of why we had to slip out of the castle, sly-like, and who this woman is."

"I marked our trail. I know the way back. I'll go back to the castle, and tell them that you ran away. They'll set the hounds on you."

"I'm not supposed to live beyond a few more winters anyway," he said with remarkable cheerfulness. "And before I die, I'll tell them all about that secret passage you just showed me. They think you spend your evenings alone, polishing the pretties, don't they? But now they'll watch, and perhaps they'll begin to wonder about your unexplained absences."

A very pregnant pause stretched between them.

"I don't know who she is!" she finally snapped.

At last, I saw the edge of her skirt out of the corner of my left eye. She had very small feet and one of them was tapping with distemper.

"Right. I'll be leaving now."

"I had a bad dream," she said reluctantly.

"I'm missing my chores and earning myself a few stripes on my back from the cook because you had a bad dream?" A snort of derision. "Did you partake of the mead last night?"

"You know full well I do not drink."

"Then tell me another one. How were you able to send me such a clear thought-picture that I knew where this place was without having to stumble about in the woods?"

The woman audibly swallowed, then whispered, "Because I was visited in my sleep last night."

"Stars," said Mouse. "Forget my threats; you're damned already."

"The mystwalker said if I didn't free this woman, she'd never leave me alone. She'd visit me every night for as long as I lived if I ignored her request." Her voice turned venomous. "To have that . . . creature . . . inside my mind. It would be unbearable."

Everybody's a hater.

"Help me free this mutt from the trap," cajoled the woman. "I'll pay you well."

"I'm wondering if your idea of payment and mine are the same, Mistress." Mouse shifted onto a knee to reach out with his stick. The pointed edge of it scratched a line along the slope of my shoulder. Cool air chilled the damp skin on my neck as Mouse's tool lifted my hair.

"See!" he exclaimed. "It *is* an amulet."

His thieving hand went for Merry, and I went for him.

The horse neighed in fright as I lurched upward, my magic erupting in streams of green florescence from both hands.

"Get Mouse!" I told my talent. Invisible to him but so very tangible to me, a coil of green magic shot out toward the teenager, who'd only just realized that not-quite dead was a very different thing from all-the-way dead.

His own eyes flew wide in shock when my magic found his neck.

Then Merry sprung, very much like that thing in *Alien,* except she's pretty and that face-chewing creature is really ugly and she's much smaller and wasn't intent on impregnating him—okay, she was nothing like that monster in *Alien.* She was Merry simply being herself: an amulet with attitude and the proven ability to spring at someone's face and latch on. I heard him scream, saw his hands go from his throat to her.

And then, that quickly, and with that much lack of compassion, I dismissed him. I didn't give a rat's ass that his cry got chopped off mid-note or that it was already turning into a choking rasp.

I didn't give a crap.

I was already rolling on my left hip, searching for his mistress. Because of the two, she was the bigger threat. She might have magic to match mine. She was—

Stars, she was the Gatekeeper.

Chapter Eight

I'm not sure if we said, "You!" in unison. It's possible, but there was a lot going on and in the end that became just another detail I never completely nailed down for the memory book.

I know we gaped at each other.

We did that much.

Then Mouse, who'd been making interesting choking, rasping noises behind me, decided tearing at his neck was useless and that it was time to put his all into the alternate option of flight. The boy got to his knees and started power-crawling away from the big bad, which in this case was me, Merry, and my magic.

My right arm had been torqued behind me—I'd rolled as far as I could onto my opposite hip in order to blast the Gatekeeper with the magic streaming from my left hand—and suddenly, without any warning, I found myself being rolled in the boy's direction.

Hell no. I was not turning my back on the Gatekeeper. She was *not* going to make another clean getaway.

"Grab her too!" I told my magic.

There's nothing my Fae likes more than a good target, and as it turns out, she's very adept at multi-tasking. Two targets? No problem: I had two hands. My chest flared hot as she quickly split evenly between the two.

"She has magic!" the Gatekeeper screamed.

Well, duh. Though having magic wasn't doing me a helluva lot of good. The boy was dragging me—*my leg, Goddess, my leg*—and Merry's chain was scoring into the back of my neck, and the Gatekeeper was struggling behind me, and with each one of her jerks my left arm flirted with the idea of separating from its socket.

It all pissed me off.

I counteracted the boy's retreat with a sudden lurch of my own, throwing myself backward so that I lay flat on my back. A second later, Mouse fell on top of me. His knee drove into my belly.

I hit him, right on top of his head. "Get off me!" He tried, but Merry was still very much engaged with torturing his nose and cheek. "Merry! Knock it off!" I shrieked. "I'm drowning here."

Perhaps it was the tone, because she dropped Mouse as if he were the plague carrier of plague carriers.

Gasping, Mouse rolled right off me.

My leg felt wrong. All that sudden movement, plus the aborted jackknife I'd attempted when the mutt had kneed me . . . it had led to a distinct sense of wrongness. The sort of awful that compels one to look. But it was so hard to see because the Gatekeeper was thrashing about as if she were having a seizure and that kept jerking me around. But finally, I got up onto my elbow and looked down.

I saw the trap and my gaze recoiled, flitting over to safer territory. The bits of blood-tacked fur underneath the chain that was attached to the thing—*the evil biting thing*—and from there to small puddles of post-change effluence, and the long, raking claw marks made by a creature who'd tried to drag herself away from the thing—*the evil biting thing*—that had held her fast all night and still held her.

Yes. Still held her.

My gaze lurched back to the thing and to the piece of meat clamped between its jaws. And finally, I forced myself to behold my own flesh—and by that I mean the kind of pink, mangled hamburger stuff you're never supposed to see.

Oh my Goddess.

I looked away, past Mouse's shoulder, to the canopy of trees. Green leaves, tall trees. Trunks wide as an old sailing ship's mast. Bark. Boughs. Sun breaking through the long spars. *Focus on that. Give yourself time. Don't throw up. Don't turn girlie. And beyond all other things, don't let your chin crumple.*

I knew I wouldn't come out of it without some scarring and had braced myself for some mangled skin, but never in my wildest dreams had I anticipated the bracelet of festering gaping holes.

Goddess, holes.

I took another shuddering glance. And when I saw the creamy glint of bone beneath the freakin' holes, my anger exploded.

I am part wolf, you know? That makes me stronger than I look. And I'm part Fae, which makes me prone to prissiness and acts of casual cruelty. And I'm indisputably a female with a mangled ankle, which needs no qualifier whatsoever.

This wolf-Fae-woman was on the point of nuclear fusion.

I flung my arms wide—spread open—just like my mum did whenever she was about to let forth a rant about kids who would not behave. My magic was still attached to Mouse by the neck and the Gatekeeper by her waist and thus we were still miserably tethered together, so they went for a very short ride.

A thud as Mouse tumbled to my right, and lighter thud as the Gatekeeper hit the dirt on my left.

I lay there, arms flung wide, flat on my back, chest heaving. And truthfully, I had zero concerns for their relative health. All I was thinking was, *Keep them off me,* and, *Oh sweet heavens, my leg.* It was a cease-fire—at least for me.

Until she croaked, "Kill her!"

Really?

Completely attuned to all the glories of me—magic, wolf-strength, girl-power—everything fell into place. I didn't have to think things through. I didn't have to speak to my magic and tell her to tighten up and get ready for the lift. I didn't have to question whether I had sufficient muscle mass to do what I wanted to do.

As Yoda taught, I thought not.

I simply did.

I raised both arms, and Mouse and the Gatekeeper went airborne. They dangled above me, living puppets kicking their heels. The boy's face was kind of purple. The Fae's boots stopped at her thick ankles. Interesting.

And then she said, "Foul creature!"

Ah, screw it.

I slapped my hands together and their noggins hit with an audible thump.

You really can knock some sense into someone, given enough reason and complete disregard for the subsequent demise of a few thousand of their brain cells. However, my strength had come from the same source that gives ninety-pound women enough muscle mass to lift Volkswagen Beetles off their beloved. And as we all know, that's usually both spectacular and short-lived.

When my arms began to tremble like they did that unfortunate time I tried Pilates, I went back to my original pose. Supine on my spine, arms flat out, right leg twisted horribly. I watched the sky—it was going to be a cloudless day—and listened to the hoarse rasp coming from Mouse. Grudgingly, I eased off on my magic, allowing the guy who was going to get me out of the trap a little air. However, I kept a pincer hold on the Gatekeeper's waist. I'd lost her once; I wouldn't lose her twice.

"Release me," she said, and the line of magic tethering us gave a twitch.

"No," I replied.

"I will free you if you let me go."

"You'll do that anyhow," I said. "I'm going to sit up. If either of you makes a sudden move that will cause me any grief—I'm talking the slightest level of irritation—I'm going to knock some sense into you again. Starting with you, Gatekeeper. Got that?"

I twisted my neck a tad and Merry's chain slipped from the groove it had cut into the nape of my neck. Another burst of sweet-pea scent. I was bleeding. Perversely, I blamed the Gatekeeper for that.

"I want this trap off me," I told them.

"I can spring it," said Mouse in a cracked whisper.

I rolled my head to squint at him. He was both younger and older than I thought. Listening to his bravado, I'd mentally pegged him at around sixteen. But now, taking in his stature and general air of malnourishment, I revised that estimate to either a short fourteen- or a tall twelve-year-old. He had an intelligent face and disordered, floppy hair that needed a wash.

"Do they feed you enough?" I asked, thinking about another mutt, one who was stolen from me at the age of twelve.

Mouse's brow pleated. "If I eat too much, I'll grow too much."

"And why is that a problem?"

"My wolf will grow too strong." Though Mouse didn't add "Are you daft?" to his reply, there had been a wealth of inflection to his comment. The statement lay there between us. An invisible insult.

"You didn't turn into your wolf last night? Are you too young?"

"I took the potion," he rasped, clearly insulted. "Like any other mutt. And will do, until my mistress decides that I've grown to enough to become a threat and that it would be better to find a new mutt to do her chores."

That had to suck.

I sat up, and a short moment later Mouse did too. I looked to my left. The Gatekeeper appeared dazed. "Are you going to give me any problems?" I asked her.

"Mutt," she hissed at me.

Some people need visuals about mutts and their powers.

"Up," I said wearily again, and merrily, merrily up she went. Her feet scissored; her voluminous skirts flapped.

"I am a Fae of royal birth!" she screeched, sharp little nails tearing at the unseen thing that cinched her waist so tightly.

More blah, blah, blah.

I twisted my wrist, and upside down my toy went, somehow reminding me of one of those wooden Russian dolls. Maybe it was the skirts; maybe it was the vest with its embroidered emblem. Or was it the stiff fringe of her bangs, peeping out from her kerchief? I couldn't quite put my finger on it.

"Can you make her bounce again?" asked Mouse.

I turned to look at him.

"Your eyes," he said in a shocked whisper. "Only once before have I seen eyes like that. Pale as the green glass bottles in the mage's tower." He reared back to sketch a hasty hex sign in the air.

"Now you're hurting my feelings," I said.

Great. The mutt knew both Lexi and the Black Mage. So much for a happy working situation. I sighed. "Listen up, you two. You're going to work together to free me from this trap. Then, you're going to put me on that pony. After that, you're going to take me where I want to go."

"Where?" asked Mouse.

"Daniel's Rock."

"I don't where it is," he said far too quickly.

Dumb kid, trying to lie to a liar.

"You do, and you'll take me there. But first," I said, gingerly turning to look at the overhang of rock where I'd left Ralph, "we're going to get me some clothing."

The horse was not a horse but a pony that had spent many pleasurable hours at the feed trough. My inner thighs ached from hugging her fat sides. Seabiscuit didn't much care for being ridden by a half Fae, half Were with an injured leg—a disapproval she aired with periodic tail flicks—but she seemed otherwise content to plod along without much steering.

A good thing, because I couldn't hold on to her reins properly, my hands being otherwise occupied with the two tethers of magic that kept Mouse and his mistress from doing a runner. The female Fae was ahead of me, those small hands so capable of firing balyfire pinned to her hips by one revolution of my magic. A looser knot was looped around Mouse's waist.

The boy took better to the leash situation than the Gatekeeper, for the most part pretending that nothing restrained him. On the other hand, his mistress had affected a few "accidental" stumbles within the first quarter hour, likely to test the bound's strength.

And after that, she'd fallen silent.

I imagine she was cursing herself for not taking better advantage of the earlier escape opportunity.

When I'd forced them to take me back to the place where I'd left my clothing and Ralph, I'd realized that I couldn't bring them into the cave. They'd see the Royal Amulet. His presence in this world should be a secret—I understood that without fully knowing why I did.

So, I'd taken a calculated risk, severing my magic and using it to surround Mouse and the Gatekeeper in a fat coil that kept them secured to the tree growing just outside the mouth of the cave. I'd done it gambling that I could retrieve Ralph before they figured a way of sliding out of their temporary bonds.

I'd been right on that. It had taken less than a minute to jam His Royal Ass-hat into my jean pockets and only a couple more to get over the heave session incurred from yanking my pant leg over my savaged ankle.

When I'd shakily hopped out of the cave on one foot I'd been afraid that they'd be long gone, but they were still there. Mouse had turned red faced from his efforts to squirm free from the magic donut, but the Gatekeeper had stood unmoving, her eyes fixed speculatively on the mouth of the cave.

Who, me? Escape? That had been the message written on her impassive face.

I suppose I was to deduce from that that she had no magic other than the ability to hurl fireballs. Yeah, right. Like she wasn't sitting on her hidden talents, hoping to ambush me later. I kept asking myself, *What else does she have? And why isn't she using it?*

Food for thought.

I'd get right to unraveling that puzzler if I wasn't so damn sleepy. "Tired" didn't cover it—I was near stupid with fatigue. Brain muzzy, eyelids weighted. Not tired, drugged. The drowsiness was an unnecessary complication. What was with that? I'd been in worse situations. Okay, I'd suffered a nasty injury. But people had become terribly keen on killing me. Getting hit, punched, choked, or stabbed was becoming the norm. Facing injury no longer put me into the danger of going into shock.

As for being tired? I'd gone longer without a nap. Not willingly, but longer.

Maybe it was the prefect trifecta of misery? Not one thing, but three. I was hurt, physically drained, *and* starving. Yep, that would do it. I was so famished, my gut hurt all the time. Hell, it bothered me more than my ankle, and you had to appreciate how bad my leg was to comprehend the hidden weird in that statement.

Despite my wolf-blood, my injury wasn't healing quickly. Though I hadn't looked in over an hour, from the smell of sweet peas blooming in the woods I knew the wound was still oozing blood.

Clearly, Lexi had taken my agony and kept it.

A piece of knowledge that held me stiff in the saddle, acutely conscious that every minute adjustment I made to my own personal comfort might be adding to my brother's anguish.

You see how each of my endless "wants" fed back onto another problem? I was hungry, so I thought of endless food metaphors, which made me all the more conscious of the squeezing pain of my empty gut. This led me to ponder on the non-existence of pain in my leg and the need to remain still.

Which, of course, made me want to move.

I could console myself that I actually was moving forward by plodding slowly toward the Two Sisters, but that didn't stop me from aching to stretch my leg. If only to kick the Gatekeeper, who every so often turned around—eyes narrowed, mouth pursed—to check to see if I was still up-right.

Exactly like she was doing right now.

I gave her a nod.

Yes, bitch. Still sitting upright.

You'd think she'd give that a rest, considering what she knew of my connections. I was the Shadow's sister—a fact she'd sussed out at first glance based on the distinctive eye color I share with Lexi—and I obviously had friends in high places. As far as she knew, I was Mad-one's one and only BFF. Think about it: with ten thousand Fae souls or more from which to choose, the Mystwalker of Threall had tapped *her* for my rescue. How's that for coincidence? The only Fae who knew how to open the Safe Passage being coerced into helping the halfling from Creemore who didn't know how to open it.

I wouldn't want to make book on that.

While the sour-faced Fae chewed over those odds, I'd reached my own conclusion. There could be only one ex-planation for the Gatekeeper's providential appearance, and it came with a gut-punch: Mad-one had delved more deeply into my memories than I'd realized, culling important de-tails such as the fact that I needed the surly Fae's amulet and knowledge to return home to Creemore.

I'd sensed Mad-one's intrusion during our talk yester-day afternoon and thought I'd rebuffed her. But now I was wondering if she'd ever truly left. What if the Mystwalker of Threall's palm was semi-permanently glued to the trunk of my walnut?

Ew.

It was entirely possible that she was listening to me think right now.

If she was, she could go fuck herself. Right after she told me exactly how much of my inner musings she was passing to the devious old bastard sharing my brother's soul.

I swallowed down some sick and rebalanced my left wrist on the saddle's pommel. Neither one of the twin cables of magic streaming from my fingers was weightless.

How much longer?

I lifted bleary eyes to the cloudless sky and marked the sun at mid-morning. Trowbridge had reckoned it was a half day from the shallow crossing to the path between the two hills. Daniel's Rock would be on the other side. But last night's run had added miles and we were coming at the two hills from a slightly different direction.

I didn't know how much longer it was going to be. And I wasn't going to ask.

Stay awake.

A few miles back Merry had instigated a campaign of pinches and jabs in an effort to keep me in the here and now, but about five dales ago she'd run out of gas too. Now, under the cover of my shirt, she lay sluggish, bouncing between the valley of the girls.

Stay awake.

I forced my eyes wide until my brows rose, and then wider again until I could feel my pointed Fae ears pull back, and then, for lack of anything better to do, I pinned my dull gaze upon Mouse. His hair needed washing, his clothing needed burning, and he had a long scar running down the inside of his arm.

My rope of magic was a glowing green coil around his waist.

Mouse shot an upward glance at me through his lashes. "Fair gave me a fright the first time the Shadow's eyes rested on me. But then I said to myself, for all his fine clothes, the Shadow was a mutt, just like me. Is he your da, then?"

"No."

"And here I thought I knew every mutt's face." Mouse caught a low branch and held it away back so my trusty pony and I could pass.

"Stop fishing," I told him, bending low over the saddle.

"Never in my life have I taken a fishing pole to the River of Penance." He let the branch fly with enough force for my hair to stir in the backdraft. "Where has he kept you? Some village sympathetic to your birth, filled with kindly souls who don't mind the Shadow's mutt among them?"

"Still fishing."

"You're a mutt," stated Mouse, his tone flat, "whoever your da may be. And they won't forget that—the Fae *never* forget that. The Shadow may have worn the silks of the court, but he was never one of them, was he? I know he's missing from the court. They say the Black Mage has their hounds looking for him as well as the Son of Lukynae. If he's sent word that he needs your help and you answer him, you're fat for the fire."

At mention of the Black Mage's name, my insides clenched, which my Fae incorrectly read as a threat. She reacted without leave, swelling until the slack, invisible rope about the boy's torso tightened into a squeezing vice.

Mouse's face set, his nostrils flared with pain. They were fine nostrils. On a boy better dressed, on a youth better loved, they'd be elegant ones.

Still he didn't try to fight the restraint. It made me think that he must be accustomed to being restrained and/or being hurt.

"Lighten up, magic-mine!" I snapped. "He's allowed to talk."

She hesitated, the shiny bits inside the stream of green flashing her reluctance; then she sulkily loosened her hold. And something changed in Mouse's expression, or perhaps better said, something was added to his carefully set countenance.

He edged closer and I put a cautious hand on the burlap sack that brushed against my knee. "Why is getting to that God-cursed rock so important that a mystwalker would sink into a shit-pool like my mistress's mind?" I didn't answer, suddenly awash with the need to move in my saddle again, and he asked with a trace of his old belligerence, "Do you think you're better than me?"

"Oh, don't get your panties in such a twist. I'm not better than you and I'm not less than you. I'm just me."

A girl with a quest and a numb bottom.

"What are panties?"

"Something I wish I'd thought to put on before I left my house yesterday." I gave the strand of hair tickling my nose a huff and it went back to tormenting the corner of my lip.

The path narrowed to curl around an outcrop of boulders about the same time as the land began dropping on our left side. I was leery of Seabiscuit taking a misstep into the ditch widening on our left, but she seemed unconcerned. Her gait never faltered; she lumbered along, seemingly indifferent to my body's tension.

I forced myself to relax my muscles and tried not to think of my chafed bits.

Mouse took an opportunity to study me from toes to nose. "You'll never make it on your own to the rock." His tone was matter-of-fact. "You're about to slide off your saddle like butter tipped from a fry pan."

"I won't fall."

He nodded toward the Gatekeeper, who was pretending not to listen but so very much was. "If you do, she'll be on you."

"I repeat, I'm not going to fall." I straightened, vertebra by vertebra. "Why are you telling me this?"

"You'll be needing friends. And mayhap, I'll be needing some."

"I have lots of friends."

He did a walking turn, arms held wide. "I don't see any."

The front of my shirt rustled. Two golden arms grabbed either side of the chain I wore around my neck, then held on for the ride as Merry shortened the length of Fae gold until her amber pendant rested upright an inch or two above my cleavage line. Too weary to climb higher but too belligerent to let such a challenge rest, my BFF hung, arms raised, the bottom of her pendant balanced on the curve of her chain. A wrestler, waiting with resigned fatigue for the next round.

Mouse stared at her with parted lips.

"Meet my little friend, Merry."

"Leaping goats," Mouse breathed. "It's the Son of Lukynae's amulet."

"Rock," I warned him when he was in danger of walking backward into a boulder.

He executed a quick-footed evasion. "Who *are* you?"

"I'm Hedi of Creemore." My gaze dropped to Merry as I spoke. With dismay, I noticed that her amber stone had a brownish cast and her inner light had faded to a pinprick of red. No wonder she'd grown quiet over the last couple of miles.

She was starving too.

Now that I focused on it, I realized that Ralph had been peculiarly quiet since I'd jammed him in my jeans pocket. Normally, he made his presence known, at least to the person who bore him, but he'd hardly twitched this last age.

Last night's dinner had amounted to a snack. There'd been no time to fully satisfy their hungers before the moon dominated the sky.

We'd have to stop, but stopping had a lot of built-in problems. Unless I could navigate my pony over to a stand of trees, get within arm's reach of a healthy branch, and let my amulets take over from there . . .

I studied the staggered ridge of firs above the outcrop of rocks.

Not worth the climb. *Merry hates spruces.*

I swiveled in my saddle.

Though the ground dropped sharply away, the forests to my left were a smorgasbord of yum: elders, beeches, and maples. Merry and Ralph could pick their choice if I could only get to them. However, we had that ditch bordering the beaten path. As an obstacle, it wasn't terribly deep or wide, but navigating its incline would prove a daunting challenge to my minimal riding skills. Up to now, any pitch changes to our road had been gradual and slow, requiring minute adjustments to my seat. Sometimes I was required to lean slightly forward in the saddle, sometimes slightly backward.

I was never going to be a student of dressage. Riding was hard. I had chafing. I'd ridden Seabiscuit without a stitch of clothing for half of a mile before I picked up my clothing, and I had chafing in places you don't want chafing.

Enough said.

Bottom line, my seat was not confident in more ways than one. Besides my being crazy-ass tired, my grip on Seabiscuit's reins was tenuous—a less than satisfactory arrangement of a tired thumb pressed hard against the loop of leather circling my right palm.

I couldn't do the ditch. I was down to one thumb; I had magic streaming from my fingertips and tethers leading from my hands. There was no way I could hang on to the pommel in an effort to keep myself in the saddle.

Maybe the ditch would shallow out around the next bend.

Goddess, I hope so.

"There is no village named Creemore," pursued Mouse.

Worried, I said sharply, "Well, that's where I come from."

At this, the Gatekeeper turned, and paused to look back at me, her eyes narrowed into unappealing squints.

"Keep walking." I gave her all my teeth.

See? My Goddess heard me again.

I saw it the moment we completed the fourth bend in the road: one very old ash whose limbs were spread out in an expansive welcome. Hell, I wouldn't even have to slide off the saddle to reach the thick, knotted branch that arched low over our chosen road. Feeding Merry and Ralph was going to be as complicated as saying, "Whoah, horsie."

"Buck up, Merry. I see lunch," I murmured in English.

Switching languages, I told the others to slow down, which earned me a quick, dark glance from the Fae. I waited until the baleful Gatekeeper was a few feet past Merry's dinner before bringing my mount to a stop more or less underneath its heavy branch.

Mouse said, "I need to piss."

At which point the diminutive Fae swung completely around, her features twisted into a full, foul glare. "Why are we stopping here?" she demanded.

"Turn around and face forward," I growled.

"I have done what was required of me. Release me or—"

"Turn. Around."

Her eyes warred with mine for three very long "Mississippis" before she complied. I studied her rigid back for a tick before I tilted my head back to gaze upward.

Crap.

Perspective had made me believe the tree limb would be horizontal to my current elevation astride old Seabiscuit once we caught up to it. And if that had been the case, feeding Merry and Ralph would have been dead easy. But now, sitting under the tree, I realized that I'd need to stretch and stand on my stirrups to pass Merry up to it.

A problem, as both of my hands were tethered to my reluctant tour-guides.

I turned to consider the ditch again.

Double crap.

Merry crawled up the slope of my breast in order to take a better look at lunch. There was none of her usual vigor on display as she attempted to heave herself into a vertical position. She noticeably wobbled, I noted with increasing glumness.

"Use my hair," I said, hardly moving my mouth.

She didn't sass me for my suggestion, and I didn't grimace when the sharp edges of her ivy leaves raked my skull as she reached for a hank of my hair. Holding on to it gave her the support she required to stand, and now, more or less upright, she unfurled another tendril of ivy from the nest surrounding her dull stone.

Without any real conviction, she stretched it upward toward her meal.

I straightened tall in my seat.

We both gave it our best, but Fae gold and semi-mortal spines can only thin so far. After we proved the point in a manner that we both found painful, her arm fell.

"It would be better if I didn't dismount," I whispered. "Maybe we'll find another tree up ahead. Or if you're really hungry, we can try the—" I was going to say "fir trees," but she suddenly slumped, turning herself from an upright stick figure to a legless pendant in one sudden and swift collapse. Her chain made a burring noise as she dropped to the very end of it—a zip line deployed without brakes. She bounced twice and then swung there.

Seemingly lifeless.

"Merry?"

Chapter Nine

I could feel the chill of her stone right through the cotton of my shirt.

"Merry?" I said louder.

She didn't respond. I had fear then, equal to that I felt when I swung out over the falls. But unlike that moment when the ground had fallen away from my feet, this terror wasn't set with anticipation—*dear Goddess, please take care of me because I'm going to fall*—this was already happening. I was in free fall.

I could lose Merry. Right here. Under the ash tree that could fix her.

I swayed, the realization so sharp and sickening, it overwhelmed me. Spots formed, and the edges of my vision started to soften again.

"Wake up!" I told her.

One of those limp hanging vines gave a twitch.

"Come on!" I said, blinking fiercely. "You don't go to sleep. You don't slip away. We stay. We fight. We don't bail on each other. Come on!"

As the edges of my vision sharpened, the light that had so briefly extinguished inside her amber belly flickered.

Then, with a shudder, those limp arms and legs retracted, shifting back into the nest of gold surrounding her stone.

"You scared me." My whisper was an accusation. Her belly was still chill. She was edging closer to a sleep from which I wouldn't be able to wake her.

She lifted a weary arm in assent.

I could see again. Her. Me. Everything.

If we stayed this course, moving forward without stopping for necessary repairs, we were finished. Sooner or later—probably sooner—we'd both pass out. And then, neither of us would be able to wake the other.

I knew it; Merry knew it.

She was spent, having depleted her reserves last night.

And though I'd tried to fight it, I was ready to slide off the saddle, likely as a result of what my body had suffered last night and this morning: copious loss of blood (it lay in pools), dehydration (panting does that), and shock (we're talking *pools*).

I gazed upward with frustration. The tree hadn't moved. The limb was still there. Just out of reach. If I fed Merry, she'd be well again. And then, with her reserves topped up, she could help me stay alert enough not to slide off the saddle. One hand washes the other.

Except, before all that necessary sudsing took place, I needed a free hand.

Dammit.

One of my tethers spoke up.

"Do you have any objections to me taking a piss?" Mouse moved closer.

I stared down at his upturned face, thinking how tired I was and how little time it would take to hoist Merry to her meal. I was already positioned under Merry's buffet. All I had to do was stand and stretch.

Why not cut the ties that bound me to him? Just for a second?

I'd used my magic as an independent restraint back at the cave. The donut had worked: the Gatekeeper hadn't summoned up any magic to defeat mine; Mouse hadn't been able to slip free of it.

Why not try it again? Except this time, fashion an individualized one, because I only need one hand free and I only required the use of it for less than a minute. I could tell my magic to squeeze the crap out of him if he tried anything . . .

I teetered on the edge of common sense.

"I really need to go," he said again, shifting on his feet.

At the word, "go," I got a vivid image of Mouse flashing me a cheery "gotcha" grin before haring off for points unknown. Back at the cave, he'd been the one making the concentrated effort to escape. If he decided that this was his last chance, and he made a sprint for freedom, running even as my magic crushed his ribs, he'd be utterly useless to me. Without his muscle, I couldn't remount Seabiscuit.

His brow pleated under my fierce scowl. "A man's got to piss. It's just a fact of nature."

My gaze moved to the Gatekeeper. I studied the fuzzy ball of her topknot, then her hunched shoulders, then the circle of magic pinioning her arms to her sides, and finally, the ends of her short little legs.

With those itty-bitty feet, she couldn't make significant tracks in the two seconds it would take me to plop Merry and Ralph on the tree. And with her arms pinned, her balance was definitely compromised. I'd watched her lurch like a drunkard over some of the rougher portions of road we'd traveled and been mildly amused at her clumsiness.

Slide off your horse and she'll be on you.

Okay, so I won't get off the horse. I'll do what I need to do—stand up on one stirrup, lift and place the amulets on the branch—then I'll sink back to the saddle, thighs weakly hugging Seabiscuit's fat sides, while they feed. I can stay alert until Merry's topped up her reserves. And here's the bonus: once filled, she could share some of that reserve with me, and this muzzy, light-headed feeling, which made thinking in a straight line so difficult, would go away.

Merry's body was exuding waves of cold again. The chill puckered my nipples and spread goose bumps around my ribs.

Yes. It was donut time.

Like the smart person I vaguely sensed I wasn't being, I went over the plan in careful detail with my Fae, visualizing the sequence—cut, donut, stay, and retether. And then, because I didn't want to give the Gatekeeper a heads-up, I thought, rather than said, my command.

I was being wily.

Cut, I mentally commanded magic-mine.

She splintered and a hundred or more particles of florescence glittered, separate and lively, unattached lights. They hovered indecisively, then opted to float over to the loop of magic around the woman's waist. They sank down onto it, joining the band of bright green wrapped around the woman's torso.

I saw the Gatekeeper's back stiffen. As the coil swelled, her shoulders tightened, moving higher to grace her ears. Slowly, she turned her head on the short stem of her neck. One brown eye stared at me for a long moment.

She knows, I thought.

I stared back at her, keeping my face blank the way I used to when my aunt Lou gave me the squint-eyes. However much the Gatekeeper may have wanted to test the limits of her new situation, she must have come to the conclusion that it wasn't worth it, for she turned back to face the road.

Good. Stay there.

I flexed my aching, swollen left hand, enjoying the release from the constant tugging weight of magic. Then quickly I opened my palm, holding it like a platform in front of Merry. "Hop on," I whispered. "I'll give you a hoist."

She scuttled over my life line.

"Eat as much as you can," I whispered in English, tipping my neck sideways to ease her chain over my head. "I need you strong." The necklace's smooth links slid up my sweating neck, gathering my tangled hair with it.

Since then, I've had time to think about all those muzzy decisions. And it has occurred to me that if anyone had chosen to take my picture right then—freezing me in that position—the pre-photoshopped elements would have amounted to one of those romanticized female studies. It was all there: the gently curved and upraised arm, the tilted head, the hair messily bundled, the eyes slanted downward . . .

Given what happened next, the last detail was the important one.

My gaze, for want of any other focal point, landed on Seabiscuit's ears. And so, I had a perfect, if somewhat blurry, view of them as they pricked forward in sudden interest.

Uh-oh.

Slow as a submarine's periscope being operated by a methodical man, the pony's ear pivoted until it faced the hills to our right. I twisted at the waist, breath freezing in my windpipe. I saw boulders, strewn on the hill as if they were a giant's abandoned toys. Beyond them, I saw the first line of the forest's firs—scabby, fat spruce trunks, needled branches sloping upward like they were a kid's rendering of Christmas trees.

Rocks, trees, more rocks, more trees . . .

Then, amid all that nature, the glint of silver.

Bob the blind bookseller had a metronome in his shop. Growing up, I never asked him why he'd accepted it along with the carton of battered James Patterson thrillers. Bob was an odd duck; he was the purveyor of used goods, and if he chose to sell a musical device that counted time then he did. It was no more unfathomable than the lariat of cowboy rope he'd tacked on the wall behind his cash register.

Often, after Bob had put the shop to bed and left for the evening, I'd sneak downstairs and use his hidden key to let myself in. While wandering the store choosing my next novel, I would occasionally detour to lift the metronome off the shelf. I'd turn the pyramid over in my hand, to wind the key; then I'd flip it around and push the metal weight clamped on the pendulum's arm all the way down the stick.

The lower the weight, the faster the pendulum would swing. I'd slide that thing down till it rested on the fulcrum. Then, I'd release the spring that held the arm in check.

And now, staring at that glint of metal shining intermittently through the trees, I felt like I was the kid I once was. Standing where I shouldn't be, having just sprung the spring.

There's a moment before that first tick—a split second of frozen anticipation before the thing started counting time.

I used to enjoy it: the hitched breath, the instant *before*.

I don't like it anymore.

Time stalled, like the bile that wanted to climb up my throat, as I stared at the source of the flashing glint of something shiny. That was a fortuitous thing because it gave my brain the much-needed space it needed to figure out what I gaping at.

Goddess.

Not a mirror, as I'd hoped, but a silver-toned sword held by a horseman wearing a familiar jacket. I recognized it at once, having seen only one uniform of the same shade of bottle blue since arriving in Merenwyn. The rider who'd accompanied Qae had worn it.

I looked past the rider. He was alone.

Qae was not with him.

Neither was Trowbridge.

You see? In the instant *before,* when time made no difference, I was able to process that Trowbridge was not there, which meant maybe he was still free, leading Qae on some wild chase on the lee side of K2. But on the heels of that happy thought, my inner voice sneered, *Idiot. He's already been captured. He's on his way to Wryal's Island in chains.*

I stopped that dialogue right there, not letting the awful possibility travel to where my emotions lived. Because I was here, in the instant *before:* when decisions, both good and poor, were made.

I dropped my arm, letting the hand that had grown into a fist around Merry slide down the back of my neck. I released her chain. Felt, rather than saw, her slide down the knobs of my spine.

From his seat at the top of the second hill, the rider studied me as I studied him. He'd already come to his conclusion. His curved blade was raised, ready to swing, or swipe or chop. His reins were gathered, and there was something about the position of his hips that told me his knees had just communicated to his mount.

Charge. That's what I got from those knees.

My sluggish brain started firing faster than the pistons on a Porsche. It calculated the distance, not in miles or kilometers or feet or yards—but in time. How long? There were two hills between us. Those slopes were babies compared to K2's. But still, he had one hill to gallop down and another to canter up and, once clear of them, shoulder-high boulders to avoid.

It sounds like a lot.

But at cavalry speed, it meant I had fifteen seconds or less before his charge became my capture. Which is when my brain leaped to the next thought—

I can't ride worth shit.

The ditch now looked like a great option, dismounting the only choice.

Tick. The instant *before* broke and the pendulum started wildly counting off the quarter seconds when the man on the horse kicked his mount and opened his mouth to utter a chilling hoot.

The horse erupted into a canter.

From that instant on, the pendulum's stick started swinging at top speed.

Tick, tick, tick. I shook off my pony's reins and lunged forward fast, flattening myself over Seabiscuit's startled neck. That gave me the leverage to jerk my bad leg over her wretched rump and roll off her. As I threw myself off her Seabiscuit neighed, then performed an agitated equine two-step in an effort not to step on me.

I was all for her two-step, doing my part by performing an evasive roll in an effort to avoid being flattened.

Tick, tick, tick.

In all my panic, I forgot I *still* had one cable of magic streaming from my right hand, and that line of green hadn't been given verbal leave to cut the connection before my hasty dismount. My Fae talent held on to her prize, and thus, when I went tallyho to the ditch on the left, Mouse did too.

Up and *over* Seabiscuit, he went.

Showing distinct promise as a trick pony rider, Mouse climbed over Seabiscuit's dancing back, still *on his feet,* both of his hands gripped around the cable of magic, his teeth clenched in determination. He never lost his balance; he simply walked over Seabiscuit.

Then, he had to ruin all that athleticism by falling on

me. I'd only just landed and was processing the fact, lying flat on my back.

Seabiscuit reared, showing her rounded belly, before she galloped away.

The next part was kind of a visual montage of quick-sliding snippets, coupled with an audio of drumming hooves. Momentum carrying him, Mouse stepped on my stomach. I rolled again, his feet tangled, and then he was half on me and half off, his weight pinning me.

We were still tethered!

"Cut!" I shouted.

My Fae talent exploded in a starburst of green sparkles. The boy gasped, choking on inhaled particles he couldn't see. I held on to Mouse's arm with an iron grip as he choked up that and my magic. It didn't take long—only two hacking coughs—before his breath was clean of anything except the sour smell of his fear.

The rider was close, my ears informed me.

In and out Mouse's breath rasped—a challenge to the cacophony of yips and hoofbeats thundering toward us. He scratched at my fingers, trying to tear them loose.

He had no magic.

"Go!" I opened my claws and gave him a shove toward the ditch. "Get into those trees and keep going!"

I didn't wait to watch him run off. Before he'd cleared the ditch, I was rolling to my feet. The horseman had disappeared, but I could hear him. The sound of his mount's drumming hooves echoed through the field of rock.

Goddess. He's already navigating the boulders.

I raised my arms toward the cloud of confused green sparkling in the daylight. "Come to me!"

Chapter Ten

All of my magic heard my call. The donut around the Gate-keeper's waist blew apart. She shimmered in a momentary cloud of confusion—bees suddenly dislodged from their hive—that quickly coalesced into a torrent of intention.

My talent hadn't left me, departing to find a better host in this realm of full-blooded Faes. It flowed right to my primed fingers

"She has magic!" screamed the Gatekeeper as the rider kicked his horse past the last of the boulders. "Beware of it!"

It better be enough.

I braced my feet to face the charge. I told my bowels to give it up—*you don't have time to cramp in fear.* I informed my rippling horror to stuff it. *Do not look at the horse. Do not feed that fear. The rider doesn't intend to crush you under its hooves. Look at his arm, how it is raised high, the tip of his sword pointed at you.*

He has no plans to flatten you. He means to cut you in two.

Stop the sword, I thought as he came thundering down the first hill. *Get his wrist.*

Plan intact, my vision tunneled, my focus centering on

the arm that held the weapon. Get the wrist and I had a chance. Miss it with my magic and I was going to be minced up like an onion on a cutting board.

"Beware of her magic!" she shrieked again.

Get the wrist.

"Cut off her hands!" she howled.

He heard her. During those last seconds, when I was trying to squelch the thought that maybe he was planning to mow me down, he pulled on his reins and canted his body to the side. Dust plumed as his mount fought to answer the command issued by his knees. And for a second, I couldn't see through the cloud churned up by the horse's hooves. All I got was a confused glimpse of horse legs, and girth, and riding boots as the animal veered for a sharp right.

Get the wrist.

I saw the flash of his arm in motion, swinging up to cut me down.

"Attach!" I screamed.

My magic surged up, a living bolt of green fire. It hit the tanned circle of skin above the sleeve of that awful bottle blue jacket and wrapped itself around it, a living manacle of my talent.

I experienced a brief spurt of elation.

Then physics fucked me.

The horse and rider were still moving, even if their trajectory was slowed and no longer in a straight line. And I was no immovable object.

The shock of impact went right through me.

"Ah!" I was blown backward, the laws of science that I didn't understand propelling me willy-nilly off the path and then off it into space—this is where the trailing *h* of my cry rose in a shriek—and still, I kept going.

Gravity made a snatch for me halfway over the ditch.

I had a brief touchdown in the curve of the pebbled gully. Then, a hot poker of pain stabbed as my shoulder's ball joint did things it shouldn't when the object I'd grabbed—the wrist of one big man with a sword—went shooting over the ditch.

I saw him fly: a blur of bottle blue, shiny silver, and flailing legs.

Then, I noticed the green bungee cord trailing after him.

Oh shit. With a sense of inevitability, I watched as the line tethering the two of us grew tauter than a tightrope. There was a snap, sharp as a whip crack. And then, I was being pulled again by my fingernails—*sweet heavens, when's it going to end*—right up and over the lip of the gully.

We didn't go far, my magic and me. Our bungee cord lesson was thankfully brief.

I landed in a patch of wild daisies.

The rider landed elsewhere. I heard a bad sound that I equated with meat being thrown on a counter: a cross between a splat and a thud.

I hoped he was dead.

My landing, though relatively soft, was a stunner—the culminating blow on top of everything else. I found myself dazed, stretched on my back. My spine hurt like it had spent some time on the rack. My shoulder was on fire, and my arm was twisted painfully over my head.

I could feel my nails; they burned with fierce pressure.

I tilted my chin and rolled my eyes for a look-see.

The landing had twisted up my Fae. Her lines were kinked, her flow all jammed up. She was the garden hose that was threatening to burst. I could sense the dam of her anger; I could measure the insult she took from being twisted and bent like a pipe cleaner.

Got to fix her.

"Chop off her hands!"

The screech came from the beaten path, where in the

instant *before* I'd sat on a fat pony named Seabiscuit. The Gatekeeper had followed our flight and now danced on the other side of the ditch, screaming encouragements. She was using her hands, punctuating her shrieks with chopping visuals.

She wasn't talking to me.

I swung my head, my gaze following the line of my magic past the crimped part. The rider lay sprawled. *Please be dead.* He looked like a corpse; he lay unmoving, though he maintained a death grip on his damn sword.

Can corpses really do that?

"Kill her!" the Gatekeeper shrieked.

His toe twitched.

No, no, no.

He sat up. A rivulet of blood spilled, hot and fast. Smelling sweet but faded.

"She has no balyfire! Use your blade!" shouted the Gatekeeper.

Where was *her* balyfire? The thought was fleeting, and I didn't pause to examine it further because the rider was shedding his lethargy with impressive speed. He shook his head, then rolled to his side, and the coil of green between us swelled obscenely into the fatter knot.

Pain in my hands.

Distress in my ears. I could hear the hiss of my Fae— *sss, sss, sss!* She was wordless with suffering. From the squeeze, from the knot.

I rolled as the rider had, in a desperate effort to unkink the current running between us. And it was a partial success; the bend started to open, and the awful growing heaviness in my head and hands—

He twisted again, moving onto one knee.

I gasped at the spike of unbearable pain.

He forced the fingers of his clenched fist open, allowing the sword to drop. He reached for it with his free hand.

"Go!" I screamed, releasing my Fae. "Hurt him!"

"Yesss!" I heard her hiss as she exploded into a cloud-burst that dappled the leaves and the grasses with flashes of bright shiny green light. In the space of one eyeblink, she re-formed herself into a stream of glittering malefi-cence, beautiful and deadly. Now, tethered to no one, grounded by none, she surged toward the rider, a hungry python.

A snap of her tail and she was a coil around his throat. She squeezed.

The rider dropped his weapon. He tore at his skin as she swelled around the purpling column of his neck. Gasp-ing for air, he staggered to stand. She bore down on him, her rage cold and cruel. His back arched, his eyes bulged. Then, he whined, high through his nose, as she cracked the first vertebra.

He dropped.

He died with the second crack.

I turned my head away from the sight of my magic twist-ing around the corpse's neck. Her color was a gloating green, her movements almost orgasmic.

"Abomination!" screamed the Gatekeeper as she scut-tled down the pitch of the ditch toward me. Her lips were pulled in a pointy-toothed grimace.

"Whore!"

I raised my aching hands to ward her off, but she had no intention of her flesh touching mine. When she reached me, she lifted a foot, twisted slightly at the hip, and swung her little black boot.

Her aim was true; her kick got me right on my wounded ankle. Though I didn't feel pain, I felt horribly, stomach-turning wrong.

Goddess, where's my strength?

Her expression darkened into a troll's leer. She took a

step back. I knew her next kick would be aimed at my head. I raised my free arm to crook it protectively in over my head as I opened my mouth to summon my magic.

The words on my tongue were never uttered.

From out of nowhere, Mouse came at her with a roar, no weapon other than his hands and his speed. His dive was a bruising tackle that swept her off her feet. As they crashed to the earth, her voluminous skirts flew, dark wings of a crow.

They landed in a tangle of dress and shouts. She jerked up a knee to get him in the balls. "Base-born scum!"

"Dog cock!" he shouted, twisting to avoid her sharp little knee.

"Touch me?" she screamed, pushing at him. "I'll have them boil your balls, you—"

He hauled off and hit her. His palm was open, but the slap was wide. Her head whipped to one side.

Goddess, where's my strength? I was sliding . . . slipping toward some place I shouldn't go. I shook my head to clear it, blinking hard to bring the scene into focus.

The Gatekeeper's cheek was no longer pale. I could see the outline of Mouse's hand: four red fingerprints, with a red smudge below them for his palm.

Her eyes were hard, black pebbles. She raised her hands—not to point or to plead. Her fists were turned toward him, clenched so hard that her knuckles gleamed. I knew it meant bad things were coming, but I couldn't remember what they were or how they would hurt me.

Or us.

Or we.

As I struggled to untangle the meaning of the "wes," and the "mes," he lunged for her wrists, snaring them in his own punishing grip. I nodded, owlishly wise. *That's right. Get the wrist and you'll be safe . . .*

She kicked out with her leg.

He twisted, swinging her around, and then he shoved her hard, and she fell, her hands briefly starfishing. Before she could rise or turn, he placed his foot on her back and pushed her down until she was flat on the ground.

Fast as a crocodile hunter, he jumped on her back, his legs snaring hers. "Chop off her hands, you said?" he said, grabbing her wrists again. "Cut them off? Shall we do that to you?"

She bucked and cursed. "Get off me! You verminous—"

He ground her clenched knuckles into the earth. "If I had a knife I'd do it. I'd chop them off so you could never use your balyfire again."

"Scum!"

"Aye, I'm scum. And wouldn't you like to singe me with your fire?" He leaned over, lowering his face so that he could speak into her ear. "But you can't, can you?" His voice dropped to an intimate whisper. "You haven't got any balyfire left. You've used it up, haven't you? Who did you lay a streak of sulfur on?"

Me, I thought. *She shot a fireball at me. She came up the steps from the Safe Passage and popped her head into my world, and then she sent a ball of sizzling fire my way. And still I followed her to this world . . .*

Why did I do it?

Mouse was shaking his head. "By all the Gods in the sky above, if I'd known that you would never have got me out of the castle. And now look what you've done. I can't go back. There's nothing left there for me but a terrible death. You bat-fowling bitch, you've killed me without using an ounce of your talent."

His hands went to her neck. From the look on his face, I knew his intent was to squeeze until her skin was the color of a boiled beet.

"Stop." My voice sounded thin.

I don't think he heard me. Shoulders bunched, he leaned into the task of killing her.

"No, Mouse!" I summoned authority, even as the world around me dimmed into shadows, and blurred light, and creeping numbness. "Don't kill her," I explained, my words smearing into a weary trail. "I need her alive."

A beautiful serpentine stream of sparkles undulated past me, drawn to the boy who wished his mistress dead.

"Donut time, magic-mine," I murmured. "Keep her away from me if you can."

The sky winked blue. Then it was gray.

Movement in my pocket. Faint warmth on my chest.

Can't be Merry. I think I lost her.

Burning in my eyes.

Only damsels in distress pass out.

Be a dame, not a damsel.

"Breathe through your mouth slowly," I heard Mouse mutter.

How long had I been out? I worried.

"The fresh air will clear your head," he said.

I gave it a try and discovered it did.

When the sky was blue again and the inclination to pass out again receded, I rolled my head toward him. Mouse sat against a tree. His legs were drawn up, and one arm was braced on his knee.

"Did you kill her?" I whispered.

He shook his head. "No."

Thank heavens. I needed her to open the portal.

Wait. Mouse was free. He could have run. He had not. Why not?

Merry!

I fumbled at my own chest, searching for her, and found two pendants. One was hot; one was not. I looked down, way past the boobs, to the place where my ribs met, and my heart beat hard. Ralph stood over Merry, his icy belly pulsing with white fire. Somewhere during the fuzzy period when I'd briefly succumbed to damsel status, he'd slipped out of his hiding place in my jeans and morphed into a stick figure on steroids.

He must have climbed my body to reach her. Her color was horrible—a mustard brown.

The end of his right "arm" was rapier sharp.

"One minute you're a dickhead; the next you're protecting her. Ralph, I'll never understand you."

"You have two amulets," said Mouse. "And one is the Royal Amulet."

"I need your tree," I said in a stronger voice.

"Why?"

"To feed my friends."

"What *are* you?"

"Same answer as before," I replied. "I'm Hedi of Creemore." I could hear someone breathing harshly. "Did you break the Gatekeeper's larynx?"

"And what would that be?"

I didn't really know, so I rolled my head in the direction of the noise.

The Gatekeeper was flat on her back, her legs wide. She was breathing noisily through her teeth. Not in pain, I thought, but in rage. My magic had correctly interpreted "donut time" and had encircled her waist.

Tightly.

Good enough. I tried to sit up the normal way, but my head was heavier than a bucket filled with wet cement. I rolled to my side and braced myself into a partial recline on one elbow.

Much dizziness ensued.

"What's wrong with me?" I asked.

Mouse tilted his head to consider me. "The teeth of the

wolf traps are coated with juka. I expect your wolf licked your wounds and the juka is inside you now. Before we set off, you should have been made to vomit and your wound rinsed well in the stream."

"You couldn't have told me that before?"

"Could have. Didn't."

Fine. "What is juka?"

He blew some air out of his pursed lips, shaking his head. "It must be a rare world you live in that you don't know about the dust that sickens the wolves. It's made from a plant. Once it's dried, they grind it up into a fine dust. A bit of it sprinkled in a wolf's food will lay the man wasted."

"How wasted? How sick?"

"You won't be up to your full strength until the juka's worked its way through your body. Until then you'll want to sleep like the dead and you'll be weak as a—"

"So bottom line, no death by juka dust."

"Aye, no death."

"Good to know." No fade into twilight, just this sludge of extreme fatigue that made lifting my noggin a piece of labor. I thought of the body lying just out of my line of vision, and then I thought of Qae and Trowbridge, and of Lexi . . . How was I going to get to the rock now? There was neither hide nor tail of Seabiscuit.

I used what abdominal muscles I owned to sit upright. *Whoa. Spinning world.*

I waited for it to clear.

"Have you noticed that your leg's been dripping blood for a mile or more?" Mouse inquired.

I knew that, but I flicked my gaze southward. The side of my foot was forked with crimson streaks. I didn't try to tug my jeans high enough for a thorough inspection. Memory of the holes—let's not forget the *holes*—tightened my gut.

What a mess.

I braced my palms on the ground, then started shimmying backward toward the closest tree. It was a maple. Merry was very fond of maple.

Sweat had pearled my upper lip by the time I'd maneuvered the three of us into the crotch of the tree's fat roots. I drew in a shaky breath, hooked their chains with a grimy finger, and pulled them over my head. For a tick or two, I let them dangle, thinking they'd untwine themselves, because feeding was going to be complicated if they didn't, but Ralph held on and Merry didn't push him away.

I lowered the knot of them to eye level and gave her the WTF squint. After a pause, she replied in her own way—a blip of ruddy orange light, small as pinprick.

Where there's life, there's an FU.

It was Merry's way.

Smiling faintly, I laid the two of them on a root by my hip before settling my back against the tree. The forest was quiet except for the Gatekeeper's indignant breathing.

"How long does it normally take for the poison to wear off?"

Mouse didn't answer. For the minute it took me to compose a bullet list of items required to make a travois he sat near me, studying his twined fingers and saying nothing. Finally he rubbed his temple with the heel of his palm in exasperation.

"I have something that will help," he said.

I gave him the same silent glare I used to direct at customers who complained about too much foam in their lattes. He lifted an unrepentant shoulder. "As I said, most of the damage was done already."

My tone turned acidic. "Before we ever set off on the trail."

"Aye—"

"Stop saying 'aye!' " I snapped. "Say 'yes,' 'no,' 'kiss my

ass,' but stop with the 'aye.' Every time you do it, you remind me that I'm here. And right now, Mouse . . ."

I rubbed my mouth with my fist.

"You don't want to be here," he finished. "Then we have something in common, don't we?" He stood to stretch. "If you're still dead set on traveling to the rock, you're going to need some of the juice."

"Sadly, I don't have a bottle of sun potion."

"I did." His belly let out a gurgle. "It's in the bag attached to the pony's saddle."

"I'll bet you had a lot of friends in the castle, didn't you?"

"I had a few." He put two fingers to his lips and whistled. A short, low note, followed by a long, high one. And curse me if not a moment later did Seabiscuit come over the rise at a trot. Tail flicking, shaggy ears forward, belly swaying from side to side.

My head swiveled as she passed me. "How did you do that?"

A slow grin broke out over his face. "She likes apples." He caught her bridle and stroked her neck. "She prefers a whole one, but a core will do." He reached for the bag slung over the pommel.

"Slow movements, Mouse."

"One push with me finger and you'd be flat again, Hedi of Creemore." He squatted, placing the bag on the ground. Then he undid the strings and reached into his bag of wonders. He extracted a wad of burlap. With great care, he unrolled the swaddling to reveal a small glass bottle of clear liquid.

I eyed it, then the bag. "What else is in that sack?"

"Three more bottles of the juice."

"You always travel with four bottles of sun potion?"

He snorted. "Of course not. I had to risk my neck stealing these from the storeroom."

The Gatekeeper rolled stiffly to a sitting position. My

magic was a fat donut around her thick waist. She reminded me of a kid I saw once at Wasaga Beach wearing an inflatable inner tube. She fixed Mouse with a steady gaze. "I will see you dead."

"Enough with the threats." I allowed myself one steadying breath, then tugged up my jeans so I could take a look at my leg.

Immediately I wished I hadn't.

"It looks worse than it is," Mouse said.

"Sure it does," I said with my eyes closed. A flood of scents—sweet peas gone rank, faded wolf musk, and the faintest whiff of crushed herbs—teased my nose.

Mouse moved close enough to take a long, hard sniff. "The bugger who set it must have coated the teeth twice, because I can still smell the juka in the gash. That gash will need to be rinsed out well, else the bleeding won't stop."

I cracked my eyes open to slits, then wordlessly pointed to the bottle of potion.

He sat back, appalled. "Not with the juice! A body doesn't splash that around. I risked my life and more to get these bottles."

"You got a better idea?"

He scratched the back of his neck while he thought about that, then heaved an aggrieved sigh. "I'll do it, then. Your hands are none too steady." He reached for my leg, then hissed in irritation when I drew it closer to my chest. "Don't be daft. I could have let her kill you."

"I kidnapped you and frog-walked you over hill and dale all morning. Why should I trust you not to take your best shot while you can?"

"Because it's too late for me to go back!" he snapped. "The loss of what I've stolen will have been noticed now. I can't return to the castle."

"You stole four bottles. You never planned on going back."

His gaze held mine, then traveled to the Gatekeeper. "Your leg will need binding after this." He got up to search the ground. "Here it is," he said, picking up a sharp stone. He turned for his mistress. "I'll be needing a piece of your skirt. Mind your kicks."

"Do not touch me, mutt," she warned.

Before it got nasty, I fake-coughed. Twice.

She subsided into a glower.

Mouse crouched cautiously beside the Gatekeeper. He caught her skirt and used the stone to make a cut in its hem. "You were right on one thing," he said as he tore a strip from his mistress's skirt.

"About what?" I returned the Gatekeeper's glare of death with a somewhat muted version.

So tired. So very tired.

"I had no plans to return." He held up the strip and measured it with his eyes, then tore another few inches. "I knew I'd never see another morning of stable duty as soon as she woke me and told me to make haste. 'Bring food for a pony and mead for me,' she said, 'then meet me in the jewel room.' When I heard those words, I got the same feeling as when I'm holding the throwing bones, except more powerful." He thumped his chest with the back of his fist. "Felt right here. I knew my future was about to cast for the final time."

"What tipped you off? The word 'mead' or 'pony'?"

A corner of his mouth tugged up. "Neither. She wanted me to meet her in the jewel room." He started walking back to me, the long strip of fabric bunched under his arm. "You see, for years, I've seen her suddenly start and touch her vest pocket. Then soon after that, she'd find a reason to visit the jewel room. She'd shut the door and stay in there for a day or more. Most thought she was doing her job polishing the pretties, but most didn't check the bottom of her skirt when she reappeared. Sometimes it was dusty, sometimes muddy, sometimes wet." He knelt beside my outstretched leg and took time to arrange the things he needed for the task ahead. Bottle of potion, sharp rock, length of bandage. "I knew there had to be an exit to the outside world from inside of the jewel room."

"That's not the type of secret you share with your servant."

"Aye, it was one she'd kill me for knowing." He touched my wound with light fingers. "I expected to be set alight with her balyfire sent as soon as I'd finished whatever task she set for me."

"Those fireballs she tosses—she doesn't have an endless supply of them?"

"Not her. She's only middling high on the royal list."

"How much magic does she have?"

"Only her balyfire. But her most powerful magics are the connections she has to important people. You don't play the fool with the Gatekeeper, and you don't expect her to play it either. Which is why I knew she meant to bury me with her secrets. So, instead of fetching water for the pony and mead for her, I broke the lock on the storeroom and took enough bottles to last me four moons."

"You couldn't have taken more?"

"That's all that was left." He slid his palm under my calf, then jerked his chin at the bottle of juice. "Will you want a sip before I start? To take the edge off?"

My trust wasn't won that easily.

"No," I said.

He picked up the rock, then inquired, "Then will you want a stick to bite down on? Whatever has been scabbed over will have to be—"

"Don't want to hear the details, Mouse."

"If you cry out—"

"Just. Do. It."

"Right, then. Best you don't look."

I averted my gaze to a nearby shrub. "Where were you going to run to?"

"I was going to seek my luck with what was left of the Raha'ells," he replied. "Normally, they have no greater use for us mutts than the Fae, but I thought they might like to know about my mistress's special door. A secret entrance into the Royal Court's castle—now that would be a useful thing to know, don't you think?"

You think?

"For someone who wanted to sneak into the castle," he added in case I wasn't following.

Fat luck. I might be dopey, but I wasn't that out of it that I couldn't pick up on the storm-the-castle significance of a back door into the well-guarded fortress. Though I wanted to make sure of one detail. "The castle's connected to the Spectacle grounds?"

"Aye, it is, and the guards won't be expecting trouble from within the castle, now would they?"

I thought of my bullet list. Finding Trowbridge was now on the top of it. Was there a place for rescuing a pack of Rahae'lls at the bottom? *No. We can't.* If we made it to the end of the list—the book destroyed, the Black Mage dead, my brother back to being Lexi—it was suicide to expect that we could free the Rahae'lls on top of all that.

And then everything Lexi and Trowbridge had gone through since I made the pact with a wily old goat meant nothing. Isn't it good enough to stop bad things from dripping into my own world?

Mouse cleared his throat and jerked me back to the here and now. "I don't need to do that now, though, do I?"

"What?"

"Seems to me I don't need to find what's left of the Raha'ells." He picked up the bottle of sun potion and pulled the cork out with his teeth. He spat it out, then gave me the same sort of smile Lexi used to send my way after he'd conceived a grand new plan. "I'm healing the leg of a girl who wears two amulets." He drizzled a thin stream of liquid into my wound. "Is the Son of Lukynae alive?"

"My Trowbridge is a hard man to kill."

"Trowbridge, is it?"

I stared at him, feeling my eyes burn.

"Will it be him or the Shadow we'll be finding at the rock?"

"I. Don't. Know." Three broken words.

He stared at me, then nodded. "I guess we'll have to wait and see, then. Now would you like a sip of the juice before I bind it?"

The path between the Two Sisters was a well-worn deer path, complete with deer droppings.

Finally. I turned in my saddle to glance at the sun.

"Keep doing that and you'll break open your wound, again," muttered Mouse.

I hadn't seen a cloud. Not a single one.

"If you're looking for a jinx, you needn't," Mouse said, apparently adept at mind reading. "They only like the pure-blood wolves. We mutts are beneath its notice. They like the Kuskadors too, but that stands to reason—for all their airs, underneath their serving uniforms they're full-blooded wolves too. The jinxes take no notice of the difference between the two. Agitators or ass-lickers, it doesn't care. They look for the pure blood. They'll skim across the sky until they find it."

Trowbridge's blood must read as a pure Raha'ell. "You're talking about the milky haze that has glittering bits inside it." I wanted to be absolutely clear that we were on the same page. "What are they?"

"They're conjures." He lifted his shoulders and let them drop. "Unnatural incubuses that feed on the hunt. But as I said, you need not bother your head over it. They have no taste for our blood."

I closed my eyes briefly. *Jinxes.*

"How many are there?" I whispered.

He nodded. "Every dawn, the mother jinx gives birth to four little ones." Without breaking pace he cupped his hands. "No bigger than that they are, when they're first-born. Full of sparkles and light. Fair wondrous, they are at first."

"They don't stay that way. They turn into storm clouds."

He grimaced. "Before the Rahae'lls start to howling in the Spectacle pens, we know the mage's hunting party is coming back with new captures. It's written in the sky. Every jinx follows her bounty, rumbling like a vengeful consort who's brought her cheating lover back to heel. My hair stands up on the back of my neck, watching the jinxes flow back into their mother's belly."

"How big is the mother?"

"She's grown as big as the Spectacle grounds. It won't be long before she'll be hanging over the castle's back walls. You'd think the court would be in a fine fettle about that, but they're so glad to see the Raha'ells being herded into the pens, none of them have said a word in public. Though who knows what they say when they're abed?"

He lapsed into a short, but thoughtful, silence during which I savaged the soft skin inside my cheek.

Bad things had begun to drip.

"I was there for the birth of the first," he said reflectively. "Me and a few lads. To be honest, little was done in the kitchen and the stables that morning. Anyone who could find a reason to loiter on the back ramparts without getting a boot in his ass for his trouble did so. We all wanted to see the Black Mage conjure his way out of trouble."

"Trouble?"

"They blame him for the night the Raha'ells broke free.

Once the dust settled and the court discovered that he'd lost both the Son of Lukynae and his own Shadow . . . he was in dire trouble." Mouse stared ahead, but I don't think he was seeing the trail or the stiff back of the diminutive Fae. "It was quiet the morning of the conjure," he said. "So quiet—"

"You could hear a pin drop," I added.

"A pin drop," he repeated, "aye, that's a good one. It was so quiet, a pin could have dropped and all would have heard it. The Black Mage walked to the center of the Spectacle grounds. He stretched out his hands, wide as this"—Mouse pantomimed a medium-sized fish—"and said that it was time to end the court's problem with the wolves outside the castle's walls. Some tittered in the back, because any stripling of the Royal Court can make a balyfire and that's what it appeared he was going to do. But instead of fire, he produced the jinx. He let it float upward, and it grew bigger and got those shiny flashes . . . tiny pretty jewels . . . and then those titters turned to silence. 'This is a jinx hound,' the Black Mage said as proud as could be. 'It knows the scent of the Rahae'lls and it will hunt, never tiring, until it has run to ground every single Raha'ell man, woman, and babe.' "

"How many of the Son of Lukynae's people have been captured?"

"I don't know how many Raha'ells have been captured, but there can't be too many left free. The pens are full and they've had to build three more. The jinxes are bringing in young ones now. And we've never seen that before. They say the Raha'ells cherish their children and would die protecting them."

A piece of information that would cut Trowbridge to the bone should he know.

I flinched. "If it finds the trail of a—"

"It won't stop."

Chapter Eleven

We met the ward before we met my twin at Daniel's Rock. As per usual, the Gatekeeper was in the lead, trudging along with the enthusiasm of an enlisted man on his first twenty-kilometer hike. Mouse walked alongside Seabiscuit and me. The trees had begun thinning, providing tantalizing glimpses of a gray rock face.

Being on my guard wasn't on my list anymore.

I've made it.

Be alive, Trowbridge. Be there.

Karma must have a hotline to every thought I've ever spun in my head. No sooner had I envisioned Trowbridge standing outside the rock, his face wreathed in relief and pride, than the entire vista in front of me—the Gatekeeper's resentful form, the tall trees, the sun-filled space beyond—was suddenly obscured by a wall of blue.

A curved one. Like someone had taken a glass bowl, poured a cup of thick blue paint in it, upended the whole damn thing, and slammed it down in front of us.

"It's a ward!" I yelled.

"Sheep's teats!" said Mouse, lunging for my pony's bridle.

The frightened pony pranced forward, heedless of the

fact that we were heading into trouble instead of moving away from it, and barreled right into the Gatekeeper.

Her shoulder hit the ward, went right through the barrier, and kept going.

It could have been any type of ward—one created to hide things, or one fashioned with the intent of filling someone with so much ill ease that they'd walk away not knowing why they felt compelled to, or even one that made no pretense at being anything other than a barrier.

But it was the bad kind. The one filled with a sticky, syrupy sort of magic that sucks you into its suffocating hold. The weight of the magic is a vise grip of pressure around your ribs and diaphragm. You're drowning in heavy liquid, and time seems to slow, so you're fully aware as you suffocate. I'd been in one such ward only once, in Threall, and there had been a point midway through it where I hadn't been sure I was going to make it all the way out.

The Gatekeeper half-pivoted toward me as she was drawn into it, her brows lifted to the sweaty fringe of her bangs, her mouth a big wide O, in anticipation of an "oh shit!" that required no translation from Merenwynian. Then, without even a pop or a slurp, she was pulled backward into the ward's treacle grip.

All parts of her disappeared except for the long green shimmering rope of magic that she'd complained about off and on all morning.

"Cut!" I cried, but it was too damn late. I was the Pekingese owner who'd been too slow to step into the condo elevator only to watch the doors close abruptly on her pet, leaving her holding one end of the leash while the happy pooch took a sky ride to the penthouse. And I can tell you now with absolute authority that the horrified owner must have thought something along the lines of—

Oh shit, there goes my bitch.

"Magic!" my Fae exclaimed. A sparkle of titillation went right through my hand all the way to my plummeting heart.

"Cut!" I hollered again, trying to control Seabiscuit.

But it was all too late. Too late to figure out how to get a panicked pony to back up—she snorted; she pranced; she danced.

Too late for Mouse. He didn't even get a chance to comment on sheep's teats before he was swallowed by it.

Too late for Hedi. The line of magic between me and the Gatekeeper drew taunt.

I sat back in my saddle and shouted belatedly, "Cut, cut, cut!"

Also too damn late.

Genghis Khan must have had at least one moment when he sat on a knoll overlooking a town and thought, *All this war and death is just too freakin' hard.* But you know what he did? He sucked it up. He spurred his trusty steed and ransacked that village anyhow . . .

If there was no reverse on this horsie, I was going in full speed.

I gifted Seabiscuit's fat flanks with a heartlessly vicious kick. She whinnied, her back quarters bunched, and then, by golly, I got my slow-motion moment. I entered the ward on the momentum of the pony's leap into blue oblivion and enjoyed the slow slide toward the back of her saddle.

For the count of three, I stayed there—hellishly caught in the no-no instant before the big fall—time no longer slowed, but frozen. I was surrounded, a culture specimen being sandwiched between layers of blue-tinted viscous material.

Pressure, all around me.

Can't breathe.

And then, inexplicably, between one heartbeat and another, it all changed. The sticky stuff dissolved around us and my trusty mount's front hooves broke through the thinning veil of blue.

Immediately the laws of gravity and principles of physics resumed.

Mouse, still grimly hanging on to Seabiscuit's bridle, broke through first, shouting a blue streak. Then the pommel gave my lady parts a farewell bruise, and then—*oh sweet heavens*—I was Supergirl, except she flew with her hands out and I was flying nose first over my pony's ears, trawling a tether of magic and one irate Gatekeeper. My arm was pulled up and backward as the full weight of the diminutive Fae made itself known.

My landing was predictably nasty and, as per usual, done headfirst. My teeth snapped together, my jaw tested the concept of dislocation, my boobs flattened, and my knee lost an inch or two of skin.

A pause, then it was the bungee cord all over again: another wince of hot flared in my shoulder sockets as she was sling-shot past me.

She landed with a thud-thump and a grunt.

In the moments following land ho, I listened to Mouse hacking up a lungful of magic, and the Gatekeeper's wet wheeze, and the sounds of Seabiscuit presumably heading hell-for-leather for the winner's tape.

"I hate wards," coughed Mouse.

"I think I love them," I replied.

Before we'd been outside of the bowl; now we were inside it. And *now* I understood why the ward had turned blue. Not only was the interior of the ward's walls tinted blue, so was the late-morning light within it. It was alive, this light, and it carried the lingering heat of an Alpha's open-throttle flare; it goosed my flesh and sent my heart into a thump of joy.

Trowbridge.

Blue light everywhere. My man was flaring.

* * *

Daniel's Rock was a twenty-foot misshapen hump of pale gray, textured with fissures and stained with vertical streaks of dark charcoal. My mate had been facing a slit carved into the rock when I tore through the ward, but as Seabiscuit cantered past him he spun around with a warrior's coiled grace, the blade he held balanced and ready to swing. His mouth was set in an ugly clenched-tooth grimace, his body language primed for battle.

I love this man—the knowledge was a fist bump to my solar plexus.

Even if dirt was caked on either side of his mouth and his expression was more furious than loving. Angry, half-naked, dirty. Less than pretty what with his warrior's leer beginning to sag in relief . . .

I didn't care.

I love this man.

I will always love this man.

He looked like he'd seen hell, left a memo on how to improve it, and then done a tour in purgatory. Since we'd parted ways, his clothing had been edited down to his jeans and those had seen a rough and drastic revision, the legs of which having been hacked off at mid-thigh. His custom-made cutoffs rode low on his narrow hips. But more significantly, he carried a sword.

My soldier of impossible causes had found himself some weaponry.

"Whose sword?" I asked in a voice that barely trembled.

His flare blazed, then blinded.

"That's all you say? 'Whose sword?'" His voice rose. "What the fuck took you so long?" He was a tall shadow on the other side of a field of fierce blue. "You should have been here! When I came here and only found him . . ."

Him? As quickly as the question formed, I tossed it aside, for I heard him take another ragged breath, this time through his nose. Trowbridge finished hoarsely with a "Jesus, Hedi."

"I had to take a couple of pee breaks."

And with that, the scorching heat of his Alpha flare eased, the fire licking away until his light felt like a warm caress. And as the light around me went from cobalt blue to the hue of the Mediterranean, I heard him huff.

It was tiny, but it was a huff.

"May the Gods preserve us," said Mouse in awe. "It's the Son of Lukynae himself."

I hoisted myself to one bruised elbow, a motion that elicited a squawk from the Gatekeeper. "Donut time again," I murmured to my magic. The weight on the end of my fingers disappeared. I sensed, rather than saw, both of my charges move to the side.

Trowbridge slowly lowered his sword.

My anxious gaze flitted over him, taking in his strung-bow tension, searching for injury. A liberal coating of mud that was half-dry and half-wet, leaving the overall impression of mottled crocodile skin, questionably enhanced his near nudity.

No wound on his heaving chest. No blood on his taunt thighs.

Unharmed.

My lip trembled, partly from the knee-dissolving sweep of relief but mostly because the instant he'd turned to face me and he'd sucked in a hard breath I'd known.

We were equal in this love business.

From this point on, they'd be no security locks on my heart. No distance allowed between us, no regrets given leave to grow. Screw all the other shit that kept stepping in between us and trying to trip us.

I knew.

Once you took away the magic and the fangs and erased the backstories and unfathomable histories . . . after you reduced the noise, the conflicts, and the confusion . . . it all came down to what was at core real and what was not.

It was so damn simple.

Here it was: I could believe in a man who swung me off a waterfall. I could pin my faith in a guy who sucked in his gut and followed me back to his own personal hell. I could pour my trust into a guy who feared water but liked showers and who would always be ever more pretty than me. When everything else was shifting, when nothing else made sense . . .

I could believe in him and me.

Because he loved me as much as I loved him—I was his.

And it wasn't because I'd tricked him into saying the vows that bound us together. And it wasn't because he was at heart an honorable man who'd decided to make the best of a less than optimal situation.

I saw it in his eyes. I was no step-down. I was no compromise.

I was his One True Thing.

There was only one response to such a declaration. I flared. I let my green light find his in the middle of that clearing because it was the fastest way of touching the essence of him—my Trowbridge, my love, my mate, my heartache and joy. Our flares touched, a prelude to a heated kiss; then at the intersection of his light and mine our colors merged. My green and his blue made turquoise, the same shade as the shoals of the Mediterranean, where the water is warm and the currents are hidden.

Love traveled in the light, the pure summation of all the good things and the bad things in both worlds.

"They're mates," I heard Mouse say in awe.

Our flares eased, then blinked out. Trowbridge heaved a sigh and with it, shook off that tension that had held him fast. He gave a hard glance at the wall of rock—almost as if he was telling it to stay—then covered the ground separating us in long strides.

He's been running. His shins were heavily coated in mud splatter.

My mate dropped to his knees before me, his legs, as is their habit, splaying to surround mine. Two large hands cupped my jaw. His palms were damp from sweat.

"You're so late," he growled. "You should have made it here hours ago. I thought—"

"I got sidetracked." My nostrils quivered as the smell of him—mud, woods, wolf, and stress—enveloped me. "But in the good news category, I got here in the end. Step one accomplished in our epic—"

He put two fingers to my mouth. "Shh." Either his digits trembled or my mouth did, because I felt a tremor between us. *He's haggard.* His chest heaved, up and down, down and up. Mud cracked with each labored breath. His kissed me, a fleeting brush of hard lips.

"You ran all night," I whispered, my bravado slipping.

"My mate needed me," he said quietly, and hell lived in those tired blue eyes. "I was crazy worried about you last night. Tink, I didn't know it was going to be a full moon."

I studied the harsh lines bracketing his mouth. "Yeah. That was a surprise."

"You got to believe me," he started. "I would never have . . ."

He stalled, his face reddening.

"Time moves so fast here." He shook his head in self-disgust. "Eighteen hours to one Earth hour. Shit, I lost half a day in my kitchen back home while I listened to Harry argue with Cordelia about who was going to pick up the Swiss Chalet chicken." He blew some air through his teeth. "My clock was set on Creemore time when I followed you through the passage. If I'd known, Hedi, I would never have left you to face your first change alone . . ."

His words trailed off, a question in his eyes.

My gaze dropped to focus on a flake of dried mud that had spiraled to the ground by his knee. I stared at it, thinking about running and traps, and then I raised my eyes to meet his again.

I saw the fear. The fatigue and the hope.

I looked away.

Then, I laid the truth out, but I did it the way I wanted to. I focused on the good. "I climbed a tree before nightfall to get a sense of where I was and how far I had to go. So I was forewarned—I saw the moon when it was still low in the sky and I knew what was coming. I had time to find a safe place to ride it out."

"That's good," he said. "This isn't the place I'd have chosen for you to face your wolf."

I heard relief in his tone.

"I didn't say that." I touched his jaw lightly, finding the hard muscle clenched above it. "When I heard the moon sing last night, I decided it was time to let my wolf meet her." Without looking into his eyes, I said, "I know. It would have been way easier to go through my first transformation in the safety of Creemore with you by my side, but . . ."

"Tell me."

"You weren't with me and I knew that you might never come."

"I'll always find you."

"I know that now." Beneath the pads of my fingers, his jaw was slick with sweat, stippled with stubble, tense with strong emotion kept barely in check. "But last night, when I saw that thundercloud following you and I knew he was tracking you . . ." My nostrils stung. "You'd told me that Qae never gave up. And that he was the one that ran you to the ground."

His eyes hardened. "Sweetheart—"

"If it was my last night of life, I wanted to understand what it felt like to be a wolf before I died. I needed to feel that connection with myself, and with you. And if you survived, I wanted you to be able to track my scent, if I had one. So, I stripped down, and I hid Ralph. Then Merry and I waited for the moon to sing." I licked my lip, remembering. "I didn't hear her sing until she was high in sky. How could I have not heard her, all these years? Her song is so sweet, so seductive. It leads you where you need to go, if you only stop fighting it, and just . . . listen." My eyes caught his. "So, I let go and I changed into my wolf."

He cocked his head and did something I'll always love him for. He didn't ask if I liked it or not. He waited like a man watching as the jury takes their seats. He didn't rush me. He didn't try to put words in my mouth.

He waited.

"Being a wolf was the best thing I ever felt," I told him with utter sincerity. "I didn't run—I flew. I have never felt so free in my life. So joyous. So focused on one thing—"

I broke off as he jerked me to him. His fingers slid through my hair, cupping the back of my head. The other hand held my jaw as his hard mouth slanted over mine.

He kissed me.

And I forgot about the rock, and the pony that still cantered around the ward's ring, and even about the Gatekeeper and Mouse. I even pushed aside the mystery of the ward that enclosed us. Right now, it was him, and me, and two hearts, and his lips and my lips, and our breath combining, and his scent weaving a bracket of love around me.

Eventually, we both had to breathe.

He broke away to lean his temple against mine. "When I got here and found that you hadn't made it here yet . . ." I felt his head move against mine and heard him swear under his breath. "Qae and the rider split up at the falls, sweetheart. You had a tracker on your trail. I kept thinking of what he'd do to you when he caught you."

We killed him.

I didn't want to think of the tracker or his body. "I thought I'd never see you again," I told my mate. "When I saw the lightning—" My voice crumbled. I leaned my cheek against his brow and covered my mouth with my palm.

I wanted to cry.

I *needed* to cry.

I hyperventilated into his ear, fighting hard not to crumble.

"Easy, Tink," he soothed. "You know I'm bulletproof. I'm here now. We're good. We're together again."

I pulled back, hand fisted, to thump him on the chest. "Don't ever play Frisbee with me again." *Thud.* "Ever. And from now on we meet danger side by side. You do not—"

He caught my fist before it could dent him again, pulling me tightly to him. Lips warm against my skin, he murmured, "You said, 'Swing me, big boy.'"

"What?"

"At the waterfall," he said. "That's what you said before I gave you the push. "'Swing me, big boy.' I watched you swing out and let go. You were so fucking beautiful and brave. I'll never forget it. That will always stay with me."

I wiped my nose with my forearm. "What happened to Qae? Did you kill him? Make him hurt?"

"My bloodthirsty mate." A faint grin flitted at the corners of his mouth, then left, leaving him grim faced. "Once I was high enough on the mountain, the chase turned into my game, not his. I knew every path that led to nothing, every ridge that led to something. I found a good place for an ambush. All I had to do was wait for him to find me."

"He had a weapon," I said, remembering the mixed-wood forest and the rider with the bottle blue jacket. "You didn't."

"Qae made me push you off a fucking waterfall," said Trowbridge flatly. "All I needed was surprise and my hands. Then the moon rose, and I was transitioning. His horse caught scent of my wolf. I damaged his horse and got one of his weapons, but not Qae. He was able to catch his horse before it bolted again and took off." His fingers raked my tangled hair. "We're going to have to leave this place soon. I made some significant trails last night, covering my tracks, but Qae might have found them, and you've definitely left traces that won't be too hard to follow."

"No one is following me," I said quietly.

"What?"

"The rider won't be coming after us. We only have to worry about Qae."

"How can you be sure?"

"The Fae with the blue jacket found me this morning. He attacked. I used my magic and she—"

"She?"

"Not she—we. I killed him with my Fae. We broke a bone in his neck, then we listened to him wheeze through his mouth, and then we broke another bone. And after that, he died."

And with that, I lost the war against the tears.

As I sobbed, he rocked me on his lap, his hand moving up and down my back in wordless comfort. I cried until I had no tears left; then I rested, face pressed to his neck. His skin was aromatic with mud and the lingering traces of his wolf.

I thought of my own blood and wondered why his nostrils hadn't caught its sweetness, then realized that I couldn't smell it either—the Fae scent of me was a floral undertone in sweet magic fragrance permeating the dome.

I moved my bandaged ankle out of his line of vision, knowing I needed to tell him about the trap and about the mother jinx over the Spectacle grounds and how four babies went out every day for a spot of Raha'ell hunting. But I couldn't. Not while he was holding me like I was the present he'd longed for and finally unwrapped, and not while his sour mud and wolf scent was twined around me like another pair of arms.

"Why are you covered in mud?" I asked instead. The crust of dried sludge under my cheek itched.

"Cloud camouflage. I tried everything to shake the thing off my tail, but that bastard followed me like I was leaving a trail of blood. Wherever I went, whatever I hid under, it found me. Nothing I did worked, until I remembered that movie you talked about yesterday. I found some mud, and took a bath Schwarzenegger-style. Then I left the cloud by the creek."

Tell him, Hedi.

"Tink," he said quietly. "We got some new shit to deal with."

Past Trowbridge's shoulder, I saw that the ward's walls had lost their blue tint. Which stood to reason—my man was no longer flaring. I could see the dark forest behind us, though this close to the barrier the objects on the other side were faintly blurred.

We're inside a ward. That can't be good.

"I'm not ready." I listened to his heart thud in his chest. I needed this. I wanted to feel safe and loved, if only for the count of forty.

Seabiscuit cantered by, searching in vain for an exit. Mouse was in pursuit. Trowbridge's chin snagged my hair as he turned to watch. "Who's the kid chasing the pony?"

"That's Mouse."

"Mouse," he repeated with a nod. "Is he a Fae? I can't smell shit over the ward's magic."

"He's a mutt."

"You don't see many mutts outside the castle," Trowbridge observed. "I see you found the Gatekeeper. How'd that happen?"

"The Mystwalker sent her to me."

"You're going to need to explain that statement to me."

I'd rather not. I changed the subject. "Why did you turn your jeans into cutoffs?"

"The pant legs kept dragging. It was pissing me off."

I smiled into his chest. "Maybe I should get the League of Extraordinary Bitches to make all your jeans into stripper pants. Velco sides. Snaps instead of zippers—"

"Just as an FYI, when we get back to Creemore, I plan to spend most of my time buck naked."

"There are laws against that."

"Then we're both going to be felons, because we're going to be naked a lot." Trowbridge nuzzled my neck for another few seconds, then spoke, his lips moving against my nape. "Sweetheart," he said reluctantly. "I gave you a minute, but time's up."

"I know."

"Brace yourself. Your asshole brother's here."

"Lexi's here already?"

"Yeah, he's here." Trowbridge rose in a shower of mud flakes, then offered me his hand. I eyed it, thinking about my leg, then gritted my teeth and stood. My left leg held, but the right felt spongy. At least I could feel it now, though. It wasn't completely numb.

On the other hand, my thoughts were numb with surprise. Lexi wasn't supposed to be here. Okay, that sounds wrong. My twin was *totally* supposed to rendezvous with us at Daniel's Rock—meeting here at this landmark was key to the execution of our epic quest.

But he shouldn't be here *yet*.

Actually, by my reckoning, he shouldn't be here for another day.

No matter how fucked up the time differences were between the two realms, the Old Mage had made it crystal clear how long I should wait before I crossed the fairy portal into Merenwyn. He'd been precise on that because the clock started ticking for Lexi the moment he planted a foot in this reality.

If my twin saw the three sunrises in Merenwyn, the soul-merge that bound him and the Old Mage would be irrevocable.

Hence the need to synch arrivals.

By my given timetable, I arrived in this realm a full twenty-four hours earlier than I should have. And yes, I was measuring that by Earth hours, which makes things complicated, but if I rendered it down and took away all the time difference calculations it still came down to one final point.

Trowbridge and I should be waiting for Lexi at Daniel's Rock, not *greeting* Lexi at Daniel's Rock. We were unsynched.

How many sunrises in Merenwyn has Lexi seen since he crossed back into this realm? How long has he been here?

"Where is he?" I asked.

"Inside the cave."

There was a cave?

"The son of a bitch," said Trowbridge, "almost got my fist through his teeth when he told me that I should wait here, and that everything was 'all in hand.' He didn't give a shit that you were out there alone with a tracker following your trail. When I said I was going to take off to find you, the smirking bastard slammed this ward down around me."

Smirking bastard.

"If I could have killed him without hurting you or me, I would have." Trowbridge blew some air through his teeth. "Heads-up, Tink. He's way different."

"He's just come out of detox; Lexi's not going to be the life of the party."

"Yeah, he's weirder than that."

The rock was, as I'd mentioned, a massive, rounded hump of either granite or some equally hard mineral. I know my trees, but I can't tell the difference between rocks. Though Daniel's Rock was basically round in shape, its surface was fissured. Trowbridge led me to one of the deeper slits in the face of the rock, which indeed turned out to be an entrance to a small cave.

Framed inside the narrow natural rock doorway was tall, fit blond man. A fireball blazed and bobbed in the air above his lifted hand.

"Hello, twin," I said as happy-happy built in my gut. Lexi looked so good. He wasn't sweating out fumes of sun potion. He wasn't bouncing on his heels like a junkie without his drug. He was calm. He was fit.

Coolly, his gaze swiveled in my direction. Green eyes, just slightly darker than mine. A long fall of golden wheat tucked behind his right ear and a three-week stubble of hair above his left ear.

No despair behind those eyes.

No devilment or welcome either.

A niggle of ill ease made itself known.

I wet my lips and said, "You can put out the fireball now."

"I will not extinguish my balyfire on a wolf's command," he said, each word a distinct bite of disdain. "Any more than I shall for yours, nalera."

And just like that, the happy-happy sizzle in my gut dissolved.

That's not Lexi. The evidence was staring at me, through

my brother's eyes. Obvious in the way he talked (given provocation and an audience, my twin would always opt for a provoking drawl over patrician enunciation) and in his stance—there was a perfectly good wall right by his shoulder, and he wasn't leaning against it.

Lexi was a leaner.

That's not my twin.

"Where's my brother?" I asked the Old Mage.

Chapter Twelve

I've hit a couple of highs and lows in the space of the last year. I'd fought for my life and won, which was a definite high. Though I'd had to kill doing it. Not once, but three times—which theoretically was a low. And I'd faced stuff that I hadn't wanted to: Threall, the consequences of my actions, and even the League of Extraordinary Bitches.

But covering that short distance to the man who wore my brother's face was right down there on the bottom of all that is awful. It's unbearable to see someone you love overtaken by another's soul. The foreign tilt of the head, the unaccustomed posture . . .

The soft downy hair on the back of my neck rose in stiff horror.

Lexi, where are you?

"Greetings, Hedi of Creemore," said the wily old goat who'd stolen my brother's body.

The fireball danced perilously close to the long sweep of my twin's golden hair. "Put your balyfire out, old man," I told him. "You know you can't kill Trowbridge or me without killing yourself."

"Didn't see that coming," said Trowbridge.

The Old Mage lifted my brother's eyebrow. "There was

no intent to kill. What you see is a demonstration of powers that a wolf cannot hope to possess. This one"—he inclined his chin to Trowbridge—"needs to be reminded that a wizard is superior in all manners to him. It shall always be so—magic shall always defeat brute strength—and yet this particular wolf has such a difficulty accepting the realities of his position."

"Keep talking, asshole," said Trowbridge. "You'll run out of gas faster."

The wizard tilted his head to study my mate. "The teeth of my balyfire's flame are deeper than your fangs, wolf."

"Go ahead." Trowbridge bared his teeth. "But when you do, I'll bring you down and be all over you. We'll both turn crispy. And then we'll talk about fangs."

I watched the wizard's expression turn to ugly amusement.

"Does he actually believe himself to be the Son of Lukynae?" he mused. "This wolf from Creemore, with his sword and armor of dirt, thinks to destroy a civilization ages older than his? With what? No magic. No army. No peculiar gifts." He laughed, and my belly clenched because his snide amusement bore no resemblance to my brother's cocky grin. "A common wolf from a realm without magic thinks himself destined to defeat a civilization such as mine. Such vanity." He made a fist, and the blazing ball flared. It disappeared with a pop, leaving scarcely a trace of smoke.

I took a step forward, but Trowbridge caught my arm and tugged me back. "Don't get between him and me," he growled.

"In public, ever the protective wolf," sighed the wizard. "Such is their nature. All bluster and false charges. And yet who came to your mate's aid last night? Who rescued her? It was not you, Son of Lukynae."

Trowbridge slanted me a hard look. "What rescue?"

I turned to the man who'd stolen my brother's body and said firmly, "Step back, Old Mage. Let my twin come forward."

The old goat straightened Lexi's sleeve cuff. "I wish to be called by my real name—Old Mage, Mage of the Royal Court."

"There's too many mages," muttered Trowbridge. "We have the Old Mage, the Black Mage—"

"Helzekiel is not a true mage," said the man wearing my brother's face. "He is a duplicitous usurper. A weak counterfeit. A cunning—"

"Seriously, bro." Trowbridge wore an irritating smile. "There's too many fucking mages." Raising his brows, he glanced my way. "I say we call this one the Old Mage just because it pisses him off so much, and the other one Helzekiel for pretty much the same reason."

Sounded good to me.

"I refuse to talk to you," I said to the Old Mage. "I want to speak to Lexi."

"Your brother and I have come to an equitable arrangement—I inhabit this body during the sunlight hours, and he takes it during the night. It satisfies both of our needs."

"I don't give a squat about any agreement you squeezed out of my brother when he was going through a drug withdrawal inside a freakin' portal passage. It doesn't hold. So step back, old man. Let my brother speak."

"We don't require your assistance to destroy my Book of Spells," the Old Mage said, his tone haughty and amused. "Nor do I need your assistance to dispatch my old apprentice whose lackluster natural talents are inadequate to the task of protecting the court."

"Stop using the 'we' word—there is no 'we'!" I snapped. "You're a temporary unwelcome guest, got it? And Lexi damn well does need my help destroying the book."

"Why? Do you know where to find the Book of Spells?

Do you have extraordinary magic or skills? No. Your talents are meager. Your presence is not required, nor is it helpful. In fact, it's a hindrance. Your twin does not need your—"

Pssst. My blood pressure skyrocketed and I drowned him out with a shout. "I'm still going to be there beside my brother—brother, not *you*—when the deed is done. That book's going to be toast before the next sundown, and then I'm heading to Threall, where I'm going to personally tear your rotting cyreath from my brother's. You made a promise to me, Old Mage, and you're going to keep it. You're gone. Once the book is destroyed, your soul is toast."

He just looked at me.

I hate reading eyes. I hate understanding things that aren't said.

I'm not leaving—that's what I saw.

Here's another thing I absolutely hate: being left wordless with frustration.

So, I made a fist and hit him.

Not-Lexi clutched his throat, rasping and gurgling. Hypothetically speaking, that should have been an entirely gratifying reaction, but when I'd gone to wipe that look of insufferable arrogance off his face I'd done so with a girlie fist—my thumb tucked into my palm.

"Shit! Shit, shit, shit, shit!" I cursed, hunching over my abused digit.

The scent of faded sweet peas swirled around me as I did the two-step.

Trowbridge sniffed sharply, then exclaimed, "You're bleeding!"

"No, I'm not! My thumb! My thumb!"

"Where are you bleeding? Are you cut? Did someone hurt you? By God—"

"I'm not bleeding! I bled! Old blood. I'm okay now!"

With a growl, he pounced on my ankle. My jeans leg was eased up and my field dressing exposed, and then things got very tense inside the very small cave.

"What happened?" my mate said so very, very quietly.

"I stepped in a trap."

"How long?" He shot to his feet. "How long did it take you to get out of it? Is that where you were all night? Were in you in a fucking wolf trap?"

"Trowbridge, it doesn't hurt. It hasn't since last night."

"Bullshit." He pivoted on his heel, his hand already closing into a fist.

The Old Mage, having long since forgotten whatever close-combat lessons he'd once learned on his father's knee, greeted the danger with a scholarly squawk and a hastily raised hand. A ball, hazy and bright, full of light, started to take shape—

Trowbridge's punch was powerful and swift, a vicious uppercut to not-Lexi's jaw. My twin's chin snapped backward so hard, the back of his head hit the bedrock wall behind him, then rebounded forward.

I swung into action, catching Trowbridge's arm, which was poised for another blow. "No! You'll only hurt Lexi!"

"That's the idea!"

Not-Lexi wove his feet for two full "Mississippis" before he dropped to his hands and knees. He hung there for a couple of moments, then tried to get up. His balance was awful, and when he put pressure on his right foot he sucked in his breath in shock.

His bleary gaze settled on me.

"Hey, Hell," he said, his tone a touch shaky.

I froze. Stared, searching for my twin. In an instant the body language had changed. His shoulders were held less stiffly and the manner in which he held his head subtly altered. He cocked his eyebrows—it was his signature move—the right brow lifting ironically higher than the other.

Hope was a tense, breathless knot inside my chest.

"Lexi?"

"None other." My twin wiped his mouth, frowning at the blood that subsequently streaked the back of his hand.

Trowbridge nudged me with his shoulder and asked, "Are you sure it's him?"

I nodded, my nose burning, my throat thickening.

"You son of a bitch!" Trowbridge roared. "That was your trap!"

And it was lights-out for Lexi.

His trap, his trap, his trap. There was no echo in the cave but a terrible one inside me.

Lexi lay limp on his side. His too-pretty hair a tangle across his face. Trowbridge touched the small of my back, steadying me. I didn't need it. I was standing, wasn't I?

"How can you be sure it was his?" My voice was very small.

"All the traps in the Oldbrooke Woods are your brother's."

That's when my knees turned to water. Trowbridge grabbed me, and before I could puddle beside my brother's sprawled form he'd lifted me into his arms.

"It doesn't hurt," I said again.

Not my leg, anyhow.

He gazed down at me and his expression tightened. Then he pressed a hard kiss to my brow and carried me out of there. He walked fast. The loose end of my bandage fluttered, ghost white, as he brought me out of the dank darkness.

Outside the cave's mouth, there was a single soft wedge of emerald green grass on which Trowbridge placed me with acute care. He touched my face. "You going to be all right if I leave you here for a moment?"

I nodded.

"Be right back."

I looked up at the sky and reckoned it was mid-morning, or thereabouts. Mouse sat crouched on the backs of his heels, the pony's reins looped through his hand, at the edge of the ward. The Gatekeeper glowered, her arms still tightly clamped by her hips, thanks to my oddly well-behaved magical donut.

All the traps in the Oldbrooke Woods are Lexi's.

Trowbridge dragged my brother out by his suspenders. Once clear of the cave, my mate rolled Lexi onto his back, so that my twin, the trap setter and wolf hunter, lay faceup. Then Trowbridge turned for me, crouching by my outstretched injured leg. He gently tugged my pant leg upward to expose Mouse's makeshift field dressing. It was dirty and covered in brownish stains.

Trowbridge sucked in a breath. "I need to see what's happening under this."

I found the peak of my ear and rubbed my thumb over it. "You're not going to like what you find. What's under the bandage is going to scar and it's going to be ugly."

"Do you think that makes a difference to me?"

He used to love my skin. And now it was marked. I had a bumpy, puckered piece of ugliness left on my shoulder compliments of a close encounter with a crossbow bolt, and my ankle would never be pretty again. When I crossed my leg, he'd notice the scar. When he draped my leg over his shoulder, he'd see it. I'd wear the evidence of my brother's actions for the rest of my life. It would be a constant reminder.

"Scars will never change how I feel about you," Trowbridge told me as he rolled up the denim. "I've got scars; do you hate them?"

"No, I mourn them."

"Don't. They're reminders of shit I survived. That's the whole deal, Tink—I lived to see the scar. So, I'll take yours and I'll be grateful for them."

I watched his hands, noting how well he used them, even though his pinkie and ring finger were nothing more than stubs.

Trowbridge set to work on unwrapping the makeshift bandage from my leg. Within two revolutions, the air turned ripe with his anger. The linen and the wound had become one, an unfortunate consequence of dried blood and Were healing properties. "We're going to need water to soak it off," he said grimly. "That prick of a bastard better not have sealed us off from any water source."

"Mouse has sun potion," I said. "He used it to rinse some of the juka off."

"Did he get all of it?"

"I don't think so. Some of it had a chance to get into my system."

Trowbridge's gaze swept to the boy who held Seabiscuit's reins. "You!" he said, switching to Merenwynian. Trowbridge and I had been speaking English, which had left Mouse in the dark, though not the Gatekeeper. She understood the language of Earth. How much could she hear from where she stood?

Mouse slowly straightened. "Yes?"

"You have more sun potion?"

"Aye," he said warily.

"Bring it."

Mouse tied Seabiscuit's reins to a branch, then unhooked his sack from her pommel. From its depths he brought out one of his burlap-wrapped bottles. He unwrapped it as he walked to us, his body language a manifesto of reluctance.

Trowbridge carefully stretched out my leg. "Hurts?" he asked in English.

"No."

"Heads-up—it will. It's going to hurt like a bitch when I remove these dirty bindings." He shook his head at the wrappings. "I hope your skin hasn't grafted to this." When Mouse approached, Trowbridge asked, "How much juice do you have?"

"I have a full bottle, Son of Lukynae," said the boy in Merenwynian.

I raised my eyebrows meaningfully.

Mouse chewed his lip. "And two more in my sack."

Trowbridge stopped picking at the strip of linen. After a pause, he said, "Don't call me Alpha."

Body braced as if he were expecting a backhand, Mouse offered the potion. Trowbridge took it from him with a gruff nod.

"I have to take it," Mouse blurted.

My mate looked up.

"If I live with the Fae, I have to take my ration," Mouse continued. "There's nothing else I can do. Even if I leave the castle and take my chances by running, there's nothing to run *to*. I might find a village where they need an extra pair of hands and weren't too fussy about my blood, but I couldn't chance meeting my wolf . . . I'd *still* have to take it. Anyone who wants to pass as Fae has to. That's why I took it. But if I knew I had a place where I could be a wolf, then I wouldn't take it."

Trowbridge regarded Mouse for a long moment. "A man's got to do what a man's got to do."

"I wouldn't take it unless I had to," Mouse whispered.

"I got that," said Trowbridge. "Go see if there's still a stream on the other side of the rock. I'll need enough water to wash my hands and rinse her leg."

"Aye, Alpha."

* * *

"Your brother looks like shit." Trowbridge pulled the cork from the bottle of sun potion. The scent of the elixir streamed from the small bottle's neck: flowers a day before the rot.

Though Lexi was still out cold, his nostrils flared.

I looked away.

Grim-faced, Trowbridge drizzled the juice over my dressing until the fabric bled. He studied the small rust puddle beneath my leg, then looked up at me. "I want you to take a mouthful of the juice before I go any further."

That shocked me. "You hate sun potion. It subdues our wolf."

"You're going to bleed, sweetheart." Trowbridge's knuckles had grime embedded in their creases. "And it's going to be god-awful when I tear this thing off. Your skin has already partially healed around it."

"It won't hurt. I can barely feel my leg."

Alarmed, he pressed lightly on my foot. "Do you feel this?"

"No, but—"

"Shit," he muttered. "Can you move your toes? How long were you in the trap?"

"Five hours? Six?" I wiggled my toes. "I'm not sure. I was in and out."

"You will take the juice," he announced.

"Trowbridge, listen. I—"

"Don't argue with me." He brought the bottle to my mouth. "I hate what this stuff stands for, but don't ask me to watch you hurt when I don't have to. Take the fucking potion."

Would it help with the pain inside my chest? Would it lift that heavy weight that made me feel a hundred years old? Take away this nagging emotional misery?

His trap.

I took a mouthful. Let it bathe my tongue, fizzing slightly, then swallowed. Trowbridge watched me keenly, his head cocked, but the familiar buoyancy that generally followed a sip of juice didn't turn my world all soft and muzzy.

After a few seconds, he raised his right hand. "How many fingers have I got?"

"A thumb, half of your index finger, a quarter of your ring finger, and—"

Scowling, he sat back on his heels. "A few fucking hits over a couple lousy days and you're already building up a resistance. This shit is worse than fucking crack."

"You're cussing a lot," I said mildly.

"Get used to it. I swear more when I'm tired."

And even more still when worried, I thought, watching him irritably scratch at the mud flakes on his muscular forearm.

"The juice will kick in." His fingers moved to his leg, where they began to drum a restless tattoo. "It always does. That's why the Fae love this stuff." He tipped back his head to squint at the ward. "At least the cloud won't find us through the ward."

"Jinxes."

"What?"

"The clouds are called jinxes. According to Mouse, Helzekiel conjured up the first one about ten days ago."

"But I was . . ."

Chapter Thirteen

Trowbridge was going to say that he was here in Merenwyn ten days ago, but he hadn't been, not really. In the interim, he'd spent time in Creemore, and that muddled up time calculations beyond comprehension.

The two worlds' time lines simply could not be stitched together.

Trowbridge scrubbed his face. "It is messing with my mind—knowing that only an hour or so has gone by in Creemore while meanwhile we've been . . ."

On the run for more than a day.

"I can't do it anymore," he said. "We're here now. We need to live by Merenwyn's clock and forget the rest."

I nodded, albeit slowly.

He smiled at me, the weary curve of his mouth telling me that he recognized my reluctance to forget home. He changed the subject with more determination than finesse. "So, what else did the mutt say about the frickin' cloud?"

"Mouse said that every morning the mother jinx gives birth to four small ones. They're sent out to hunt wolves and they don't return until they've found their prey." I lifted my shoulders. "That's it."

"Only wolves?"

"It can't track mutts. Only the full-blooded Rahae'lls and Kuskadors."

"So it hunts by scent."

"I think so."

Mouse returned carrying his dripping shirt and a drenched wad of what looked like the wrappings he'd used to protect his sun potion bottles. "We have no cup nor bucket. But I thought you could use this lot to wash the crud off you."

Trowbridge took the sodden shirt with a nod. Mouse stayed, shifting his weight on his feet, as Trowbridge began to clean his hands.

Without looking up, my mate said, "That will be all."

Mouse nodded. "Yes, Alpha."

Trowbridge waited until the boy was back beside Seabiscuit before he muttered, "I told him not to call me that."

"He's very curious about us."

"He's looking for a pack." Trowbridge worked the cloth over his palms, then dropped the shirt. Gently, he retested the bandages wrapped around my ankle. "These wrappings are looser, but not by much." His expression turned regretful. "Tink, we got to get this done. These dressings have got to come off and we can't wait for the juice to kick in. We have to leave here. This ward might protect us from the cloud, but it also keeps us trapped. If Qae's found my trail, I've led him right to you. You never stay long in one spot when you're being tracked. I don't want to walk out of this bowl of magic and find a surprise waiting for us."

"Do what you have to do. I won't feel a twinge of pain. Lexi took all of it last night."

Trowbridge lifted startled eyes.

"No, that's not the juice talking." I gave him a bittersweet smile. It was time to tell him of the trap, and Mad-one and Lexi's visit. "My brother came to me last night while I was in the trap and he assumed my pain."

"He *came* to you?" repeated Trowbridge, his voice dipping into a dangerous drawl. "And he left you there? I'll—"

"No!" I said, catching his arm before he could lunge for my comatose twin. "Not like that. He wasn't really there. Not in body and form." I winced, knowing I was going to have to try to explain something that I didn't have a handle on.

Trowbridge looked up to determine if the Gatekeeper was within hearing distance. She'd been fluent enough in English to spew insults at me back at the Peach Pit, on our first introduction, before she'd turned on her heels and hauled her ass back to Merenwnyn. He jerked his chin at the boy who stood nearby, worrying the edge of a hangnail. "Mouse," he called, "take the pony and the woman to the stream. Water the animal and watch the woman. Got it?"

Mouse brightened. "Yes, Alpha."

When we were alone except for my comatose twin, Trowbridge resumed the interrogation as if it had never been paused. "Was the dickhead there or not?"

"Lexi's voice was there; his body was not." I crinkled my brow, remembering. "Though I could feel his hands, stroking my fur, and that was more than a little weird."

"If he touched you, he was there."

"Ghost hands, Trowbridge. That's what it felt like."

He swore under his breath.

"I don't know how to explain what happened, but Lexi was able to talk to me through Mad-one. The important part is that he came when I called. And that he tried to make it better for me. I was . . . not good."

"Big of him," Trowbridge snarled. "Did the ghost-bastard happen to mention that the trap mauling your leg was his?"

"No."

"Ball-less wonder."

"I want you to listen to me, okay? Because what I'm

going to say is important." I waited for his glare to turn from Lexi to me, then said, "Once we've done what we need to do here, I need to believe that we're going home to Creemore. And I want the life that we should have had: you have your pack and me, and I have you and what's left of my family." I drew in a long, shuddering breath. "I want peace, Trowbridge. I never thought I'd want a quiet life again, but that's what I want. And if you can't put aside how you feel about Lexi . . . if you and he are fighting all the time . . . Creemore will turn into a new battleground."

"He traps his own kind."

"I know!" I hissed. "My leg is proof of it!" I stopped to swallow again, pushing down the knot that kept rising. Then I said, more calmly, "But when I needed him, Lexi tried to help me. He gave me the language—I understand Merenwynian now; didn't you notice that?" I nodded in the direction of the Gatekeeper and Mouse. "And he sent those two to set me free."

Trowbridge twisted to follow my gaze. "You told him everything about the Gatekeeper and the Safe Passage?"

"No!" I wanted to howl in frustration. "It wasn't like that. We weren't talking like you and I are talking now. It was a stream of conscious thing, with Mad-one acting as a conduit. The Gatekeeper issue was random. Either Lexi or Mad-one must have gone deeper into my mind and seen things I hadn't anticipated them seeing."

"Are you telling me you were mind-fucked by your own brother?"

I studied the fury growing on his face.

"No," I said slowly, ice forming in my heart. "He didn't 'fuck' my brain. Only mystwalkers can screw people's brains without their permission. So if you're talking about brain-fuckers, then you're basically talking about me."

"Bullshit," he said, returning his interest to the bandage.

"You'll never get your kicks out of messing with people's heads."

"How can you be sure?" For once I had, if only briefly.

"Tink," he said, teasing the edges of the wrappings. "A lot of us have abilities we wish we didn't have. I'm good at killing. I didn't know how good I was at it until I came here. I'm also a champ at warfare. That's who I am now. But I don't kill for fun and I never will. Does that make you want to run from me?"

"No." My eyes burned.

"So . . . ditto. But I'm not giving your brother a pass for him going where he had no business going. And you shouldn't either. He's a predator. He took from you because he could. He'll keep doing it. I keep telling you: the kid you knew is long gone. What you have now is a manipulative son of a bitch who you shouldn't trust farther than you can throw. There was—"

"He felt remorse." I touched my chest with my fist. "I felt it right here."

"You felt what he wanted you to feel." Mouth flat, Trowbridge took the bottle and poured another thin stream of liquid over the dressing.

"Yeah?" I jackknifed over my leg and pressed down on the gummy bandage. In response to the pain, Lexi moaned low in his throat, his features twisting. "He took my agony." My gaze held my mate's. "I told him I was lost and scared and he sent me the Gatekeeper." I switched into my mother's tongue. "I told him that I didn't know the language and he gave me the gift of Merenwynian."

A terrible flatness crept into Trowbridge's eyes.

"I know he's done some terrible things," I whispered. "To you. To the wolves. To me. And I'm angry that he's done them. *Really* angry. But I can't hate him . . . and I can't leave him here. If he's a bad guy with no redeeming features, then none of this makes sense. I need to believe he's salvageable."

My mate studied my toes as if an answer lay in them. Then he shook his head. He lifted his gaze to mine. "You also need to hear this. It's going to break your heart and leave a scar, but I'd rather tell you the truth and leave a scar than tell you a lie and watch you die. Hedi," he said grimly, "there was ash in his fire."

I stared at him in confusion. Ash? In what world was that important?

"Whose fire?" I asked.

"Your brother's." He softened his tone to the pitch a doctor uses when giving really bad news. "Lexi spent the night here. He made a fire, and he burned wood all night—there was too much ash for it to be a morning fire. Unlike you, he wasn't injured, and he wasn't lost. Oldbrooke Forest is not that big. If you know where you're going, and how to get there, you can cover the ground pretty quickly. I'm guessing he could have reached you in three hours, tops, and done it without breaking into a sweat. He could have sprung you from the trap. Been the hero—the whole nine yards. But he didn't."

I felt sick. As if I'd eaten something that hadn't agreed with me and now it was stuck in my craw, like a fur ball. When Lexi had said he couldn't come to rescue me, I'd understood that to mean that he was still in the Creemore portal, being healed of his addiction.

Because that's where he was *supposed* to be.

Being healed. Getting over his sun potion addiction.

I stared at my twin, my brain searching for a plausible excuse. "Maybe Lexi crossed the portal last night, as soon I called for help? He traveled as far as he could to get to me, but he'd stopped when he realized that the Gatekeeper would get there first?"

Still in dreamland, Lexi's arm was curled over his head as if to protect it.

"The geography's wrong," I heard my mate reply. "He'd have used the Creemore portal. That's hours northeast of here. And he would have had to detour around the Faelands to get here, which would have added more time. No way could he have done all that and still burned a fire all night. I'm sorry, sweetheart, but when he was 'talking' to you last night, he was doing it from Daniel's Rock."

My hand went to the ball of Merry and Ralph. I felt a flash of heat and a flicker of cold and knew that I had touched both.

"There's more," he said, his tone heavy.

I didn't want to hear more. I wanted my brother to still be redeemable.

"There's always fur and crud left over following a Were's transition. But there's nothing here. Not in the cave, not anywhere inside this ward. Lexi didn't change into his wolf last night. It was a full moon. The only thing that would stop the process would be a dose of sun potion. So, I'm thinking your bro might not be clear of his juice addiction."

"What is Lexi playing at?" I whispered.

"I don't know. But for both of our sakes, don't put your trust in him." He studied the sodden bindings; then tenderly—oh so gently—my mate pinched the end of the linen between his grimed fingers. "So you sure you don't want another hit before I do this?"

"No." I lifted my gaze to meet his. "*I* won't feel it."

Trowbridge's gaze moved to Lexi. "Works for me."

And with that my loving mate ripped my bandage free.

My twin cried out like a man who'd been branded with a hot iron. Chest heaving, he shot upright to a sitting position. For an instant he was awake.

He saw me. And I saw him.

Ashes in the fire, I thought.

My twin's eyes rolled up toward a heaven he didn't deserve to visit, and he fell into another deep faint.

Chapter Fourteen

Despite Trowbridge's judicious use of light slaps and "hey, asshole," Lexi's slow crawl to consciousness was a frustratingly long process. When my brother's eyes finally opened, he stared blankly at the sky for a long moment. His nostrils flared—the air was heavy with a perfume of rank flowers and bruised sweet peas. Then he rolled his head toward us.

Purple circles under his eyes, dots of sweat beaded his forehead. The illusion of health the old wizard had presented to us had disappeared when the old goat had stepped back to let my brother take his hits.

Lexi moved his jaw to test for breakage. "Your boyfriend sucker punched me."

"It was your trap," I said.

My brother briefly closed his eyes before reverting back to a study of Merenwyn's unblemished sky.

I studied my leg. My skin had made an effort to knit together since the juka had been thoroughly rinsed from the wound. Healing was in progress. Holes that should be filled had. Though not completely, and probably the indents would always be there. An ankle bracelet I'd carry forever.

"The first fifteen minutes after you hear the snick of the

jaws closing on your hind leg are pure, stark terror," I said, my tone conversational. "It takes an hour or more for your wolf's panic to ebb into exhaustion. That's when you start thinking. You've really got two options. You can wait for the hunter to come to check his trapline—"

Trowbridge interrupted. "Which, if the lazy bastard is strung out on sun potion, could be a couple of days."

"Or you can go for door number two," I said. "You can chew off your own leg. All things considered, that's the kind of internal conversation you don't ever want to have." Still no comment, except a tightening of my twin's jaw, so I went for the lash. "Dad was a wolf. Would you have set your traplines for him too?"

"I can go back to sleep," Lexi said quietly, "and you can find yourself talking to the wizard inside me."

"You know, I'm not sure how much of a threat that is. I'm not fond of either of you right now. He lies. You lie. What's the difference?" My hands curled into fists. "But since you're here, why don't you tell me how much time we have left?"

"For what?"

"Lexi, I'm done with games. I know, okay? Last night you weren't communicating with me from some portal between this world and the other. You were here. In the cave behind you. Sitting by your fire. That's why I heard you so clearly. Which means that we're already out of time, or we're *almost* out of time. So which is it? Are you and the old wizard a permanent couple? Have you seen three sunrises in Merenwyn yet? Or do we have some time left to get this thing done?"

He didn't say "doh" or smack his head in surprise. "There's time."

"How. Much?"

My twin delayed answering—a piece of recognizable leftover childhood behavior—filling in the taunting pause by raising himself onto one elbow to scowl at his right boot. He moved it slightly and bit down on a wince.

Hurting much, Lexi?

"I've been in Merenwyn for a day and a night," he said, switching back into the Fae language. He dipped his head to swing his long swath of hair over his shoulder. "If the deed is to be done, it must be completed by the end of tonight."

"So, you weren't in the portal's passage last night." I answered him in the same tongue and was proud that my tone was matter-of-fact.

"No. I was here." Wearily, Lexi sat up, his movements slow and careful.

"You useless son of a bitch." Trowbridge pushed himself away from the wall, the scent of his anger curling into a scorpion's tail.

Three words. Three devastating words.

"You left me there all night," I whispered.

Lexi stood, and as he did every bit of healthy color leached from his face and his green eyes shone as if inner-lit by a supernatural force. Not a good look for my twin: Dean Winchester would have gone for his stabby-knife. Still, he was Lexi, which meant that he'd go down with a sneer and challenge. "Take your best shot, Son of Lukynae."

Trowbridge gave him the once-over. "Why waste the energy? You won't feel it. You're still cranked on the juice."

Lexi stared at him for a second, a bitter smile flitting. "That craving has been cleaved from me."

My twin's eyes moved to study mine. He gave me a long, measuring look, acutely similar to the one my dad used to give me when I did something inexplicable.

I took in a breath, short and swift. And at my tiny in-hale, the mask Lexi held as he'd examined me—this twin who'd pushed him into an unaccountable hell—slipped.

I saw betrayal in his eyes.

It was my due, and even though I was still torn between hating him and loving him, I accepted the weight of it. My mouth opened, a jumble of words poised to spill.

Trowbridge spoke, breaking the moment. "Don't believe any of his bullshit. The son of a bitch didn't turn into his wolf and it was a full moon last night."

"Unlike you, wolf," Lexi replied, "I don't have to turn into a dog who lifts his leg to mark every bush he encounters. I have access to powerful magic, and it protected me from the moon's call."

"You sorry bastard," said Trowbridge. "You've turned your back on the best part of you."

"The best part of me?" Lexi arched one mocking brow. "Only a Raha'ell would spew those lies."

"Don't fight," I said, suddenly drained.

But Lexi had gained his second wind. "What did he tell you about the life of a wolf in Merenwyn? Did he spin you yarns about the glories of the hunt, the blood, the brotherhood? Did he mention that belonging to the Raha'ell pack comes with the dues of starvation and death?"

Trowbridge's scent spiked. "You don't know anything about it."

"But you do, Son of Lukynae." Fist coiled, Lexi took a step forward on his "good" leg, narrowing the space between himself and my mate. "You know exactly what a Raha'ell can expect from this realm. And you let her come anyhow. I should carve out your heart and serve it to your hounds."

I knew he was going to swing at Trowbridge and that was going to be the beginning of a major brawl. But before my twin could release his anger with the punch he so clearly wanted to throw, he froze.

For a second, he just stood there, a living statute.

"Stand back from him, Tink," Trowbridge said softly.

A tremor shook Lexi; then, the snarl on his lips slipped

and his arm slowly lowered itself to loosely dangle at his hip. His anger, his belligerence, his very essence, melted away in front of my eyes.

He's gone.

The Old Mage cocked his head toward Trowbridge, though I don't think he saw the Son of Lukynae. The expression on the wizard's face was distracted—that of a physicist whose preoccupation had been snagged by a new and troublesome possibility.

"The one named Qae has breached the ward," he said.

Oh crap. Not now.

Trowbridge grabbed the sword. "Where?"

The Old Mage pivoted to point to the right. "Where the water runs."

"Stay here," Trowbridge told me.

Seriously, when had I ever "stayed"? I surged to follow him, pushing aside the man—not Lexi, not Lexi—who hurriedly stepped to block my path.

"No, nalera," he said. "Let the wolf—"

"I'm not your nalera," I spat. "And you're not my brother."

My top speed is significantly slower than Trowbridge's. Within three long strides, I was left in his dust. I followed anyhow, sprinting as fast as my size 6s could take me, pausing once to flatten against the rock as Seabiscuit cantered past.

By the time I rounded the fat bastard that called itself Daniel's Rock, my Trowbridge had already met his nemesis in the small field near the place the water ran.

They'd already begun the dance, warily circling each other.

Trowbridge was taller and better built. Both men gripped swords. Qae's was demonstrably longer, but Trowbridge's reach was greater.

I don't know if that made for an even match or not.

But the hair at the back of my neck bristled.

Qae held the dark in him, I sensed, and he took that quality of sewer and stealth with him wherever he went. He had rat-like features—small eyes, a long, pointed face—and the similarity was emphasized by the way he moved. His steps were small—tiny, scuttling adjustments to Trowbridge's more graceful movements.

There was only a tiny blip of light to Qae, and that came from the pouch he wore attached to his belt. Something bright glinted inside it. I wondered what it was, but the tracker chose then to make a slight swipe toward Trowbridge with his blade. The magic-scented air stirred, and I realized Qae carried a faint scent about him. He was not full Fae. He was something else.

Unbidden, my gaze jerked to the ward. But beyond its wavering shield, there was no rat pack as feared, no cadre of cavalry. Just the backdrop of Oldbrooke forests and another smaller outcrop of rocks.

But still . . . there was dark here, in the northern lee of the rock.

As my lover circled Qae, my gaze swept the area, searching—

I blinked, not believing what I saw.

The Gatekeeper squatted in the S-bend of the stream that coursed through the narrow gap of two boulders. She still wore her donut of magic, but the glittering pieces within it were sparking in distress. Magic doesn't like such close contact with water.

The Fae woman's skirt was wet and bunched up around her hips.

She's peeing? *Now? While all this is going on?*

Then my heart—which had been doing a frantic *thump, thump, thump* compliments of my dash around the rock—stalled mid-beat as comprehension swelled.

No. She was not taking a piss.

She was sitting on Mouse's body, and if he wasn't dead yet he'd soon be, because one of her knees was pressed hard on his neck. The boy who longed to belong to a pack was unconscious, his face turned sideways, water sheeting over his nose and slack mouth.

She trying to drown him.

Qae chose that moment to lunge toward Trowbridge. The curve of Qae's blade flashed in the mid-day sun. My mate feinted backward, one hand spread, the other balancing his sword.

I had a choice, though the question and its answer flashed so quickly that the action that followed felt less like a decision and more like a drive that couldn't be squelched. Question: Save Mouse, or interfere in that delicate dance between a warrior and his tracker?

Save the mutt.

He needs your protection more.

I skirted the men and flew on silent feet to the stream that ran crooked in the lee of the big rock. As I broached the Fae, her head snapped up, her eyes widening in surprise. She opened her yap—I'll never know what she meant to say. It didn't matter anyhow. She could have hexed me with a mouthful of incantations and still she wouldn't have been able to slow me. I was locked and loaded and moving at mach speed.

I vaulted over her, and as I did, I grabbed a handful of the fuzzy topknot that had taunted me all morning. Over the last twelve hours, I'd learned a thing or two about momentum. Thus, I didn't let go of that fuzzy handhold when I lost my balance and I didn't let go when my shoulder screamed as it assumed the weight of her and I didn't let go when I heard my Fae start shrieking inside my head.

"Water!" My talent screamed in very real fear. "It will burn us!"

In a different slice of time, perhaps I would have answered magic-me with a comforting shush or mayhap I'd have paused to consider the source of the sudden biting pain on the upper arm, but hello—the laws of momentum were still in effect. Hedi of Creemore was a projectile in motion. As I shot over the Gatekeeper, my fingers sank deep into her topknot, her head snapped back, and she let out an anguished howl.

Together, we spiraled into the leggy brush that bordered the stream. As soon as we stopped rolling, I topped her. It was easy to get the upper hand—my manacle of magic already incapacitated her.

It should have ended there.

The Gatekeeper had no hands free to gouge my eyes, no balyfire to burn my flesh. But the bitch had teeth. She sat up and used them, her pointed canines snapping at the exposed skin above the gaping neckline of my T-shirt.

Wolves do that. They go for the blood pulsing at the throat.

She should not have done that.

Not to me.

Not to my wolf.

My bloodlust surged, fed by the magic, and the danger, and the black evil I sensed all around me. I felt for one of those slick, slimy stream rocks, tore it free from its anchor of pebbles and packed earth, and without pausing, brought it down hard on her head.

She jerked away, twisting her shoulders and neck to the right, and thus, instead of crushing her venomous mug into pulp as I'd intended, my strike simply grazed the side of her head.

Chest heaving, I slowly lifted the rock, poised to strike again.

The woman deserved to die.

"Yeess," breathed my Fae. "Kiiiiill her."

I could feel death's presence pressing on me. It was everywhere on this side of the rock—heavy, dark, and inevitable.

The stone was heavy.

"Kiiiiill," my magic insisted.

"No." The bloodlust waned. I dropped the stone weighing my hand and rolled off the Gatekeeper. Wearily, I knuckled mud from the corner of my mouth. "Detach," I said to my magic.

The donut of magic crushing the Gatekeeper's ribs considered that command a fraction too long for my liking. I stared at her, thinking she was both beautiful and stubborn. "You answer to me. Not I to you." My tone turned knife-sharp. "Do it now."

She broke apart into a haze of agitated magic.

A cloud of temporary obedience, she ghosted over me as I entered the stream again. She flashed and flickered as I snared Mouse's left arm. She hovered high over me, emitting sparkles of false docility, as I heaved Mouse over.

Don't be another Varens.

I righted Mouse's body so that his mouth was no longer filling with water. Then, teeth set, I dragged him from the shallow stream.

His hair was plastered to his cheek.

A wolf by any other name.

He will live.

We will make him live.

I reached for Merry and lifted her over my head. Ralph came with her, his chain catching my chin. "Don't get in her way," I warned, my tone rough and awful. I twisted my neck and yanked them both off me and then laid them down on the dry ground. Asrais don't like being wet either, and healing is best done skin to skin.

Mouse's chest was undeveloped for his age; his skin, pale and thin.

A wolf by any other name.

I used the driest portion of my shirt to blot the wet from his flesh, then fitted the ball of Merry and Ralph into the hollow below Mouse's slight pectorals.

"He needs you," I told her. "I need you. Please do what you can."

Then, placing my trust in my Asrai's instincts, I pivoted back to Trowbridge and Qae.

While I'd been wrestling with the Gatekeeper, my mate and the tracker who'd followed him over hill and dale had stopped feinting.

Now they fought in earnest.

Somewhere during the three minutes it had taken to rescue Mouse, the balance of who was the stronger opponent had been tipped. The pouch swinging at the tracker's waist had been opened and the contents pulled out and put to use.

Qae had a net.

It was as supple as the lacework of Cordelia's filigree knit sweater and hardly much larger.

But it was silver.

The suffering my wolf had endured last night had rendered her weak and silent, but now she growled inside me.

Silver.

Qae swung his net of awful at my mate. Trowbridge curled his body into a comma to avoid its stinging touch. Qae pounced, lunging forward to slash his weapon across Trowbridge's leg.

A line of red beaded my mate's thigh.

I am wolf; I am Fae; I am me.

And silver doesn't mean shit to any of us.

* * *

"Magic-mine," I whispered to those dancing flecks of untethered magic over my head. "You want to do some damage?"

I am the Queen of Sparkles.

My talent answered without hesitation, and what had been unfocused and separate—those dancing flecks of untethered magic above me—quickly funneled into a single coil of magic.

She floated, her body flexing, eager for my command.

Qae swung again. His silver net stretched in flight. The trailing tip caught Trowbridge high on the shoulder. A rash of red blisters broke out across my mate's deltoids.

My wolf's rumbles reverberated through me, sending shocks up my spine.

"Kill?" inquired my Fae.

"Soon." I pinched the fingers of my right hand, in a come-hither, and the coil above me undulated to them. I welcomed the flash of pressure on my nail beds as the heavy coil of my magic attached herself to my person, followed by a sudden flutter in my heart as she poured her essence into my blood.

Yes. Fill into my blood; join the wolf inside me.

Let us spill blood.

Let us make mayhem.

I flicked both hands. My magic unspooled in a gleeful arc, and as she did my wolf and I gave my Fae a mixture of commands. Their order was disjointed and illogical, but the meaning was there.

Kill. Maim. Destroy.

And together—wolf, Fae, mortal-me—did all three.

Chapter Fifteen

"Sweetheart," I heard Trowbridge say. "Let go of the dead guy."

I blinked.

Sparkles, sparkles, everywhere.

I lowered my head toward where they seemed to cluster, a horde of busy flies, over a clump of something torn and shredded. He—*mate, lover, mine*—caught my chin and, *slowly, sweetly, tenderly,* raised it so that I was staring blankly at a wall of rock.

"Don't look over there, okay?" I felt him brush my hair, a long, soothing swipe. "Why don't you tell your magic to rest now? Because it's over. It's really, really over."

My hands throbbed.

"Everybody's safe. Mouse is okay; I'm good." My mate's touch moved from my tangled hair to my aching shoulder. He rested his palm there for a "Mississippi" or three, as if to let me grow accustomed to his touch. "Your arms must be tired," he murmured, sliding his palm along my taut biceps. "Why don't you rest them?"

Through downcast eyes, I studied the long fingers circling my arm. Sometimes I forgot that he's missing some

of them. When he touched me—*slowly, sweetly, tenderly*—
I never noticed it.

But now I did.

Only two of his digits were unscarred, though they were
coated in blood and dried stuff that was once mud. How
could a person forget those scars? He carried evidence of
his wounds all the time, and I'd let my consciousness dismiss it.

I shouldn't do that. But maybe you need to do that.

Forget stuff.

"That's it," he said, gently forcing my arm down. "That's
good."

I *was* tired.

"To me," I whispered. I endured—*welcomed, needed,
wanted*—a brief flare of fierce hot pressure as she flowed
back into me.

"That's it, baby," he said, easing me back to him. His
chest was solid against my back. His legs cradled my hips.
His arms curled around me.

Safe. I let my weapons drop into my lap and studied
them. I had all my fingers. There was no blood on them.
What did I do? I twisted my neck to look.

"No," said Trowbridge firmly. "You don't need to see
that."

"Did I do something . . ." *Bad? Terrible? Bloody? Necessary? Good?*

"No," he said. "You did what had to be done."

He slid an arm under my legs, and then he was rising
with me in his arms. I was limp, like a rag doll, and it
seemed to take much effort simply to roll my head so that
it fit in its customary place on his shoulder.

"You carry me a lot," I whispered as he strode toward
the rock.

"You get banged up a lot."

"Wait," I said, lifting my head.

"What?"

"I left Merry and Ralph by the creek with Mouse and the Gatekeeper." I tipped my head back to look behind us. But Trowbridge was walking fast, and twisting my neck like that made everything go fuzzy. I couldn't see Mouse or the thing I'd killed. Only a wall of rock.

"Hey, kid," Trowbridge called without losing a step.

"Yes, Alpha." Mouse's voice sounded thready.

"You alive?"

"Yes, Alpha," Mouse replied with definitely more life.

"Bring Merry and the weapons, leave the net, and the Gatekeeper, and follow us." My mate's arms tightened on me. "And be careful of the blond Fae. He's no friend of ours. He gives you any problem, you holler."

"Yes, I will be glad to holler," said Mouse. "Whatever 'holler' means. I shall be—"

"Just shout, kid."

"I can do that, Alpha."

Trowbridge's strides slowed as we broached my brother, who stood in the shade provided by the rock. My brother's arms were folded near his waist, one hand clasped over his wrist. He wore an expression of academic interest as he returned our regard. From where he stood he must have watched the whole thing go down, and he hadn't lifted a finger to help.

Not Lexi.

The man wearing my brother's face took a step forward.

Trowbridge shook his head and pushed past him. "Buddy," Trowbridge growled, "your wizard's showing."

My mate eased me back down on the soft patch of earth outside the mouth of the cave. "This time, I want you to stay."

"I don't stay."

"I'm beginning to realize that." He touched my hair. "Feeling better?"

Yes. No. Yes.

Mouse came hurrying around the northern end of the big rock. "I have them!" He speed-walked toward us, holding his right arm rigidly extended, probably to keep the cargo resting on his palm as far from his soft body parts as possible.

The boy was wet, and he had a lump by the side of his temple.

The Gatekeeper must have surprised him. I asked him if that was so, and he said yes and that when he'd seen the tracker through the ward she'd sprung on him. She'd hit him with a rock, and that was all he'd known until he woke to find the amulets on his chest.

Trowbridge snared a chain. "Ralph, you're with me. Merry's going with Hedi. You want to cuddle up later, that's fine. But right now, that's the way it's going." The authority in his voice brooked no protest and Ralph offered no opposition to the plan. Trowbridge separated them without any effort. He threw the Royal Amulet over his head, then leaned forward to ease Merry carefully over mine.

"You've got food in that sack of yours," he said to Mouse. "Bring it."

Mouse had food? All that time when my gut was squeezing in hunger, there was food in the damn bag dangling by my knee?

I hate Merenwyn.

A pause followed, during which I inspected Merry for damage. She was pale, and there was mud in her crevices. Frowning, I twisted the tail of my T-shirt around my finger. I began to daub at the grime.

I should have opened the damn sack.

"It's not much, Alpha. It's only . . ." Mouse's voice trailed off.

"Your last biscuit," Trowbridge said. "From the smell of it, it's not very big, and not very fresh."

"I have nothing left but a few crumbs."

"Then bring me those. My mate needs to eat, and she needs to rest. And I'm going to make sure she does both before we leave this place. Got it?"

The Alpha of Creemore was already talking to the air.

I looked up. "I need a shrub for Merry and another for Ralph. They could do with a snack."

Trowbridge called, "Kid, she—"

"I heard, Alpha!"

Mouse's dash to Seabiscuit was slowed by the necessity of making a wide circle around Not-Lexi, who walked toward us with the air of a man on a mission.

Oh hell no.

I refocused on getting Merry tied up. My hands shook. My twin didn't own his body anymore. They were his legs but the old man's will moved them.

"What do you want?" Trowbridge growled.

"It is a matter between myself and the girl."

"I'm no girl." Had I ever been one? I could see Lexi's boots and his tight pants, now sporting a small tear in one knee. Had he ever had a chance to be a boy?

The wizard cleared his throat with an irritated cough. "The presence of the wolf is an unnecessary complication. Despite his strength, and obvious willingness to use his fists, this is not a situation where either of those qualities is useful. Destroying my book before Helzekiel has fully appropriated the contents as his own is the only vital aspect of this journey. We should not risk being apprehended before we have accomplished this task. Traveling to the castle in the company of the wolf known as the Son of Lukynae will only add unnecessary danger to a situation that is already fraught with danger. We must leave him here, inside the ward; otherwise a jinx will detect the scent of his wolf."

It was too much. I snapped.

"Enough!" I cried. "Go away, Old Mage!"

Was that all I had to shout? "Go away, Old Mage"? Or did Lexi manage to struggle back to me on his own? Later I'd wonder about that.

But then I didn't think. I didn't ponder. I simply watched, gut twisting, as my brother's expression cleared until it was a blank canvas, devoid of any emotion. For the count of four "Mississippis" he was neither Not-Lexi nor Lexi.

He was empty. Flat. Dead.

Then, he blinked.

I knew him to be my twin again.

He stared at me for a long moment, and I got the feeling as he did that he was mentally reviewing everything that had happened when he was gone. When he spoke, his voice was pitched softly and there was not a shred of mockery to it. "Go home, Hell. Before this world marks you further in a way that—"

"Shut up," I whispered. "Just . . . shut up."

Trowbridge stood up, his stance protective, but Lexi's gaze never wavered from mine. My brother said, "You need to trust me to take care of what needs to be done here."

"Trust you? I don't even know who I'm talking to."

"*I'm* talking to you," Lexi said. "I'm here now. And I'm telling you that you need to go back to Creemore. I can't keep you safe here."

"When have you kept me safe?" I shook my head. "You didn't come to my rescue last night. You didn't jump in and help us a few minutes ago when Trowbridge and I could have used your muscle. You watched from the sidelines! Why? Why, Lexi?"

Hope flared and died as I searched my twin's face. "Was it because the wizard wouldn't let you? Or because he told you not to?"

He had no answer for me.

I rubbed my face, suddenly exhausted beyond words. "I don't know how much control you have over what you do anymore." I raked my hair behind my ears and straightened. "But I can't think about that right now. I have a job to do, and I'm going do it. And then I'm going up to Threall, where I'm going to finish what I started. You tell the wizard that I'm going to hold him to his vow."

And that will be enough.

I can't bear any more. I've bitten off more than I can chew.

Lexi said softly, "Spoken like a twenty-two-year-old who has never seen anything more dangerous in her life than the playground at our old school." His tone firmed. "You do not speak for me. It is my life, my choices, and my fate. And if I decide there are benefits to this situation you have forced upon me, you will not interfere."

I understood then why instinct had compelled me to cross the portal from one world to another. At some intuitive level I'd known that I couldn't trust Lexi around the one thing he'd desired above all—having his own magic. And not just any magic, but conjures and spells that would delight and terrify. Could I even trust him to destroy the book? If the Old Mage gave him a reason not to . . . if they played the game differently . . .

My tired brain couldn't come up with scenarios that didn't include destroying the book, but my instinct was pinging like Trowbridge's sonar. I couldn't trust either farther than I could throw them.

"It's never been *your* fate," I replied. "It's been ours. We've shared final destinies from the moment we were born. We just didn't know it."

My eyes filled.

"Get the hell out of her face, Shadow," Trowbridge growled.

"You don't talk to me, wolf."

"Make me stop."

Lexi tossed his chin and spread his hands wide. "So Robbie Trowbridge wants to talk. Why don't you tell her why you really came back to Merenwyn, Son of Lukynae?"

Enough.

"Trowbridge is here because he loves me," I told Lexi flatly.

My brother's gaze rested on me for a contemplative moment. "Hell," he drawled. "Do you remember the history of Lukynae?"

"Be careful, asshole." Trowbridge's body coiled. "You can travel to the castle one of two ways: conscious or unconscious. Neither one makes much difference to me."

Lexi lifted his foot and placed it carefully on a log, then kneaded this thigh for a moment before he spoke. "The first Lukynae was a half-bred Raha'ell who turned a civil uprising into the War of the Weres. Peace only came to Merenwyn after he was betrayed by one of his own and captured. His punishment was exile to our world. Not just to Earth—but to Creemore." He turned his arm to show me his wrist. "His blood runs through the entire Creemore pack. Trowbridge has it. You and I have it, though of course ours is diluted."

He dropped his arm.

Here it comes.

"You hurt her," said Trowbridge in a low voice, "and I'll beat you until there is no more you."

My twin's expression hardened. "The Rahae'lls believed the Son of Lukynae would return from exile. They would know him by his blood and by his flare. And when he returns, he'll fulfill the prophecy's prediction."

"So," I said. "I don't see what this has to do with me. Trowbridge has already fulfilled the prediction. He came back and turned the Raha'ells into a great fighting force. The deal's done. Prophecy fulfilled."

"Not by half," said Lexi.

I turned to my mate. "Trowbridge?"

My mate said bleakly, "The Son of Lukynae's light is supposed to lead the Raha'ells to the promised land."

"What promised land?"

"Ours."

There it was. Ever since I'd watched the Fae slaughter three Raha'ells at the shallow crossing, I knew this was coming—that ugly place in time when all forward movement paused and I was forced to examine the yawning chasm between the well-intentioned Hedi and the real Hedi.

As gaps go, it was the crevice that led to hell.

You see, two days ago well-intentioned Hedi thought she saw the big picture and understood how she fit in it. Talk about a two-for-one. If she saved her brother's soul, she'd stop bad things from dripping into her world.

Doable.

All one needed was a match and a bit of luck.

But then we'd gone and stumbled onto the Raha'ells and I'd been forced to watch a kid die from having a spear—a *freakin'* spear—skewered through him, and my heart had had hurt so bad it had felt like a giant clam was squeezing it, and a fierce ugly red anger had stirred deep in the core of me, and that's when my inner voice had whispered, *Hey, Hedi, this is the* bigger, *big picture.*

And you know what my instinct had told me to do with that?

Shut. It. Down.

Because saving the Raha'ells had never been on my list. This world, these conflicts, this brutality, was all too big for me to fight. I was too small. Only a giant could take care of all that.

Anyone could see that I was no giant.

A fact further emphasized when I stepped into the trap. Since then, the real Hedi had been quietly whittling down her objectives to three basic points: *Get into the castle. Get out of the castle. Get your ass home.* Or, in other words, *save your brother's soul and call it quits. Let someone else kill the Black Mage. Go ahead, bad things, commence dripping. Let someone else lead an uprising of Raha'ells.* I wanted to go home to Creemore.

Stars . . .

You can't go breaking people out of holding pens—fucking *holding* pens—without causing an uproar. People notice that type of crap. Forget about a stealthy retreat. You're going to have archers; you're going to have horses; you're going to be pursued.

Running on foot through enemy-controlled territory. Miles of farms and villages—that's what Trowbridge had said. Yeah, right. The average Fae wouldn't happen to notice a pack of desperate wolves streaking for the Safe Passage.

"Hedi," said Trowbridge.

I held up a hand. I heard, rather than saw, his harsh huff in response. Well, sue me. I'm a slow, circular thinker and I was so not finished thinking.

Say we did manage to break them out of the castle—maybe Lexi's wizard did an abracadabra and everyone in the castle except me, Trowbridge, the Raha'ells, and Lexi fell into a brief sleep.

Like that's going to happen.

As Trowbridge and his troupe of desperados still couldn't travel through the Fae land—even my imagination

can't come up with a spell to put an entire realm to sleep—
we'd be forced to retrace the detour Trowbridge and I had
taken. Find the same shallow crossing and head to the
safety of the mountains.

*Where we'd presumably subside eating lichen and the
odd goat.*

Of course, the jinxes would follow us all to K2 . . . No
problem. We have mud. We'd be mud-daubed desperados.
Screwed the first time it rains.

Oh shit. Oh shit.

"Twin," said Lexi.

"Shut up!" I snapped, worrying my ear.

Clearly Karma was no longer going for the belly laugh.
Now she was working the ironic life lesson. Devious de-
ity. Just when I'd finally gotten the big message—there really *is* no place like home—she'd snatched my ruby slippers
and waltzed off with them. *Come back.* I want Toto, and
Auntie Em, and the chance to click my heels together.

Because Creemore never looked so good.

You piss off someone in southern Ontario, they don't
send a hailstorm of arrows at you—they shoot nasty looks.
And they don't kill you for having the wrong blood. All
right, I did get tied to the old oak tree and I *was* knifed,
but let's reexamine the how and why of that.

Knox went for me because he was an asshole, looking
to pin his own crime on me. And though my pack had
helped chain me to the tree, they did that not because of
who I was but because of what I'd done or, more pertinently,
not done.

The night I'd pushed Trowbridge into this realm, I'd told
his pack that I was their Alpha-by-proxy. Had they gone
to the back shed, found their spear, and skewered me
with it?

No.

They'd fallen on their knees and accepted me. They'd

found me a trailer and set it up—exactly as I'd asked them to—even though they'd have much preferred to see me installed in the Trowbridge manse. And when I'd said, "I need a cookie," they damn well had smothered me with sweets. For *months*.

During those golden days, they'd sent me invitations of all sorts, from dinners, to store openings, all the way to eighth-grade graduation events. They'd bruised their knuckles on the door to my silver trailer, searching for my advice.

They'd waited for me to embrace their life, their pack.

But I never had. Alphas prowl their territory, alert to any threat for their people. Not me. I'd let others handle the disputes and I'd let others worry about possible dangers. And eventually, I'd begun entirely avoiding any interaction with the wolves of my pack because—oh, the insult!—they hadn't loved me just for being me.

Worse—I'd refused to meet my wolf. She'd been right there, waiting for me to let her free. And that bitch was freakin' awesome.

As Trowbridge had said, I'd missed out on one of the best parts of me.

And that, Hedi, is what led you to the old oak tree.

Crap. And double crap.

Trowbridge's scent touched me with questing fingers, but I backed away from it. I was on the cusp of turning the page in my own book of painful learning and if I let his essence wrap around me I was going to fold like a baby and the decision would never be mine. And I was not a know-nothing infant. Not anymore. Going, going, gone. I rubbed my ear harder, my thumb stroking it so fast it was surprising a puff of smoke didn't erupt from its tip.

Well, well.

So here we were. Despite all my efforts in keeping my

life down to me and mine, we'd arrived at the *Casablanca* moment. Rick's standing on the tarmac with Ilsa, and heroic Victor's waiting by the plane. Do the problems of three people amount to *more* than a hill of beans in this crazy world?

Goddess. Big pictures suck.

They fucking *suck.*

"Hedi," my mate said softly. "We need to talk."

"Can't," I said faintly. "Feeling a tad light-headed."

My brother, aka the shit-disturber, got in another shot. "Tell her what's supposed to happen to your flare and you."

There's more?

"Shut up!" yelled Trowbridge. "I swear to God, I'll—"

Faster than a cobra, Lexi struck. "It's supposed to become as bright as a blue flame, and as hot as the sun, and then, it's supposed to explode."

I whipped around to face Trowbridge. "You're going to explode?"

"I'm not going to explode," he said tautly.

Chapter Sixteen

I sat down. Or rather, my legs folded and I decided to go with it.

"I am sorry, twin," my brother said.

I lifted heavy eyes. "For?"

"He should have picked you up and carried you right back to your world. He knew you weren't equipped for Merenwyn."

There was so much objectionable in all that, I didn't know where to start.

I fixed Lexi with a quelling stare. "I got this far."

Evidently, not the response my twin was hoping for.

Lexi limped-stalked to Trowbridge, who was leaning against the rock, in a way that at first glance might have been construed as casual—arms folded over chest, hips jutting forward—but wasn't in the least: neck tendons rigid, balance positioned for a quick takeoff. Heedless to the simmering danger, my twin shoved his face into my mate's personal space and said accusingly, "You should have taken her home."

Trowbridge got points for not immediately nailing my twin. He slowly straightened from the wall and collapsed the distance between himself and my brother until his breath warmed my brother's nose. When Trowbridge spoke it was through lips that barely moved and his tone was lethal-soft. "She's got her heart set on saving your soul. Personally, I think they beat the good out of you and there's nothing worth breaking into a sweat over. You should remember that when you get in my face."

"Lexi, move back," I warned. "You're not helping."

The Shadow remained where he was for another taunting second, then took a few jerking steps back, his hands spread. Lexi's smile would have made Gandhi foam at the mouth. "Did you ever tell her about Wryal's? Or of any of the dangers she'd face there?"

That sounded like a disease. "What's Wryal's?" I asked my mate.

My One True Thing's gaze was still locked with my brother's. "It's an island," he answered tightly. "Both the castle and the Spectacle grounds are on it."

Of course they are.

Not only did we have to rescue the Raha'ells from freakin' holding pens, but now we have to get them off an island? It wasn't like the wolves could swim across—Weres can't swim.

"Is there a boat?" I asked. "Or a ferry?"

"There's a bridge." Trowbridge's nostrils flared in and out. A racehorse before the jockey dug in his heels. "Very long. Nice drop to the water."

"I was playing up to now, wasn't I?" I asked, my voice small. "Thinking that if I wore blinders and didn't let my head turn left or right, kept my eyes on the prize . . ." No one leaped to the fool's defense and I couldn't blame them. I chewed the skin on the inside of my mouth. "This is all so much bigger than me."

Trowbridge walked to where I sat. He stood over me, looking down. Expression inscrutable, except for the tiny sparks of blue glinting in his eyes. His scent was spiked and sharp with musk. It did not try to weave itself around me.

"I'm scared," I told him.

Wordlessly he sank down into one of his graceful crouches, his weight balanced on his heels. Three inches closer and his knee would have grazed my elbow. He plucked at some creeping weed, then tossed it aside. Then he swept the sandy loam with the side of his hand to make a canvas. With his finger, he drew an elongated oval. "This is Dhesperal Lake."

He drew me a map.

"Not a puddle or a pond," he said, "but a lake." The lines bracketing Trowbridge's mouth seemed carved. Inside his "lake" he drafted another irregular shape. "This is Wryal's Island." He brooded over his diagram. "With me so far?" he asked without lifting his head.

"One lake, one island."

He made a large four-sided box that took up most of the available space on the island he'd sketched. "This is the castle." Then, so close to the castle it might as well be appended, he fashioned a far smaller square. "And these are the Spectacle grounds."

I tried to make sense of the scale. The lake seemed oversized in comparison to Wryal's. "Where's the bridge?"

The tip of his finger added an L-shaped line from the castle to the shore. "There."

Seriously, Karma? The crooked bridge was on the south end of the island. As far away as the place where they're holding Trowbridge's pack as possible.

Trowbridge had sat back on his heels. "The Spectacle's a quarter acre surrounded by wooden walls that are too slick to climb and too thick to batter down. I've seen some crap in Merenwyn, but those holding pens . . ." He shook his head. "I've seen junkyard dogs kept in better conditions." Gaze downcast, he said quietly, "The worst goes down in front of the viewing stands. The Fae watch shit happen and hoot like they're at some fucking football game."

Lexi stared at my mate through slit eyes.

I remembered the grandstands. Though I'd never physically been on Wryal's Island, I'd visited the Spectacle grounds via my niece's dreams. Through her eyes, I'd seen the Fae in the stands. Not a rabble, but an elegant and cruelly detached assemblage of those who believed themselves rightfully privileged. They wore cloaks and sat in high-backed chairs.

"There was a cage too," I said. "They put you in it with Anu and she was afraid of you."

My mate's head jerked in surprise and I realized that he'd forgotten that I'd seen the Spectacle grounds through some dream-walking. Trowbridge studied me for a beat; then he said, "Yeah," and his gaze returned to study the lines he'd drawn in Merenwyn's earth. "I knew I was pretty much fucked when I woke up inside it."

"You didn't look frightened."

"I was," he said simply.

He rose and jammed his hands inside his back pockets, and those damn cutoff jeans slid low as he walked away from me. But this time I didn't fixate on the patch of skin on his lower back. Instead I noticed those jutting hip bones and the hard, masculine planes of his muscles.

A warrior's body honed to the bone.

His back pockets stretched as he made fists. "They have archers up on the castle's towers whose only job is to keep their eye on the Spectacle grounds, and more men patrolling the pens. The Fae are armed; you're not. Unless you can think up a miracle, you're shit out of luck."

"So you're going to sacrifice yourself to be the Raha'ells' miracle?"

Say no.

His back muscles tensed; then he slowly swung around to look at me. "It's going to take a miracle and more just to get into the castle." Blue sparks in his eyes. "But if we get that lucky, *after* I'm sure you're on your way back to the Safe Passage I'm going to stay to do what I can to free them."

"You'll die."

"I'll try real hard not to get killed."

I rubbed my temples.

Was this how it was going to go between us? I'd connive behind his back and then say, "Oopsy," and then he'd do the same to me? Back and forth? An endless game of tennis without rules or even a winning number of points?

"We have to stop doing this," I told him, and I was surprised at the sound of my own voice, because it was quiet and firm.

He tilted his head. "This?"

"This modus operandi we have of jumping first and then saying 'sorry.' This thing we do of only telling half-truths. It isn't working anymore."

"It isn't working?" he repeated, his voice too soft, too low. "You've been playing that call since we met. You jump, I follow. What's your frickin' problem?"

"You should have told me what you were planning to do. Our destinies are entwined, Trowbridge. You know that."

"I *would* have told you."

"When?"

"When the time was right," he said tightly.

"You mean when it was too late for me to stop you."

"You really want to get into this? Now?" He jerked his chin toward Lexi. "I'm not doing this in front of him, so if you want to *explore* this topic," he said, playing a biting emphasis on the verb, "I suggest you take your sweet ass to the cave."

"Fine." I stood up, weaved for a second because I momentarily saw spots, then stomped into the cave. Okay, it was more of a stagger-stomp, which, I devoutly hoped, hurt Lexi. Once inside, I didn't explore Lexi's cave. I went in as far as I needed to go to get a fraction of privacy and still be able to see the trees. But still, that put me a stone's throw away from Lexi's old campfire.

Trowbridge followed.

"What the hell do you want from me?" he said harshly.

It was a small, contained space. "Hell" echoed.

I snapped back. "I want us to be honest with each other. I want to know when you're planning to risk your life."

"Like you warn me when you risk yours?" he growled.

He'd never been that angry with me before. I took a step backward, and my good heel crushed one of the charred remnants of Lexi's fire.

And *whoosh*. Trowbridge's thin control splintered. "You want honesty?" he shouted. "It tore my guts out to stay on the ridge, and watch my people be mown down by the fucking Fae, and not do anything for them! I was their Alpha! I should have been there with them. Down at that shallow crossing fighting with them! But I put you and your fucking epic quest in front of my pack! I put you in front of everything! God dammit, I came back to Creemore for you!"

I took a step out of the fire. "You couldn't have done anything to help the Raha'ells; they—"

"Also because of you!" he shouted over me.

My turn to draw in a sharp breath through my teeth.

Trowbridge spun around, presenting me his back. He pressed his hands against his temples and rocked as if his head were about to split open. "Jesus, Jesus, Jesus," he repeated.

I breathed into the back of my hand. How did this fall apart so fast? "As I recall it, I didn't stop you from going down that hill to their defense. You stopped me."

With a sigh, he dropped his arms and turned around to face me. "You'd have died before you made it halfway down the ridge. I thought of telling you to stay, but you never stay. I thought of going to fight without you, but how could I? You don't know how to survive here."

"I have magic. You keep discounting how useful it can be."

"Can it stop arrows?"

No, it couldn't.

Wearily, he leaned against the wall. "You got us involved in what you keep calling an 'epic quest.' FYI, I don't want to ever hear that phrase again." He frowned at Lexi's fire. "It's not epic; it's just fucking impossible. We haven't got a snowball's chance in hell of coming out of this. And if that's what it is—if that's what's going to go down—then we've got to destroy that book before it happens." He raised his head, stared at me, little flits of blue light sparking in the dim light. "If I can't save the Raha'ells, I'll damn well save my pack in Creemore. I can't die knowing I let both of them down."

"But you want to do both."

"Of course I do."

"You always going to be such a tough guy?"

"Tough guy?" He dug his fists into his pockets. "You're killing me, Hedi. You keep walking into danger. Some bitch opens a portal and throws fire at you and you jump right through it after her. You didn't take a gun. You didn't take water, food, or shoes. You just . . . jumped."

"St. Silas's man had a gun on me." I looked down at my feet and then away. Ash coated one of Varens's moccasins; blood stained the other. "You should have told me about the prophecy. You should have told me that you always meant to fulfill it."

"I can't abandon my Raha'ells here without trying," he said. "I won't be that guy. It's not who I am anymore.

I fought to claim them as mine. I'm their Alpha. You don't toss that back."

I used my thumbnail to push back the cuticle on its twin. "You loved Varens."

He nodded.

"And you love the Raha'ells."

"Yes."

"And you love me."

"*Yes,*" he said with quiet emphasis, "I love you."

I knew that.

"Being an Alpha is what I'm meant to do," he said. "It fits. But you fit me too. You and me . . . it's more than just sex and mating pheromones. You remember me the way I was before everything went to crap. You see the screwup I was and the man I've become. You don't expect an Alpha, or the Son of Lukynae. You don't even want them. You see me. And I see you."

His gaze roved over me.

"Yeah, you fit me. The way your skin slides under my palm, the way you make me laugh. Even when you piss me off or scare me so bad I want to punch the wall." Tiny flickers of blue light spun in his eyes. "I had a taste of you before I came here. And I wanted it back. Every night I'd go to sleep thinking how I could get back home. And every morning I'd wake up in my camp knowing I had to find a place for my Raha'ells so they won't be hunted like fucking animals anymore."

I folded my arms around my waist, hugging myself.

"Believe me," he said. "I was never planning on bringing you here. I knew it would be dangerous, and I knew you weren't ready for it. I was going to buy a few kilos of iron shavings, pack them in a backpack, and use the fairy portal in Creemore on my own. I thought I'd be back before you knew it. But then the witches screwed up that plan and you had to jump through the Safe Passage, while I was handcuffed to a fucking fence. I saw you going, knew what was waiting for you . . . Nothing could have stopped me. I would have brought the entire fence through the passage if I needed to."

Wonderful words, but his back was still braced against the wall, his shoulders stiff, his fists hidden inside his pockets.

He rocked a bit. "I can't go back to being just Robbie Trowbridge. And I can't pretend I don't know what I'm leaving behind me if I don't try to make this better. You talk a lot about Karma and fate, and all that Fae stuff. Maybe this is my destiny."

A wave of weariness did the obligatory wash.

Well, well, well.

There's that stinking word: "destiny." Seriously, seven months ago, standing by the apartment window, I would never have believed that my future would lead to anything other than a long stumble from one poor-paying job to another. But in those days, I didn't like looking into the crystal ball. From what I could see, my life was going to be nothing but a wasteland of loneliness and wanting.

I couldn't say that anymore.

Now I had the ingredients for everything I'd ever wanted. A mate. A brother. Friends. A place to belong in a pack— something I was never aware of how much I'd secretly yearned for.

But of course, having it, even briefly, came with a terrible price tag.

Because Trowbridge was who he was and I was who I was. He meant it when he said that he couldn't live with himself if he turned his back on his pack. A year ago, I might have been incapable of understanding such a sense of duty, but my slacker conscience had been a bur under my butt ever since that day My One True Thing walked into my Starbucks.

I don't know how he did it—how he could be the cata-
lyst for so much change in me. But he was. Loving him
made me love more. And now I was thigh deep in a freakin'
epidemic of love: I loved him, I loved Lexi, I loved Merry
and Cordelia, and given time, I'd probably be awash in
gooey sentiment over Anu.

But damn if all that loving didn't come with side dishes
I don't recall ordering, the most onerous being an inescap-
able feeling of responsibility. That sense of duty was getting out of hand, growing faster than Boston ivy over
crumbling brick mortar. I felt culpable for Lexi's fate, I felt
an uncomfortable obligation about Mouse's future, and—
damn, damn, damn—I now freakin' well felt answerable
for an entire race of people.

Wow, someone hit the reset button.

I am so not the hero type.

And yet I couldn't pretend the life of a wolf in Merenwyn wasn't as bad as all that. I knew the truth. I'd seen
the hunt. I'd spent a night in a trap. For crap's sake, I wore
Varens's slippers. Could I walk away from the Raha'ells
and still be me? Could I force Trowbridge, using my questionable skills with feminine tears and whimpers, to give
up on them too?

No. I couldn't. I wouldn't want to live a life with a man
who turned his back.

Crap.

All or nothing. A long life of nothing much special or
a short life filled with—*oh, someone just shoot me*—higher
purpose.

Crap.

Life without loving people isn't much of a life, is it?

I performed a brief mental burial of me-first Hedi and
walked over to my man. He watched me warily as I placed
my feet between his.

"I can't, Tink," he said. "I just can't."

"Shut up," I said, scraping some mud flakes from his throat. I pressed my lips against the beat of his artery. His blood was warm; his pulse, strong.

My blood runs in his blood. My life ends with his.

I turned my head to rest my cheek on his chest. "I'm no hero, Trowbridge. I don't like being hungry, I don't like being hunted, and I really don't like feeling threatened all the time. It scares me to think what might be ahead of us. But it is twisted, what they do to the Raha'ells in this realm. I thought I could walk away from it—I really wanted to—but I can't. I can't un-see what I've seen. I guess I'm not that girl anymore either."

"Tink," he whispered.

I pulled back; then I cupped his face with my hands. "Listen up, Balto." I tilted his jaw downward until his lips were out of easy kissing range and I was staring at him eyeball to eyeball. "You should know that if we make it through whatever hellfire is facing us, I intend to be a fully participating Alpha's mate. I stand beside you." He started to smile; I could feel his skin crease under my palms. "I'm not going to take every word you say as a done deal; I'm going to want to discuss."

His arms slid around me. He pulled me until we fit together, my hips cradled by his, my chest crushed against his. "You mean situation normal."

"Don't be a smart-ass. So let's discuss—and come up with a plan for breaking your pack out of jail in addition to doing everything else on our list. And let's make it a good one, because I want at least a three percent chance of walking out of the castle relatively intact. My last breath is absolutely *not* going to be taken in a place called the Spectacle."

A comet spun in his blue eyes. "Sweetheart, even if we survive—"

"Don't like the word 'if.' "

"There's no guarantee you'll ever see Creemore again, Tink."

I called up a wavering smile. "Guess your mother's wallpaper got a reprieve." I brushed the corners of the Son of Lukynae's firm mouth with my fingertips, then shook my head. "What a surprise package you turned out to be. I thought I was hooking myself up to rebel without a cause and what do I get? Maximus and Robin of Locksley, all rolled into one."

Robbie Trowbridge lifted his brows. "You're talking movies again, right?"

"*Gladiator* and *Robin Hood*."

"Saw *Gladiator*. Crap ending." He leaned to kiss me again, then he stopped and lifted his long nose. He sniffed, and sniffed again. "What the—"

I'm not sure what level of profanity my mate was going to tag onto that question and I never got to find out, because a dark form chose that moment to sprint past us for the relative safety of the outside of the cave.

Not fast enough.

My mate was thoroughly capable of disengaging from me and grabbing Mouse's collar before the kid managed to scuttle out of striking range. Trowbridge hauled the kid and gave him a ruthless shake.

"Hasn't anyone told you what a dumbass move it is to spy on an Alpha?" shouted Trowbridge.

Chapter Seventeen

"I wasn't spying!" squeaked Mouse.

Trowbridge had hauled him out of the cave. Mouse stood with his clawed hands bunched at his waist, his shoulders hunched under our glares.

My tone was flint. "What I want to know is how he got past us. He was by Seabiscuit not ten minutes ago."

"It's what I do." The kid's fingers spasmed. "I slip in and out. Quiet as a mouse."

"Open your hands very slowly," Trowbridge told him, "and show us what you have."

With a wince, Mouse obeyed, opening his cupped fists and tipping the contents of his palms. Gray ash plumed as the small charcoal remnant of Lexi's evening fire bounced along the stone floor.

"What were you planning to do with that?" Trowbridge asked too softly.

"Hedi of Creemore never got to eat her crumbs." Mouse blew at the blister forming on his palm. "I thought I could make a fire. Then if I could find some game . . . a squirrel or other creature. Her belly's been grumbling all morning. She needs feeding."

Trowbridge cocked his head. "Do you know how to use a bow?"

The teen's cheeks reddened. "No."

Mouse's tattered dignity clawed at me. "I haven't eaten for over thirty hours," I said. "Does that qualify as being a long time between meals in Merenwyn?"

"Yes," said my Trowbridge. "That's a long time between meals."

Thank heavens, because it was twenty-six hours longer than my previous starvation record. "I could eat a squirrel," I said. "If it was skinned and cooked over a fire." Another bad thought occurred to me. "I don't have to skin my own squirrel yet, do I?"

"No," said my mate softly.

Had it come to this so quickly? I was actually looking forward to tearing into a meal of charred rodent on a stick? I scowled at the streak of ash marring Varens's moccasin. "How long will it take to get to the castle from here?"

Lexi spoke up. "It's two hours south."

Is that all? A quarter had been flipped, but it had not fallen and now it spun, caught in a loop of an endless rotation. I needed that sucker to land. To read the verdict, be it heads or tails.

I could wait to eat.

I turned to Mouse. "You said that the Gatekeeper took you through a tunnel that brought you out of the castle."

Trowbridge stiffened with interest.

"Aye," said Mouse. "And you want me to tell you where to find it."

"Yup."

"Make me one of you. I heard every word you spoke in the cave. And I know that the Son of Lukynae and the Brave Hedi of Creemore have come to lead the Raha'ells to a better world or die trying to do so. I want to fight with you."

You see? This is precisely how myths are made. A wisp of truth is taken, gilded with gold leaf, threaded through a silver needle, and sewn into a cloth fabricated by half-truths and complete fantasy. Mouse had listened, and processed incorrectly. And now—poof—I'd gone from a girl caught in a trap to "the Brave Hedi of Creemore," the most unlikely addendum to a prophecy you'd ever meet.

His gaze burned mine. "Make me a Raha'ell."

Right. Like I had the power to do that.

Mouse continued his pitch. "Don't trust my mistress to show you the right way into the castle. She'd rather die at the hands of the Son of Lukynae than face what the Royal Court will do to her for her treachery. But I know where it is—she showed me. I'll take you right to it. And once inside the castle, I can get you food," he bargained. "Meat for the Alpha and all the sweetlings you could wish for, Hedi of Creemore. Clothing too. Whatever else you need. Let me be there to see the walls come down. And after that the Fae can kiss my backside. I'll be one of you."

One of you.

My gaze went to Trowbridge's. His expression was hard to read, but his eyes asked me silently, *Can we trust him?*

Mouse waited for my verdict. Thumbs up. Thumb down.

Would it be kinder to leave him? To let him carry on until he drank the last drop of his stash of sun potion? For if we brought Mouse into our epic quest, his blood would be almost certainly staining my hands.

These were the sort of decisions an Alpha makes.

You asked for equal partnership.

You got it.

My nod to Trowbridge was slight and far more reluctant than sage. The Son of Lukynae considered the teenager, then said, "I only take men who are willing to fight."

"I am willing to fight."

"And willing to die."

Mouse didn't so much as blink. "That too."

"Say it."

"I'm willing to die."

My stomach twisted again.

"You'll have to find your rank among them," said Trowbridge. "You'll be at the bottom until you prove yourself deserving to be higher. Now, do you want to be known as Mouse or by another name?"

"Can I think on it?"

"For a bit. Tell me about the Gatekeeper's tunnel."

The tension in Mouse's body visibly drained. "You get to it through the room of riches. There's a—"

"Traitor!" shouted the Gatekeeper.

Mouse gleefully shouted back, "You're longer my mistress! I'm one of them now! I'll tell them what I want!" And so, with flushed cheeks and the promise of a pack behind him, he did. "There's a secret tunnel under the lake! I know where to find the entrance and how to open it!"

There's a tunnel under the lake: I really, really wanted to do a fist pump and scream, "Bingo!"

Trowbridge did not seem to share my joy. "What side of the lake?"

It took me a second to understand the importance of the answer to that question. According to Trowbridge, all the lands to the south of the castle were cultivated and teeming with Fae farms and towns.

Please don't say "in the village square."

The teen walked over to the tiny map etched in the dirt and studied it, head tilted. Then he bent forward to drill his finger into the loamy sand. "There," he said, straightening.

"Am I looking at that right?" I whispered to Trowbridge.

"When you come out of the tunnel," Trowbridge asked Mouse, "you're on the mainland, looking at the back of the Spectacle?"

"Aye," answered Mouse. "You can see it plain as day. It's straight across the water."

Karma freakin' loves me.

My brother, the perpetual killjoy, spoke up. "Do you have any idea how many armed men there are within the castle? Or how much magic any member of the royal house has? Have you considered that Trowbridge's face is known? Or that he's the most wanted man in the realm?"

"Your face is twice as recognizable as mine," said Trowbridge.

Lexi's eyes flickered. "If your mate comes with us to Wryal's, we'll never get close enough to the book to destroy it. That's what brought you here, isn't it, twin? Or have you forgotten that?"

"I haven't forgotten," I replied. "Putting a match to it comes first."

"So let me see if I understand the sequence of events. After you've slipped into the castle, unobserved, and gained access to the Black Mage's rooms, unobserved, and destroyed the book . . . you and Trowbridge plan to stroll through the castle to the Spectacle, where you intend to free his wolves?"

Put like that, it did sound insane. And he hadn't even mentioned the part about going to Threall to save his soul.

I gave him an abrupt nod.

My twin sucked in his cheek. With barely held patience, he said, "I won't help you commit suicide. The Raha'ells are more animal than human. Do you think they'll welcome you? They will kill you based solely on the fact that you're my sister."

Trowbridge's scent spiked. "They will revere her as my mate."

Mouse cleared his voice. "I don't want to anger the Son of Lukynae for speaking out of turn, but I know how we can distract the court so your consort won't be needing her brother's help."

"I can set fire to the Great Hall," Mouse said gleefully. "It would be a rare pleasure to set the place alight."

Trowbridge cocked his head. Lexi narrowed his eyes.

And I said, "What's the Great Hall?"

"The most important room in the castle," Lexi said with a flicker of real interest. "It's where the court gathers to feast, it's where they toast, and it's where your social status is known. Fortunes have been lost and won depending on the seat assigned to you at the long table."

"Go on, Mouse," said Trowbridge.

"When you and Hedi of Creemore are finished in the Black Mage's tower, you give me a nod across the way. I'll be watching for it. Then I'll set my torch to the hall. The place is full of wood and fine table linens; it will burn easy. The gold will melt off the ceilings, and the magical tapestries . . ." His brow crinkled. "I don't know exactly what will happen to them, but it can't be good."

Lexi cut in, "How will you get in?"

"The same way any servant enters any fine room in the castle. Quietly, so as not to be a distraction. Carrying what needs to be carried." Mouse's grin was wide, and his teeth shone. "A noble can't be walking into the hall before it's time for the evening's feast without someone remarking on it. But someone like me could enter, hours before I was needed, and it wouldn't be noticed."

"Except by your quartermaster," I pointed out. "You stole sun potion. I heard you tell the Gatekeeper that you couldn't return to the castle."

"He has no business there. And as long as I stay true to my name, he won't find me. At least not for the hour or two it will take to destroy the castle, the grounds, and, I expect, the whole court too." Mouse's gaze flitted from me to Trowbridge, then very briefly to Lexi, and back to me. "You're worried that someone will come upon me while I set the fire. Don't. The Spectacle is not until tomorrow night. Today's a quiet day for those royal born—they'll be up all night tomorrow. All of us below stairs will be expected to work our knuckles to the bone. The kitchens will be busy for two days straight. No one expects a meal in the Great Hall tonight."

"That's true," murmured my twin.

Mouse showed his teeth to the Gatekeeper. "Once the fire's lit, they'll send every servant, every man or woman wearing a uniform, and every person with the magic to quell the fire to the hall. As for the rest, they'll stand and gawk, and while they do you and your lady can be opening the gates to the pens."

"Where's the room of riches in relation to the Great Hall?" Trowbridge asked.

"It's on the opposite side of the courtyard," Mouse replied. "Their backs will be to you."

Lexi said to Trowbridge, "There's still the postern gates—the sentries won't leave their posts. Not even for a fire in the Great Hall."

"What are postern gates?" I asked.

Trowbridge said, "An exit at the back of the castle. That's how you get to the Spectacle grounds. Through the alley between the castle and the palisade."

"More guards," Lexi objected.

Trowbridge lifted his chin in irritation. "We're outnumbered, but we have surprise, and everything we need to do is in a straight line. The Gatekeeper's secret passage is on the east wall. The mage's tower in on the southeast corner, and the postern gate on the south wall."

Through which were the Spectacle grounds.

I stared at the rough sketch he'd drawn of Wryal's, quelling an inexplicable bout of nausea.

Lexi offered one final objection. "Once we leave the protection of the ward, Trowbridge's presence is vulnerable to detection by a jinx. It hunts wolves. Your mud is not going to last long as a shield. You're already sweating it off, Son of Lukynae. I can smell the stench of your wolf."

"You know what I find interesting?" Trowbridge turned to me, his eyes slits. "For a guy who's been in deep rehab, your brother knows a shitload about jinxes. I spent nine winters sitting around a campfire listening to wolves trade more war stories than I can remember. And no one ever mentioned clouds that hunted wolves. Or used the word 'jinx.'"

Lexi smiled. "My mage and I saw one as we traveled here. He recognized it as the embodiment of a spell he conceived but never put to use."

"Why didn't he put it to use?"

My twin replied, "I do not know."

"The old goat's almost as helpful a bastard as you, isn't he?" Trowbridge mused, rubbing his neck. "We've got to get through a shitload of things over the next couple hours, and it starts with someone collapsing this ward. So, can you do it or do I need to go knock-knock on your skull to call the guy who can?"

When it came time to bring down the ward, Lexi limped to the place where Trowbridge had drawn his map. My twin used the heel of his boot to scuff away the etchings, claiming he needed to do his conjuring on a patch of bare earth. I'm not sure if that was true or not. If communing with the soil were an integral part of the process, wouldn't he have taken off his boots?

How much did he need to lie now? I wondered about that as I watched him raise his hands shoulder high, then spread them as if he were prepping to tell the story about the one who got away.

My brother's a striking man. Even when he's pale, sweating, and dirty. Even when his "bad" side is presented to me—the right side—with the dark shadow of a paw print definitely visible beneath the three-week stubble of his hair. Yes, he's handsome and likely always will be. That being said, every jewel has the right setting, and Lexi found his when he began to conjure.

Gilded by the mid-day sun, his hair glowed brighter, and his green eyes—so pale, so translucent—seemed to intensify in color, borrowing from the nature surrounding him. He tipped his jaw slightly toward the sky, and I watched the arrogance that he habitually wore as defense fade and be replaced by the type of confidence borne by a man who knew himself to be great.

I moved closer to Trowbridge, my heart hurting, and his heavy arm carved around me to tuck me tightly to his body.

Lexi rolled his wrists, so that his palms were turned upward and his fingers were loosely curled. Then my brother let loose a long, lyrical stream of words that were neither Merenwynian nor English.

Pressure spiked in my ears.

I flinched against it, and Trowbridge drew me closer until my cheek rested against his warm chest, then cupped my ear with his palm. The trees outside the parameters of the ward blurred and magic unseen moved to my brother's call.

There was no pop, no explosion of glitter bits.

I knew the ward was gone, because as swiftly as blowing out a candle the throbbing pressure in my ears died and the scents of magic, and pony, and sun potion and blood dissipated, caught on Merenwyn's ever-present soft breeze.

But mostly I knew it was done because my brother's

loosely clawed hands turned into tight fists and an expression of glorious bliss lit my brother's beautiful face and I saw what he could have been, and what he wanted to be, and what he could never be.

Chapter Eighteen

We found the creek before a jinx found us, which was a minor miracle, since much of the crusted mud that had turned Trowbridge's back into a crocodile hide had long flaked away and what was left had turned to a slick film of taupe.

Murphy's Law: the day had turned stinking hot and muggy. My One True Love's scent disguise kept sliding off him.

Trowbridge took a step off the bank into the lower edge of the stream where the ground was covered with a layer of last year's leaves. He kicked aside a heavy mat of rotting mulch, then sank to one knee to dig into the foul-smelling mud. With an expression of acute distaste, he slapped a handful of goo on his chest.

I grimaced in sympathy. Then, biting down on a wince, I cupped my hands and leaned forward to slurp up a mouthful of creek water. It was sweet and cold and left an aftertaste of freshness. I splashed some on my face, then tipped my head back, letting the icy water sheet down my throat and cheeks.

"So. Much. Better," I informed Merry.

My amulet-friend, intent on feeding on tender shoots of elder, commented with a tiny blip of primrose light. Merenwyn's sun was still strong and its powerful rays shone right through the heart of her, turning an amber belly into a gleaming golden one.

Ralph was in the shade, quietly supping on a nearby branch.

Seabiscuit let out a soft whicker.

"Keep the pony quiet," Lexi told Mouse. After taking his fill, he'd pulled off his boots and now cooled his ankle in the icy current, a few yards downstream of Seabiscuit and the teen. My sibling's gait had de-evolved over the last few miles from a smooth glide to a hitched limp. He hadn't complained, but then again, he hadn't spoken much since we left Daniel's Rock.

"'Tain't my fault if she's talkative," muttered Mouse, stroking Seabiscuit's neck.

I stood, gritting my teeth. My butt was on fire and my thighs one spasm away from a full-blown muscle cramp. I'd covered the ground astride my trusty Seabiscuit. Certain private parts of me that were *supposed* to stay tender and plump felt puffy and bruised from the saddle burn.

Still, I'd take those muscle aches over walking. The over-hill, over-dale potion of our journey had flattened the Gatekeeper's mouth into a seam of fatigue. She sat on a rock, a squat toad, impatiently waiting for me to release her from her restraints so that she could drink from the stream. Lexi had volunteered his belt, which I'd used to secure her hands behind her. "I'm thirsty," she complained again as I sloshed past her.

"Then drink."

"Do you expect me to lap water like a dog?"

"Up to you."

I couldn't stand her.

Her and her fuzzy topknot.

Trowbridge twisted around as I approached. He'd already applied the scent screen to his chest. The soft thatch of hair between his nipples was matted with mud.

I bent to scoop up a gritty handful. "I'll get your back."

He rotated to face the woods, his arms falling to his sides. Though the river sludge smelled rank, it was relatively easy to spread. I smoothed a thin layer over his bulky shoulders, noting the tension stored in his muscles that he'd striven to hide from us.

Unlike the forests we'd gone through yesterday, this terrain had seen fire and was covered with regrowth. Instead of a forest of fat trunks, layers of green obliterated the sight line, a fact that clearly troubled my mate.

"What is it?" I asked, following the deep groove of his spine. "Your instincts talking again?"

"Pinging like sonar." My mate checked the sky, then eyed the ridgeline to the south. "I know a place where I can see the lay of the land better. It's not far from here," he said thoughtfully. "It wouldn't take me more than twenty minutes to make a quick recon of the area."

Silently, I ran a line of sludge along the edge of his waistband.

Trowbridge tensed his belly muscles until his navel stretched into a taut smile. Victim to gravity and the lack of love handles, his cutoffs slid so low they were admirably indecent. "It won't take long. And I won't leave you if you're—"

"I'm not scared."

And I wasn't . . . much. I just didn't like being parted from him again. On the other hand, I respected his instincts. If they were saying, *Danger, Will Robinson,* then we should be on alert. And taking the whole crew for a look-see— the slow-moving Gatekeeper, the noisy pony—would defeat the purpose of Trowbridge's scouting mission.

I gave him an ass-pat. "Done. Turn around; I'll do your face." He pivoted and bent his neck so that I could reach his face. He'd rinsed off the old layer after drinking. His skin was still slick. He looked like a cover model who'd been artfully disarranged. *Beautiful, beautiful man.* I started at the bridge of his long nose. "What if you walked into something?"

A posse of Faes. A group of hunters. A pack of wild boars.

"Same deal as before, Tink," he said, trying not to move his lips as I took swipes at the grooves bracketing his mouth. "The Fae might rough me up, but they won't kill me. They'll take me to the castle."

My fingers paused.

He touched my chin gently with his knuckle. "If I do get captured," he said softly, "I'll be expecting you to come rescue me."

My gaze jerked to meet his fierce blue eyes. "What? Again?"

A lopsided smile from the man wearing the mud mask. "As often as it takes." He reached to draw me to him, then stalled, grimacing at his mired palms. He took a rueful step backward. "Tink, I swear I'll be back within a half hour."

A foot separated us and I already missed him. "I have no watch."

"See that tree?" he asked, pointing to the tallest fir to the west. "If I'm not back before the sun sinks behind it, you come find me."

I closed the gap, winding my arms around his slick neck. "Deal."

He pulled my hips to his and grinned down at me. "I'm going to kiss you now."

I smiled as his mud paws came up to cup my jaw. "Just out of curiosity, are all your kisses going to come with advance notices?"

He lowered his head until my lips could feel the warm flow of his breath. "It builds up anticipation."

"Trowbridge," I whispered, "you had me with the cut-off jeans."

"Geezus," he murmured against my mouth, "you're easy."

"Keep that in mind."

He didn't slide his fingers through my hair, and I didn't plaster myself to his body. There was an audience: I could feel Lexi's penetrating gaze piercing my back. There was slime: the aesthetics of mud wrestling will forever be a mystery to me. And there was a sense of déjà vu.

How many good-bye forever kisses can you do in the space of two days?

Our lips touched and melded. I tasted him (salty and somewhat muddy) and he supped from me (salty and less muddy) and the passion that was always there, ready to flare between us, was nothing but a gentle promise.

Later.

Please, Goddess. Let us have some laters.

His gaze swept over my features, lingering on my mouth, then moved beyond me to my brother. I would have bet my last dollar that silent communication between my mate and bro was never going to happen (with the possible exception of *fuck you* and *fuck you back*), but as their gazes locked I re-formed my opinion.

Trowbridge lifted his chin in a question.

"What?" I said, my eyes moving from mate to twin.

Lexi answered with a slow, silent nod.

My guy squeezed my shoulders. "Be back soon."

"Do that." I smothered a smile watching him leave. The seat of his cutoffs sported a perfect handprint.

Mine.

A watched pot never boils. Unless of course, you're on the phone with the cable company and then the sucker suddenly foams over between one automated command prompt and the next, creating crud on your stove's elements.

Similarly, the sun seemed frozen in the sky. The lower edge was almost, but not quite, touching the tall spire of the fir in the west. It felt like it had been there, poised to sink, forever.

Hurry up, Trowbridge.

I paced by the Gatekeeper, pointedly ignoring her fulminating glare.

"Mutt," Lexi snapped at Mouse, "if you're so worried about your satchel, why don't you unhook it from the saddle and take it elsewhere?"

Shrugging off his braces, Lexi waded out of the stream.

Mouse moved protectively in front of Seabiscuit. Something, I realized now, that my mutt-pal had been doing ever since we left the rock—keeping himself between Lexi and the sun potion. "There's two bottles and an empty," Mouse replied, his chin lifted, his tone steady. "And I'll smash them all before I let you have them."

"Why?" Lexi took a seat on a nearby log.

Mouse's gaze flicked to me, then to the tall fir.

Lexi sighed and shucked off his gray shirt. "Out of curiosity, how would you plan to stop me?" He balled up his shirt and bent over his feet to dry them. "With your magic? Or perhaps your brawn?" He lifted his head to study Mouse. "Now you're silent. Except for your body language, and that's talking louder than your mouth. You're as proud as a Fae coming from a whore's room. You stole three bottles of the juice from the store master's locked room. Quite the thief," he drawled.

"Except I can't steal magic, now can I? Not like some who have no talent of their own."

Lexi's smile was chilling. "Never forget that you've already served your purpose. Or that you have no gifts to offer us other than what we already have with the Gate-keeper."

"Mouse, take Seabiscuit into the shade." I waited until my would-be defender did—reluctance stamped on his thin shoulders—then went to the stream to rinse my hands. The water clouded, the silt swirling around my digits.

"Nice," I murmured. "Was that necessary?"

Lexi shook out his shirt with a snap. "The boy shows his hand too easily. In the Fae's world, those with power rule; those without serve. A servant has to be smarter than his master. He needs to weigh the risks of his choices before he acts. I'm surprised he hasn't already been checked and checked hard. You shouldn't encourage him."

"It's a moot point, isn't it? Mouse isn't going back to the Fae."

"Do you think Trowbridge and his Raha'ells will put up with his insolence any more than them?" Lexi pulled the garment over his head with a grunt. "The mutt acts before he thinks," he said as the top of his head emerged, "and he leads with his mouth."

Actually, at present, Mouse led with passive aggression. He'd unhooked his satchel from Seabiscuit's saddle and presently had his arm sunk elbow deep in its burlap depths. He rummaged noisily, glass clinking, then pulled out the spent vial of sun potion. Using his teeth, he pulled out the cork and then spat it out. All innocence, he lifted his gaze. "Thought I'd get rid of the empty. That is, if it *is* empty." He upended the bottle.

It was. Not a drop fell from its mouth. Mouse pitched the spent vial into the bushes.

I shook my head. "You got to admit, he'd make a great Stronghold."

"He won't survive long enough to carry the name." Lexi grimly felt for his braces. "Mark my words: he'll be the first one to fall."

I noted the beads of sweat dotting my brother's forehead. "Do you still want to drink the juice?"

"I have magic now." He stretched for his boot. "Sun potion is unnecessary."

It didn't escape me that he'd sidestepped the question. "All that power's temporary," I said quietly. "You're not a mage, Lexi."

"But I could be one."

"You're *not* one of them."

"Not a Fae? I can't fault you there." He sat down on the log, boot in hand. "I'm definitely not a full-blooded Fae. But I could and *should* be a powerful wizard. We were born to it, Hell. It was a destiny that was denied us."

"To use your word: bullshit."

"Our citadel grew from the seed of a black walnut," he said, obstinately returning to the thorny subject of would-be wizards.

"You've seen our tree in Threall," I said slowly.

"No, I haven't. But my mage explained the significance of our citadel's species. Only those with the power to wield great magic are born from such seed."

My spine stiffened every time Lexi used the possessive and spliced it to the word "mage." "I hate to break it to you, Lexi, but you are not Harry Potter."

Lexi jerked on his boot. "Who is Harry Potter?"

"He's a—never mind." My tone turned flat and hard. "What else did the Old Mage tell you about Threall? Did he mention that his cyreath squats on top of yours? That his soul-ball is doing its best to smother yours?"

A muscle worked in his jaw.

"You have a beautiful cyreath. The light that shines from it is complex and jewel toned. Rich reds, beautiful blues."

And bruised purples.

"I'll take your word for it."

I studied his face. "Is your leg still throbbing?"

He reached for his other boot. "No."

If he was still dealing with my pain, it was going to hurt like blazes pulling that tight-fitting leather over his ankle. That is, unless my wound had healed leaps and bounds since my last sip of the juice. I looked down at my bandaged leg. Some of the swelling had gone down; the wrappings were definitely looser. Was it better? I started to pick at the knot on the bandage.

"Must you?" he said tensely.

"It still hurts?"

"Not a bit," he said with his lying face.

And there you go—he'd pushed me away again, so I pushed back when perhaps I should have waited for more privacy. "You know, I remember what it's like to have the old man inside you. I've felt the panic of not being able to control my own body. You don't have to put up a front for me. Not for the pain in your leg, or how you're feeling."

"I'm a man now." He carefully eased his foot into the leg of his boot. "Not the boy who used to share his every thought with his sister." He raised his brows. "Do I look panicked?"

"No. But sometimes you seem distracted. Like you're having a one-sided conversation. Is that what's happening? Is the Old Mage a worm wriggling in your head?"

"A maggot in my brain? That's a picture I could do without." Gritting his teeth, he jammed his heel into the boot. It was a moment before he could add, "You'll be relieved to know that I am worm-free."

Miserably I said, "When he steps forward, I can't see you anymore." My twin lifted his gaze to mine, his brows squeezed together in confusion. "I'm looking at your face, and listening to your voice, but I can't find you. You seem to disappear underneath him. Are you really there? Listening but mute?"

"Sometimes."

Oh, Lexi. "And the rest of the time?"

My twin's gaze slid away.

"Where do you go?" I whispered.

He stood up, favoring his right leg. "I'm not sure. I don't seem to have a body. I'm floating, surrounded by a wall of blue fog that I can't see past." At my gasp, he sent me a flicker of a smile meant to be reassuring. "It's not frightening."

I knew those mysts. "He's sending you back to your soul-ball in Threall."

He let out an amused huff. "That accounts for the swaying sensation."

That's how Lexi met Mad-one. And how they were able to see into my mind while my wolf was drifting in and out of consciousness. I said as much.

" 'Met'? That wouldn't be the word I'd use." He started tucking his shirt into his trousers. "She visits sporadically. What does she look like? Her voice sounds young, but you can never tell with the Fae. Would I want to bed her?"

"Listen to me!" I said sharply. "This isn't funny. I don't know what feel-good vibes the old geezer's flooding you with, but resist. Don't go to Threall. It's dangerous for you."

"I told you—I feel no fear when I'm there."

"Can't you see that he's doing his best to ease you into a permanent coma? Promise me that you won't let him send you there again."

"He's not sending me." Lexi squinted at the sun. "I'm choosing to go."

I sucked in a shocked breath.

"Every time I leave this world to visit your special realm, the Old Mage shares more of his knowledge with me. You can't even begin to appreciate the depth of what he understands. He's let me see so much . . . you couldn't imagine . . . conjures and concepts." Lexi touched his mouth, unable to sum up the awesome with words.

"You know the magic won't stay."

"But it is!" His features lit up. "Everything's staying—*everything's* sticking. Within two days, I've learned as much as Helzekiel has over a lifetime. A few more hours in Threall and I'll have enough to bring him down. Did you see the ward I placed around Daniel's Rock? Do you know how much effort it took for me to do that?" His teeth flashed, and he pinched his thumb and forefinger, leaving a scant eighth of an inch between them. "Less than this. And I could do it again. Right now, right here, if I wanted to."

Old Mage, you're a devious bastard. So that's the deal the old geezer was offering Lexi: get his sister to agree to walk away and the Mage would give Lexi endless and equal ownership to everything he's learned. Lying buzzard. He'd welch on the deal as soon as soon as the soulmerge was final. Though I doubted that Lexi could see that. My twin was animated, flushed with excitement at the mere talk of magic. "Lexi, he's a wiley old goat. You told me so yourself. If he's offering it to you, it's only because doing so works to his advantage."

"He didn't offer to share his knowledge. I bargained for it. I made him give it to me."

"He's manipulated you into wanting it."

"You don't know what you're talking about. *You* were not there."

"I know he's shadowing you. Influencing your thinking." Lexi's neck was blotchy with color. I tried another tack. "You know what I've been asking myself all afternoon? Why didn't *you* come last night, Lexi? You've already admitted that you were there at Daniel's Rock. I pleaded with you to come. Get me out of the trap. You said that you *couldn't*. Who stopped you?"

"You needed the Gatekeeper to return to Creemore. It was a good decision."

"But it wasn't your first instinct, was it? When we were kids, no one could touch me when my twin brother was around. I had a hard time fighting my own battles. You were my self-designated protector. But this time, when I asked for help—begged for it—you sat back and sent someone else."

"You have to stop comparing me to the boy I was."

I thought back, trying to piece my cloudy memory of last night into a more solid picture. "You were shouting at the Old Mage. You told him that you didn't care what it cost you. You demanded that he let you take my pain." *My twin's voice had been so urgent, so desperate.* "What did it cost you? What did you have to give up to him?"

"Just leave it, shrimp."

"I'm going to enjoy ripping his cyreath from yours." I leaned forward until my face was in spitting distance of my twin's. "Can you hear that, old man? I'm going to hold you to your promise! I will not release you from your vow!"

A deep, dull flush spread over Lexi's cheeks. "If I ask you to release my mage from his vow, you will."

"Don't count on it."

"It is my life." Flickers of green light spat from my brother's translucent eyes, a presage of a full flare.

Frustration searched for release and found none. My head throbbed with the urge to pound my brother. I drew in a shaky breath. "Can't you see that the Mage has mined you for your weaknesses? He's preying on your desire for magic. He keeps moving the magic-carrot, and you keep following it all the way into the blue fog. Don't go there again. You'll get lost in Threall and his magic and you'll never come back."

"I need a few more hours." He stretched out his leg.

"Why?" I exploded. "Haven't you learned enough magic to satisfy yourself? You just told me that you know as much as the Black Mage! How much more does any man need?"

"I need to ruin Helzekiel as he's ruined me."

Oh, Lexi. Is that how you see yourself? My tone softened. "You're not ruined. You're just a bit dented."

He stared at the toe of his boot for a long time, then said, "You don't know what he did to me."

"No." My voice was a thin whisper. "But I can guess."

He paled and looked away.

"Come home with me," I said. "We'll leave this world behind us."

"You won't be going home."

"Yes, we will. And when we do, you can start over."

"I can't be a wolf in your mate's territory." He shook his head. "My beast will challenge Trowbridge."

That would be very, very bad. "You can control your wolf."

"Not without sun potion. He's inside me. Pacing all the time. Waiting to get out again." Lexi pulled at the sheet of moss coating the log. It came away in his hand, the size of a slice of Wonder Bread. He squeezed it, testing its density. "I only met him once—just one night—but it was long enough for me to know that he was dominant. And he's far more aggressive than I ever remember Trowbridge's father being. He wants to rule. He wants his own land, his own pack. He'll risk everything, kill anyone, to get it."

"We'll think of something." A very strong steel cage or a plot of land way up north far away from other people.

"Give it up, Hell." He tried to re-place the moss. It sprung back, refusing to knit itself back into the wound he'd made. "We both know I don't belong in Creemore. I'm like one of those antiques in Sharron's Secret Treasures." He got up, then limped to the stream. "Is that shop still there on Elizabeth Street?"

"No."

Nodding, he tossed the sheet of moss into the stream's current. "Your world has moved on. I didn't fit much before, but now I really don't fit. Cell phones used to be the size of walkie-talkies and only the rich and stupid had them. Now everyone's got one. People watch movies on portable computers. *Portable* computers?"

"You'll get used to technology."

"I doubt I can even remember how to read English." He scrubbed at the bristles at his right temple, unconsciously scraping his clawed fingers over the wolf inked above his ear. "I need to *be* someone. And who would I be in your world? A drifter with no land or position. If I stay here, I can start over. Once the court witnesses the power I can wield, every person who used to hide a sneer behind a smile will tremble in my presence."

"Lexi, the Old Mage will *never* let you use his magic independently."

"You do not know what he will do or won't do." A bead of sweat ran down Lexi's throat, joining the dark line around his collar.

"Then prove it. Do something your own. Produce something magical just for me."

"I'm not a knave who performs for the satisfaction of others."

Weariness slid over me. "I'm right on this, Lexi. He's too possessive of his skills, too vain about his status as Old Mage, mage to the Royal Court, to ever allow you to wield *his* magic as you wish. Your mage will never let you have full control."

"Don't forget that I made the ward over Daniel's Rock."

"With or without the old geezer's permission?" I didn't wait for an answer—I thought I knew it already. But there was a concrete test for my hypothesis.

Please, Lexi. Let me be wrong.

Merry covered territory as she ate, frequently moving higher to graze on tender shoots. It took me a moment to find her in the elder tree.

"Are you finished feeding?" I asked.

She answered by lazily untwining a golden tendril from the twig she'd entwined herself around. A food-satiated Merry is a temporarily benevolent person, though I probably had minutes before her bonhomie began to erode. I offered her my palm. She hooked my thumb and dropped gracefully onto my offered platform.

Her supple chain spilled over the edge of my hand. I stared at its swaying length for a second, thinking of all the times her golden links had warmed my neck. Once, my only friend. I couldn't have shouldered the isolation of my existence without her friendship.

I stroked her stone, and she spoke back, her amber depths turning gold-red with affection.

"Did you hear any of that?"

Her answer was a curious blip of yellow light. Feeding is a noisy business and her hunger had been pressing. She hadn't caught the conversation.

"Lexi says he's got autonomy over his actions, and that he's got almost as much power as Helzekiel. If that's true, he should know how to unbind you from the curse that's kept you captive."

Merry's temperature rose to near blistering. Her stone pulsed purple.

"You're mad at me for waiting!" I hissed, my finger curling in pain. "I should have asked him to do this right away. Before we left the rock. But I wasn't sure if I was going to be asking a favor of the Old Mage or my brother. I'm still not sure, Merry."

A grudging pinch.

I'd received worse from her.

"It's time for the big question, Merry," I whispered. "Are you ready?"

The points of her golden leaves turned pricker sharp. She lifted a thin arm and pointed it to the nearby tree. Ralph had morphed into a stick figure, and he stood upright on the tree's limb, arms akimbo, his stone shining brightly in the muted shade.

"Him too?" I asked.

A blip of hot red from the center of her amber belly.

I brought both hands together. "Hop on, Ralph."

With a marked swagger, the Royal Amulet swept his chain up and tossed it over his stick arm. Then he leaped, landing neatly on my left palm. He stalked over my life line, jumped the seam between both hands, then kept going, pushing Merry up on to the Delta of Venus below my right thumb.

I shook my head. "Ralph, no one's ever going to call you smooth."

Chapter Nineteen

Lexi's brows rose when I called him.

I scanned the ground for beetles, found none, and placed the amulets on a patch of tamped earth where once—ten or twelve days ago judging from the remaining musk—a small mammal had spent the night.

Prey, said my wolf.

Merry rose to her feet first. Ralph took a fraction longer—pausing to redistribute some of his gold so that his legs were a half inch longer than hers. The reallotment of his finite gold resources made his head proportionally smaller than Merry's, but I guess the whole point was to appear taller, not brighter.

Lexi joined me. "What is it?"

My twin needed to understand what our mother's amulet had grown to mean to me. "The first time she ever spoke to me," I said, my gaze focused on Merry, "I was trying to smother my tears into a pillow. A leaky kid really pissed off Aunt Lou." I crossed my arms over my chest. "I was doing a really lousy job of crying quietly. I kept thinking that she was Mum's sister; she had to share some of the qualities our mum had. She didn't, but it took me some time to convince myself of that."

I'd kept challenging her in those early days.

Merry's amber took on a definite orange cast. She remembered too.

"Anyhow. Merry must have gotten tired of my tears. She pinched me under the chin." I rolled my eyes, shaking my head. "You've got to remember I was alone in bed and Merry had never so much as twitched an ivy leaf before. Goddess, Lexi, I sat up so fast you would have thought the headless horseman had knocked on my window." I slanted my eyes at my brother. "Do I have that right? When Mum wore her, did Merry ever move or talk?"

Lexi thought about it. "I don't think so."

"That's what I thought." I shook a finger at my amulet-friend. "Your sudden animation scared the crap out of me and you know it."

Two throbs of orange from her lion-heart.

My eyes burned. "She's not an amulet. Or a piece of jewelry. She's a person. She once had a voice, and use of her arms and legs. She had free will, and a life, and all that was stolen from her the day she was cursed to live the rest of eternity as a speck inside a hunk of amber."

"I don't see what this has to do with us."

"You know exactly what it has to do with us. There's only three amulets of any note in the Fae realm. Merry, Ralph, and the Gatekeeper's. It's pretty obvious to me that only a very powerful mage could have worked the spell to enchant an Asrai. If it was a garden-variety conjure every Fae from the Royal Court to a farm peasant would have an amulet. So, it takes a great mage or a great mage in training to entrap a living being." I raised my accusing eyes to his. "Which are you? You say you have free will—you say the old goat will let you use his magic at your will. If you won't perform a party trick, then do something important, something right. Prove to me that you have magic of your own when he's not at the wheel." I waved my hand at Merry and Ralph. "Undo the spell that holds them in this prison. Give them their freedom."

Red flags high on Lexi's cheekbones. "It's not as easy as that."

"Could Helzekiel do it?" I spat.

And bingo. I may not have conjuring skills to match my brother's, but I sure knew the magic words. The air fairly crackled between Lexi and me as he sank down to my level. He settled his weight on the backs of his heels and cleared his throat.

Ralph edged close to Merry, whether to protect her from any further evil or to get first in line for a stint of spell breaking I couldn't tell. But both amulet hearts—one golden, one icy blue—tilted upward toward my brother as his long hands began to move in a circle over their heads.

I leaned forward, excitement tightening my gut, as my brother's lips parted.

Do it. Release them.

I don't know how long it was supposed to take or how hard he was supposed to work for it. I could only report that Lexi tried harder than a kid with a painful stutter to get those spell-breaking words out. His throat strained; his mouth grimaced.

But he couldn't push a single syllable past his tongue.

Not for seven "Mississippis."

On the eighth, my twin's shoulders sagged and his gaze grew unfocused and I knew that he was speaking to the wizard who lived inside him.

Merry cried out—a flash of vermilion. And Ralph's arms lengthened into sharp points—twin rapiers ready to pierce flesh.

I saw all that. Peripherally. Just like I was aware that Mouse had edged closer and the Gatekeeper had struggled to her feet. I was aware of everything and nothing. My gaze was locked on Lexi's. I was looking straight into his eyes when his soul dimmed and the hot emotion that had twisted his features into a mask of frustration began to melt away.

"Don't go," I whispered.

I doubt he heard me, for his soul had already flown away on battered wings.

Gone.

Ralph surged forward, into the valley of death, his small swords flashing.

The Royal Amulet took an unexpected solo flight into the unknown as the Old Mage's countermeasure against amulet charges hit him dead-on.

The mite-sized balyfire threw sparks as it impacted with Ralph's jewel. He flew, a blue comet with a long golden tail. He met the earth face-first, then torpedoed through a heavy layer of mulch, his progress unchecked until he burrowed into a tree root. I heard the clunk and saw the thatch of compost light up as if someone had hidden a string of LED lights under it.

"Ralph? You okay?" I asked.

A leaf twitched and then lifted, pierced by a needle-sharp strand of gold. The Royal Amulet sat up groggily, disdaining Merry's help.

I spun around to give the old man a glare. "Was that really necessary?"

The Old Mage shoved Lexi's sleeves up, his movements fast and irritated. He inspected the scratch marring my brother's wrist with a puckered mouth. "You and your 'friends' are vexing creatures."

"Then bugger off."

Evidently that suggestion required no thesaurus. He drew himself up to my brother's full six feet, except Lexi never stood as if he had a poker up his ass. "I am here to offer you terms for a new agreement."

Said the devil to the dimwit. "Go away, old man," I replied.

"You desire the Asrais' freedom."

Of course. Nothing came for free with the Fae. I lifted my narrowed gaze.

The wizard smiled faintly. "Though I cannot break the spell surrounding the one you call Ralph, I can easily destroy the enchantment that holds the female Asrai. With one pass of my hand, and a few short words, I can break the conjure that has long held her captive."

Suddenly I felt heavy. Like I'd become hollow when I'd watched my brother's soul flit off and now that void was being filled by liquid that was neither life sustaining nor pure.

Ugly water. Fouled and spoiled. I could taste it on the back of my tongue.

"Let me guess," I said woodenly. "All I have to do is agree to release you from your vow. Merry's soul for my brother's."

"Precisely."

Merry stepped closer to Ralph, her body suffused in a horrendous orange-red. "Why isn't Ralph part of the offer?" I asked on her behalf.

"The enchantment holding the Prince of Asrais is far superior to that restraining the female. Breaking the spell holding him would result in an explosion that could be heard and seen for miles."

"It would kill him?"

"No. He is an Asrai."

Nice to know, except I didn't have the faintest idea of what constitutes being an Asrai. Except for the attitude. Both Merry and Ralph had plenty of that. Though the latter's fell more into the "I'm entitled" category. Wait a minute . . .

"Ralph's really a prince?"

The old man lifted both shoulders in a supremely dismissive shrug. "Of the Asrais."

I studied his self-satisfied smile, feeling a sick curl in my gut. "Who set the enchantment down on Ralph?"

"I did."

No wonder Ralph reacted so violently to the Old Mage.

"What about Merry? If you break the conjure holding her, won't there be an equally big kaboom?"

"No. Her prison is not a blue diamond of the greatest clarity, but a piece of common amber, riddled with air bubbles and flyspecs. It will fracture easily."

Really? If I pried up a rock, could I use it on Merry? One smash and she'd be free?

All I needed was blunt force. I scanned the area for a suitable hammer and spotted one near the edge of the stream. It was half-buried in the earth, but the general outline of it looked promising. It was substantial enough to deliver a shattering blow but not so large that I couldn't pick it up with two hands.

I started digging it out.

"It is a pity about your friend Merry," the Old Mage said with a thoughtfulness that sounded wholly manufactured. "While the prince waged war against those he shouldn't, her mistake was trivial in comparison."

The mage had the pole, he had the hook, and now he was baiting it. I knew he was dangling a lure in front of me and I knew it was going to hurt like hell if I bit down on it, but just like that lake bass, I still opened my mouth.

"What did she do?" I asked, raking away the damp earth.

"She ventured too far from the safety of their sacred hollow and her path crossed that of Helzekiel."

"That's it?" I lifted my head. "She was in the wrong

place at the wrong time? Helzekiel cursed her just because he could?"

I'll never call myself a Fae again.

"Helzekiel performed the conjure to prove his worth," corrected the Old Mage.

Merry was a freakin' merit badge?

I swallowed down the snarl rising in my throat and bent my head again. "Is that part of your basic mage accreditation?" I gouged at the earth trapping the stone. "Screw over an Asrai and you get your wizard's cap and gown?"

The Old Mage kneaded Lexi's right thigh as if it ached. "Long ago, I made an error in judgment that a few viewed as a crime of treason. It was decreed that I should be punished. But as in all things, the Royal Court was divided. Half were poised to select a mild censure, as they feared losing their mage. Half were in favor of the Sleep of Forever, as they feared my growing powers. The outcome of the vote rested on Helzekiel's potential. Could he, in time, become *almost* as useful as I? Naturally, I was aware of my assistant's ambitions, and so I never allowed him to witness a spell completed in its entirety."

"Then how did he know how to do the nasty to Merry?"

"The court demanded that the Prince of Asrais' punishment be performed in public as a caution to those who considered waging war against them. Unbeknownst to me, Helzekiel took secret notes of every word and gesture."

Merry's belly was effused with bloodred light.

"Behold the result of Helzekiel's ability to follow instructions," the Old Mage drawled. "Note the substantial differences between the two amulets. The Royal Amulet is a blue diamond set in a meaningful design. Your friend Merry's setting resembles a robin's nest. The knave could not follow a simple sequence without erring." He clucked his tongue against my brother's teeth. "Fae gold shouldn't be squandered so."

"Yeah, I feel real bad for the Fae gold."

Now that I'd dug around all the margins of the rock, I realized it was both heavier and larger than I'd thought.

The old man lowered himself into a squat beside me. "She has suffered," he said.

Tell me something I don't know.

"If you use brute force in an attempt to break her loose from that which holds her, you will not be freeing her. She will not be her true size, nor will she have all her talents."

I'd seen her shape under a magnifying glass. She was no bigger than a piece of rice. Unless that's the true size of an Asrai? Maybe they truly were mite-sized? The Old Mage was as adept at lying as I was.

What if she really was smaller than the *i* at the end of my name? Would I be freeing her to live the remainder of her life as a shrunken tiny version of herself?

"No one truly loses," he continued. "In return for this Asrai's freedom, I can give your twin a life such that you could never provide him in Creemore. I can place him at the highest table of the court, giving him prestige, power, and influence. He will live a very long life—and never again will he threaten the longevity of your own, or that of your mates."

With the Fae the devil is in the details. For instance, "I can" does not mean the same thing as "I will." Perhaps once my twin would find himself seated at a place of honor. But soon enough Lexi would start spending more and more time in Threall. Awash in his new addiction, he'd hardly notice as the length of his "not-here" moments stretched to eternity and beyond.

My brother's an addict. He'll always be one.

"I will see the book destroyed," the old geezer promised. "You can leave this realm now assured of the continued safety of yours."

As if it were that easy. "That doesn't save the Raha'ells or Ralph, does it?"

"Are we bargaining, nalera?"

"So far you haven't said anything really tempting."

He rubbed one thumb over the other, his gaze shuttered as he thought. "What about the Raha'ells?" he offered abruptly. "As soon as I have taken my rightful place as mage to the Royal Court, I will petition the king for their freedom."

Yeah, we all know how useful petitions are.

His eyes glinted. "I give you my word that the Raha'ells will return to their hills and their hunting grounds. You can return to your world with a clear conscience. Knowing that no evil will seep through your portals."

I cocked my head, finally struck by the non-specific nature of the last threat. "What bad things are we really talking about? Locusts? Plagues? Evil mage magic? What precisely is written on the last page of the Book of Spells?"

"You would not understand it."

"Try me. Go ahead. You can use little words."

He considered the wisdom of answering. Then with a slight lift of his chin, he said, "The results of my studies into realm dimensions."

"More mumbo jumbo. Get specific or get lost."

"I was testing the elemental boundary dimensions between one world and another."

"Whose world?" I asked sharply.

"Not yours."

There really were other dimensions? The physics geeks would be agog. "So," I said slowly, "what you're telling me is that you left DIY instructions for creating portals like the ones between Merenwyn and Creemore?"

If so, what was the big deal? Earth didn't have wizards, but it had many covens of witches. Wards could and would be purchased. Every known portal could be contained within one. Kind of like double-bagging the grocery bag weighted by the juicy steak. Countermeasures could be taken to reduce seepage.

"Those were early studies," he said with disdain.

Early? I turned my head to stare at him. I'm not a student of higher learning, but I'm becoming very good at decoding facial expressions, and the gleam of acquisition in his eyes set all sorts of alarm bells tolling.

"You went past that, didn't you?" I evaluated the satisfied curl of his mouth and felt hope die. "Did you leave step-by-step instructions on how to slip into other universes on that last page?"

A pause, then he answered proudly, "Yes."

I thought it through. "So, Helzekiel wouldn't need a portal to visit me in Creemore. He could just snap his fingers and appear in my local Tim Hortons."

"Yes. That is my fear."

No, it wasn't.

"One day you'll need to rule," Trowbridge had told me once. "And some of the decisions you have to make will damn well kill you."

He was right.

My gaze slowly traveled from the embedded rock to Merry.

You'll never know how sorry I am for what I'm about to do.

I spoke to her. Not the guy who squatted in my brother. Not the audience of the Gatekeeper, and the pony and the half-blooded kid named Mouse. I spoke to the brave soul who had stood by me all these many years. I spoke to the person I was going to betray.

"This isn't about Lexi anymore," I said. "It's about what a man like the Old Mage will do if he's not stopped. He's a wizard with a score to even up and a reputation to reestablish. Once he's taken care of Helzekiel—and trust me, he *will* take care of Helzekiel—he'll move on to eliminating those in the court who sentenced him to the Sleep of Forever. I don't think they're good people, but without them there's no one to check his relentless curiosity and ambition."

I wet my lip. "No one except us, Merry."

Oh Goddess, her color is turning black as a witch's blood.

"He'll start walking the world again," I told her, my words tumbling. "But his ego and curiosity will keep pushing him to expand his horizons and soon walking through universes won't be enough. You know I'm right, Merry. You know he'll start tinkering with those other worlds. Those people won't see him coming. They'll be as unprepared for him as you were for Helzekiel."

Forgive me, I pleaded with my eyes. "He's so much more dangerous than the Black Mage. I can't release him from his vow."

She stared at me for a long moment. And then, the bright fire inside her—one that was fed on a hope so edged with yearning that it could have lit a hundred homes with its brilliance—slowly extinguished itself. When the light in her belly was no more than a muted glow, she did something she'd never done before. She deliberately turned her back on me.

Ralph extended a golden arm and drew her close.

My eyes fell to the mucked-up earth and the piece of rock that was bigger than I'd ever anticipated. Had I really thought it would be as easy as that? Forget the mumbo jumbo, just break the stone? One strike and the entire my-best-friend's-enchanted problem would shatter? If that were the case, Merry would have led me to the closest rock pile as soon as she got me used to being led around by her golden leash.

Idiot.

I used to think she followed me. That wasn't quite right, now was it? We went together. Sometimes me leading, sometimes her leading. Both tethered by links stronger than Fae gold.

Broken now.

I pushed the earth back, knowing there were more truths to face. I forced myself to check the tall fir in the west. I knew what I'd see—my mental clock had never stopped ticking. The sun had sunk behind it.

Something's happened. Trowbridge should be back by now. They've caught him, and right now, even as I stand here, they're leading him to Wryal's Island. Panic, a sickening flutter in my chest. *I'm the leader now. I'm the person who has to see this through.*

Ralph curled two arms around Merry when I crouched beside them.

"You heard him. Every piece of magic he knew up to when he was sentenced is written in his journal. The Book of Spells holds the key to releasing you. I'll find it. I'll tear it out. There has to be someone in this world or ours who can free you."

Merry swiveled around.

"I can't do better. I wish I could." I offered my hand.

It took four "Mississippis" for her to disengage from Ralph. Another two for her and the glowering Ralph to step onto my palm. My throat hurt as I picked up their chains and placed them over my head.

They hung from my neck. A burden of guilt and love.

I turned around to stare at the old man.

He said, "I need not be your enemy."

"Oh, we're far too late for that."

"Perhaps I shall leave you to ponder my offer."

"Don't let the door slam on your ass."

Clearly, another insult lost in translation. I needed a Merenwynian lexicon of smart put-downs for the Fae.

"You will need me soon."

I got off my knees and stood. "Door. Ass. Bye-bye."

There is dusk and there is dawn. Both can bleed. Both can have a terrible beauty. Watching the soul-light resume in my twin's eyes was as hard as watching it fade. Losing him had evoked pity. Gaining him back brought anger.

I was furious. Coldly and implacably so.

I knew the moment Lexi was back, for his expression changed. And I knew when he'd finished replaying what had happened in his absence, for the look in his eyes turned from fuzzy to shamed. His gaze cut away from mine.

"I am faint with thirst," the Gatekeeper reminded me.

"You had a chance," I said curtly. "Mouse? Bring me your burlap sack."

He brought it to me. Just like that. No back talk, no "what about," no pauses to sift possibilities of action. It's something I liked about the boy: you gave him an order and he did it. "We lose the pony here," I told him, untying the bag's strings. "She's too noisy. Take off her bridle and let her go. We're leaving now."

"But the Son of Lukynae is not back," said Mouse.

I stared him down until he looked away. Balance of command restored, I extracted the two bottles of juice from the burlap bag and threw the now-empty sack behind some bushes. One vial went into my right pocket.

Lexi finally spoke. "Trowbridge is not back?"

What, didn't his *mage* give him the entire 411?

"Trowbridge said it was less than an hour to the castle," I said tightly. "I want to do it in fifty minutes, tops. But you've been limping." I jerked my chin at his leg. "I take it that's because of the pain?"

"You may not find him in the castle," he said quietly.

No. That's where I'll find him. I have to find him there.

"Answer my question. Can you keep up?"

"He could have met other dangers. He could be—"

"Or do you need a hit of this?" I held up the bottle of juice. "Because nothing is going to slow us down, got that? Nobody is going to stop me from doing what I said I was going to do. Not you or your leg. Not the Gatekeeper. Not the Fae. Nothing and nobody."

You'd think I'd just offered him a capsule of cyanide.

Well, Lexi could take his sense of betrayal and stuff it. My anger was a wooden roller coaster, shuddering upward toward a precipice.

Blotches of color mottled Lexi's neck. "I don't need it."

I jammed the bottle into my other back pocket. Good enough. One of us might. Trowbridge. Me. Mouse. "If you have anything you need to do—like check to see if you still have your balls—I suggest you do it now. Because we're leaving as soon as I get the Gatekeeper fitted with her new harness."

I turned for the Fae woman.

Though the belt cinching her arms behind her back had taken care of any instinct she might have felt in passing to toss a few balyfires at me, it didn't do much beyond that. She was not working with us. She'd lagged wherever she could; she'd been a monument to passive resistance. And I meant it about moving fast: if the truculent Fae needed motivation to hotfoot it to the secret entrance, I was the girl to give it to her.

I prodded the magic inside me. "Donut time," I murmured.

The Gatekeeper was going to lead us to the secret entrance. She was going to do it before the sun slipped below the horizon.

"Hell, do not turn your back on me and give me orders," said Lexi.

Oh?

I slowly pivoted to face my twin. "Okay, I'll give them

to you face-to-face. You've got one job from here on: shut up and walk. When we get to the castle, you're going to show me where I can find your mage's book and then we're done. You'll come back to Creemore, but then you go your way and I'll go mine. It's over. Whatever we had is finally done."

"Don't give me commands."

"Really? I'd think you'd be used to them, because you just demonstrated how easily you come to heel. Not five minutes ago, your mage said get lost and you went away. You tucked your tail between your legs and slunk off."

"I—"

"Shut up. You failed two tests, Lexi, not one. After you realized that you couldn't break Merry's spell, you should have stuck it out. You should have faced Merry and me. Admitted that you were wrong, and told Merry you were sorry. But instead, you just melted away. I watched your face—you didn't even fucking fight it. I don't give a shit why you left. Maybe you were ashamed; maybe you felt beaten. The point is: you left."

"I—"

"I don't want to hear it," I said harshly. "I know now what Trowbridge didn't have the heart to say to me. You are a freakin' grenade with a loose pin. One day you're going to explode, but I'm not going to let you do it until I've crossed a few things off the list. My world—the one you were born into, the one that I'm probably never going to see again—is going to be safe. The mistakes the Stronghold twins made aren't going to impact the people I care about. Your daughter is going to be safe. Cordelia's going to live out her life without worrying about world-walkers, and mages. From now on, there's only one thing I want from you. Try to be a Stronghold, okay? Just for one more freakin' hour you keep the Old Mage on lockdown. You get that? You have the backbone to keep him away from me. I don't want anything messing with my head. We're going to go to the castle right now, because that was our plan—the one that I made with my mate. We're not going to sit here and reflect on why Trowbridge hasn't made it back. If he could have, he would have. Speculating on how to stop the Fae from executing him isn't going to get it done. We're going to follow through. But that's what he'd do. That's what leaders do."

Even if some of the decisions kill you.

I told my magic to do what it had to do. She flowed through me, through my blood, through my will, to accumulate at my fingertips. "Leash her," I said, casting my magic at the Gatekeeper.

My magic flew to her, green and so very alive. The Gatekeeper flinched as my magic's kiss touched her chest. She leaned away from my magic as she curled herself around the Gatekeeper's torso.

I walked toward her, the magic between us tightening.

"Get up," I said.

She shook her head.

I bent so that she could read the conviction in my eyes. "Get up, or I'll tell my magic to tighten up and break a few ribs."

She got up.

I'll find you, Trowbridge. I swear, my love, I'll find you.

Lexi said, "You're making a mistake."

"I'm a Stronghold." I gave the invisible lasso a motivational jerk. "That's what we seem to do."

What my brother would have said to that I'll never know. For that's when Mouse cried out, "Beware, Hedi!"

Chapter Twenty

The three hunters materialized so quietly from the flora and fauna, they could have been wraiths. One male was bearded, well over six and a half feet tall, and had abs that could send a handful of change bouncing. The female was about five inches shorter than Very Tall Guy and had no visible body fat.

They were Raha'ells—easily identified by their long dreads, general air of ferocity, and the liberal application of mud.

How'd they know about the mud?

Mouse spoke out of the side of his mouth. "I don't like the looks of this. Particularly that one."

I agreed: "that" one was giving me the willies. Though all of the Raha'ells were armed, the third man—a clean-shaven, auburn-haired specimen of scary—was the only one with his bow primed and his target chosen.

Why is it always me?

His right fist was bunched on the midpoint of the bow's long shaft, and his left fist was bunched at his jaw. The string was taut, the arrow primed. He observed me through a single eye. Presumably, he had another, but my focus had narrowed to his bunched fists and the die-bitch intent in his unforgiving eye.

I flexed my fingers on my free hand, mentally stripping some power from the donut surrounding the Gatekeeper. Magic streamed back up my arm, surged across my shoulders, and pooled at the tips of my nails. If they fired at me— if they hurt me, or Mouse, or anyone in my party—the last thing they'd feel was the slow throttle of my magic.

What happened next always made me think of when jazz dancers strike a pose just before delivering that sudden flick of fingers that turns their closed fists into starfish.

Jazz hands.

Yeah, that's what I was thinking when Scary Guy let loose his arrow.

Jazz hands—that and *I hate Bob Fosse*.

There was nowhere to go. On the bell curve of fast-moving things that are going to kill you, arrows are right up there with speeding bullets. All I could do was duck, tuck, and pray.

Please be a lousy shot.

Please be the worst marksman in the whole pack.

I heard a soft sound—not a thud, not a comical *boing,* but an impact of sorts, which was quickly followed by a surprised cry. Heartless creature that I am, I put the two sound effects together and came up with "not me."

Good.

Mouse!

I spun around.

Not Mouse, but the Gatekeeper. She'd chosen the dumbass option of backing away. *Never run from a wolf.* Now her little head was bent, to best examine the arrow that was buried in the center of her torso. The marksman's arrow had neatly pierced the fancy emblem embroidered on her vest.

A kill shot.

Very slowly, the small woman looked down at the thing protruding from her chest. Then, she lifted her stricken gaze to mine. "Don't move," I warned her, but she took another step backward and the rope of magic between us tightened until my arm rose and my fingers stretched tautly into a terrible mimic of a plea.

A feeble flicker of flame erupted from her fingertips.

"Don't!" I said, shaking my head.

The second arrow pierced her throat neatly, with the minimum of blood and gore. It went through flesh and found tree and pinned her tightly to the trunk, a butterfly mounted for presentation. Though the Rahae'lls couldn't see my magic, I could, and it's an image that I'll never be able to erase from my memory—the Gatekeeper wavering on her small feet, one arrow through her breast, the other through her throat. Grappling against the unknown, she lifted her arm weakly to claw at her throat and in so doing brushed against the coil of my magic.

It was a rope, green to my eyes, invisible to hers. It was not a lifeline. It could not hold her here in her world.

But the Gatekeeper caught it and clung to it as her eyes glazed.

"Cut," I said through my teeth, and my serpent of magic severed its ties to the dead woman. Green sparkles flickered around my face and my fingers buzzed. I spread them and bit down on the surge of heat as my magic returned to me. Hurting my knuckles, quickening my heart.

"He killed the mistress," said Mouse, sounding more astonished than aggrieved.

"Fae filth," said the archer.

Oh, crap. He's got another arrow.

* * *

When I was young and completely unaware that my life was going to flip from happy as a Hallmark Valentine's Day special to as dark as an HBO series finale, I knew one fact: Lexi was faster than me. At navigating the birth canal. At crawling and standing. At figuring out punch lines and exit strategies. At calling rock to my scissors.

And, of course, at running.

My sibling slammed into me, or rather, he slammed into Mouse, who stood between us. Before I could go ass over teakettle, Lexi's steely arm swept around us to squash Mouse and me to his chest. "Meh, meh, his-her-blah-blah-blah!" he shouted in my ear (or something like that). As he spoke the words of conjure, he did something with his right hand, which I couldn't see, because my face was smooshed into his shirt.

I've blundered into a ward, twice. And I've seen one created, once. But I've never actually been inside one as it fell around me. I thought my ears would pop or I'd feel something equally distressing—a prickling of my thumbs, an ache in my sinuses. But there's really no sign or sound when a ward falls around you. No sonic boom to reference the fact that you've just become the oxygen-dependent life-form zipped into what might be an airtight plastic Baggie.

Also: it's invisible. Lexi's hand gesture must have tipped off the she-bitch with the longbow.

"Magic!" she cried.

I didn't turn to say "you betcha" because on the heels of that announcement I heard three zings—the depressingly familiar sound of arrows set to flight. I curled my body over Mouse's, and Lexi's arm tightened painfully around both of us. But the ward held. The zings were promptly followed by a trio of muffled thumps as the three projectiles thudded harmlessly into Lexi's shield.

I pushed away from Mouse and my brother's embrace, to turn to inspect the damage.

The three arrows were buried, flange deep, into the invisible barrier.

Relief, followed by tension. I don't like small places. And in comparison to Lexi's last conjure, which took in Daniel's Rock, part of the field, a stream, and a cross section of woods, this protective shield was horribly cramped. Most wards are bell shaped. If this one followed the general shape and form, the total circumference couldn't have been more than five feet. I tipped my chin upward, wondering if the ceiling was even lower than that estimate.

"Faith!" whispered Mouse. "This ward's as small as a shroud!"

Not quite, but damn close. "Make it bigger," I said in a low voice.

"Can't," Lexi replied. "The mage has given me enough magic to support two people, no more."

"Why?" I hissed.

"To prove a point."

Mouse cleared his throat. "But there's three of us."

"The old man bade me to expel you."

The space was so intimate I could hear Mouse's breathing hitch. I snagged his shirt. "You're staying."

Lexi snapped at me, "I don't take orders from the Old Mage!"

"Since when?" I maintained my death grip on Mouse's homespun.

My twin's jaw set and his eyes—usually so cool—turned so hot that the close air felt stifling.

Very Tall Guy broke the spell of sibling anger weaving between us. "This is an unexpected prize. The Shadow and a sweet curvy Fae morsel to tempt my tooth."

Mouse cleared his throat again.

"Beware of your sweet tooth, Brutus," said the female

Raha'ell. "The girl is the Shadow's get. Look at their eyes. Both of them are as pale as a lizard's belly. A man would rather lie in a nest of vipers than rut between her thighs."

"I swear, I'm standing right here," muttered Mouse. "Do they not see me?"

The scary auburn-haired guy scanned the clearing, his brow furrowed. He took a deep sniff; then he walked over to where Trowbridge had stood to reapply his disguise. Brow furrowed, he used the side of his foot to overturn the thatch of matted leaves. "The Alpha was here not long ago, Lily. He covered himself with this muck again."

"Perhaps we should do it again too," said Lily. "We've hit every mud hole he's hit. It's kept the terror of the sky away."

Very Tall Guy, aka Brutus, tramped over to Scary Guy. Brutus inhaled long and lustily and then looked over his shoulder at me. "Viper's nest or not," he said thoughtfully. "He plowed her."

Oh, ew.

"More than once," added the nose police. "Though not today."

At *that,* Lily's eyes bugged and the string holding her arrow quivered with tension. "The Son of Lukynae wouldn't sniff at a Fae's pussy unless the whore wove a spell over him. Tell him, Danen!" she demanded of the scary auburn-haired guy.

Choosing to avoid the who-plowed-who issue, Danen moved to the Gatekeeper's body. He pushed her head back with the tip of his bow so that he could study her face. Then he turned back to us and silently stared at me, then Lexi, and then nothing at all. He picked a spot over our heads and gazed at it blindly, and it was during that that his expression turned from speculative to bleak.

She-bitch with the longbow missed it. "Tell Brutus that our Alpha wouldn't touch one such as she," she asked again.

"Enough with the slut shaming," I said.

Mouse, whose vocabulary didn't include a reference for "slut shaming," jumped to my defense. "Hedi of Creemore is not a Fae. She's a mutt like me."

Apparently, that wasn't an upgrade. Lily went Bob Fosse, and another arrow hit the ward with a zing.

"What did you do that for?" Mouse spluttered.

The woman glared at Lexi. "Mutts grow up to be monsters. They should be killed at their first cry."

I'm so done with this.

Brutus's bowstring was tauter than Joan Rivers's smile. He pointed the head of his arrow at Lexi. "What do you think the Shadow is worth? Do you think the Fae will trade all of our pack for him?"

"Not for him," said Danen, his voice as cold as ice. "But they'll pay a heavy ransom for what the girl wears."

The female Raha'ell sucked in a shocked breath. "She wears his amulet!"

"Look further, Lily." Danen's scent had turned musky and pungent. "She wears the Royal Amulet as well."

I should have tucked Merry and Ralph inside my shirt, but with all the bows and arrows I forgot. Too late now, particularly as Merry was already on the move. She cinched in her chain, zipping faster than an express elevator to the hollow beneath my throat. From there, she rope-walked over to my shoulder. This was normally when people's eyes bugged out; few expect a pendant to become animated.

"Merry, where is our Alpha?" asked Lily.

Well, Merry *had* spent nine years among the Rahae'lls. It made sense that they'd know that she's a sentient being.

Lily prowled closer. "Have they hurt you, Merry?"

Unbearably.

"Shall I make them suffer before they die?" Lily asked.

As Merry thought about that, I pointed to the arrows

embedded in the invisible shield. "Knock yourself out." I gave Lily the Elvis smile. Lip curled just so.

She sneered right back. "You'll run out of air soon enough."

My eyes rolled toward Lexi. "Is there something you want to tell me?"

With an utter change in expression, he shook his head, which in sibling-twin talk could be loosely translated to "hell, we're totally screwed."

Merry sat down on my shoulder—as spiny sea urchin—then crossed her legs.

I rubbed my face.

"Quiet!" Danen cocked his head like a spaniel noting the rustle of the treat bag. "I heard something."

Damn, damn, damn. I glanced upward. The sky was hazing gray as it does before the sun fully sets, but no cloud befouled it. But if Trowbridge had been taken, then the Fae hunters were here, in these woods, right now. And with them, came jinxes.

Brutus lifted his chin and sifted the air for scents. "There," he said, his gaze narrowing on a very small rise behind Danen.

I heard no sound, even when Trowbridge crested the small hummock and paused to briefly assess the scene. Though blue comets fired in his eyes, he held his blade loosely in one hand.

"Our Alpha," breathed Lily.

Indeed, it was the Raha'ells' Alpha who walked down the slope, straight into the line of their fire. Walked—like he was a king, born to the role of leader, assured of his reception. Walked—as if he knew himself to be arrow impervious.

You brave fool.

The comets spinning in my lover's eyes burst into flare

of blue light. A cone of illumination, not blinding, not searing, but gentle and loving. His flare held the warmth of cupped hands cradling your face. *I am your leader,* it crooned. *I am your father,* it said. *You are loved.*

Lily moaned and instantly lowered her weapon, her face wreathed with relief.

Brutus wavered for another two terrible seconds before his shoulders relaxed. "Alpha," he said simply.

It was one word: a simple title. But my stomach tightened at the undercurrent of meaning in his tone, for I knew in one stunning flash of insight what being an Alpha truly meant to the Raha'ells.

The word was both a benediction and an abdication.

Such a vastly bigger deal than being the Alpha of Creemore, where pack members gathered for meetings and moonlit runs but lived hidden among mankind. Sure, the Ontario pack liked to bring a deer down every four weeks, but they still had their television remotes, and paychecks, and favorite sides of their queen-sized beds. For them, "Were" was a concept modified by civilization, leaving them with a tribal sense of belonging but a certain measure of autonomy.

"Alpha" held such a different resonance in this realm, where survival was not a given and comfort was measured by the number of people who had your back. It meant: "You lead. You decide. You bear responsibility for our deaths."

Goddess, can I be an equal partner to that?

My wolf was a hot ball inside my gut. As I wondered whether or not she was going to do more than expand, Danen spun around, presenting Trowbridge his back. And once more, I found myself staring into the auburn-haired Raha'ell's unforgiving eye.

My inner-bitch growled.

"Stand down, Danen," Trowbridge barked.

"No. I'll not acknowledge you."

Do it, asshole. I've got a she-bitch inside me and she's not happy.

Brutus tossed his head. "What's this? We've been following our Alpha's trail all night, hoping to free him from the Fae, and now you turn your back on him?"

"Free him?" Danen's knuckles were white. "Where are your balls, Brutus? Are you too stunned by his Alpha flare to ask him questions that any simpleton would? The scent of the Shadow's get is all over him. Look at him! Has he been beaten? Hurt in any way? Ask yourself why a Raha'ell would ever cut his hair but to—"

"They shave us for the Spectacle," said Lily.

"Yes, they do." Danen stared at me, and in his expression I saw grief, and rage, and deep fatigue. "But here he is, alive and well, weeks past the last Spectacle. And in whose company do we find him? The Shadow and his whelp."

"She is my mate!" Trowbridge's flare surged, but now it was hot, fierce. "You will treat her with respect."

Lily—*seriously, Lily?*—let out a mewl.

Danen's coldly furious gaze swept over me. "This green-eyed wench is the one you called for in your delirium?" He shook his head. "You abandoned your pack for a half-bred Fae!"

"You might want to ratchet back your Fae-hatred," I told him. "I've had a very bad week."

Pulling out his sword, Trowbridge started walking toward the Raha'ell. "You are my second, and once my best friend. I do not want to do this. Put down your bow, Danen. Turn and face me."

"Put your blade down first, then douse the magic spilling from your eyes." Disgust twisted Danen's face. "What did you have to sell for your Alpha's flare? Did you give the Black Mage your soul?"

"The flare is my own." Trowbridge's face went taut. "By birthright I own it."

"I don't believe you anymore. By the God's teeth, we made it easy for you to become one of us. We welcomed you right into our midst."

"You tried to kill me," said Trowbridge. "I fought you and won."

"Lie after lie we accepted, even though we knew that they could be naught but tall tales. Like children, we swallowed those stories, choosing to believe that you traveled through the portals when everyone knows that they've long been closed. What knaves we were. The Son of Lukynae came from a different world—one so filled with game that no wolf knew hunger—and he'd come to ours to lead us to our new destiny."

"I did come from another world," said my lover. "As did my mate."

"You told us the portal closed behind you. How did she get here?"

Trowbridge covered another three feet, moving slowly. "Let me explain."

"I've had a bellyful of lies."

"Don't challenge me, old friend." Sorrow and determination showed on Trowbridge's face. "You know you'll lose. And I need your help. Our pack waits to be freed from the pens."

"I'll not believe your tales of fantasy any longer. There is no land of plenty—this is our destiny. The bow. The blood. The end."

"Danen—"

"I know the truth!" the Raha'ell shouted, spittle flying. "I saw your capture. I watched him"—he jerked his chin at Lexi—"run you down with his horse. You didn't look like a leader then. You were a trapped wolf, surrounded by the Black Mage's men. But still, me and my boy followed you. We trailed you and the Shadow all the way to the castle, hoping for a chance to help you escape." He shook his head, his dreads rasping in reproach. "But there was no chance to set you free, and when they dragged you across the Wryal's bridge, my boy said, 'Pa, it's the end of all of us.'" His jaw worked; then he said, "I clapped my hand on my son's shoulder and told him that nothing could hold our Alpha. But Joshua knew the way of it. Not long after, the terror in the sky came to hunt us. The riders swooped in and took him from me. He's in the castle now, waiting his turn at the Spectacle. Where were you when Joshua was taken? Was it you who told the Black Mage where to send the cloud that hunts the Raha'ells?"

"I will never betray my people."

"Then tell me—tell us—where were you when the terror came?"

My mate's gaze flicked from Danen's back to me. I shook my head slightly—no. Telling the angry Raha'ell that the Son of Lukynae went back to the land of plenty for a small vacation when things got rough here was a myth destroyer of A-bomb proportions. We didn't have time for the fallout.

Use your sword, I mouthed.

Danen, adept at lipreading, slowly turned to face Trowbridge.

My man looked at his old second for a long beat. "I was in Creemore."

Danen said, "I can't miss. Not this close."

"Neither one of us can," replied Trowbridge.

"Break the ward, Lexi," I told my brother.

"Trowbridge can handle it."

Like hell. My mate had already had ample time to attack Danen but hadn't. Some misplaced piece of logic or sentiment was getting in the way. At that moment I didn't give a rat's ass why. All I knew was that he was putting himself—and, come to think of it, me—in danger.

I tapped into my magic, and she streamed from my hand to test the strength of the ward with her blind mouth. Iridescent green sparkles shimmered with each lick.

"Break the ward, Lexi." I could barely hold on to my flare.

"He won't let me," said Lexi tautly, referring to his hidden wizard.

Lily raised her bow.

Trowbridge must have caught the movement out of the side of his eye. "The first person to draw a bead on my mate will die," he said.

Colored light filled the interior of the dome, bathing the magical walls. Slightly darker and more layered than my usual neon hue.

"Break it!" I shouted.

Chapter Twenty-one

The ward didn't funnel down into Lexi's palm; it shattered in a blinding flash. The scent of magic exploded too—so strong and floral it was sweetly choking. I heard Lily's cry, and Danen's grunt, and Brutus's mutter about Gods and prophecies. And I sensed movement—things flying away from us like someone had tossed an explosive device onto the ground between us. But I couldn't see because light was everywhere. Around me and beside me—doubly bright.

And yes, somewhat dimly, I noted the tonalities, the multi-layers of green, the forest shades softening my usual electric tone.

But it was a footnote, okay? Because my mate's light was stretching for mine, a wave of ocean blue surging to meld with my flare. Our lights met and began mold and marry, and then I heard Lexi's small gasp—the sound he used to make when he'd noticed something marvelous and unexpected; the inhale of delight that would escape him when he spotted a new adventure—and that's when I realized that some of the green illumination was indeed coming from my left.

And more important, the source of light wasn't an electric or neon shade. It was the green of the woods, the shade of the firs, the dappled, mottled, and varied tones of foliage. Lexi's flare was the essence of him before the mages, before the addiction, before the kidnapping.

It was the thing left untouched.

And it was freakin' beautiful.

"The prophecy!" Lily cried, dropping like a stone.

Yes, sink to your knees. See us for what we are.

Lexi's hand reached blindly for mine. I caught it and held it. It was warm and far larger than I remembered, and it gripped mine like it was a vise.

And Trowbridge?

He was taking it—he was accepting both of us.

Look at us. Feel us. Understand us.

Brutus followed Lily, a convert unable to stand in front of such beauty, but Danen held upright. Not terribly successfully; he was visibly weaving. One good huff and he'd fall over, but still, I had to give him a grudging point for staying vertical.

That is, until the ingrate opened his mouth.

"Do you not see?" Danen said, his breath coming hard. "This is not the prophecy, but evidence of their unholy union!"

"Seriously, asshole!" I exclaimed. "How much more do you need?"

"Hedi," I heard Trowbridge growl.

"No, screw this! Danen needs to wake up and smell the magic." I yanked my hand from Lexi's grip and chopped the air with my arm. "Everybody douse the wattage, okay? I can't see the man for the flares."

If anything, Lexi's and Trowbridge's flares grew fiercer. Light danced over Danen's auburn dreads—the blue of an angry ocean; the penetrating green of a dark woods.

The sharp smell of magic was explained. Something—or rather someone—had stripped Danen of his weapons. His bow was up in a tree, his arrows broken. And the knife he'd probably hoped to use to gut us was stabbed into the heart of a pine.

Matter of fact, everybody had lost their weapons, even my Trowbridge. The Old Mage might be miserly with his magic, but when push came to shove he wasn't taking any chances with Lexi's body.

Danen's body language broadcast barely controlled violence.

"This guy is mine," I said.

I didn't look at my mate, though I sensed his coiled tension. Nor did I do an auto-check of Lexi's mood, though I felt him take a step closer to me. I just stared at Danen, who in turn was gazing fixedly at the ground.

"Danen is a strong fighter," murmured Trowbridge. "He's never lost a challenge."

I lifted my shoulders. It had to come down to this, hadn't it? If there was a tomorrow and a hardscrabble future among the dreadlocked wolves, I had to show them that I wasn't (a) the girl most likely die or (b) Trowbridge's sex buddy. Better to prove myself as a force to be contended with now. Better to do it here, against Trowbridge's second, then in a series of scrimmages against lesser wolves.

It was all or nothing.

I've got magic, Trowbridge. Don't forget that.

In case he needed his memory jogged, I flexed my spell-casting fingers, which my serpent took as permission to investigate. She undulated across the five feet separating me and the dreadlocked Raha'ell and began to sniff at his moccasins.

The bits of glitter inside her coiled length flickered.

Tasty, was he?

"You're right, dickhead," I told Danen. "It's an alliance. Me, my mate, and the man you call the Shadow. We're all in it, and it's time you all understood that, and the fact that it's going to take the three of us to defeat the Royal Court and the Black Mage."

Lexi's flare had intensified and focused itself solely on Danen. The Raha'ell blinked hard, and a tear trickled down his cheek. My serpent followed the column of his throat and nipped in to taste the salty wetness.

It was a fleeting touch, but Danen flinched, then glared at me. Naked hatred.

Or fear.

I could work with fear.

"Why didn't you free your Alpha when you saw him captured?" I asked Danen as my Fae slipped from his neck to twine herself in an airy circle around his chest. "You watched them put the Son of Lukynae in chains. Why did you skulk along, hoping for an opportunity for rescue that never came?"

For a moment, I thought he wasn't going to answer.

"There were too many Fae," he finally spat out.

My serpent of talent glittered, a band ready to tighten. "He's weaker than us," she hissed. "For he has no magic."

"There's always going to be too many Fae," I bit out. "They. Outnumber. You." The man's scent turned a tad more pungent. "The Fae have magic, and horses, and more archers than you'll ever be able to breed. They intend to wipe you out, and by numbers and magic they will."

"Fine words from the Shadow's get," he sneered.

Oh snap. At the exact moment I thought about crushing the attitude out of the man, my Fae decreed "tasty" and squeezed hard.

"Witch!" cried Danen, clawing at his chest.

I heard a crack, knew it was his rib.

"I am no witch," I growled. Not me. No mage, no wizard, no coven of three. However, I was possessed. By my own sense of inevitability and urgency; by my wolf's desire to crush any opposition; by my Fae's interest in general mayhem. And baby, it was well past time to demonstrate that I had more than words at my disposal.

Lift him, but don't crush him. Toy with him, but don't destroy him.

My coil of magic suddenly cinched his torso and the Raha'ell let out his own growl—a savage beast sound that raised the hair on the back of my neck.

Growl at me?

"Up!" I shouted.

Theoretically, 190 pounds of muscle, and dreadlocks, and deerskins should not go "up" easily. Not when it's being lifted by a five foot two inch woman whose idea of a workout consists of sprinting to the corner store for another handful of candy bars. There are laws of physics involved.

I broke them.

Up that howling bastard went.

"Yesss," my Fae crooned as Danen thrashed against our hold.

"Higher," I demanded of myself, of my Fae, of my inner-bitch. My magical talent was already with the program, and she chortled when my wolf surged inside me, reaching for our magic, binding herself to mortal-me and Fae-me.

Animal power, magical power, girl power. We were bitch to the power of three.

Freakin' invincible.

So higher Danen went. We lifted him until I could have counted the stitches on his moccasins, if he were lax, instead of scissoring his legs like some freakin' three-year-old having a tantrum. We gave him a reproving shake. "Get this straight—I'm not the Shadow's get, or his whelp or his by-blow!" I shouted. "I'm his sister. And I'm not just some girl Trowbridge plowed; I'm his *mate*. Got that?"

Mulish bastard should have said, "Got that." He didn't,

and I heard another snap of cartilage or bone. Was I going to have to break him bone by bone? In front of Trowbridge?

I'd do it. I wanted to; we wanted to.

Lexi's flare was now the dark green of the deepest forest, where children are lost and predators prowl and bad things can slip between tree and tree. Trowbridge, on the other hand, had not moved, except for his chest, which rose and fell higher and faster than usual, and his nostrils, which were flaring like those of a racehorse ready for the bell. And yet for all that, the rest of him was immobile.

"Give me one reason why we need this guy!" I snarled.

"Danen's the only one ready to take over the pack," he replied. "If something happens to us, the Raha'ells will need him."

"Like hell they will. He's already blown that. You left Danen the dickwad in charge for a couple of weeks, and he let the jinxes take your people." *Stupid, dumb wolf. If he'd only done his job . . .*

My Fae tightened and Danen groaned.

"Why couldn't he have figured out the mud trick earlier?" I demanded of Trowbridge. "It took you what? An hour to realize that you needed to cloak your scent? He had days! Days! Why couldn't he have taken your people to some caves? Or the very least, why couldn't he have sat it out until you got back? The dickwad's next to useless. He can't lead them like you can lead them."

"No. But I can't find game like Danen," said Trowbridge. "He's an expert tracker. He kept the pack from starving the winter Helzekiel sickened most of the game."

"Well, bully for him. The man drew on you. I still want to break him like kindling." I was already halfway there. Danen's lips were blue tinged, and his legs had gone from wildly thrashing to weakly twitching.

"I know," said my mate.

And that was all Trowbridge said. He didn't try to

convince me one way or the other. He'd stated his side and now he was letting me work it out. Kill Danen or let him live. My choice.

Danen's eyes were dazed slits.

The man weighed a ton and my shoulder was on the verge of dislocating. I lowered him until his soles flattened, then slightly loosened the rope of magic around his massive chest. The Raha'ell folded at the waist, limp as a puppet on a loose string, then braced his hands on his meaty thighs and did some heaving.

"You need to get some facts straight," I said over his tortured breaths. "Fact number one: I have killed for your Alpha, and will kill for him. Should anyone try to hurt him again, the last thing they'll feel is my magic shattering their ribs." I was shaking with fury. "Fact number two: no one pushed the Son of Lukynae through the portal this time. My mate came back to Merenwyn—to a realm where he's the freakin' first name on the kill list—of his own free will. He chose. To come here to this place . . . where they hunt you, and trap you. Where they treat you like you're some sort of sub-species. Goddess, I can't believe I was ever proud of being half Fae." My anger swelled my serpent of magic, and the man encircled by her groaned. "Your Alpha could have stayed in Creemore. A lesser man would have."

Lexi's light flickered and then died. He blinked hard before he took a threatening step toward Danen.

"Don't," I said.

Lexi paused.

The wolf's lip curled, and he forced himself to straighten slowly.

"The man you call the Shadow is my brother." I watched the wolf's reaction carefully, my control thread thin. "If I let you live, you will call him by his true name—Lexi Stronghold. He is my sibling, stolen from my family when he was just a child, and brought to Merenwyn by the Black Mage. He couldn't find a way back to Creemore, any more than he could escape Helzekiel—"

"Who's Helzekiel?" Lily murmured.

"He's a murderous bastard who deserves to die slowly."

"They know Helzekiel as the Black Mage, Tink," said Trowbridge. His flare was softening, soothing, not scorching.

"Who's Tink?" asked Lily.

"Shut up!" I nailed everyone with a glare. "My *brother*," I repeated in a harder voice, "couldn't escape the life he'd been forced into. Not until he met Trowbridge, and realized that together they could open the portal between the two worlds. Together, Danen. Not separately. Trowbridge and I may know the location of two portals—the one over our territory in Creemore and another—"

"What other?" Danen asked sharply.

"The Safe Passage. It's how we came here."

Danen's expression turned speculative. I moved to add, "But neither Trowbridge or I know how to open the portals. Not without the words. Only my brother knows the words."

At least I was hoping he knew the words to open the Safe Passage, because otherwise I could kiss Kit Kats and Cherry Blossoms good-bye forever.

"I don't believe the Shadow is here to help us," Danen said belligerently. "And you are connected to him by blood and bone."

"I'm not here to help," said Lexi. "I care nothing about the Raha'ells. You could all die for all I care. I'm here to put a match to a book."

"What book?" asked Brutus. His mud disguise had fallen victim to his body temperature; patches had greased into a slick taupe film.

"The Book of Spells," I answered. "If is not destroyed,

then Helzekiel's power will know no boundaries. He'll be able to walk between worlds. All worlds."

"Including yours," Lily added shrewdly.

I gave her the stink eye. "Including the one that the Raha'ells are hoping to take sanctuary in." Danen held his arms strangely akimbo, and I realized that he was loath to allow his flesh to touch the invisible band wrapped around his chest.

My wrist ached. "You really are one dumb, stubborn wolf."

Mr. Too Dumb to Cave just stared at me.

I let my breath out through my teeth. "Cut," I said. My serpent gave him one last hiss-inducing squeeze and then broke. "If you still want to challenge your Alpha or me, go ahead. Die fighting. Robson Trowbridge will kill you. He'll fight to defend me, just like he's fought for the chance to lead his people back to the world from which we came."

I saw the longing in the wolf's eyes.

"There really is a land of plenty where wolves can live in peace and children can grow up with full bellies and no fear," I said slowly. "And even though you're proving to be an asshole of major proportions, neither of us will leave Merenwyn until every Raha'ell is free to travel with us back there."

"You don't have our blood," Danen said. "Why would you risk your neck for ours?"

"I'm done," I snapped. "Kill him, Trowbridge."

"She'll stay because she's decided her people are my people," said Trowbridge. "That's all it takes, Danen. Once a Stronghold closes a fist around a person's heart and claims it, they'll go to the ends of the world to protect that life. They'll risk everything. They'll face anything. They'll do what must be done. They'll hold."

Danen cast a look at Lexi that needed no interpretation, then turned to Trowbridge.

"Lexi loves his sister," said my mate, his tone hardening. "I left her in his care, because I knew that he would have taken an arrow for her." My mate held Danen's gaze, then moved to mine. "*He* will not betray us."

Message received. The Old Mage was a different game.

Danen thought; then he sighed and pressed a hand tightly to his side. Awkwardly he got down on one knee. He shook back his dreads, exposing his neck. "I offer you my blood, once more, Son of Lukynae. You may spill it as you wish."

"We'll need it, Danen," said Trowbridge. "We're going to walk into the castle, and we won't walk out of it until everyone is free."

"Mutts too?" said Mouse quickly.

"Mutts too," I said.

Damn, my own eyes were watering now. Too much flaring, too much emotion. I savagely dried my cheek with the back of my free wrist. "Before you guys start singing your kumbayahs, I want his word."

Danen turned. "I am yours to command. Yours to—"

"No, not that. That's a given." I scanned the group. "What I want is to never hear the word 'halfling,' or 'mutt,' again. If we make it back to Creemore, none will judge me or anyone else by their blood. You will judge us by what we do. Who we are. Can you all do that? Because that's the price of entry to the promised land."

Danen stared at me for what seemed like a very long time; then he nodded. "Aye," he said with a slow smile. "We can do that."

Danen's irises were an amber brown. His lashes were sparse and his right eyebrow was caked distractingly with dried gray mud, but once the deadly intent was drained from them what were left were kindly eyes.

He nodded to me, as if we were ending a long conversation instead of three seconds of mutual appraisal, then turned to Trowbridge. "Is there a plan?"

"There is," Trowbridge replied.

"Right, we'll recover our weapons and refill the water skins." And with that, what was left of the free Raha'ells set about doing just that—all three of them bypassing what was shaping up to be a group-hug moment to break apart into satellites set on a mutual goal.

Rearming themselves. Evidently, big muscles and quick reflexes weren't enough. Brutus picked up an arrow, checked the feathering at the end, and tucked it under his arm. Lily walked past the Gatekeeper's body without looking at it.

I just stared down a Raha'ell. And there's a body pinned to a tree and I'm not even wanting to throw up. Wow. I'm a badass.

Lexi glanced at me, then grabbed Mouse by the shirt. "Come on."

"Where are we going?" squeaked Mouse.

"Lily's going to have to climb a tree." He pulled the boy over to the fallen leg, pushed him down until he sat on it, then slowly collapsed himself. He stretched out his legs and crossed them at the ankles. "This should be good."

Lily passed them, showing her front teeth.

Lexi lifted one brow.

Reality was setting in. I jammed my trembling hands deep into my jean pockets.

Trowbridge crossed the ten feet separating us and cupped my face. His right thumb stroked my jawline. "Proud of you," he said.

I bit down on my lower lip. Held it there, firmly snagged

by the pearly whites, until it stopped with the annoying quivering. *Geez Louise. Don't lose all the ground you gained by swooning in front of the troops. Real heroes don't melt in the aftermath of a battle. They raise their paws for a fist pump. They shout, "Hell yeah!"*

Trowbridge's fingers tightened almost painfully. "Steady," he whispered.

His scent swept around me, another set of arms, surrounding us in a fog of musk, and woods, and man, and—oh yes—Trowbridge yum. My lids fluttered closed, and my wolf moaned, and somehow her earthy response slid right up my throat.

I could take him here. Right on the ground.

Only his fingertips touched me. I leaned into them, imagining them moving over me. Touching my neck. Dipping into—

Lily coughed.

My eyes flew open. Trowbridge was staring down at my upper lip as if it were dewed with honey.

"You like my mouth," I said breathily.

A lopsided, tight grin. "It has its moments." Suddenly somber, he fingered the limp curl at the side of my neck. "But it almost gave me a heart attack again."

"You had my back." I lifted my shoulders. "You would have killed him if I—"

Expression grim, he shook his head very slightly. "You challenged him, Tink."

"Yeah, but—"

"*You* did," he repeated.

"But wouldn't you have—"

"Shhh." My lover turned me around so that I faced the tall tree in the west, then wrapped his arms around me. It gave us the semblance of privacy. The undersides of my breasts rested comfortably on his corded forearms. My mate pushed aside my hair to reveal the tendon he'd once bit down on. He pressed a warm kiss there, then nuzzled my temple.

"If I stepped in," he whispered into my ear, "you would have been perceived as weak. Not my equal. Someone I fucked."

Holy crap.

I sagged against him. He was hard as a rock.

"You are one crazy Tinker Bell." He sounded prouder than a guy who scored a Shelby off a vendor who didn't know their Mustangs.

My heart thudded against my ribs.

The sun was a sphere of fire behind the tall spire in the west. Streaks of it, long slashes of pure gold, tried to reach for us. "There's no holding back the night once it begins," I said, knowing the cover of dark would be an asset once we were inside the castle.

"No," he said, and his arms grew tight, tight, tight.

My mouth went dry as I realized a fairly big-assed complication. I rubbed my tongue against my teeth, then asked the question I feared to pose: "Will there be another full moon tonight?"

He stopped nuzzling and half-turned us toward Danen. My mate tipped up his chin in a silent query.

"Tonight's the second night of it," his second replied. "Tomorrow's the last."

We'll be wolves. All of us. Four-legged animals can't strike a match to set a book on fire. Lupines are useless with longbows.

Lily scowled at the longbow hooked on a bough high above her reach. "It's poor hunting here. The Fae have taken all the good game."

"And we'll have to be wearing the mud again," said a brooding Brutus. "My wolf hates it. It's not natural."

"We can't—" I began.

Trowbridge said quietly, "Time to talk Plan A." He gave my neck one more nibble, then moved away. Planting his foot on a rock, he said, "We're not going to answer the moon's call tonight. Each of us will take the juice."

Brutus growled low in his throat.

My mate didn't even bat an eyelash. In a calm voice, he said, "Every Fae takes for granted that the Raha'ells will turn into their wolves during a full moon. We're going to use that. The Fae won't be prepared for Raha'ells who walk like men but kill like wolves."

Danen fingered an arrow, then shook his head. "We'll be staggering, not walking. None of us have the head for the potion."

"Not if we time it right," replied Trowbridge. "There's a rush after you've taken a swallow, but it passes. Once inside the castle, Mouse will find us a good place to gather what we need for our attack. We'll take the juice then. By nightfall, we'll all have clear heads."

"They say it makes you stronger." Brutus's scent was growing pungent.

"A little," said Trowbridge.

"I stole the juice," said Mouse, seeking some praise. "Three full bottles. From the store master's locked pantry. Had to get past two guards to do it."

"How about it, pack? Do we take the sun potion?"

Brutus's grin showed all his teeth. "Well, there's no game here. I didn't enjoy my meal last night; the rabbits in these woods are so stringy it's hardly worth the effort."

"That was *my* rabbit," said Lily. She turned in exasperation and glared at Lexi. "You put my bow up in this tree. I want it back. Use your magic to bring it back down."

My brother folded his arms behind his head.

After all the weapons had been retrieved, the Raha'ells hunkered down to watch Trowbridge play Picasso with a stick again. The tiny silence that fell after my mate finished his sketch of the island was broken by Lily's audible inhale of anticipation.

Her cheeks were flushed, her eyes bright. "How many Fae do you think I'll bring down before I make it across the bridge? Ten? Twelve?"

"We won't be using the bridge," Trowbridge said absently, intent on adding details to his rough diagram. "There's a secret tunnel that goes right under the lake. No one will know we're inside until we're on our way out."

"There will be plenty of Fae inside the castle, Lily," said Brutus. "Now, where's this secret tunnel, then?"

My gaze jerked upward to Trowbridge's. *The Gatekeeper.* In all the fuss, and drama, and near-death experiences, I'd forgotten how essential she was.

Mouse pushed between Lily and Brutus. "I know where it is." Then he gave Lexi a shark's grin and said, "*And* how to use it."

There was a pause; then Danen said, "And once we're into the castle, what happens then?"

I left them to it. I needed to get something from the Gatekeeper.

The Gatekeeper's chin rested on the arrow piecing her throat. I forced my eyes away from that horror and focused on the gold chain around her neck.

No coin, no safe passage home, I reminded myself. Swallowing hard, I reached forward. The chain was slick.

"You haven't done this much, have you?" said Mouse, coming up behind me. "You'll have to break the arrow first, else you'll never get the necklace over her neck."

Body-looting tips from a teenager. *Sweet heavens.*

What followed next was done with shaking hands and a bout of dry heaves. Once my gut was more or less stable, I examined my bounty. The pendant bore no features

I associated as amulet-ish. No stone, no articulated arms. It was just a decorative disc with a bit of etching. I held it out to Merry, brows lifted.

The light within her amber heart issued a disgusted flash of yellow.

So, not an amulet.

"I'll check her pockets," Mouse said, proceeding to rifle through them. He passed me a golden spoon ("you'll need to melt it down, as it has her mark on it") and a small square of chamois, which he carefully unfolded ("she used that to polish the jewels, she did").

"Found anything of interest?" said Lexi.

Mouse's paw was burrowed deep inside the skirt pocket. He started at Lexi's voice, then rose, wiping his mouth. "I'm going for a piss," he mumbled.

"Nothing of value in the pocket?" Lexi called after him.

Mouse spun on his heels and spread his hands wide. "'Twas empty, Shadow." Then Mouse cleared his throat and headed for the trees. His amble was deliberately innocent; he knew his departure was being watched with squint-eyed appraisal.

"His feelings are hurt," I said to Lexi.

My twin lifted a shoulder. "Feelings are expendable."

I glanced over my shoulder. Trowbridge was going through the diversion. I dropped my voice to a whisper. "The Safe Passage is sealed. I watched it close. I tried Open Sesame and it sure as hell didn't work. We're never getting back home."

He lifted his shoulders, very much the big brother. "I can open it. The portals are the mage's creation. And remember, I know what he knows. I know the words to open the portal."

Home!

This time I was leaving nothing to chance. "What are the words?"

He spoke another long string of gibberish.

"What freakin' language is that?" I asked in frustration.

"Mage speech. Impossible to teach or to lend."

Swell.

Chapter Twenty-two

"Sheep's tits," said Mouse in a stunned voice. Past the thin line of young trees that delineated forest from field, Dhesperal Lake shimmered.

Trowbridge said, "Son of a bitch."

Lexi said, "That's unexpected."

An appalled pause ensued during which I could have inserted my own comment. However, for the life of me I couldn't have strung two words together as I stared at the complication across the lake. Granted, I was winded. We'd damn near sprinted the last mile because Brutus's sweat was broadcasting his scent. But still . . .

Seriously?

My wild imagination had added far more acreage to Wyral's than the island actually boasted. The Raha'ells' Alcatraz was actually modestly sized and made visually smaller by the fortress that had been built to dominate it. The Royal Court's castle was tall, large, and square; its presence was formidable. But it was beautiful too, what with the late afternoon sun bathing its smooth stone walls with gold. Tall, square towers—the type you expect to see flags fluttering from—anchored each of its four corners.

I'm sure anyone approaching the castle's front gate

would be suitably impressed by its grandeur. However, we were looking at the back end of the castle. The palisade enclosing the Spectacle grounds had not been built to delight the eye and was a harsh visual contrast to the elegant castle that rose behind it. Merenwyn's sun had unevenly leached the color from its wood, and some Fae handy with an axe had taken the time to whittle each log's top into a sharp point. But it looked like what it was—a brutal feudal prison.

The prison's grimness was further enhanced by the shadow of the mother jinx. She hovered high above the Raha'ells' stockade, a voluminous storm cloud whose interior sparkled with hints of pink, and purple, and red.

That was scary because every single one of the Raha'ells had a touch of *l'eau de lupine* about them, and yet it still wasn't the thing that had rendered me nearly speechless.

I sagged against a beech. "Why are there so many people? I thought the castle was supposed to be quiet today! What happened to everyone preparing for tomorrow's Spectacle?"

There had to be hundreds of Fae—the visible portion of the L-shaped span that linked the island to the mainland was completely clogged with a mob of people. Considering our twofold plan to destroy the status quo at Castle Fae was highly dependent on stealth, a big fiery diversion, and the willingness to take out anyone who got in our way, those numbers amounted to a hell of a stumbling block. Goddess, we'd need a machine gun to mow them down.

"I don't know. I've never seen this many gathered before." Mouse nervously knuckled his nose. "Every village for ten leagues must be on the bridge."

"More important, the entire Royal Court's gathered on the postern," said Lexi grimly.

"What's the postern?" I asked.

"The middle tower."

Geez Louse. How'd I miss that?

Part of the castle's back wall boasted a square tower. A story higher than the top of the palisade, it loomed over the place where the Raha'ells were imprisoned, which made it a great observation lookout for the assemblage of brightly dressed Fae clustered there. I squinted, trying to pinpoint the Black Mage by his somber dress. It took nary an instant to find him. *There.* His back was turned to us and the mother jinx; he faced the members of his court.

My gut clenched, and my wolf rumbled.

How could anyone saunter into the Spectacle grounds unobserved? The tower overlooked the palisade; Trowbridge would be in full view of the gathered Fae when the rescue attempt was mounted.

My fingers crept to my mouth.

Just then, the bridge crowd issued a collective gasp. Arms were lifted, fingers pointed, to the jinx that scudded toward the castle. The wolf-hunting menace moved at breakneck speed, and its hue was a rosy creamy blush, not a stormy gray.

I held my breath because I was sure that the terror would find us. It would catch wind of Brutus's scent, or Trowbridge's, or even my brother's—for I could swear I could detect the faintest essence of wolf wafting from Lexi.

One Mississippi, two Mississippi . . .

The miniature jinx zipped cheerfully across the lake and never changed course or speed as it approached dear old Mom. It plowed straight into the heart of her, and then it was gone, egg whites folded into the cake mix with a twist of the spoon.

The Fae erupted into a cheer.

It went on and on, that rah-rah of happiness. It was wilder than the crowd's roar as the glitter ball fell in Times Square and louder than any football celebration I'd ever witnessed. It was joy; it was relief; it was the end of bad times and the beginning of good ones.

Trowbridge grabbed Mouse. "Where's the tunnel's entrance?"

The boy couldn't find it. Mouse advanced the gap between a clump of birches again, arm held rigid, clearly expecting to push upon some invisible obstacle. Instead, he kept walking, step by hesitant step, all the way through the space between tree one and tree two, and nothing happened. No sparkles of fairy light, no trumpet of horns.

Nothing.

"The terror's going to discover us!" said Lily. "Brutus, stop sweating! The mud's come clean off the back of your neck!"

Sweat dotted the tall dude's upper lip. The rest of his face was red, and the skin on his throat glistened. "I sweat a lot," he said. "I always do!"

While Mouse blundered blindly, a jinx struggled to detach from the huge cloud hovering over the palisade. It was a presence, merely a bubble of gray. But if it detached— no, *when* it broke apart—it would find us within a heartbeat. Brutus was seven out of ten on the stink-o-meter. Lily a five. Danen only a two.

But my mate . . . He wasn't sweating, but his perfume was that of an Alpha. The more impossible the odds, the more dominant his personal signature became. His scent trail beckoned, a mixture of man, wolf, and leader. But to me? All Trowbridge. Woods. Wild. Sex.

Mouse threw a frantic look at us over his shoulder. "I swear on my mother's soul that it was here!" he cried. "I marked the tree. See the nick in the bark? This is it! It's here!" He slapped the tree in frustration. "I know it is!"

Danen pulled an arrow out of his quiver. "What'll it be, Alpha? Retreat or forward?"

"There's no going back," said Trowbridge. "We're not running from their dogs." My mate shot me a burning look and my gut roiled because it was pretty much the same look he gave me before he left me at the damn waterfall. "Just one thing," he said, shaking his head. "Can't one fucking thing work out for us?"

"You and I did," I said. "That's a miracle I didn't see coming."

"Hell," said Lexi suddenly. "The coin you took from the Gatekeeper! Give it to me!"

Frantically I dug into my jeans pocket and brought it out. When Lexi snatched for it, I jerked my hand back. I saw hurt flash in my brother's eyes before he drowned it with anger.

"Then you hold the coin out!" he said.

I did, and immediately the space between the birches changed, as if there was gas in the air and it was evaporating into a wavering, heat-spawned shimmer. Wisps of myst began curling around the white bark-coated trunks, and then the gap in between them hazed over into dark gray film.

Hey, presto: A doorway revealed itself. It led to a chasm of darkness.

Gasps behind me and the definite sounds of three bows being strung with arrows again.

"I'll go first," said Trowbridge.

"She has to go first," said Lexi. "She has the coin."

"Not on your life," countered my mate. "She's not walking into that."

Oh, screw this. My twin and mate were fully capable of bickering their way right up to the moment the prince of the underworld waved "Hell-o." I sucked in a breath and held it, because Goddess knows what that milk white haze would do to my lungs, and then stepped through the veil.

I'd feared water, expected earth, and was surprised to

discover that the tunnel was more like a mine shaft than anything else. The ground beneath my feet was solid and the space dark. A hand came to rest on my hip and Trowbridge's scent wrapped around my waist. He pushed me forward. Lexi came next, shoved through by Danen.

On their hurried entrance, a long string of fireballs popped up, one after the other, as if someone with a torch ran ahead of us down the tunnel lighting each one.

The tunnel was long and low. I could not see the end of it.

"Do you hear singing?" Brutus asked.

Trowbridge's back is large and his shoulders wide. I doubt the Raha'ells could see past them, and thus the first quick glimpse of the room of riches was initially mine, then his. It was a square room, filled with display cabinets. Some were glass fronted, some not. Behind the panes, jewels shone, silver sang, and gold hummed.

Yes, hummed.

We were rushed; we were hurried. Danger behind us and the unknown was in front of us. Still, my eyes went right for the source of that strange music.

It beckoned.

Inside a large glass case set on the flagstone floor was a living pyramid of the raw precious metal. *Fae gold's alive*: I'd known this since childhood. Put like that, it's the sort of comment that has a "sky is blue" association. A fact, neither good nor bad.

But when you witness it, when your wolf-sensitive ears are assaulted by the precious metal's low and sorrowful dirge, when you see its magical spires restlessly trying to reshape itself to freedom, it's not a neutral statement; it's the preface to a crime.

Ralph issued a burst of white light, and the articulated tips of Merry's leaves flattened. Trowbridge moved past me,

Lexi followed, and then as Lily and the others pushed their way into the room, I heard it over the low hum.

A female's gasp of horror.

I spun on my heels. A servant girl cowered in the corner to the left of the door, her spine pressed so hard against the joint between one wall and the other that her shoulders were protectively hunched together. She'd pressed the back of her hand hard against her open mouth, likely in hopes of smothering another betraying sound. But as they say, the cat was out of the bag, whereupon Brutus proved himself to be remarkably fast for a very tall dude. He surged past me, diving for the girl.

She had enough time to screech blue murder, but she didn't. And in the end, her choice of silence saved her life. If she had cried out, she would have died instantly. If she'd put up a struggle, I think the same would have happened.

I saw, you see. I saw Brutus spring at her like a wolf, not a man.

Trowbridge barely paid them heed. He slid past them to place his ear to the hallway door. There he listened, his brows pulled together, before carefully easing it open a crack. Sound poured into the small room, many voices blurred into an indecipherable babble of goodwill. My mate studied the world outside the room, then very gently closed the door.

He silently jerked his chin at Danen and Lily, then held up two fingers. They edged around a display shelf filled with silver daggers to join him by the door. Danen leaned his longbow against the wall. Lily followed suit.

The captured girl breathed noisily through her nose.

A scant few seconds after the door was quietly reopened, the two uniformed Fae who'd been standing in the hallway died relatively quiet deaths. Yes, there was some foot writhing before their necks were snapped—*oh Goddess*—and one guard dropped his weapon in surprise (*don't let anyone hear it!*), but over the babble of voices?

No one noticed the passing of two souls.

When they dragged the bodies in, the heavy crown the servant girl held slipped from her grasp. It fell, and Fae gold sang high during its brief flight of freedom until it landed with a metallic clatter on the flagstones.

"Strip them," Trowbridge told Danen and Lily. "We'll need their uniforms."

I stared at the bodies, feeling oddly detached. Dead Fae look exactly like dead humans or Weres. Nothing magical about them. Ugly, though. Seeing death so close up. They were people, who'd done us no wrong. Except they were the wrong *sort* of people and their kind have done mine wrong.

We're at war.

There will be deaths.

"What about this one?" Brutus held the terrified girl pressed to the wall, her head sharply tipped back by his hard grip on her hair. His blade rested on the long column of her vulnerable throat, a dull metal against the milk white of her skin.

"Don't kill her! She can help us," Mouse said, his words tumbling over one another in his haste. "She has access to things you'll need. Clothing. Water. Cloaks like the one she wears. Don't hurt her!"

"Who is she?" Trowbridge asked softly.

"Gwennie," Mouse answered. "She's a Kuskador—a personal servant for one of the king's daughters. And a friend."

The girl was very slender, a year or two older than Mouse. Muted clothing, covered by a very thin gray cloak. Eyes a few shades lighter than the silk, alive with fright.

"She can help us," said Mouse again.

Trowbridge shook his head very slightly. Brutus's blade

eased, but not before a thin trickle of red ran down the girl's throat. When he stepped back, Gwennie very slowly straightened her head. She flattened herself against the wall. Her eyes darted to the door, to the dead guards, to Lexi and Trowbridge—her gaze lingered on the Son of Lukynae for a horrified tick—then the tunnel's doorway. It was a rectangle of black, mysterious and frightening, for those mysterious lights had self-extinguished.

"What have you done, Mouse?" she asked in a small whisper. "They're turning the castle upside down looking for you and your mistress."

"It's all right, Gwennie," Mouse soothed. "You'll see. No one's going to hurt you."

I wasn't sure about that. We were all becoming expendable, one way or the other.

Lexi reached for the heavy crown. He tucked it under his arm and walked to an ornate display cabinet. Part of me was on Lexi alert—I wasn't a hundred percent sure how much my brother was in control of himself. I dimly noticed that he was moving slowly and that, once he'd splayed open the cabinet doors, he stared at the interior with a peculiarly fixed expression, as if it and it alone were important: the girl who cringed from him didn't matter; the dead bodies by the door were of no consequence. But I didn't earmark his preoccupation as vastly important. It was, after all, a near-empty cabinet. Inside it were three shelves. The first two were bare, save for a naked jewelry stand, and the third was lightly burdened by three simple crowns.

"The tunnel!" Brutus suddenly rasped.

And again, everybody spun around, pretty much in perfect unison, to stare in varying degrees of dismay at the wall from which we'd just emerged. Sure enough, the doorway to the tunnel was shrinking, the crisp, dark edges of it melting into the walls.

Typical.

"It's closing!" Lily, intent on stripping a corpse of its uniform, dropped the dead guard's arm and surged to her feet. With an inarticulate cry, she shoved her way past Mouse and barreled past me, all in the faint hope of reaching the melting doorway before all trace of the exit disappeared. It sealed itself before she'd finished rounding the Fae gold's glass container, leaving no visible trace of its existence. "No!" she hissed, pounding on the stone wall.

"I have the coin," I soothed. "I can open it again."

She spun around. She was visibly angry, needing to condemn someone for the claustrophobic fear spiking her scent.

"It's a trap," she growled.

"If so, we walked into it on our own," Trowbridge said.

"Mouse lied!" she accused. She pointed toward the girl cowering in the corner. "He said only the dead Fae was supposed to have a key to this room! And it's supposed to be locked from the inside. So who is she? And how did she get into this locked room?"

"The king's dresser also has a key." Lexi closed the cabinet door with a click. He stood, studying the crown, his hand flattened on the glass, and the twin-sensitive portion of me stirred again.

Lexi's expression is too blank. He's thinking deeply or he's listening to an internal dialogue only he can hear.

My brother slowly turned to examine the girl. "But you are not the king's dresser."

The girl's response came fast, words compressed between rapid breaths. "He sent me here to fetch another crown. The one the king's dresser chose for the princess hurts her scalp—that's why she never wears it, not matter what the celebration. She's vexed with him, so he pulled me aside and bade me to come here and get . . ." Her words failed. She swallowed hard then showed us the crown she held in her shaking hands. "She wanted this one. It's plainer and lighter," she said. "And—"

"It doesn't dig into her scalp." Lexi's hair swung forward, and he tossed it back over his shoulder, the motion reassuringly his and his alone. "But the king, and his consort, and the other princesses? Are they wearing their ceremonial crowns?"

"Yes. If I don't return, the king's dresser's going to send—"

"Some more guards." Lexi's tone was decidedly bored, but his expression was as bleak as a Toronto winter sky. "The crowns she speaks of are worn only for momentous occasions—marriages, the celebration of spring, the end of a war. Whatever the Royal Court is planning to do to the Raha'ells is going to happen tonight. It will be massive and final."

Mouse asked the girl, "Is it so, Gwennie? Have they pushed the Spectacle forward to tonight?"

The Kuskador servant gave an anxious nod. "When the first jinx came home empty-handed at noon, the crowds started forming. The roads are clogged with people coming to the island to witness the final purge of the Raha'ells. I heard my princess say to her sister that their father fears controlling the common folk. Have you not seen them outside?"

"Aye, we've seen them." Danen pulled a boot off the guard's corpse. "Lily, come help strip the other body."

As Lily moved to obey, Mouse appealed to Gwennie. "We need your help. We need clothing, some shears to cut their hair, perhaps a cloak or two. We have to get the Son of Lukynae to the holding pens, and Hedi of Creemore and the Shadow to the Black Mage's tower."

"You can't," Gwennie said, completely aghast. "You couldn't even get as far as the courtyard—never mind the holding pens or the mage's tower! The quartermaster's got his people turning the castle upside down for you! He said you stole sun potion from his stores and that when he finds you you'll be fed to the Spectacle."

"He won't find me. I'm Mouse. I can slip along these halls as silently as—"

"With them?" she scoffed, her gaze swinging to Trowbridge. "I know who he is—he's the Son of Lukynae!"

Mouse beamed proudly. "He's come to lead us—"

"He's got the Shadow with him!" she cried. "Right now, there's only two men more wanted than you and you brought them right to the castle! The guards are everywhere: at the head of every staircase, at the entrance to every door! You can't move a foot without tripping over one of the brutes. You can't involve me in this. I want no part of it. You have to go back from where you came!"

Lily huffed. "So that the terror in the sky can hunt us?"

Lexi pinned Trowbridge with a simmering glare. "You should have gone through the Safe Passage when you could have. Turned around, taken my sister, and left."

"Your sister is a hard-ass. There's no taking her anyplace she doesn't want to go."

"The Kuskador girl is right—you'll never walk out of this castle alive. Neither of you will." My brother's gaze slowly swung to mine. "There's no winning today, Hell, only captivity or death."

Brutus said, "If that's the case, I plan to kill twenty of them before I die."

"So few?" murmured Lily. "I'll match that and add twenty more."

Lexi kept staring at Trowbridge. "You could have kept her safe."

"She wouldn't have let me."

My nails bit into my palms. Plan A was in tatters. I'd known it upon my first glimpse of the castle. I'd seen the crowds and almost immediately my brain had started to go down the "uh-oh" path, but I'd stopped it. Because things were moving too fast and contemplation was only going to be frightening. I was running down a tunnel, leading people toward the culmination of a destiny I'd started when I'd bargained with a mage.

I needed to come up with a Plan B.

I'm responsible.

Lexi moved to the display case of Fae gold. He drew a box with his finger across the glass, his mouth thinning as the Fae gold moved to follow the heat of his skin. "So, it's check and mate," he murmured, shaking his head. "The old man's cleverer then you, and he's wilier than me. He laid this out so well, I didn't even see it until—" Lexi suddenly hissed. He rocked against the pain, his fingers pressing his temples.

I wanted to touch him, for I knew the head-splitting agony one suffered when the Old Mage delivered an attitude adjustment incentive, but fear caught me and told me not touch my twin's shoulder. I didn't want to force him to lift his eyes for my scrutiny. For I didn't know who'd be looking at me through them.

Lexi breathed slowly through his mouth for what felt like forever before he straightened. Slowly, he lowered his shaking hand, bracing it against the edge of the display cabinet. "My mage is the only person who can get us out of this," he said woodenly. "You need to make another deal with him, Hell."

Chapter Twenty-three

"No fucking way," said Trowbridge.

Lexi's eyes burned into mine, little spits of green fire seeming to make them snap. "My mage knew you'd turn down Merry's freedom for his soul. Just as he knew you'd come back to him later when you realized the bigger implication—he told you that you'd be in need of him before the night was over." Lexi clenched his teeth again, his face contorting with another spasm. "Hell— don't trust him completely. Look for the holes in the deal. He plans to—"

Lexi's speech ended with a harsh groan of pain.

I surged to catch him before he fell to his knees. Trowbridge intercepted me, swinging me around into his arms. He pressed my head against his shoulder and held it there. Into my ear, he said forcibly, "Tell me what's happening to him."

I pushed at Trowbridge's chest. "Let me go to him—"

"Tell me what's happening." Trowbridge caught my face between his hands. "Don't look at him. Look at me. Tell me what's going on."

"He's being punished, all right?" Out of the corner of my eye, I could see my brother struggle to stand. "The old man didn't want him to say whatever he was going to say. It feels like someone's taking a knife to your skull. Stabbing you with its blade over and over. It burns so hot . . ."

"You felt that?" Trowbridge whispered dangerously.

I caught the edge of my lip between my teeth and nodded.

"Son of a bitch." Trowbridge's scent wrapped around me, another layer of a protection against magic that knew no boundaries. His thumb moved over my lower lip. "Sweetheart, remember? New rules of engagement? You don't hold back from me; I don't hold back from you. What's the deal he's talking about? When did the wizard make contact with you? I had Mouse watching; I was watching. The only time I left you alone was—"

"At the creek," I finished. "When you had to go scouting."

Trowbridge shot a glare at my twin. Under the heat of that condemnation, Lexi slowly lifted his head. A trickle of blood leaked from his nostril. He knuckled it away.

It smelt of sweet peas.

My mate's attention returned to me. "What's this shit about Merry's freedom?"

"It was a bargain—he said if I forgot about destroying his cyreath, he'd free Merry from the curse holding her imprisoned."

"But you didn't take it."

My cheeks heated. "No."

"That's it?" Trowbridge probed. "Our amulets' freedom for his?"

Ralph flashed a sulky blip of muted light.

"Not amulets, plural," I corrected. "Amulet. Ralph's freedom wasn't on the table." I stared at Ralph, and as I did the comprehension that had evaded me started to prickle. I was on the cusp of something important, if I could only untangle it. "The old buzzard said that he'd only release Merry from her curse, and not the Royal Amulet, because—"

I stopped right there with a sharp, quick inhale, for my brain had been darting back and forth, from creek conversation to Spectacle, from Merry to Ralph, from flares to prophecies.

And I finally saw it; I was Einstein squinting at a blackboard. "We're going to live, Trowbridge," I whispered.

"I'm not following any of this," Brutus said.

"Of course, we'll live," said Lexi in a low voice. "Our mage requires it."

My fingers bit into my mate's biceps.

Home, home, home . . .

"Hedi," said Trowbridge sharply.

I replayed the scene in my head. What had the old man said? "The wizard said the curse on Ralph was a lot more solid than Merry's and that breaking it would result in an explosion of light that could be seen for miles. That's why he wouldn't release Ralph from his curse—not because the conjure holding Ralph was beyond his capability to remove but because destroying the curse would bring unwanted attention to us at the creek." I gazed at my lover's beautiful face and saw a future that didn't end with him blown apart. "Goddess, you won't have to go kaboom."

"Good to know," he said slowly.

I wanted to laugh, to twirl about and shout in glee. "You're not following any of this either, are you?"

"Break it down for me."

"The Raha'ells believe that your flare is supposed to lead them to the promised land. That's the prophecy, right? According to it, your light is supposed to become as bright as a blue flame, and a hot as the sun, and then, presumably, you're going to explode, and somehow that will lead them to the promised land. But they have it all wrong, don't you see?"

"Keep talking."

"It's not the Son of Lukynae who has to explode to fulfill their prophecy—it's the enchantment holding Ralph prisoner." I jerked my chin at the amulet shining on Trowbridge's chest. "*That's* the light that will lead the Raha'ells to their freedom." My gaze jerked to Lexi's. His head was bent, providing me with a three-quarter profile. "How bright will the explosion be when Ralph's spell is broken?"

A muscle moved in my brother's jaw, and there was a significant pause before he answered. "Those who do not bury their heads in their hands will be temporarily blinded and incapable of following evidence of your trail for an hour, perhaps more."

Trowbridge's face went very still. "Blinded?"

Lexi raised his chin to give Trowbridge a slow nod.

"Trowbridge," I said excitedly. "We won't need the Gatekeeper's secret tunnel to escape the castle. We can walk right out of the Spectacle and then right through the castle's gates. The prophecy will be fulfilled—you will lead the Raha'ells straight to the Safe Passage. But you won't have to explode doing it. We could be home in hours!"

"I like it," Brutus said, one large hand rubbing his chest. "I don't understand it, but I like it."

"Aye, but it will be a cursedly slow exodus," grumbled Danen. "Our people are in the prisoners' pens. After the amulet explodes, they'll be as blind as newborn pups."

Trowbridge kneaded the back of his neck. "Not if they're warned." He stared blankly at some spot over my head; then in a low voice he asked, "Mouse, can you get Danen, Lily, and Brutus inside the Spectacle grounds? Close enough for them to get to the pens?"

Mouse considered it for a second. "I think I could get them past the castle gates, into the enclosure, with Gwennie's help, but getting them close enough to the pens—"

"I'm not helping you!" the servant girl squeaked.

"But Alpha"—Mouse lifted his shoulders apologetically—"your face is too well-known. If you come with us, I couldn't get farther than the pig's trough . . ."

The skin around Trowbridge's eyes tightened. "I'm not coming with you."

"Eh?" said Brutus.

Trowbridge gave us a smile that wasn't. "I'll create a distraction—during which the three of you will give our pack their warning—then I'm going to let them take me."

No.

Danen rose, the dead guard's clothing in his hands. "You'll let yourself be captured?" Disbelief rolled in his words. "The Son of Lukynae?"

Trowbridge nodded, his gaze shuttered. "And when they bring me to the Spectacle grounds before the king, I'll be wearing the Royal Amulet."

No and no. "But Ralph's going to explode! You'll lose your head!"

The amulet on Trowbridge's chest let out a series of white flashes.

"I'll survive," he replied. "I'm a Were."

"No! That's a stupid plan." My blood rushed to my head. "Why can't we just sneak Ralph into the grounds, and hide him somewhere he'll do the most damage?"

Trowbridge's expression turned hard and stubborn. "I have to be wearing him when I'm brought into the pens."

"Well, to quote you, 'bullshit'! And where the hell do you think I'll be when you're creating your big distraction?"

His tone was ice. "You'll be with your brother, destroying the book, like you said you would." When I sucked in a shocked breath, his eyes softened. "We both have our jobs, sweetheart. Neither one's going to be easy."

"We're supposed to do things together."

"But this time, we can't."

"Your mate will indeed survive." Head bent, my twin had gone back to tracing patterns on the glass case. The gold followed the sweep of his finger. "He must. Because our fates are all connected, and it is the wish of our mage that we all live."

"Does he have to talk?" asked Lily.

Lexi lifted his head to coolly stare at my mate for a long beat. "You'll have to be convincing. The king of the court must believe you beaten; else he won't be tempted to personally inflict further punishment."

"Do you hear yourself, Lexi?"

While my twin considered my question, he allowed his palm to rest on the display cabinet. The small moving mountain of gold within it pooled against the inside of the case, seeking contact with his touch and being denied it by a thin layer of glass. "Yes," he replied. "I hear myself speak." Then he continued, "The king's presence at the Spectacle grounds is crucial. He and his court have the most magic; they represent your biggest peril. Thus your mate must be facing the king when the spell is broken. Not just facing him, but in close contact. The king and his court must be blinded." He raised both brows at my mate in an unspoken challenge. "You must lure him very close."

"I can do that," Trowbridge replied grimly.

My gut plummeted, and I opened my mouth to register my alarm. But the words—the usual chorus of "no-no-no"—froze in my tight throat. I'd had my big aha moment, hadn't I? Back at Daniel's Rock, where I'd embraced the wisdom of bearing the awful for the greater good. Two people's problems don't amount to a hill of beans, right?

Trowbridge's scent bloomed, so pungent it bordered on foul.

Instead of talking, I swallowed.

Danen held up the dead guard's jerkin, testing it for fit. "How will we know it's time to cover our faces against the blast? We can't all stand there, crouched over, our hands covering our eyes, and expect that no one will notice."

Lexi's attention returned to the display case and the gold that ceaselessly moved inside its glass prison. "Once the book is in flames, she'll give you a sign from the window of the mage's room. It is in the northwest tower, and has a fine vantage of the Spectacle grounds."

Sweet heavens, from that window I was going to witness Trowbridge being dragged into the Spectacle semiconscious. His head lolling, his feet leaving drag marks in the dirt. I'd have to watch Trowbridge being abused.

My hand went to Merry. She curled a tendril tightly around my thumb and gave it a squeeze.

I couldn't do it.

You have to.

Arms braced on the cabinet, Lexi looked up to Trowbridge. His eyes shone, and underneath the bristle of hair above his right ear the dark shadow of his tattoo could be seen. "Prolong your capture, Son of Lukynae. Give them a hell of a fight. Hedi and my mage will need time to get to the tower."

Then Lexi seemed to droop, his back bowing, and to my ears his next words seemed forced out. "I'm counting on you to get her to the Safe Passage."

With that, whatever worry I'd had about Lexi's health status faded. *Oh shit.* In all the dying and running and arrows and strange and nasty clouds I'd forgotten one very pertinent piece of information. "I still don't know how to open the Safe Passage," I said, appalled at my own carelessness to detail.

"T'ahara," whispered my brother.

So much for it being a long string of magical words, impossible to remember. "Like 'Sahara,' except with a *T*?"

He jerked his chin down in a curt nod. "Use the coin; say the word. Then go home."

"I—"

"You'll need to deal with my mage from here on," he said.

I started forward, intent on touching him, perhaps holding him here with me, in this room filled with jewels, but he lifted a hand and showed me his palm.

It was pale, like he was pale, and it was firm, like he was firm.

Stay back, it said.

"I hate good-byes, so let's not do it, okay?" His eyes studied me, their expression pained and haunted. "Just be who you are. All the way. I'm counting on you to do what you normally do."

Before I could ask what he meant by that, Lexi formed a fist and brought it down hard on the glass. The case shattered, the gold skittering away from the broken shards. "My contribution to the anarchy that will follow. If I were you, I'd set fire to this room. That will attract attention, and give you and your Raha'ells a chance to pick your places."

He pushed the long sheet of his hair over his shoulder. "I'm going to go now," he said simply.

Then he closed his eyes.

The moment the Old Mage stepped forward, my brother's body language changed. It gave me no comfort to spot the difference between the two souls, because it was still my brother's lips that moved into a superior curl and his voice that drawled, "You have a boon to ask of me, Hedi of Creemore?"

I've lost him and I may never see him again.

Lexi.

Trowbridge moved closer until I could feel the heat of him warming my back. That and the acute hate I felt for the man who wore my brother's face made my mouth curl. "I ask you for no favor. We're brokering a mutually beneficial agreement."

"Then speak." The Old Mage fussed with Lexi's sleeves. "Let me hear the conditions."

"Here's the deal: I will release you from your sacred vow if you break the spells holding the Prince of Asrais *and* Merry on my command, and open the Safe Passage on my request."

"On your command?"

"Yes."

"And in return, you will not harm my cyreath."

"I didn't say that." My Fae was on alert; I could feel her press against my throat.

He considered me, then smiled. "Do you think to test your meager magic against mine in Threall? Think carefully, nalera. You are but an ant to me. If you travel to that realm, I will trap you, like the insect you are, and you will spend the rest of eternity sitting under your tree, talking to your brother."

"You can try."

He chuckled, and I clenched my jaw. And I was glad I did, because that's when my twin's face began to shimmer just like the space between the two birch trees had before the magic doorway had materialized.

Trowbridge's arm curled around me, bracing me for what followed.

The shimmer was just the warm-up—a watch-this-bitch alert. For right after that Lexi's expression slackened and the challenging light in his eyes faded to black. And then that ugly shimmer turned to a frightening ripple of skin and bone and tendon.

I've seen Were transformations. I've seen bones elongate and fur grow.

But this . . .

I stood there, in that small room, smelling Were and magic and fear, and knew that I could do nothing to stop my brother's features from reshaping into something ugly and worn—his firm skin turning into thin crepe, the line of his strong jaw blurring under pouches of hanging flesh.

Don't weep.

I bit down harder, clenching my jaw until it hurt, forcing the gasp of pain and horror inside my chest to remain trapped behind the enamel of my teeth as I watched all remaining traces of Lexi's physical presence—from his Regency-hero boots to that long spill of blond hair—be wiped out as effortlessly as a dry eraser on white board.

There's gone and there's *gone.*

I thought it was bad when the old man stepped forward and used my brother's tongue to form his words, but . . . fuck . . . this was worse. Standing near the shattered glass cabinet was an old man whose white-cropped hair hadn't seen a brush in a millennium or two.

The Raha'ells drew their bows. *Goddess, I'm getting used to the sound of that.* Then Gwennie moaned and slid to the ground in a dead faint. *Wimp.* Trowbridge drew me tighter against his strong, steady heat.

"Steady," he said.

"I *am* steady," I replied.

The illusion was solid. Lexi's physical presence in this realm had been replaced by an old man who wore a wizard's robes and a pitiless expression.

Brutus gaped at the old man. "Who is he?"

Mouse lowered the ornate shield he'd grabbed from the wall. "It's him."

Brutus nodded, arrow pointed at Lexi's chest. "And who's him?"

Don't think—do.

"Brutus," I said, "allow me to introduce you to the Old Mage. He's the prick squatting inside my brother. Don't get too close to him. Because I'm going to kill him later today."

Now...

Chapter Twenty-four

My lover dozed, head resting on my lap. I wanted to sink down to curl into his embrace, but I was doing my bit. Watching the door, and the twisted old geezer, as my Trowbridge shook off the effects of the swig of sun potion he'd taken.

The Son of Lukynae and I had decided, following the obligatory who's-the-Old-Mage conversation (the Raha'ells had been of the opinion that Lexi was a whacked-out druggie, not a pitifully possessed soul), that I'd be the last person to sip from the bottle of sun potion. Other than Trowbridge, none of the assembled pure-blooded wolves had ever taken it, and the first hit of the juice was guaranteed to be the most potent. I'd taken two doses over the last week and was half-blooded Were: it was a given that my recovery time would be swifter. Proof: Gwennie and Mouse had hardly blinked after swallowing their dose.

But the Raha'ells . . . Ah, they were neophytes to the potion. As feared, they'd slumped into varying degrees of slack-jawed inebriation after taking their first sip. Quite the anti-climax. Here we were supposed to be storming the castle and they were snoozing on the tile.

I carefully folded the letter I'd composed to Cordelia and

lifted a hip slightly to slide the letter into my jeans pocket.
For all my stealth, the movement jostled my lover. He
roused from his deep sleep enough to mutter something
indistinguishable under his breath.

I hummed, lightly using my nails on the bristles of his
shorn hair.

His expression calmed at my touch.

It was a small thing, but it made me happy.

Plan B's details had been fixed before the bottle of juice
had been tapped. Mud would be removed, hair shorn, and
disguises donned. Mouse, Danen, and the others would
gain entry to the grounds through the kitchen and the war-
ren of passages that led from it to the prison yard. They'd
be carrying water buckets and wearing the dead guards'
uniforms. While they passed liquid refreshments among
those unfortunates in the pens, word would be spread.
Meanwhile, Trowbridge would be busy creating his disruption.

But before this happened, I would accompany the Old
Mage to the tower and the rooms that he once called his
own. Where I'd watch from a window as the old buzzard
put a match to his book—my greatest contribution to my
new pack's liberation being to give the cover-your-eyes-
and-tuck signal and say the single word that would break
the enchantments holding Merry and Ralph prisoner.

Yes. After this, it would be all action.

Though perhaps—Goddess willing—my heroic part
would be played later in Threall. If not . . . I checked my
pocket superstitiously and felt minutely better when I heard
the crackle of paper.

In the meantime?

I might never get another opportunity to watch Trowbridge sleep. *He's so freakin' beautiful.* Watching his chest
lift was more soothing than listening to a cat purr, more

peaceful than watching leaves sway. Up. Down. Up. Down. A slow rise and fall.

My eyes burned and I looked away, wondering for the sixteenth time what was with the old man and his sleeves. He kept fidgeting with them. If their length bugged him so much why didn't he make a minute adjustment to his illusion? After all, what I was seeing amounted to mage-glamour, right? The long cowl-like sleeves, the white, disordered hair, the rope belt that cinched his tunic—all those items were no more real than his slightly yellow teeth.

My twin's still there. Submerged beneath this piece of visual trickery.

Though the glamour was a telling thing about the old wizard's personality, wasn't it? He must have a very sentimental attachment to his former body. Why else would he reproduce a wrinkle-for-wrinkle replication of it? Seriously, had he ever looked at himself in the mirror? He's ancient. Given that he could have produced a highly fictionalized version of himself, he should have gone for a few minimal upgrades. A sorely needed face-lift. Some muscle definition. A few very necessary vertical inches.

And what's with the wizard robes?

Dumbass. How can anyone run in long skirts?

Guess running away wasn't his response, was it? Come to think of it, the Old Mage's go-to reaction seemed to be magic and treachery.

Remember that. He's not physical: he doesn't jab with the fist or kick out with his legs.

Whereas I am.

Perhaps my relatively new acceptance of violence would work for me in Threall. If I moved fast and got in a few strikes to his throat and nose, maybe I could incapacitate him before he nailed me with a firebolt or one of his curses.

Sweet heavens. To be imprisoned like Merry. Not

being able to run free, not being able to break loose. Not knowing how long the misery would last. The horror of those thoughts sent a ripple of claustrophobia right through me.

There were penalties for losing epic quests. Deaths and imprisonments. Sorrow and prisons. I didn't want to spend eternity in Threall any more than I wanted to die at the hands of the Fae. I just wished . . .

That I could wake up and realize that it had all been a bad dream.

I rechecked the Fae gold's slow progress across the uneven flagstones. Either instinct or intelligence had sent it creeping, inch by inch, toward the hidden doorway in the wall. What would it do when it got there and found its exit sealed?

Could gold weep?

Trowbridge suddenly snorted in his stupor, then sat up, rubbing his eyes with the heels of his palms. Muscles flexed and mud crackled as he stood. He grimaced. "I need to get cleaned up."

"Gwennie and Mouse brought water and some rags." I stood and nodded to the bucket set in the corner. "It should be still warm."

"Where are she and Mouse?"

"They went back out in search of a third uniform." The Kuskador servant's reluctance to abet and aid the Son of Lukynae's freedom force had been taken care of with one quick session with the Old Mage. He'd snared her frightened gaze, stated what we needed, mumbled five words, and then said, "You'll fetch those for us, won't you, girl? And you'll say nothing to anyone as you do. Not by word, or sign, or thought."

And she'd blinked, very slowly, and replied in a doll-like voice, "Yes, I'll do that."

Could the old wizard glamour me into accommodating

his wishes as easily as that? I shivered, thinking about it, and moved closer to my man. I put down the blade and burrowed into his arms.

"Scared?"

"Scared spitless. Aren't you?"

"Yeah, but that's normal. Fear keeps you alive."

"Do you think we'll live?"

"Don't know."

I nodded. "I guess what will be will be."

"You're pretty calm for someone who says she's spitless."

"I can't stop thinking that we were meant to be here. Meant to meet again, meant to love, meant to mate. Ever since we arrived, I've felt it inside my chest—a sense of destiny, acute as déjà vu. I'm supposed to be here. There's a reason I was born with the talent to mystwalk and an explanation for the fact that Lexi was given the ability to borrow magic, but not to keep it."

"So you think this is all a replay, another swing at the bat?"

"Maybe. Maybe in the last life, we lost."

"Not this time." Trowbridge smoothed my hair away from my face. Blue eyes, framed with black eyelashes, studied me. "You'll need to take your dose now."

Would this be the last time I touched him before the next replay of our destinies? The last chance in this life to feel the warmth of his breath on my temple?

"I need to kiss you first," I said.

The request was simple, but it wiped the warrior from his face. He stilled and there was nothing sexier and more potent in that half moment he stared at me and his eyes spoke of want, and love, and sex, and an emotion nearly indefinable to anyone other than a fellow wolf. The closest to it in human-speak are the words "mine, mine, mine."

Then he reached for me, but this time I intercepted him,

for it suddenly seemed so important that I claimed him before he claimed me. I stood up on my toes, twining my arms above his. My palms ran over his shoulders, enjoying the curves of his muscles, the small hollows between tendons. Up to his neck they traveled, my fate line rasping across the shadow of his beard. I cradled his hard jaw between my hands.

Lean muscle under bristles. Hard bone under skin. *Mine.*

He inhaled sharply as my finger ran over his lower lip. "Breathe," I murmured. He exhaled and hot breath warmed the pads of my fingers. *Delicious.* I touched the moisture rimming the inside of his mouth and wet the full lower lip that I meant to claim as mine.

It glistened slightly, and that was all I could see.

Not the room, not the old man who was witness to our kiss, not the terror, nor the future.

Just Trowbridge's mouth, wet and ready for mine. My breasts flattened as I leaned into him. He was aroused and hard. His legs widened, coaxing me to come closer, and I fit myself to him. Soft belly to hard cock. I pulled his head down and brought those lips to mine.

I kissed him.

Small biting kisses to a mouth so willing to open. A nip to the bottom of a full lip. Desire rolled over me. I lifted my mouth till it hovered a scant centimeter above his. Our noses rested against each other, and we breathed as one.

He's mine. He'll always be mine. Through life, through death, through beyond.

I touched my tongue to his.

At that first touch of wet to wet he turned into the Alpha that he was. His hands moved down to my ass. He cupped my cheeks and pulled me punishingly hard to his length.

He was ready. Pheromones spiced his scent, rutting heat radiated from him.

Then he kissed me. Not softly, not sweetly.

He took; he claimed; he imprinted.

He *memorized*.

We could have been lost—the not-here forgotten. And perhaps for a few seconds more we were. Then fresh air cooled the back of my neck and I heard a feminine gasp, followed by the quiet click of the door. I jerked my mouth from his. Twisted my head to check for the source of the noise.

Mouse and Gwennie stood against the door. She looked horrified; he looked fascinated. The old man looked intrigued. They knew. They could smell the sexual want, see it in our flushed faces. Five minutes more and I would have let Trowbridge take me against the wall. In front of *the mage*. With dead bodies on the floor. With Fae gold working its way toward a sealed door.

It is always that way between us.

It always will be *that way*.

Trowbridge's hands slid off my ass and tightened into a locked fist at the small of my back. He lifted me, turned so that his back was facing them, and then he walked us over to the corner, barely missing the stream of glinting gold at his feet.

I tightened my arms around his neck.

He lowered his head so that we could talk. "You know what I'd be without you?"

"A very pretty corpse."

"I was going for heartbroken, but yeah, you had to point out the obvious."

I issued a faint smile. "Being subtle is for pussies, Trowbridge."

"I love you," he said, plain and simple.

And then he kissed me again, except this time tenderly

on my forehead. He eased me back to the floor. "Now take your hit." He pulled out the bottle from his cutoffs' back pocket, uncorked it, and brought it to my lips. I could smell the scent of the other Raha'ells on the rim of its glass neck. Woods, earth, wolf. I smiled for him again—this time showing teeth—and took my medicine.

The potion left a trail of warmth down my throat that warmed my belly. My wolf started to pace, anxious at these new sensations, and my Fae began to nod in happiness, and me? I leaned against my lover and let him hold me as the potion's pleasure swept mildly over me. I was getting too used to it—the high faded faster than an interrupted orgasm.

When I felt relatively normal, I said, "Time to do this."

The Son of Lukynae released me. He straightened his cutoffs, then walked stiffly to the door. He checked the corridor, then jerked his head at Mouse. "How far to the first staircase?"

It was where we'd part. Trowbridge and his Raha'ells would go their way to face their individual destinies, and the old man and I would head toward ours.

While Lexi would sleep.

"It's close," said Mouse. "Follow me."

As it turned out, "close" was an understatement; there was a staircase fifteen feet to the right of the room of riches. It was circular, windowless, and steep. Mouse led the way. Sword in hand, Trowbridge followed, then me, and then the rest of our posse.

Okay, I couldn't help it. I flashed to *The Princess Bride*.

On the ninth stair, the whole file of us came to an abrupt halt when Mouse suddenly flattened himself against the wall. He mouthed something to Trowbridge, then disappeared around the corner. Trowbridge's arm swept backward to press me against the staircase's wall. Danen edged past me, dagger drawn.

"Come back, you!" I heard someone shout.

Mouse came haring back up the staircase, moving so fast past me and the other Raha'ells that I could swear he left a vapor trail. A guard wearing a red uniform came clattering up the stairs in pursuit. Danen's dagger found the guard's heart before he had a chance to do more than widen his eyes.

We left his body there, crumpled on the fifth riser. There seemed little point in hiding his corpse. We had set fire to the jewel room. Already the scent of smoke was wafting its way up the staircase.

Let the mayhem begin.

Four more stairs and we hit the landing. The old man and I were to take a right here, following the corridor until the next staircase, while Trowbridge and his people would continue downward to the ground floor and then part—Mouse and Gwennie taking the disguised Raha'ells to the kitchen; Trowbridge going it alone.

I didn't feel much like the Princess Bride anymore. There's no romance when your stomach spasms in jittery fear, no soft focus against the brightness of blood on Danen's blade.

Besides, Trowbridge and I had had our kiss. I couldn't bear to know that the old man witnessed the intimacy again, noting that this time my hands shook and my lips trembled.

So I said, "Don't get yourself killed."

And My One True Thing said, "Ditto."

Then we—the Romeo and Juliet of Creemore—went our separate ways.

Destiny called.

The utter bitch.

Chapter Twenty-five

"What is the delay?" inquired the Old Mage as we stood in front of the door to his old lair.

"The door is locked." The metal flange bit into my palm. I placed my other thumb on top of the one already set on the handle and tried it again. Nada.

Open up, you freakin' door.

I shook the handle. I needed to be inside. Positioned by the window so I could stare down at the Spectacle grounds and witness whatever would happen. Be ready to give the sign. Say the word.

I'll kick you into splinters if I have to.

"It's not locked; it's magicked. Stand aside. I will open it." The old man moved before I could; the sleeve of his cloak brushed my shoulder and the length of my brother's muscled arm grazed the side of my neck.

Sickness rose.

He flattened his hand on the wooden door and said something low under his breath that I couldn't catch. Sparks—their hue a color-match to the cable of green that streamed from my own hand—flashed between the seam of his fingers.

Me and magic-mine jerked back.

With a small smile the mage worked the handle, and the door swung open as easily as if it had been greased. Pride of possession was stamped by the set of his shoulders. These rooms once belonged to him.

"Enter," he said quite unnecessarily.

I squeezed in sideways, taking care not to touch him.

The square room was a pack rat's delight. Shelves lined the available space of the mage's lair, and they were filled with bottles, some dusty, some gleaming, and books, some with spines soldier straight, some left cracked open.

Despite the clutter, the furnishings were meager. A hard-used pine table, its wood nearly buried under a haphazard pile of dried herbs. A few baskets on the floor filled with twigs and pinecones. A tall stool, the middle rung of which had been worn by a few centuries of foot use. And in the middle of the room, a wooden lectern, on which a heavy book lay open.

The wizard hurried to the lectern. "The insufferable, ass-sniffing toad," he muttered, flipping through it. "Helzekiel's perused all but five pages." His cheeks reddened and his jowls seemed to quiver, an old man enraged. "How dare he claim my work as his?"

He used my brother's voice. And he carried the scent of my blood on him. And the sour stink of Trowbridge's mud shield. And the faint aroma of Danen. And the sweetness of old magic.

I hated him with such a sudden surge of heat that my own face flushed. "Start working on the wards," I said through my teeth.

"Time," he murmured. "It is ever your enemy, is it not, nalera?"

I'd like to kill you now, I thought, watching him push up his sleeves and bend over the book.

Later.

I swung away.

The tower room had two windows. One was full of light, offering a picture of rolling hills. The other was dark, the late-afternoon sun seeming unable to pierce the depths of the mother jinx, whose roiling mass was just visible at its top corner.

Shrugging off the cloak I'd worn to cover my non-Fae-issue jeans, I went to the dark window. It was sealed, and the glass was watery. I found the casement's crank and turned it slowly, inching it open.

Hot air slid into the room and with it the pungent perfume of the Raha'ells.

Their combined smell could be reduced to wolf musk and woods, but Goddess, there was so much more. The scent of the people in those pens spoke to me in a language I no longer needed an interpreter for.

With emotion. Anger. Fear. Desperation.

Maternal grief.

I looked down to the Spectacle grounds.

The area contained by the palisade's towering wall amounted to a patch of land, not much bigger than Trowbridges' front lawn. There were three holding pens, lined up like a row of matchsticks. Each was long and narrow. A press of men had been crammed into the first pen. The next was filled with female Raha'ells and their children. The third was empty.

That's all?

There's so few of them.

Over the last day, I'd grown to think of them as a small army—a hundred strong or more. But now, staring down on them, I realized I'd made the mistake of equating the strength of their reputation with the size of their pack.

There couldn't be more than fifty of them.

How many men were crammed in the first cramped pen? Twenty? Twenty-five? It was difficult to guess, as no one was lining up for a roll call. A few of the men were wounded. They sat slumped at one end of the corral, using the wooden rails as their backrest. The rest were ambulatory, but they milled about restlessly—the fluid grace I expected from their lupine heritage missing. I frowned, studying those men, and realized all of them held their necks stiffly.

Oh Goddess, they'd been collared with silver.

My gaze moved on to the next tight corral. The Fae must have run out of collar restraints, because none of the women wore them. Again, I tried to count heads but soon gave up, because most of those women kept pacing, constantly moving from rail to rail—penned wolves pacing off their prison.

There was no sanitation.

And the Fae had kept the Raha'ells thirsty. The day was hot, despite the approach of sunset, and the splintered bottoms of the water troughs placed between the three pens were bone dry.

I twisted my head and turned my focus to the cluster of Fae who were gathered on the back wall's terrace. The Black Mage stood at the edge of them, easily identified by his somber clothing. Unlike those around him, Helzekiel's interest was not pinned on the cloud over him. He watched the grounds, and the wolves, and his guards.

Next, I searched for the king and found him by the grandeur of his crown. Unnaturally pale, he was a tall man with very long straight platinum hair. He wore a blue jacket, the edges of its sleeves almost as heavily encrusted with jewels as the crown he wore. He stood alone, surrounded by a fan of women.

Behind me, the Old Mage cleared his throat.

"Mutter, mutter, mutter," he began.

Within those three indistinct words the room's temperature abruptly plunged from warm to chill. Then, sparks—lime green, gold green, and citron yellow—started circulating over the Book of Spells. The wizard waved his gnarled hand over them, and those lively glittering bits blew apart in a bright flash that turned his face a grassy shade.

One page down.

His thin lips began to move again.

I swung back to the window and the Spectacle beneath it.

Where was Trowbridge? And how long did it take to go through the kitchen and grab a bucket? Shouldn't Danen and the others be there by now? Had someone stopped Gwennie and Mouse? Had Plan B been scuttled before it had a chance to spread its sails?

Mutter, mutter, mutter.

Another pop, definitely louder than the first.

Two down.

My heart leaped as Mouse finally walked into the grounds, accompanied by Danen, Brutus, and a barely recognizable Lily. A large pole had been strung with buckets. Danen had one end of it braced on his shoulder; Brutus, the other. Lily trailed after them, her head down, her weary posture transforming her into a lowly servant tasked with taking water to the animals in their pens.

I heard a page turn.

Reaction rippled through the prisoners in the first pen as Danen and Brutus drew close. My gaze darted to the guards. Surely they'd notice the stiffening of the wolves crammed in the corral. Surely they'd notice how one of wounded men struggled to his feet. Couldn't they smell the scent of hope was rising?

And sure enough—one did. He started to turn toward the pens, but Mouse approached him, offering a dipper of water. He accepted it, for the day was hot. Mouse pointed to the sky, and the guard nodded. They both looked up.

Good boy. Keep distracting him while the word is passed.

Behind me—mutter, mutter, mutter.

It was Lily who told the men in the pen. I could tell, even though her mouth barely moved, because those lining the rail closest to her seemed to lean forward as one, straining to hear every detail. Then, one man turned to mutter to those who stood in a close press behind him, and from that word spread faster than virus in a classroom.

Their scent changed, defeat sinking under a layer of hope.

Pop!

Three wards down.

"Where's Trowbridge?" I whispered to Merry.

Just then, Brutus looked up, searching for my window. When he saw me, he widened his eyes meaningfully and he looked toward the castle's back gates.

Had he heard something with his ears that I had not?

The answer to that was simple.

Hell yes.

From outside the tower there was a hoarse shout, and then another, and then the guards were sprinting toward the inside courtyard while the archers on the back wall turned as one to train their bows on the disruption.

Don't fire on my mate!

The Black Mage raced to the terrace's wall and braced his hands on it, stretching to peer down at whatever was taking place. Those of the court members closest to the inner wall followed, anxious geese clucking in alarm.

In my mind's eye, I saw Trowbridge's diversion in torturous detail. My man alone, swinging a sword against a horde of armed men. My mate falling, his body pierced with arrows . . .

Don't let them hurt you too much. Don't let them—

More shouts.

Behind me, mutter, mutter, mutter.

Pop!
That's four.

"Talk faster, Mage!" I pressed my cheek painfully against the window's stone surround, craning my neck, hoping for a glimpse of the inner courtyard through the gates.

Anxiety was a gorge rising up my throat, ready to spill into a shout of frustration. But before it could spill out of me, the Raha'ells began to keen as one.

I closed my eyes in relief.

The Son of Lukynae had been captured.

My mate entered the Spectacle grounds heavily flanked by a bevy of guards.

He appeared incapable of walking.

Two Fae dragged him across the rough ground. They gripped him just above the elbows, a position that forced his arms to twist back painfully. As he passed through the gates, Trowbridge lifted his head just enough for me to catch a glimpse of his battered face. Ralph was cinched close to Trowbridge's throat. The gold of his pendant writhed, and his amulet shone so brightly, it was hard to look at.

A woman's voice cried out, "Alpha! We are yours to command!"

The guard trailing behind Trowbridge slammed the end of his staff into the muscles between my mate's shoulders. My mate's face twisted in a rictus of pain.

I can't bear this.

I wanted to be down there with the Raha'ells, growling low in my throat as they growled. I wanted a staff of my own, which I'd use with extreme prejudice. I wanted to grow wings. Huge black ones like an avenging angel's. Wings so powerful and filled with such dark promise of retribution that the guards would tremble and cower as I swooped toward them.

But those are wishes.

And wishes never really amount to squat.

Not when you're standing by a fucking window. My magic flared inside me, hot and wicked. It rose up, up, past my heart, down my shoulders, coursing through my veins, to burn the ends of my hand.

Pop! The fifth ward snapped with a sharp crack, the dispelled magic briefly tingeing the mage's lair acid green.

One to go.

They brought Trowbridge to a patch of beaten earth and forced him to his knees. Then, they all turned expectantly toward the gate.

King Jaden was all about the show. He was the peacock in full display as he sauntered across the grounds, followed closely by his entourage.

"Hurry up, Mage!" I hissed over his mutters.

My love's mouth was bloody, his teeth red rimmed.

When the king stood over the kneeling Son of Lukynae, he raised his voice so all could hear him. "On your belly, dog."

For this, my mate mustered a short, but pithy, reply. "Fuck. You."

Jaden gave an amused huff and raised his arm high over Trowbridge's head. Then, smiling, the king started to lower his arm, a few inches at a time.

Very, very slowly.

As if he were pressing down on a great weight.

From what I could see, the Fae didn't have anything in his hand. No weapons, no whip. Nothing except his magic. But it must have been powerful, because Trowbridge flinched as if he'd been struck.

"We are with you, Alpha!" shouted that Raha'ell female again. Except this time she added, "Resist! Resist!" Which prompted another of my mate's pack to begin chanting, "Son of Lukynae! Son of Lukynae! Son of Lukynae!"

Yet another pack member picked up the chorus, and then another, and then they were all chanting, their clenched fists pumping as if they were at a concert, instead of an execution.

"Son of Lukynae!" they howled as Trowbridge's body began to shake.

I'll never know whether Trowbridge allowed it to happen or he couldn't stop it from happening. But part of me crumbled as my mate finally bowed over his knees, his hands flattening on the earth. Then, some unseen force gave him a final heave and threw him violently forward. He sprawled onto his gut, his legs spread, his cheek pressed to the ground.

He did not get up.

The king of the court leaned over Trowbridge's prostrate form to thrust two fingers between Ralph's chain and his neck. Jaden worked the amulet up over my mate's chin and then ruthlessly yanked it free. Then the Fae straightened, and in a dreadful mimicry of the Raha'ells' raised fists he lifted Ralph high in his own.

He pumped his arm twice—smiling to the fading chants of "Son of Lukynae! Son of Lukynae!"—and then pivoted from the waist to play to his audience of entourage.

Yeah. He waved Ralph like he was a freakin' prize.

Blood from Trowbridge's torn ear snaked across his jaw.

"Mage!" I warned in a dreadful voice.

Mutter, mutter—

The final ward broke with a deafening boom, followed by a flash-bomb of cold light that bathed all the items in the rooms—the wizard, the pine table, the once creamy pages of the book and me—with a horrendous lime green.

"Torch the book!" I screamed, reaching to pull Merry off my neck.

The old man conjured up a miniature fireball, as easily

as I might flick a lighter, and tipped his hand sideways. The tiny burning ball fell on the book's curling pages.

Whoosh.

That easy. The Book of Spells was aflame.

"And now my vow to *my* Maker is complete," he said, staring at the blaze.

Bully for you. I swung back for the window, prepped to do my part and see the prophecy through. And as I did, I heard the old wizard speak again and I smelled magic, but it was magic of the dreadful sort, sweet as cane sugar, as oddly thick as an overripe banana.

Then I got hit with a custom-made conjure.

Chapter Twenty-six

I was struck, mid-torso, by a blast of pure energy. No sparks, no light, no blare of trumpets to warm me. It felt as if Goliath had made a fist and punched me in the gut. It hurt so badly; there was an element of disbelief to the pain. Ever hit your shinbone hard enough to feel light-headed?

My magic surged from me as I staggered backward, and without even thinking we reacted. *Take this.* My talent whipped across the room, a green serpent cast on doing some damage on a lying piece of shit.

But as she flew, the wizard swiftly made a motion. A shield! It was too late to issue a magic-recall and far too late to recalculate the GPS. She hit his ward with an inarticulate cry of horror. Instinctively I wrenched my hand back. Instead of popping free, she stretched obscenely, her nose firmly attached to that thing he'd cast.

"Give me the word!" I shouted. My magic rippled and rolled, panicked to free herself from the sucking ward that held her fast. My arm bucked with each of her gyrations. "The king's going to kill Trowbridge!"

"Not yet," the wizard murmured. "He'll toy with him first."

"You son of a bitch! Give me the word!"

"Be calm. Accept your fate."

"Death?" I choked out. "We die, you die."

"Rest easy, nalera." He brushed the soot off his sleeve. "Neither you nor he will face an execution. There is no need, for there are alternatives to death." He glanced down at what remained of his book. "Punishments that inflict no physical pain. Prisons that have no bars."

My magic thrashed at the end of my line, a tuna running on the hook. I both felt her wild gyrations and didn't, because my brain was taking the pieces of his word puzzle and putting them in awful order.

"The Sleep of Forever," I whispered.

The Old Mage nodded. "Precisely so."

Trowbridge and I lay in some dark and dim room, our bodies useless, only our brains awake. Two wolves caught in a forever trap.

The wizard picked up a page, grimacing when it crumbled to ash. "Rest assured the Royal Court will not risk losing their only wizard. In light of the circumstances, they will be agreeable to condemning both of you to an eternal rest."

"But you're not their only wizard."

He looked up. "I will be."

I could hear my talent inside my head; she was screaming.

"You planned this," I said shakily. "Right from the beginning when you forced me to switch places with Lexi so your soul could share his body and not mine. You wanted to claim his muscles as your own. His legs, yours; his voice, yours. You never intended to share, not for three days, not for a week. Before I even agreed to your bargain, you were calculating how to smother his soul."

He pushed himself from his lectern. "You give me an omniscience I do not possess. One might anticipate the future, but one may never fully control it. A mage must always react to new circumstances, choosing the best option among the opportunities presented. But yes, the demise of your brother's soul was certainly predetermined as soon as our pact was sealed. I cannot share a body with one who is unwilling to take care of it." He studied me for a moment. "Will you accept your destiny calmly?"

"No."

He snapped his fingers.

And with that gesture, the fire that always made my fingers tight and my blood race began to cool. *Sweet heavens . . . no.* In front of my eyes, my talent's color—that glorious vibrant shade—faded from a flashing florescence to a watery, icy green.

"Stop it," I said.

"As you wish." He waved his hand, and the suction that had kept her blind head attached to the invisible wall seemed to break. She slumped, limp. Using both hands, I hauled her toward me, trying to gather her thinned body into the safety of my embrace. But with each tug, she frayed and split a bit more.

And then, she broke apart into fragments.

Pale flickers of bits of magic sought to form a shape and failed. Without direction, they rose in a disorganized cluster, seeking an exit and not finding one, because the one that had hurt them stood between them and the window. So they went higher, streaming toward the tower's domed ceiling, stopping short of it at a rafter. One bit attached itself, and then more layered on, until they resembled a swarm of honeybees.

"Magic-mine," I whispered, my tone broken.

"Now you have no more magic than your brother," he said.

I tore my gaze from her and saw that hidden smirk. "I'm going—" I didn't finish the threat; I just went for him.

The pine table was between us.

He flicked a finger—just one—and that table flipped over, not a slow slide but with supernatural speed, and not as a result of Newton's law but at the wizard's behest.

The harvest table became the flyswatter and I the fly.

It carried me for a few feet. Merry went with me, tumbling and bouncing against my chest. Then, it flipped over to crush me under its weight.

It was just an old pine table and everybody knows that pine is supposed to be a light wood, but I could barely breathe under its supernaturally oppressive weight. I could barely turn my head, the fit was so tight.

Merry scrambled up to the hollow of my neck, her feet stiff with distress.

Have to get it off me.

I am wolf, and I am girl, and those two words put together mean "powerful," but the wolf had been half-starved and well beaten and the girl . . . she'd been beaten too. The best she could do to raise the ponderous load was a shortened arm curl. I gave that a try, and the animated table pushed right back with a brute force devoid of sentiment or empathy.

Oh Goddess, I'm going to suffocate.

Every inhale only encouraged the table to bear down harder.

We're trapped. Again. The memory of the wolf trap and that horrible fear was too fresh. I started to panic, pounding on the wood with my fists, calling for my magic.

Help us!

With three we're stronger.

"God's teeth," he said irritably. "Cease your struggles."

Words almost guaranteed to send me into a tizzy of rebellion. But taking out my fear and frustration on the cursed object squeezing down on me hurt me much more, because the table took insult to being beaten by my fists.

Calm down. You're only hurting yourself more.

I told myself that I didn't need as much air as I thought I needed. That I had to take shallower breaths. Think my way out of this. *Don't pant. Don't panic.* I fought to adjust. To the table's weight. To my terrifying vulnerability. To the fact that I couldn't hear my magic and that the coil of her was no longer a warm weight attached to my hand.

I needed a focus point. I rolled my eyes toward the Old Mage. The toes of his shoes curled upward. The hem of his robe was rimmed with dust.

You stole my magic. And now, you're trying to hijack my destiny.

No.

This is NOT how it's going to end.

"I must reintroduce myself to my court," he murmured, strolling over to the window. For a second or two, he just stood there, checking things out at the Spectacle grounds—a handy target for an arrow or a meteor shower of fireballs.

Come on. Take him out.

But not one single shaft whistled through the window's open arch. Even when he propped a bony hip on the window ledge and leaned an arm out.

Somebody shoot him.

What he did next was simple and awful. He opened his palm—pretty much like someone checking to see if it was raining—and said, "To me."

Just like I said "to me" when I talking to my talent.

Except the world doesn't tremble when magic-mine and I have a one-sided conversation. People don't shriek in abject terror. Skies don't rumble, and lightning doesn't flash. And the stink of ozone doesn't squash the scent of every living thing.

The Old Mage backed into the room, holding out his arms stiffly, and as he did the barometer plunged inside his lair and the magic pressing down on me became unbearably heavy. Above his lined palm was a thin curl of cloud smoke—foul smelling, spitting red bits of ugly stuff.

I forgot about not panting. I forgot about being calm.

Goddess, he's brought that evil into this small box of a room. With growing horror, I witnessed the mother jinx's tongue touching his fate line. She tasted it, and when she found the dry skin agreeable I watched her give herself to him.

She streamed into his flesh.

She poured into his palm.

And the rest of her—the huge, stinking, thunderous mass that boiled in the sky above the Spectacle grounds—followed.

It was a small room, not built for that much magical energy, and the mother jinx funneled through the open window like a twister coming in for a touchdown. Her noise was the howl of a crazed wind, the shriek of magic unleashed. She circled her mage, and the old man smiled broadly, his head turning to and fro, as he watched the mage-loving tornado turn around him.

Other things were caught in the vortex of that evil. Baskets, pinecones, glass vials, books, dried small animal parts, herbs, and, strangely enough, a perfectly upright stool.

But not the harvest table.

Nor the girl being panini-pressed beneath its weight.

Or, for that matter, a hive of stunned bees, clinging to a rafter.

When the wind began dying and the ozone began clearing, the breakable items that had been pulled into the air fell and broke. Glass shattered; baskets rolled; the stool landed with a thud, its legs sticking upward.

"Yes." The Old Mage's back was to me. "Now, they've noticed me."

I felt another rib go.

"Magic-mine," I gasped, "come to me."

The wizard leaned out of the window to shout, "I have come back from death, Helzekiel! How dare you parade my accomplishments as yours, you whoreson!"

Helzekiel had a response for that.

The old guy saw it coming, and faster than I would have given him credit for being capable of doing, he jackrabbited back into the room, narrowly avoiding the fireball that whizzed through the window.

Whoosh. The Black Mage's balyfire imploded on the wall near the doorway.

Sparks burned through the denim on my right leg, and a sheet of them cascaded from the lip of the table pressed upon me. *If they start whizzing fireballs in here, I'm going to be Joan of Arc.* Helpless, I watched the old wizard straighten his clothing and smooth his hair with the hand that wasn't clenched into a tight fist.

"And now, we wait," he said, sounding satisfied.

"I'm going to kill you," I promised.

The table grew heavier by another ton.

I may or may not have had a brief time-out there. I couldn't move my head anymore, not from side to side, anyhow, and soon the overall pressure became intolerable. Dots formed; blackness encroached . . .

The thudding of many feet roused me from my daze.

They're coming, I thought. *The court, the guards . . . all of them . . . and all our plans . . .*

It's done. Our epic quest is finished.

Trowbridge, I'm sorry.

I gazed up at my talent and condemned her for her cowardice. We could have been stronger together. We could have fought together.

The three of us: Hedi. Wolf. Magic.

Couldn't she see that?

Then, strangely enough, I heard echoed shouts from the bottom of the stairwell. A loud argument ensued, though the words were mostly indistinguishable. The dispute was followed by a pause, then the sound of a single pair of feet mounting the stairs at breakneck speed.

One man. Not an army.

How fast could someone climb seventy-two stairs if he was hauling ass?

I concentrated on my magic, willing her to hear me. *There's still time,* I told her. *We need you.*

And you need us.

Helzekiel might be Mr. Evil Black Mage, but taking those stairs at a gallop winded him. From the hall I could hear him struggling to catch his breath. It was overloud, a scorching inhale followed all too quickly by a hoarse exhale. He took but a moment to collect himself before trying the door's latch.

I heard it swing open.

"You!" he hissed.

With the weight of pine pressing on my temple, I couldn't turn my head to personally witness what new hell was coming my way. But I knew it was the Black Mage, because he carried with him a presence of darkness.

Let one of them kill the other. It will give me time. My gaze moved from the hive that glimmered weakly, out of reach—*hear my call, magic-mine*—to the Old Mage, who stood framed by the window.

Intent was written on his face, and his clenched hand . . . it glowed. The clouds had fed on the hunt and supped from the Raha'ells' pain. And perhaps it had taken not their lives and their hurts but a portion of their soul-lights too.

Could that be done? I don't know.

But magic turned dark, glowered inside his palm, red

and angry, making his flesh appear pink and translucent. His finger bones gleamed, long gray-white ribs, and his knuckles—

Oh, shit.

Those knuckle bones tightened.

The old man flicked his wrist and threw.

The curse's flight was soundless. But as it whizzed over my table, the entire room seemed to flex in its wake. The burden crushing me briefly lifted, the table being caught in the suction of the aftershock. I hauled in a much-needed quick breath before the ponderous weight crashed back down on me.

Another rib broke.

When the Old Mage's curse hit, it exploded over the door, not the assistant.

There was whomp of pushed air like a giant's hand wiping a slate clean, and then I was experiencing the horror of being trapped and helpless as the tower room's heavy oak splintered into a detonation of dagger-tipped shards.

Old wood was turned to toothpick tinder and spikes of javelin-sharp terror—and it felt like three-quarters of it was rat-tat-tatting into my pine table. But by divine intervention, not a single shard ripped into the body of the girl who lay beneath the pine slab's protection.

However, one long-tipped missile found a soft target.

The Old Mage cried out and folded at his waist. Big hero that he was, his bandy legs held him for a half second; then he slumped slowly to the floor near me. He fell to his knees, his legs splayed wide open, his hands clutching his belly. Then, his chin lifted and he stared at me in wounded and childish surprise.

Good, I thought savagely, knowing with one glance that

it had to be excruciatingly painful. The splinter of wood was driven deep into his side. *You haven't felt pain for a long time, have you, buddy?*

Some men—be they Fae, or mortal, or something in between—aren't born heroes. They're plotters, quick to spot the opportunity. Thus, in the face of agony, the mage did what he was inclined to do naturally—he stepped back from the source of his pain and let someone else endure it. His illusion started to melt away. Jowls firmed; the pore-heavy skin smoothed; the eye pouches lifted.

Bit by bit, the man beneath was revealed.

One long sweep of matted hair, one pair of haunted eyes.

I stared at Lexi.

You look so battered. So pale. So sickly.

"Lexi?" I gasped.

"Shhhh." My twin made a fearsome face, his features twisting in extreme effort, the way they once did when he was a kid and deeply focused on something.

All I could think was—

Don't die. Not in front of me.

Not while I can't do anything for you but watch.

He grunted through his teeth, and suddenly the punishing weight on top of me went away. Without any visible abracadabra, the table ceased being a three-ton curse and returned to being a table.

I could breathe. I could twist my head.

I flattened my palms on the pine slab and pushed. Seconds earlier it had been a heavy torture, but now it lifted relatively easily, if one didn't take into account a few broken ribs. It raised with my effort, a foot at first, then more—enough for me to brace my knee under it. It took a howl of pain and another heave to breach the table's point of balance.

It tipped over and crashed to the flagstones.

I was free.

Arms hugging my ribs, I rolled to sit up.

Lexi was so pale. The only thing bright was his blood.

He said five words. "Get out of here, Hell."

Chapter Twenty-seven

Helzekiel stepped over the door rubble, pausing only to pick up a particularly sharp and stabby piece of wood. You didn't need to be a Mensa member to figure out what he was going to do with his splinter of oak.

He walked straight past me, his gaze fixed on my brother.

You're not staking my brother.

I rose silently, half-bent at my waist. I had no magic, and my sense of direction seemed tilted toward the left, the result of one or the other of my recent beatings. But damn, I could move my arms again, and I had a hard head and 120-odd pounds of force working in my favor. Plus, let's not forget, enough hatred to fuel a nuclear reactor. Put bluntly, if hate was all I had I could transform my body into a mage-seeking torpedo.

I went for the tackle.

He heard the soft pad of my moccasin-shod feet. As I flung myself at Helzekiel's back, he pivoted quickly on his heel, his arms opening to receive me.

We toppled.

I landed on top of him in a terrible mimicry of intimacy,

my breasts flattening on the chest of the man who'd broken my brother. My eyes lifted and locked with his.

Helzekiel's irises were a half shade lighter than his black pupils.

I watched those dark circles widen.

"Your eyes," he breathed.

I head-butted him. Forehead to nose. Cartilage cracked, and blood smeared, and then we were rolling. Briefly he was on top. My wolf snarled, and then I was on top. Over and over, we rolled, dried heather crackling beneath our struggling bodies.

I had nails and teeth. I went for everything I could reach. His neck. His cheeks. The skin above his wrist.

I was the honey badger of revenge.

He slapped me. My head whipped to one side. Another blow and he was on top, his knees pressing on my shattered ribs. I screamed, drumming my heels. Merry was a hot coal scuttling up to my chest. Above his head, I saw movement on the rafter. A swarm of tiny lights. Faint pinpricks, getting brighter, purer, sharper.

Greener.

"Come," I urged to my talent, parting my lips.

Helzekiel's eyes grew darker, speculation swimming with sex hormones stirred by his questionable conquest. He lowered his head, putting his mouth on the place that Trowbridge had marked. As I struggled, Helzekiel's tongue wet my skin with a long, insulting lick—a sickening prelude to what he planned next.

But there, at the base of my throat, his tongue met something unexpected. Hot. Metallic. Moving. He stilled. Slowly his head lifted. He stared at the taunt, flexing golden links, his brows pleating.

"Recognize the gold chain, do you?" I purred.

Merry sprung.

* * *

Orange-red was her belly; needle sharp were the ends of her articulated vines. She latched on, pinching his cheek with her pincers.

More blood dribbled, sweet as freesias.

I went for his eyes again. With a grunt he captured my clawing hands, snaring them together with one of his. Once he held them in an iron-tight grip, he slapped the heel of his other palm on my jaw, keeping my head firm to the flagstones, and pushed away from me. The links of Merry's chain were piano wire against my neck. I felt the burn and then the cut, and then the air was twice perfumed with freesias.

I'm going to lose my head.

And it was going to be cut off, far less neatly than Marie Antoinette's.

So be it. I wanted to tell to Merry to not stop, no matter what. To keep torturing the bastard who'd imprisoned her inside a hunk of amber, even if I lost my head. To never let go of his jaw, to never cease her efforts to gnaw her way to his carotid artery.

Kill him if I cannot.

A nice sentiment, but I was inarticulate with pain, close to passing out.

Already I saw moving spots above me.

Bright glittering bits of green.

Goddess. Magic-mine.

I opened my mouth to the small cloud hovering over me. My Fae talent thinned to a stream and came back home.

Reduce, reuse, recycle. Never had a PSA seemed so applicable. I did not allow my magic to sink to my gut. She was a tool of war, like my brain was a tool and my wolf's strength was a tool. Separately we were broken; melded together we amounted to half-broken.

But it would do.

I'd make it do.

Merge. All of us together. Sister-wolf, frightened Hedi, magic-mine.

Take from this; take from that.

Merge.

Through my bloodstream my talent surged, and she brushed against my will and took from it direction, and she slid against my wolf's feral heat and took from it muscle.

A fine specimen of wrath, she erupted from my fingertips.

New. Improved. And oh-so-very deadly.

My gaze went to his, then beyond him. I bared my teeth—a feral wolf, a bloodlusting Fae.

Target found.

Go. Grab. Use.

My pearly whites were the last things Helzekiel saw before my magic brought the marble mortar down on his head.

My twin had used that instrument daily to grind herbs and the eye of newt. That was his part of his job description, along with hunting wolves and being the Black Mage's Shadow. It was a familiar tool for Lexi. But now it was my mine.

Five pounds of stone make for a good cudgel.

Blood sprayed.

As it does.

The mortar lifted and fell. On each lift, it felt and looked a bit different. Wetter, heavier, uglier. Bash. Grunt. Bash. Grunt. I repeated the cycle until we could do it no more, and then we released our cudgel and heard it crack in two as it hit the floor.

Helzekiel's body lay partially over mine, an unforgivable weight on my ribs. *Get him off me.* Whimpering, I pushed his broken head off my shoulder and wriggled out from under him.

I rolled away from his corpse to face the window. *Blood and death used to sicken me. And now the only thing that sickens me is my own pain.* Magic-mine moved, tugging my hand to slide toward what interested her. My gaze numbly followed her progress to Lexi.

She nosed his boots.

All the wailing should have stopped, I thought, but it hadn't.

Lexi's head was bent, in contemplation of the wound and the stick, and the long smear of blood that coated his shirt and the top portion of his pants.

What is that noise?

I fought to place it. I could hear Lexi's shallow breaths, and my own fast breathing, and the sound of Merry curling a few of her vines into a crazed and complicated awful nest around her red-orange belly. But over that, something louder.

I turned my head to locate it. It came from outside.

"Son of Lukynae!" I heard them chant. "Son of Lukynae!"

Trowbridge.

"Lexi!" I shouted, rolling to my hands and knees. "Break Ralph's spell!"

My twin blinked very slowly, as if wakening from a dream. As I crawled to him, his head turned slowly to me. He looked dazed.

"Say the word!"

His brows pulled together.

I grabbed his shirt. "You told me at the creek that you could see some of the stuff the Old Mage sees, know some of the stuff he knows. Especially when he's concentrating hard. You must know it. We need the word!"

My brother's face shimmered, glazed, and then a haze went over it. My brother's firm, sharp jaw sagged. The skin below his eyes grew fleshy as the Old Mage struggled to take over his body again.

"Go away!" I screamed. "Go away, Mage!"

I shook my twin as hard as I could. "Lexi!" I pleaded. "You're strong—dammit, you're a Stronghold. We hold. We don't give up. You hold for me. You push him back. Find me the word. Break the spell."

Keening cries from outside.

Tears clogged my voice. "Everything we've gone through. Everything you've suffered and I've suffered. The way Dad died, and the way the Fae executed Mom. She bled out on our kitchen linoleum, Lexi. She died in front of me. And I couldn't stop it. I was trapped inside the cupboard. All of life has led to this. Fight back."

He whispered, "I always fight back."

"Then keep doing it."

"Jaden is at the bottom of the tower. It will come down when the curse is broken."

Two twins stared at each other.

One taproot, one destiny.

I nodded. "Then let it."

"Warn them," he said simply.

I dragged myself over to the window and pulled myself up, holding on to the lintel. Shakily, I yanked Merry over my head. I placed her on the windowsill. I tried not to look at what was being done to Trowbridge, to look beyond that. But he felt me. He had to have, because he raised his anguished gaze to mine.

"Wolves!" I yelled. "Beware!"

"Aisce!" screamed Lexi.

One word. One short, single consonant blew apart Merenwyn.

I'll never know what it actually looked like.

Before Lexi had uttered the word, I'd already thrown my arm over my face to block the oncoming explosion of light and swung away from the window. I was facing the interior of the room when the twin curses blew apart.

There were two shock waves. *Whomp. Whomp.* One lifted me clean off my feet; one slammed into my back.

As I hurtled through the air, I knew nothing.

Not my name. Not my destiny.

Not anything.

I was alive. I knew that because I hurt really badly.

Ambient noise was gone, replaced by a strangely muffled quiet. Dust motes hadn't finished their dance. They hazed the air around me, blurring details.

Had the tower come down?

The domed ceiling had a portion blown out of it, and a long vertical tear drew a jagged line down the tower's wall. I could see light through the doorway where there should be no light.

Somebody was going to need to call Mike Holmes.

My hair was in my mouth. I lifted an arm to do something about that, then noticed that bits of my magic coated me, a green shimmer on my pale skin. Healing me, I decided. Soothing the small cuts on my arm, the many nicks on the back of my hand.

All one again. My wolf's heat warmed my core.

"Lexi?" I whispered, turning my head to the side. A shred of bookbinding peeped from under a drift of heather. It fluttered as I breathed, so I pursed my lips and blew a whistle of air. It rolled away, a fragment of spent evil, coming to rest at the heel of Lexi's boot.

He was facedown.

"Lexi?" My heart skipped a beat, taking in his immobility, and then kick-started again when he groaned. I rolled to my hands and knees. The glow of the setting sun illuminated the open arch of the window. Its casement hung from one hinge, twisted and paneless.

Trowbridge.

I crawled across the rubble to the window, grabbed the stone ledge, and used it to haul myself to a semi-upright position.

Below me, the birth of a legend.

Bodies everywhere. Moving bodies, dead bodies, people soon to be dead bodies. Ralph's blast had mown down those closest to it. As the base of my tower, the corpses of the Royal Court lay strewn in an outward fan. Their colorful clothes were tattered; their legs and arms were posed in ugly attitudes of death.

But beyond, in the Spectacle grounds proper . . .

The area contained by the palisade's tall walls wasn't a theater of death. It was the scene of an ongoing massacre. For Ralph's blast had not just killed and blinded; it had mown the Fae down. And now a race of people denied respect, the right to peace, and the basic right to life had broken free from their pens.

The Raha'ells were on a rampage.

I searched among them and found Trowbridge, easily identified by the ring of warriors who surrounded him. The guard he was choking was in his final death throes, and as I watched Trowbridge finished him off by snapping his neck.

"Son of Lukynae!" the wolves roared.

Frenzied and fueled by the complete belief that every brutality they wished to do was deemed both just and right and had been predicted by a prophecy made long ago, the Raha'ells fell upon the rest of the Fae.

We can be animals, we wolves, even when we wear mortal skin.

"Hell," I heard Lexi rasp.

I spun around. My twin had pushed himself onto his knees. A braced arm kept him from falling flat again. His head was bowed, and his long golden hair hung over his face.

"Do it," he said hoarsely. "Go to Threall and finish it."

Bloodlust in my veins.

Yes, we are predators, we wolves.

Chapter Twenty-eight

A fierce desire to protect and a darker wish to spill some blood while doing so can turn a mystwalker's soul-soaring flight into mach-five super-drive. All of my usual let's-go-to-Threall teleportation routines—think up, think fly, think there—were telescoped into one fluid rip of the incorporeal from the physical.

Without the usual agony, I was *there,* up in Threall.

That fast.

I came to consciousness before my corporeal shape had fully formed. Kind of ugly, watching my soul-light being encased by the layers of things I understood my body needed: bones, and arteries, tendons and muscles.

Instead, I focused on the stumps studding the small clearing. Perhaps that's how the old wizard had untangled the magic required to conceive his spell of glamour. He'd spent centuries watching new mystwalkers materialize in the clearing. Lots of time for him to study the process and to deconstruct it for his own use. By the time the pool of test-subjects had thinned, he'd figured out how to create an illusion of a body.

Then, he sat back and waited for a sucker.

I'm going to hurt him bad.

"Come alive," I heard Mad-one say, her tone urgent. "You must make haste."

I gave myself a self-check. I was almost good to go: I had legs that I used to stand. I spun in a careful circle, searching through the mysts for Mad-one. "Where are you?"

"Where I have been this age," she replied sharply. "Guarding your citadel. If you have the belly for battle, make haste to me, for I grow weary."

"I'm almost ready. Give me a second to grow another arm."

"Are you strong, Hedi of Creemore?" she said in a softer tone. "For you will need be."

"I was born strong," I said without any irony.

"Then prove it so," she told me.

I didn't have a good comeback for that one, so I kicked off and took to the air, the Tony Stark of Threall. Streaking across the tops of the trees, piercing through blue mysts, moving so fast that the cyreaths cradled in the boughs of the old trees below shuddered in my wake.

No loving heart had I. My thoughts were simple.

The old bastard hates pain, does he? Well, I'm going to whack his soul-ball like it's a piñata holding on to the Earth's last cache of Cherry Blossoms.

And then I'm going to tear his soul to shreds.

We are one tree, Lexi and I.

Two black walnut seeds that had spliced together, producing one taproot and a trunk. But as the citadel of our souls grew toward the sun, the stem of the tree split in half and the heart of one tree turned into two very distinct trees.

My half of the black walnut is stunted in terms of upward growth, though I'm not ashamed of its lack of inches because it's obviously healthier than its twin. Solid limbs, thick curving branches, heavy foliage. Also, my soul-ball is enviably firm; the hues that spun from it are green-gold, with intermittent flickers of brilliant blue.

As a soul-light, I'm stunning.

However, it was obvious that I was never meant to be a mage. For my side of our shared tree had never sought to stretch impatiently for the sky and the colors of my cyreath hadn't been mixed from a royal palette of reds and purples and blues.

On the other hand, my twin's citadel was a sample of what happened when three fairy godmothers named Fate, Karma, and Destiny warred over a man's future. He stretched for what he couldn't reach, and his health suffered. His walnut tree was raddled. Stripped of bark in places, and with broken branches.

It was very, very quiet in the little hollow where our tree grew.

Not even the wind sighed.

"Hello, my name is Hedi of Cremoore," I murmured. "You tried to kill my brother. Prepare to die."

I floated, eye level to the soul-balls that hung from Lexi's side of the tree. Mad-one had been right on the money: I'd arrived in Threall not a minute too soon. The old man's sagging cyreath was collapsed over my twin's, turning two distinct shapes into one deformed blob. The interior of the mage's soul-ball emitted a steady throb of a red-tinged purple light.

Ugly.

I couldn't see much of Lexi's soul-ball, except for what meager amount was visible beneath the old man's smothering weight: a half inch of firmer material and a thin wedge of jewel-toned light.

Talking of Mad-one, where was she?

I pulled back, my gaze roving the small clearing, in

search of her. A visual sweep of the shadows cast by the trees and the tall grass didn't produce her. I narrowed my search to the ground directly below my hanging feet. There I saw a flash of blue and followed the hem of her gown to the shape of her, kneeling at the base of our tree. Her eyes were closed; her hands were flattened, the palms on our joined lower trunk.

She looked up, her face screwed in pain.

"Hurry," she gasped. "Complete your task."

I nodded, returning my attention to the pressing problem of parting the two soul-balls. *Forget going for the piñata stick.* I couldn't beat the old man without harming my brother's soul. I was going to have to get my hands dirty to remove him.

My flesh crept at the thought.

Touching meant intimacy.

Fully anticipating a blast of wizard nastiness, I reached for the old man's cyreath. But instead of hearing the old man nattering in my head, demanding what the hell did I think I was doing, I heard the low hum of distant two male voices. A mental shield had been placed around me.

Thank you, Mad-one.

I scooped up the old man's sagging soul-ball—grimacing at its faint dampness—and raised it carefully. It stretched as I pulled upward, elongating into a teardrop shape. I increased the pressure by increments, hoping for the sweet spot, where his soul-ball would slough off Lexi's easily. And it was working, or I felt it was, until I encountered resistance.

Crap.

"Mystwalker," groaned Mad-one. "Make. Haste."

I shoved the limp mass of the old man's cyreath to one side and bent to look at the place where the two souls touched. What I saw at first glance was a lot of mushed-up goo. *Don't be joined.* I ran a finger through the wet stuff

and found a faint seam. I followed it, heart dropping. Goddess, the skin on Lexi's cyreath was so thin. If I tore it
wrong, the essence of him would come spilling out of his
soul-ball.

Suddenly the Mystwalker cried out.

The old man's thoughts had been focused firmly on my
twin's sudden inflexibility, but now he turned to inspect me,
caught with fingers where they shouldn't be.

He sent a hot poker through my temple. It didn't matter
if he didn't actually have a hot poker—that's what it felt
like. I couldn't see through the pain, but my hands kept
moving. Pleating up the fabric of his soul-ball, following
the seam line.

I can endure this. I will endure this.

He switched weapons. "Wolf-loving whore."

His tone was low, pitched for a dark mutter and at odds
with his usual patronizing patter.

So he'd dropped the pretense. He was as he truly was.

"Half-born, half-baked, half nothing," he continued.
"Not worth taking to Merenwyn with your twin."

My fingers stilled for a second, and the wrinkled weight
of his soul rested on them.

"The value of your existence was weighed the night Helzekiel executed your mother. You know that, even though
you've told yourself repeatedly that he did not know that
you were there, hiding in the cupboard like a little mouse."

I returned to work, but this time I did it humming "Silent Night."

"But you knew. He heard you," the old man continued
in that horrible whisper. "Gasping in fright. A little mouse,
cowering behind your mother's protection ward. He knew
you were there, but he left you to burn. Because you were
not worth his trouble. Another half-bred wolf to feed? One

with such weak talent? You were not worth his effort. Let her burn."

That's bullshit. I don't believe any of that.

"You lie to yourself, nalera. I can see into you. Part of you is convinced of our low worth, though you have struggled much to push the thought aside." He fell silent, then said, "Now you focus on—"

He broke off to laugh. "Your One True Thing?"

"Shut up."

"The wolf does not love you. Why would he? You trapped him into bonding with you—and you know much a wolf hates a trap." His tone turned guttural. "But perhaps you really don't, for you're not a full-blooded creature. You are neither this nor that. An embarrassment to the man you call mate. An anchor of Fae iron strapped to his back. He wishes to run, but cannot run. He will never run free again."

This was how the old man had broken Lexi down. He found the fears, and the little voices a person can't quite smother, and he used them.

Goddess. Lexi.

"No, your brother's will was surprisingly difficult to conquer. Half-truths would not have worked. Only the bare truth would break it."

I'd found the end of the seam. I needed to concentrate. To pull the old man's stinking carcass off Lexi's gently, taking great care so as to not tear my brother's soul.

Focus on that. Not these lies.

But the voice went on. "When your twin woke in the passage, he demanded answers. He could not understand why he was with a mage—he fears mages—or what was being asked of him. His confusion was not surprising—he was sent into the portal drug raddled and insensible. I informed him that his sister had betrayed him, and had used his affection for her to trick him into a life of sacrifice. I told him how quickly she'd leaped at my offer once she'd realized the scope of her loss of independence."

Lexi, if you can hear me, it's not the full truth.

"Half-truths, full truths. You are ever adept at rationalization."

"Go on, talk it up, asshole." I started peeling him away. "Because I've almost reached the point of separation."

I shouldn't have gone for the cheap shot.

"Hedi!" cried Mad-one.

I looked down just as the old man materialized at the bottom of the tree. He made a sharp gesture, and Mad-one fell over with a cry of pain.

Instinct bowed my body over my brother's vulnerable cyreath. *Freakin'* instinct. If I'd only had time to think about it, I would have realized the safest thing to do would have been to put those cyreaths in the line of fire.

But my instinct to protect is impossible to deflect.

This time, when the old man's hands curled to shape the ball of his curse I could actually see it form into a sphere of purple light, the interior of which was filled with red-tailed comets.

He uses his soul, I thought. *And then this—oh, shit.*

Unlike a ball of fire, there was no whizzing trail of fire, providing me opportunity to calculate trajectories and likely impact zones. The wizard simply jerked his hands again, and that quick movement released his dark conjure, and suddenly I knew real pain.

"Oh!" I cried.

Then, all was in motion. I was a ball, spewed from the mouth of a cannon, flying fast over the wedge of tall grass that bordered the forest. Unable to stop, I tore into woods, hitting trees, breaking branches, and cracking twigs. And with each shiver of leaves, and snaps of green wood, I tore through the mindscape of slumbering Fae.

My run ended abruptly, eight trees in, when I finally

came to rest hanging over the limb of a linden tree. It belonged to a Fae of middling importance to his local village's prosperity. I could taste, as if it were mine, his terror at my sudden intrusion into his sweet dreams.

I was his nightmare.

I pushed myself off the linden branch and fell a foot or more before I remembered how to fly. I heard branches crack to my left. I looked up and saw a torpedo of wizard robes and white hair streaking toward me.

Oh Goddess, he can fly too—

The Old Mage flew as fast as a bird of prey, his talons outstretched.

Indifferent to the soul-balls he left swinging in his wake, he tore a straight path through the tree canopy. He didn't apply his air brake as he came in; he hit me at full force. An eagle's dive-bomb on the field mouse.

It was the type of strike that rattles you right out of your body. Grappling for my face, he grabbed me while I was still spinning. Two surprisingly strong hands pinioned the top of my head, thumbs tight on my temples.

I flailed, striking at him.

His grip was worse than a pit bull's locked jaws.

I couldn't shake him. And I started to hear his mutters again. Louder this time. The long, pitiless stream of them, all strung together without rises or falls.

Fear slashed through me. If he got inside me this time, I'd lose it. I'd lose my mind here, in this forest of strangers. I'd never find my way home. I'd stay here, madder than Mad-one and twice as lost.

No.

I won't let it happen. I want to go home.

I hooked both of my legs around his waist and wrapped my arms around his body. And then, I made us fly. We zoomed through the torn canopies, following the same trail

we'd broken not moments before, heading to the light—
there must be light—to the place where no trees grew except a walnut with a split trunk.

We came out of the woods in a burst of leaves.

I looked down and saw the patch of waist-high grass,
where not one single sapling grew. With a smile as wide
as an avenging Valkyrie's, I dropped us like a bomb.

On impact, we bounced apart.

Those terrible thoughts stopped, chopped off in mid-
stream. I knew I should hurt, but I didn't even feel my aches
anymore. I was beyond that. I lay in a crop circle of flattened grass, breathing through my mouth as if I'd run a
very long race.

Out of the corner of my eye, I could see the wizard's
form. He lay in deeper grass. His illusion had remained
intact; he appeared as corporeal as me. He was immobile.
Flat out. Not moving, not talking, not shaping curses with
his gnarled hands.

But his eyes were slit open, and as I watched his lashes
fluttered.

I crawled over. Pushed aside the long grass, then rose
on both knees over him. I clasped my hands together and
raised them in a knot high over my head. His eyes widened. I saw the color of them and awareness too. *Good.
He'll feel pain.*

And then, without much thought, I brought my clenched
fists down.

Two. Three.

Four times should do it.

Any job worth doing at all is worth doing well. I added
two more blows. Then I pushed myself to my feet—
strangely clumsy—and walked away from that thing I'd
battered. My brain slowly worked to reason it out. Why
wasn't he dead? Why hadn't hitting him like that completed

the job? Because it stood to reason, if he still had a form in Threall—albeit broken, bloodied, damaged—he still had life.

Or at least, access to a soul.

I concentrated on pushing the tall grass apart so I wouldn't crush its stalks under my feet, and on walking slowly and deliberately so I wouldn't tumble ass over kettle, and finally on moving purposefully and forward in the direction I needed to go.

To the light.

I knew how to finish it.

Mad-one lay curled like an infant not far from the base of our tree. Her palms were pressed hard over her ears, and tears ran unchecked down her cheeks. "He won't hurt you anymore," I told her as I passed. "He's not going to hurt anyone anymore."

I tipped back my head and searched for Lexi's cryeath. I could see my twin's soul, a jeweled source of illumination peeping from under a burden of ugliness.

Up, I thought.

It's easy to hover, but it was easier to sit astride a thick branch as I set about finishing what I'd started. I took a handful of his damp vellum and began once again the careful process of pleat and pull.

I could sense the old wizard's presence.

He'd only just realized that he'd attacked a fellow eagle, not a mouse.

I spoke to him as I worked. "Every record of your explorations into magic has been destroyed. No one will ever read it; no one will ever know how far you went. Your apprentice is dead, and with him, the recollection of your best spells. Your name—if it is ever spoken again—will be forever linked to a terrible moment in the Royal Court's history."

I bent my head sideways to consider the seam between

my brother's soul and his. I could see the difference between them now. I don't know how I didn't before.

Their souls had not fully joined.

"You fear that you will be forgotten." I pulled the vellum of his soul-ball taut. "But you were already forgotten, long before you ever attempted to steal our souls. Your importance was dismissed the moment you were sentenced to the Sleep of Forever. Life went on without you." I chose a spot above the seam. "As my life shall. I will forbid your name from ever being spoken in my presence. I will enjoy whatever fate brings me, living among my wolves with my brother, and the only memory I'll allow myself to dwell on concerning you will be this one."

Holding the fabric of his soul tight as a canvas, I stabbed it with my nail.

I tore a hole right through it.

Chapter Twenty-nine

I watched, for once well satisfied to be a witness, as a thin lance of purple ugliness poured from the tear of his cyreath. Then, the skin split and the rest of his foul soul escaped—in a rush—like a two-buck bottle-rocket.

I waited until his soul had spiraled into nothingness before I dispatched what was left of his soul-ball's sheath. Then I bent over my brother's cyreath, focused on the more important task of cleaning all traces of the foulness from it. When I was finished, I ran a gentle palm over it. Patches of his outer shell were thinner than others, where the old man's cyreath had rested hardest, but overall his soul-ball was intact.

"I think you're good, twin," I whispered. "A little dented, but good."

CROSSING FINAL ITEMS OFF THE LIST

Side by side, Mad-one and I slowly flew back to the place where the mage's trees once hulked on the edge of oblivion, the clearing rutted with stumps and bordered by a straggling hawthorn hedge. As we glided over the latter, soul-balls glowered from within its thorny branches.

As I kept Mad-one company, I felt the tickle of Trowbridge's call.

Soon, my mate.

The Mystwalker of Threall's speed slowed as she drifted toward the fence made from branches that had been cut or broken and long stripped of their leaves. They'd been pile-driven into the mossy soil at a forty-five-degree angle, then layered, stick upon stick, until they formed a high, circular wooden fence around an ancient beech.

Mad-one waved her arm, and the branches pulled back, chittering like tiny teeth. She didn't immediately welcome me into her private space, instead hovering by the doorway with an indecision that didn't sit well on her. "None will ever know what wars were fought in this realm," she whispered. "The names of those chosen to defend the Royal Court have already been forgotten." She stole a strangely timid glance at me. "We are the last of our kind. There are no wizards to train those born with the ability to dream-walk."

"Given what I know, I'd say that was a bonus."

"Who will protect these souls?"

"Souls are better left alone to make their own errors and to learn from them."

She crossed her arms, staring at the old tree. "I'm not sure I will return to Merenwyn."

"I'm not coming back, Mad-one. If I leave without you, you'll stay here forever. Alone."

A tendril of blue myst wreathed through a crevasse in the wall of branches. As sinuous as smoke, it undulated past me. My eyes followed its progress as it slipped into the heavy foliage of the tree inside her fence.

It was ancient. Gnarled limbs. Twisted roots.

Was she old? Was that her deal? Was everyone she loved gone?

"Is that your citadel?" I probed.

For a moment I thought she wasn't going to answer.

Then, I saw her throat move and she surprised me by shaking her head. "Not mine. But one who is infinitely precious to me."

Confused, I studied the tree and then the silk damask divan that was placed close to its trunk. I thought of her lying on it, touching the bark of that old elm.

"That's the citadel of your One True Thing."

Her nod was slow and solemn. "Five hundred and more winters have passed since I have stood beside Simeon. And during all those days, he has guarded my body. Fed it nourishment. Bathed it. Protected it as I have protected his citadel from harm." She fingered the belt around her waist. "This body is how I remember being, but I do not know if it is what I still am. My true shape may be as withered as his citadel has become gnarled. I may be—"

"Beautiful. Or ugly. Does it matter?"

"It may."

"If you have aged, then so has your lover. Does the thought of seeing Simeon with thin hair and a stoop disgust you? Would you turn from him?"

"Never."

"Then it's time to go home."

She wet her lip. "I don't remember how."

It was really tempting to tell her to click her heels three times together, but I refrained. She'd become a friend, this woman of the haughty expression, the girl of the tragic past. She was what I could have become. I chose my words carefully. "For me, my mate is my anchor. He's my piece of reality that kept me connected to my real life. So when I need to go home—and Tyrean, we *need* to go home—I think of him; I listen for his voice. He's been calling me for a few minutes. His voice is faint, but I can hear him. And if I block out all the noise around, and all the fears, and the what-ifs—if I search for it and cling to it, I can follow it all the way back home."

She shook her head. "A thousand times I have spoken to Simeon. When he wakes at dawn in Merenwyn, I bid him good morning. And when he tells me that the light has fallen and the stars shine, I wish him sweet dreams and tell him that I will protect him. But none of those conversations has ever brought me home. Thoughts do not take you home."

"Have you tried to follow his voice home?"

"No. I could not. If the mages followed me, they would—"

"The days they could hurt you or those you love are over. Touch his soul, Mad-one. Tell him it's time to bring you home."

She stared at me, chewing her lip.

"Don't trade one master for another. Don't let fear rule you. Let's be brave for the rest of our lives, okay? All the way to the end."

She laid her hand on the rough bark. She closed her eyes. Her communion with her love was silent, but the light in the cyreath that hung from a crooked limb near the top of the tree suddenly brightened.

The Mystwalker of Threall's face softened. She opened her eyes and looked at me, and then her mouth broke into a tremulous smile. She was Tyrean, young and hopeful. "Good-bye," she whispered as her body began to shimmer.

"Safe travels," I replied.

Chapter Thirty

Trowbridge's breath was warm on my mouth. I could taste the essence of him. Courage. Honor. Wolf. Inside my mouth, on my lips. *Am I dreaming? No.* Because his scent surrounded me, cocooning me in its possessive embrace.

Woods and the wild.

And something else.

"Wake up, Hedi!" My One True Thing shouted hoarsely in my ear. And then the ungrateful sod slammed his fist in the center of my chest. Hard. Really hard. "Breathe on your own!"

It damn well hurt. I struck out blindly, the side of my hand meeting hard bone, and then I gasped and curled in pain. My ribs were broken.

I'm back in real time and things hurt just as badly here as they do in Threall.

Reality sucks.

"I'd say she's breathing on her own now," Mouse said.

Yeah? Well, breathing suddenly got incrementally harder, because on the heels of that pronouncement I was dragged onto a pair of hard thighs and I found myself being held tightly—way *too* tightly—and rather violently rocked.

"Ribs," I croaked.

His grip eased.

Trowbridge was alive and strong and now making an effort to cradle me gently in his arms. This was a good thing. I squeezed open an eye. I saw this—my mate's corded throat splattered with Fae blood, and the shadowed walls of the mage's room.

Some of my jubilation dimmed.

Well, Hedi, you're still in Merenwyn.

Gone were the battle sounds—the grunts, the growls, the high-pitched cries. However, the land of the Fae wasn't silent, at least not in the wizard's lair. I could hear Trowbridge's harsh breathing and beyond that the oddest hum.

I pushed slightly against Trowbridge's chest, and he eased me away with acute care, like I was broken or fragile. Which I'm not—recent events having proven that I'm nearly indestructible.

A ring of faces looked down on me. Mouse, with Gwennie peeking over his shoulder. Danen, with his expression set to grave. Brutus and Lily wearing Super Bowl smiles.

I tested my voice. "Did we win?"

"We won."

Gwennie shrank back as a wolf—dark snout, bushy tail—thrust himself into our midst. Lolling tongue. Blood on muzzle. Battle-gleam in his amber eyes.

I did not know him. "Who's this?"

"My son, Tenu," said Danen proudly. "One of our best hunters."

Uh-huh.

The wolf had a wide face and a scent far more pungently lupine than any Creemore wolf I'd ever spent some time with. Tenu stretched his neck to sniff at Varens's moccasin, then darted back when Trowbridge rumbled a warning.

This is my life now. I will be sniffed; I will have no privacy.

I looked up at the man who held me.

Blue eyes glared down at me, the comets in them as bright as the stars.

It could be worse.

"You wouldn't wake up," Trowbridge growled. "Your heart was beating so slow I couldn't hear it until I put my ear to your chest." His fingers dug into me. "Is that the end of it? No more going to Threall? Because if—"

"I'll never go back," I whispered. "I shut that place down."

Which was more or less the truth. For centuries, the mages had searched for those born with a gift to mystwalk. Now there were no more mages left and, for at least a generation or two, none to step into the Old Mage's empty shoes. Plus, given the scary stories and attrition rates associated with being a mystwalker, I couldn't imagine a lot of people voluntarily going there. From infancy they would have heard and believed the tales spun on their mothers' knees: Threall was a terrible place, with curved tentacle hooks that never let go.

Home to women who were lost and slightly mad.

My gaze moved from Trowbridge's, taking in the disaster left in the wake of the explosion. Broken bottles, cracked crockery, strewn straw, a dead mage, and an overturned pine table.

Then suddenly I remembered taking Merry from my neck. Placing her down on the window ledge, turning from her, preparing the blast.

Goddess.

"Where's Merry?" I whispered.

That's when *she* spoke, and my thudding heart forgot how to beat all over again.

"I am here," she said.

* * *

Imagine hearing an angel speak. A voice like a crystal bell quivering in the gentle wind.

My gaze had flown, searching for the source of that sweet voice, and had found her.

"You're so small," I said.

"Shut up," she sang.

"You're like the size of a Barbie."

Absolute truth. Like the pose-able doll, Merry was all long hair, small waist, tits, and ass, but that's where the similarities ended. For despite her lilting speech, my bestie had attitude written all over her. And instead of being Malibu blonde she was the burning shades of maple leaves in fall, brown skinned, her rippling curtain of dark hair streaked with vibrant oranges, searing yellows, and fiery reds. She wore a scowl and a simple long gray-taupe dress.

Lovely. Merry was utterly lovely.

I blinked, then searched for Lexi and found him slumped against the wall, his legs spread out. Soot on his jaw. A scorch-mark on his shoulder. His wound had stopped bleeding. His wolf was healing him.

"Hey," I said.

Lexi looked at me for a long moment. "It's so quiet," he said with an air of discovery.

"That's how it should be," I told him. "Can you walk?"

"Of course I can," he replied, a Stronghold through and through.

I turned back to Merry.

"I want to get this over with."

Two tiny perfect eyebrows raised in query. "Ready?"

For what?

She rolled her shoulders forward; then with a grimace, she snapped them back.

My mouth dropped open. "You have—"

Her finger lifted in warning. "Not. One. Word."

I said two.

"Angel wings!" I crowed. "You're like every myth come to life. You're the real Tinker Bell, complete with the—"

I jerked back in alarm as the appendages in question blurred in indignation, hummingbird fast. She zoomed upward until we were more or less nose to nose and eye to eye. She had soft brown irises and large pupils.

"Snap out of it, Peacock," she said, dead serious. "You have a window open, but it will close soon. Do you hear me? It will *close* soon."

Automatically, I glanced to the mage's window. Night had fallen; the stars were shining. "How long was I gone?"

"Too long," said Trowbridge. "At least a half hour."

It had been minutes in Threall. None of the time lines synched.

A form flitted past the window, then returned to hover. The Asrai stared at me, arms folded, wings blurring. He was Ken-sized, wearing a blue jacket, thigh-high boots, and what was either a pair of hose or some really tight pants. His hair was white, and it flowed down past his hip.

"Ralph?"

He dipped his head in a curt nod. And with a small motion I knew all I needed to know. But in honor of my mom, who was a princess and a woman who always had a gracious word, no matter what the provocation, I said, "Thank you for all your help."

His eyes shone white.

That's creepy.

I was glad when he flew away.

My friend Merry had tiny, tiny white teeth. "You must leave. Now. We could kill only those we could reach. Those who are blinded will recover soon and your chance to leave this world will end. There are three miles of Fae land to cover before your people are safe."

"Agreed," said Trowbridge. "Mouse, if you've got people

you want to bring, you get them now." He gazed at me. "Ready to book it to the Safe Passage?"

Oh hell yes.

Lexi was unsteady on his feet, so the best horse in the Royal Court's stable carried him all the way to the Gatekeeper's swaying rope bridge. And there, in front of his Merenwynian pack, my lover did something extraordinary. When Brutus moved to help Lexi off Jaden's personal mount, Trowbridge stopped him.

"I'll do that," Trowbridge said.

He didn't say that Lexi was forgiven for his dark past. He didn't have to. The pack watched as the Son of Lukynae looped my brother's arm over his shoulder, and then they followed their Alpha, and Lexi, and me across the swaying bridge and up the mountain, all the way to the narrow stairs cut into the rock face and from there up to the wide ledge that looked over a vista of improbable beauty.

I understood another truth during that hurried retreat to the Safe Passage: what people do means more than what people say.

And perhaps Merry figured that out too, because she stayed beside me, her wings a golden blur, her presence a continuation of a lifetime of belligerent devotion. Yes, she stayed by my side—seeing me all the way to my own freedom—but she didn't sit on my shoulder. She hadn't touched me, not once, since she'd gained hers.

An uneasy silence had fallen between us.

She was the being who'd witnessed every good thing I'd ever done—a ruefully short list—and all the bad things I'd ever done: the thefts, the lies. She was the sister who had been there for all weak moments in my life, to comfort me through the whimpers, the tears, and the fears.

I knew that I was going to lose her.

I was both glad and heartbroken.

* * *

It's ridiculously easy to open the Safe Passage once you have the right word and the right coin. I paused to toss another pebble through the cave's mouth. The wind caught the piece of quartz and took it fast, and judging from the pings and dings echoing down the black tunnel and the sudden sweet burst of scent that followed the eventual silence, the current had carried the small stone all the way back to the Peach Pit.

I inhaled deeply. "Smell that?"

Trowbridge nodded. "Apple pie."

I blinked hard against the sudden burn in my eyes.

"You go first," Trowbridge said. "Show our pack the way. I'll watch for the Fae, and be the last through."

Oh Goddess, this was it.

I looked over Trowbridge's shoulder to where Merry hovered. The motion of her wings caused her hair to feather. It was bewitching to watch, as colorful as the maple trees in the fall when their leaves rustle in the wind.

Trowbridge rubbed his mouth. He jerked his head at Lexi and Danen. "I need to talk to you before we start the evacuation. Let's take a little walk." He led them to the edge of the promontory. Mouse kicked a clod of dirt, then followed.

Chapter Thirty-one

"Alone at last." I lifted my shoulders at Merry, helpless in the need to find the right words to say. I needed good ones, multi-layered and multi-meaning. Ones that were easy to say because I had a freakin' lump in my throat.

She flew closer, bridging the gap between us until she was so close I could have balanced her on my palm if I'd lifted it and turned it upward in appeal. I didn't. I wouldn't. I looked past her, to the trees. "You're not coming with us to Creemore, are you?"

"No," she replied, her voice a musical sigh.

I couldn't get used to hearing her talk. I'd imagined her voice so many times—my fantasies providing her with a gruff growl or perhaps a rasping purr. Never once had I given her a celestial one. And yet why hadn't I?

She'd been my angel with bloody knuckles.

"This is where I belong." Her arms rested by her sides, oddly lax. Those years of forced immobility had left her stiff. Perhaps one day her limbs would move as fluidly as her amulet once did.

I just wouldn't be there to see it.

"I don't see Ralph anywhere," I said with a touch of bitterness. He'd stayed long enough to make sure that the King of the Royal Court was thoroughly dead—according to Trowbridge Ralph had taken a piss on Jaden's body—before he'd flown away, without so much as another kiss-my-royal-ass good-bye. "Couldn't he have waited to accompany you home?"

Unless she wasn't welcome home. And if that was the case, then—

"I don't need to be led home," she said.

I picked up another pebble and jammed it into my pocket. "I don't either."

Silence greeted that.

I glanced to her.

She looked away first, refocusing her gaze on Meren-wyn's hills. "It's so green," she mused. "I've seen every-thing through brown glass. The colors of my home world almost hurt my eyes."

My grip tightened on the stone.

"The Asrais have been without the prince's leadership for a dozen or more of your lifetimes," she said, returning to subject of Ralph. "He has returned to gather them into a strike force."

"Lucky them."

Her profile was to me, but her mouth lifted in a faint smile. "The Royal Court has, to use your language . . ."—she paused to make a deliberate switch into English—"got their asses kicked. This is a wonderful opportunity for my people."

"The Asrais are going to war?" I asked.

"We've always been at war." Her gown swirled as she pivoted back to face me. "It is our way."

"You're too good for him," I told her, meaning Ralph.

"I know."

"He doesn't deserve you."

"I know that too."

"And if he doesn't—"

She interrupted me. "There are people I have missed," she said. "Ones that mean the world and beyond to me. I'm going to find them, and when I do, I will stay among them for the rest of my life. I don't want to travel anymore."

"Your family."

"My loved ones."

Did she have a Trowbridge? "You've missed them."

"Always."

"I'm so sorry," I whispered.

And then, because she was who she was despite how she looked—and that meant forever fiery, feisty, and impatient—and because she would always be who she was, whether imprisoned inside a hunk of amber or free to roam the worlds, my dearest friend delivered upon my cheek one of her trademark slaps.

"What was that for?"

"Don't get weepy on me. For I can't cry. None of the Asrais can."

Perhaps not but they can express themselves. As I watched, the hues that twisted in her hair—the burnt browns, the bright golds—became suffused in a warm flush of red.

"That changing-color thing—that was never part of being enchanted, was it?"

"No," she said simply.

The color of love is, and shall always be for me, a deep hearth red. The same shade I'd seen beating from the heart of Merry when I was just a dumb kid, scared of the shadows in my bedroom, and all I had was her light.

A red, protective, loving glow.

I swallowed against the hurt in my throat. "I'm going to miss you forever."

Her mouth thinned in pain; then she said in a tone so low that I knew only I could hear her, "Try not to get into too much trouble. I won't be there to fix you anymore."

"I know."

"We do not say that we love," she whispered.

I nodded.

She didn't say good-bye; she just patted my face again—an angel's kiss—before she flew away. I held on to my tears until she was naught but a tiny fading light in a sky full of celestial lights.

She was going home.

It was time for me to do the same thing.

THE LEAP HOME

I took one big step into the portal, holding Lexi's hand, leaving behind my love, and the gathered throng waiting to take that fateful step into the Safe Passage.

The first twenty feet of the windy ride back home were horizontal and painless. Then, the Safe Passage curved sharply downward and Lexi and I were free-falling.

Lexi and I plummeted in absolute dark, with no sense of how long our descent would be. I'd used up all my breath on my first shriek and was sucking in the required oxygen for my next when I saw a faint light below. That source of illumination grew as we whistled toward Earth, and made it possible to note the Safe Passage's walls in better detail.

They were highly polished.

I thought I saw shadows moving behind their reflective surface and I swear, I heard people crying from behind that smooth wall of rock. Those lost cries should have wrung pity from me, but all I could think of was this: *Get me the hell out of here. I want to go home. Back to Ontario, and the Trowbridge manse, and even the League of Extraordinary Bitches. Please, my kind and wondrous Goddess, return me to the small-world worries of Creemore, and let me enjoy once more the blessed world of cars, and refrigerators, and chlorinated water that came out of a tap.*

Yup. Totally done with the hero shit.

Lexi's legs were longer; thus he hit the ground first with a grunt and a pillow of dust. My own landing was a trifle softer—mostly because I fell on him. He swore in Merenwynian, then choked out, "Move your knee."

My knee complied, which earned another pained hiss from my twin.

Four shallow stairs led to a doorway and my own particular promised land. Through it daylight spilled and blue skies beckoned. Cold air stretched icy fingers toward us, announcing that it was late fall in Ontario.

Home, home, home.

I shoved Lexi playfully aside to double-time up those stairs. But since I knew what obstacles were waiting for us aboveground—the preserve of stone statues, the miniature train tracks, the chain-link fence, the total glory of the Peach Pit—I slowed down as soon as I cleared the last step.

My twin didn't. He'd found his second wind, and he thought he was home, you know? He could smell pie. And earth. And—

Lexi skidded to a stop a scant five inches from the iron rails. He stared at them for a split second, his expression perplexed; then his eyes slowly rolled in disbelief to the wolf monuments and thence to the fence.

Trowbridge had torn up the chain-link fence when he followed me to Merenwyn. Two posts had been completely unearthed. They lay on their sides, their ends heavy with cement. A third and fourth post had been partially excavated; these leaned drunkenly to one side, still connected to the twisted carnage of the remaining chain link.

However, in our absence repairs had commenced.

An open-bed truck had been driven down the Peach Pit's sloping hill (the bakery's owner was going to have a hissy fit about the flattened grass) and parked on the pedestrian pathway between the exhibits. The printing on the side of the Chevy read: "Gene's Fantasy Fences." In smaller print, it said: "Unique custom wrought iron."

Poisonous cold radiated from the truck. With it came my halfling reaction to the Fae's kryptonite: numbing fatigue and shivers. So much iron inside, all of it nearly pure. A barrier made from such pure iron would slow down a horde of incoming Fae.

If not kill them.

New postholes had been dug. But the shovels had been abandoned. And what we had left was a pack of Weres milling about up in the parking lot, none of whom looked all that friendly.

I knew them.

For they were Creemore Weres.

Crap. I knew that Trowbridge and I would have to eventually face the itty-bitty problems we left in our home world. I just didn't expect them to be *waiting* for us. My gaze scanned the half-dozen wolves standing in the parking lot up the hill, noting the presence of my old enemy, Rachel Scawens. Standing beside her was her daughter, Petra.

Petra wore a neutral expression.

I couldn't say the same for the rest of our greeting party. Two days ago, the sum of the Creemore Weres' aggressive scents and brow-lowering scowls would have made my sphincter tighten. But I'd seen stuff since then, you know? I'd seen people fight for their lives, not just because their feelings were hurt or because they were hoping to upgrade their position in the pack, but because they had no choice.

It was either fight or die.

And it was like that for the Raha'ells every freakin' day of their lives.

Rachel had a rifle. Typical.

Two other Weres had brought their boomsticks too.

Also typical.

I smothered a sigh. "Last time I saw you, Rachel, you were walking away from me, leaving me and the others to duke it out with some bikers. And now here you are, with your daughter"—I nodded relatively benignly to Petra— "and a few Creemore wolves. How'd that happen?"

Petra answered, "Cordelia called from a pay phone and said that our Alpha and his mate needed us. Then my mom called my cell and said she needed to be picked up. Once we got her, we came back here because it's the last known location for our Alpha. We found St. Silas and his men digging a new fence."

Succinct and to the point. Man, Petra should write for Coles Notes.

I didn't see the French-Canadian council member of the NAW among the assembled. I asked where he was. And again, an answer that was both prompt and fulsome. "St. Silas and his men are in the bakery, waiting to see what happens." Petra slid a warning glance toward her mother. "We're all waiting to see what happens," she repeated evenly.

Behind, from the Safe Passage, came a lupine yelp and heavy thud.

The first Raha'ell had landed.

Rachel's knuckle tightened on the trigger of her Remington. "Where's my brother?"

"He's coming." My magic shot down my arms, branched out to both hands to painfully simmer at the base of my nails. I eyed the rifle. Rachel couldn't shoot me without hurting her brother.

She knew that.

Another thud behind me, followed by a low growl, and with it the aggression streaming from the Creemore Weres spiked again: a sour sharp scent that completely overwhelmed the scent of pie.

"Sheep's tits!" I heard Mouse say from inside the portal.

And here we go. Once more, a nice visual of my wavering life path splitting into two forks. One way led to waiting for other people to smooth out problems for me. The other—dealing with this lack of respect right here and now—might lead to a non-threatening, but painful, bullet wound.

Seriously?

I'd fought for my life and the lives of those I'd loved, waging war against two Fae mages and a Royal Court, and I'd won. And now I knew without a doubt what and who I was beyond the titles. (Not to get repetitive, but here they are: Daughter of Ben, the wolf, and Rosylyn, the Fae. Sister to a twin, who may or may not have magical powers, once the dust settles. Consort to the Son of Lukynae, mate to the Alpha of Creemore . . .)

All those titles? They're merely notations in my history.

I'm Hedi of Creemore pure and simple. My blood is sweet with Fae magic and rich with lupine pride.

I'm one perfectly imperfect Hedi.

I wasn't going to surrender a quarter inch of the recognition I'd clawed to myself. Not from the hands of my future sister-in-law. And definitely not at the freakin' Peach Pit in front of a handful of fast-food-fed wolves.

I felt my brother's presence beside me and movement to my right, which I knew was Mouse taking a flanking position. I did not take my gaze off the Creemore wolves, who were visibly tensing with each thud-growl coming from the interior of the Safe Passage. The Raha'ells were landing faster than suburban stork deliveries nine months after a blackout.

If they perceived the Creemore wolves as threats; if they thought themselves without a leader . . .

"To me," I said softly in Merenwynian to my pack.

And then I held my breath.

The Raha'ells, still in their wolf forms, slunk up the steps. For an instant, they stood shoulder to shoulder at the portal's entrance—a hundred percent feral—blinking against the sunshine.

Stand with me.

For the record, I *know* I didn't say those words out loud. But as I thought them, I summoned up a visual of myself standing amid a milling throng of wolves. A freeze-frame image of what I wanted, what I needed, what I expected.

To my utter astonishment, less than a fractured heartbeat later I received an image. And then another, and then a flurry of them, as if someone had tossed a handful of vividly painted cards at me.

The images were so clear, so freakin' disorienting. So much like the thought-pictures shared between Lexi and me. Some were color; some were black and white; some were—

Oh Goddess. They're all from my Raha'ells.

For a second or two, or perhaps three, I allowed myself to absorb them, completely oblivious to anything other than the images flooding my mind. Because, sweet heavens, all of those wolf thought-pictures were of me.

Of me.

Images of Hedi of Creemore as seen by her wolves. A young woman standing in the window of a tall tower. A pair of green eyes lit with the unearthly fire of an outraged Alpha. Small hands, knuckles grazed. Her grimed face filled with determination and strength, and—*oh Goddess*—fierce beauty.

"Hell," murmured my brother, his tone shaken.

So he was receiving them too.

The rest of the Raha'ells funneled up the stairs. Lips retracted. Tails rigid. Fight pheromones broadcasting louder than a trash-talking Jersey girl. The first responders hip-checked me in their eagerness to get close to me; the new arrivals weaved in front of Lexi and Mouse, leveraging for a chance to stand closer to me.

I'd called my wolves to me and they'd come.

I'd had this opportunity with the Creemore pack, and I'd let it go.

Never again.

I lowered my arm, letting my hand drop to the wiry coat of the male wolf on my left. His fur was dense under my touch. He leaned into me, just slightly. *When this is over, I will learn his name,* I promised myself. *I will know his family. I will learn everything about everyone in this pack.*

As I will with the Creemore wolves.

"These are the Raha'ells," I said in a loud, firm voice.

One of the Creemore wolves swore softly under his breath. I recognized him—he worked in the city but came home on the weekends. I stared at him, understanding his fear. It was daylight; the moon was long gone. Only the most dominant Creemore wolf could hold on to his animal self after sunrise. And here I was, standing in the bright sunlight, flanked by wolves, not naked people looking for clothing. The Creemore Were had to be calculating how the Merenwynian refugees were going to affect his standing among the Ontario wolves.

Get used to it. Things are going to change.

"These wolves belong to Trowbridge and me. And we, in turn, belong to them, heart, body, and soul. When Trowbridge arrives we'll discuss how these two packs will merge, but in the meantime, Rachel, I'm giving you two seconds to lower your weapon."

Her eyes glittered. "I'll wait for my brother."

"I'm not giving you that option, Rachel." I stared at her for a beat. Then, I said very quietly, "One."

"Mom," said Petra, "you should to do what she says."

"She can't even change into her wolf!"

"Oh, but I can, Rachel. I did it in Merenwyn. And I plan to do it again, every single month. I will run with the wolves because I am one of you."

"She's not the same," Petra warned her mom. "Can't you see it? Everyone should put their rifles away, okay?"

"Not until I see the Alpha of Creemore," Rachel said firmly.

I'm going to enjoy this.

Magic-mine was curling above me, glittering in anticipation. I flexed my fingers, smiling wide, knowing that my face was lit with the lust and joy of battle. "Two."

Epilogue

Sometimes families break up. You don't want that to happen to yours, but all too often it happens anyhow and those who you thought defined you are taken from you.

And you're lost.

At least you think you are. But that's a bunch of crap, isn't it? You know where you are—stuck in some shadow place where grief rules. In the meantime, you're still breathing and you're still moving through the real world, albeit slowly, and sometimes as you go about your daily life your shoulder may brush against another's.

A girl's got to pay attention to those accidental life intersections.

That's how new families are born.

We need them. For without family and friends, our lives are hollow.

I smelled Trowbridge's approach before I heard his tread on the first stair. I expect that's going to be the way of it for the next seventy or eighty years—his scent will reach me before he does. Today, it was a mellow perfume. The sour tones of anger, stress, and unhappiness were missing.

Sooner or later—though not today—I'll tell him that his

personal signature has changed. I don't consider the new element off-putting; its presence is merely another layer to a complicated man. But I hope he won't prod me for details, because I'm having a hard time coming up with a good scent comparison. The smell is not sweet like flowers, and it is not ripe like a wolf returning from his run. But it is as persistent as the lingering scent of charcoal from a recent fire.

Bluntly put, Robson Trowbridge is no longer just "woods, wild, sex, and yum."

He's more.

Merenwyn had forged Trowbridge. It had taken the free-floating gifts that hadn't found a place to stick—like valor and commitment and honor—and made them stick.

Maybe that's what I'm detecting.

I guess we're both more now.

My mate entered our master bedroom, wearing boots, a pair of perfectly fitting faded jeans, and a T-shirt, which he was already in the process of tugging over his head. He dropped the jersey on the floor as he passed the laundry basket. "I need a shower; I smell like a pig."

He didn't. Not one bit.

But he sure loved hot running water. The aluminum rod over the tub needed replacing courtesy of our fun last night. I made a mental note to add "new shower curtains and rod" to the list.

I inserted my chipped nail under the wallpaper's seam and lifted.

Yes.

Carefully, I pinched the hangnail of paper and gave it a test tug. It was all about how gentle you were. Slow is the way to go with twenty-five-year-old wall coverings.

Yes, yes, yes—

It was coming off the drywall in a sheet, complete with the most satisfying tearing noise, and I knew brief jubilation until the inevitable began. The glossy side of the wall-paper started to separate itself from its backing.

No, no, no.

Once it's begun, you can't stop it. As I continued to lift, the paper went from sheet, to thinning strip, to nothing. What the hell did they use to stick this stuff to the wall? Cement glue? I sighed and dropped the paper to the small mound beside my knee.

"So, I'm guessing they found a pig for tonight?" I asked, because I could feel Trowbridge's gaze boring into my back.

"Yeah." His scent curled around me, a coaxing embrace. "All that's left is to figure out where to put the roaster."

"To the right of the barbecues."

"You think?"

Intent on the job, I nodded. "Uh-huh."

The sash made a horrible squeak, and cold air poured into the room. I heard Trowbridge call out the bay window, "Hey, Bill."

"Yes, Alpha?" A voice floated up.

"Tell Lexi that Hedi wants the spit placed to the right of the barbecues."

I glanced over my shoulder. "Close to the driveway."

A hand braced on the sash, Trowbridge twisted to look at me for a second. Then he stuck his head outside again. "Make it close to the driveway—"

"But not too close," I murmured.

Trowbridge drummed his fingers on the wooden frame. With a hint of humor, he said, "Bill, did you get all that?"

"Yes, Alpha."

"Good enough." Trowbridge pulled the sash down, closing the window on the cold air and inquisitive ears. Hands dug into the depths of his pockets, he studied me again. "Shower?"

Tempting. I'd developed such a weakness for nooners. And my mate was a Goddess-appointed natural attraction, standing there shirtless, his jeans riding low on his hips. I made some calculations based on past experiences. "We'll never make it down to the barbecue in time."

"I'll chance it."

I gave him a wistful smile.

"I need to do this right, Trowbridge. It's our first formal gathering. It's important to me."

Resolutely, I went back to the paper, selecting a new piece of forget-me-nots. I gave it a firm—but gentle—upward tug. Success was all about keeping the tension level. Never pulling too hard or too fast.

Say good-bye, little blue flowers.

"You know you're leaning toward obsessive with the DYI, right?"

"Yep," I replied.

Our master bedroom was in the process of a significant face-lift. The work had started nine days ago, after the Alpha of Creemore had entered the room to find me standing in front of its bay window, chewing my thumbnail to a stub as I watched the road.

He hadn't said anything, but he'd slipped between me and the glass. Strong arms hard circled me. For a while, we'd stood melded together, his chin a solid, comforting weight against my temple. When most of my anxiety had drained away, he'd asked, "What do they call all this flowered shit?"

I frowned. "Chintz?"

"Chintz," he murmured with a nod. "I think I'm done with chintz."

There's an antiques store not too many miles from Creemore filled with furniture pieces from an earlier time. My mate brought me there, and I'd wandered the dusty barn for a good two hours, my hand trailing over the pine, the oak, the cherry, and the maple.

And now we have new old furniture.

I like it very much. We've also replaced the old comforter with a hand-pieced quilt. I knew the beauty belonged to us the second I saw the border's embellishment: tiny stitches forming a pattern of entwined ivy. Since Trowbridge is basically a hot-water bottle, we've never actually slept under the quilt, but I'm partial to the sight of it covering our new bed—just as I'm quietly thrilled every time I walk into the room and see the floor.

That I totally love.

Seven days ago, my mate took a break from his Alpha duties to personally rip up all the carpeting. Once Lexi and Petra had taken the pieces away, my Trowbridge had worked on through the rest of the day and night, restoring the oak floor with a professional-grade sander, a few gallons of top-quality polyurethane, and a Dumpster full of choice cusswords.

He wouldn't let me help.

It must be a guy thing.

But now the floors gleamed. Old wood, with old memories, brought back to life.

I'd spent most of my free hours doing the rest. Repainting the trim—*victory!* Making a stab at recovering the easy chair—*not quite a victory!* Then, scrubbing everything that didn't smell like us with a solution made from two cups of hot water, ten drops of thyme essential oil, and a quarter of a cup of borax.

The only lingering trace of Mannus and the eighties was the wallpaper. It had to go. I couldn't wake one more morning to those blue forget-me-nots.

Because, you see, it had been ten days.

Ten *freakin'* days.

I wet my thumb and rubbed it over the film of backing until friction rolled it into tiny cylinders. They fell—*rat-a-tat*—on the plastic sheet I'd placed to protect my oak floors. I started working my nail at the wall covering's seam again.

The bedsprings creaked. I heard a boot drop. "You almost finished?"

"As soon as I'm done with this panel."

"Thought so," he murmured, getting up to disappear into the bathroom. Over the scratch of my *pick-pick-pick,* I heard the sounds of drawers of being yanked open and slammed shut. Then, my nose crinkled. I smelled ammonia.

He was cleaning the mirror? Well, that was a first.

The tap squeaked; water ran.

Trowbridge came out of the washroom carrying a Windex bottle filled with clear liquid. He sank into a crouch, his heavy thigh brushing my shoulder.

He scored the top of the wallpaper with his wolf-hard nails.

"First you have to scuff it up so the water will penetrate. I'll get Jack from the hardware store to bring you a scourer so you don't mess up your manicure any worse than you've already done."

My knuckles wore a line of scrapes.

Balancing on the backs of his heels, he aimed the nozzle at the wall. "After that, you need to wet the paper." He began squirting hot water on the strip next to mine. *Squish-squish. Squish-squish.* "You know, we could easily get Jack and his crew to do this."

"I told you. This is our private place. Our room. Our bed. Our walls."

Squish.

"Yep. Thought you'd say that too." He squeezed the handle a few more times, spritzing the paper until all the blue flowers were slick. "Now, this is the important part," he told me, setting the bottle down. "You've got to let the water do its work." He let his elbows rest on his thighs, hands dangling between his knees. "All you have to do is let it sit."

Staring at the wall, he began a tuneless whistle.

"How long?" I asked.

"About twenty minutes." He gave me a wicked smile. "Maybe less."

I heard a lawn mower start up. Then another.

"You're talking about a quickie."

"Mmm-hmm." His voice was warm butter.

That had possibilities. I let my gaze roam over my mate again.

Thanks to his super-fast-healing Were genes, his buzz cut was fast on its way to becoming a very bad memory. Small black curls swirled at the nape of his neck. And a lot of the gauntness that had produced such spectacular hollows under his cheekbones was gone. My man was rapidly filling out.

It made me happy.

And not just in the "my world's finally going right" kind of way. Nope, the feelings flooding me at that moment were far baser. Trowbridge's shoulders have always rated as a strong attraction, but now they are freaking awesome. My gaze dwelled on them for a second, then moved on to where his jeans hugged the curve of his butt cheek.

My gut tightened. "What's that in your back pocket?"

"A box."

I could see that now. Also this—that it was a very small and very square.

Growing solemn, Trowbridge shifted his balance to extract a ring box. It was royal blue, and someone had wrapped a clumsy bow around it.

Little butterflies—I was positively *aflutter* with little butterflies.

Trowbridge stared at the box for a brief moment, and I got the sense that he was having a bout of minor misgivings.

Come on. You can do it.

He slid off the ribbon. It drifted—thin white crushed silk—to our floor. "I was thinking about your mom's Bride Belt a week ago," he started.

For half my life, I'd worn my mother's Bride Belt around my hips, hidden underneath my clothing. Its chain is made of soft supple Fae gold and the clasp that secures both the belt and the soft leather pouch is jeweled. I always took comfort from its familiar weight. Rattling inside the pouch were five diamonds, each about the size of a desiccated pea.

To me, the stones weren't diamonds; they were relics of spilled tears—specifically, my mother's and my own. Perfect stones born from the tears we wept at the lowest and highest points of our lives.

A birth. A great loss. An instant of great joy.

As sentimental tokens, they were irreplaceable. However, nostalgia is a lousy substitute for having food in your belly and a roof over your head. Ten days ago, I gave the belt to Cordelia and told her to hawk the rocks.

Now Trowbridge set his thumb to the lid. "And that made me think about your tears."

Please don't offer me a diamond ring. Make it anything else. A sapphire, a ruby, an emerald. Don't give me a diamond.

Nothing could replace my tears.

He flicked the lid open. Then he turned his ravaged hand toward me, the jewelry box balanced on his palm like it was an offering, instead of a good thing on the cusp of going very, very wrong.

My gaze dropped on the ring sitting on the satin cushion.

It was a custom piece. Any dimwit could tell that with

just one glance. Made of dark gold, eighteen carats or higher. Not dainty so much as airy. Someone who'd never met Merry might have thought it was a miniature bird's nest. Until they looked at it carefully, and then they'd see that the twigs weren't twigs at all but very delicate vines.

It was exquisite.

"I'm going to miss her too," he said.

Oh, Trowbridge.

"I know the ring hasn't got a diamond in it yet." With some fascination, I watched color spread over his high cheeks. "I looked at the stones the guy had, but they were all shit. None of them was as bright as one of your tears." His neck moved as he swallowed. "If you want one of those diamonds," he said levelly, "we can go look at them together—I'll get you whatever you want. It will fit right in the center and if it doesn't I'll get the guy to make it over again so it will." His gaze dropped to my mouth, then traveled slowly back to my eyes. "But I thought . . ."

"What?" I whispered.

"That we should wait until you get your Bride Belt back."

My voice was a thread. "Trowbridge, I don't have my Bride Belt anymore."

"But you will."

I stared at him.

He nodded slowly. "You will, sweetheart. Promise."

Be careful of those, My One True Thing.

A spark flitted in the depths of his eyes. "You need to believe that people are going to be there for you from now on."

I already have, I thought. *I believed in a man who pushed me off a waterfall. I believed in my wolf, and my magic, and the people of our pack.*

And I believed in myself.

But if—when—my belt was returned and the stones were mine: that was the issue. The concept was sweet, but wearing one of my tears, letting total strangers gape at evidence of my greatest joys and sorrows . . .

I inwardly winced.

He took the ring, pulling it free of the bed of satin. Held it, pinched, so that the twists of gold rose above his scarred knuckles. "I know this isn't Fae gold. And this isn't Merry. And I know that if you wear one of your tears in your ring, we might attract attention from some dickhead who should know better than to mess with us."

Blue comets started to swirl. "But Tink, if that's the case, let them come. We'll take care of them. This is our place and our rules."

His maimed hand moved to my jaw and then upward to my temple. He pushed aside the hair I'd arranged, and tucked it behind my ear. "I don't want you to hide these around the pack anymore." His thumb swept my ear's pointed tip in a gentle caress. "And I say if you got Fae Tears, you should wear them. They're the most beautiful diamonds I've ever seen." His gaze lifted, to wander the room. "This home we're creating—it's just the beginning. We're going to make a pack that's never been seen before. But it all starts with us. Right here. We're the glue." He pulled his brows together, searching for the right words. "We need to make another stand. This time without any mages, or arrows—"

"Or crossbow bolts and bullets."

"Those too," he said. "Life can be short, sweetheart. However long ours last, I want the world to know what you mean to me."

I snared my upper lip to keep it from trembling.

"You are my chosen mate. Stand in front of our wolves with me at the next moon? I want to say the words again. This time with witnesses."

I released the strip of paper I'd twined around my thumb and watched it flutter to our newly stripped bedroom floor.

Tiny blue flowers on a background of cream. Old oak burnished to shine. He'd been married before, to a girl who wore a fussy dress. "I'm not wearing white."

"Tink, you could wear nothing but your Bride Belt and I'd be proud."

I held out my left hand.

He slid the ring over my knuckle. It was heavy. And beautiful. One day—soon—I'd put a tear in it. My eyes burned. "Robbie Trowbridge," I said, not lifting my gaze from my beautiful ring.

"Yes, sweetheart."

"I *really* need a shower."

The Trowbridge drive is a long one and the front lawn large enough that it took two Ontario pack members over two hours to cut the grass. In my opinion, mowing the grass was a wasted effort. After all, it was very late in the growing season and it was Sunday.

Trowbridge had disagreed.

Sometimes, a wise mate knows when to throw her man a bone. Thus, the grass got cut in time for our first "Sunday at the Trowbridges'." Hah. As I'd thought, it was a *totally* wasted effort. Who could see the lawn? Those who couldn't find a place for their vehicle along the drive had parked their cars on the grass. The rest of the front yard was devoted to long tables with fluttering plastic tablecloths, people, and grills.

It took a knowing eye to spot it, but the two wolf packs had carved out their own territories. The Creemore Weres had claimed the gas barbecues. They were proving how very manly they were by cooking chicken, ribs, and premade Angus burgers.

The Raha'ell territory was definitely to the right of gas grills where a rented rotisserie had been set up to slowly roast the pig. The Merenwyn-born wolves were in high spirits and had been since their nose hairs had first quivered with the scent of pork. To them, this Sunday lunch was the perfect combination of two new favorite things—food you didn't have to bring down yourself and useful human technology (i.e., battery-operated spits).

Yes, I was working the pack. Which reminded me; I bestowed a nice smile Rachel's way. If she was going to be my actual sister-in-law instead of my metaphorical SIL, I could make the effort.

She flinched and looked away.

You'd think she'd get over it.

All right.

My new life in Creemore wasn't going to be Camelot.

I have a bitch of a future sister-in-law who'd added to her list of grudges a broken nose and a fractured jaw. And the two wolf packs hadn't merged yet. But that will happen; I know it will. Eventually emotions or hormones will come into play and the tipping point between the Raha'ells and Ontarians will occur. There'll be a lot of drama and perhaps some blood.

But we've faced worse, Trowbridge and I. We'll work it out.

That's what we do.

Anyhow, I wasn't going to worry about it today, because it was Sunday and hellooo, I'd just got engaged, and plus, I had things occupying my attention. Like, for instance, keeping myself away from the grill area entirely, as I didn't want charred meat scents to taint the hand-knit sweater that Mickie Kellerman had left in a gift-box on our porch.

Back in the summer, I didn't know Mickie's name. As far as my memory served, she was the Creemore bitch who spent a lot of time at Sandra's Knitting. I have since memorized the face and name of each member of both packs. I know their mates and families. I know their ages, their occupations, and whether they're into baking.

This was one of my new occupations. Besides being Trowbridge's sounding board, I deal with the people-side of the pack.

I know, who knew?

But you know what? As Trowbridge had pointed out, eventually you have to stop thinking that Karma is out to get you and choose to believe that she's pushing you in a better direction. Life can get not only better, but it can also get good.

I am already a complete believer of that philosophy because the benefits of the Stronghold–Trowbridge union are multiplying faster than bunnies on fertility drugs.

Example?

When I'd dropped by to thank Mickie for the present, she'd taken an obvious shine to me. She and Bert were childless and had developed a special interest in the Merenwyn mutts, particularly Mouse and Gwennie. For some reason, Mouse had convinced the Kellermans that I walk on water. The end result is that I'm now happily anticipating mittens and a matching toque for winter.

Yes, life is good, though I'll always miss Merry. No one had remarked upon the ring on my hand, but the sweater's sleeves were long enough to hide it and I wanted to enjoy the secret for a day. Now I rolled the ring with my thumb, turning it until the nest of gold was warm on my palm. I made a fist, wistfully wishing Merry could see how my life had turned out.

And strangely, I felt better.

"Do you find these biscuits dry?" asked Mouse, chewing slowly.

"They're called cookies here." I took another swig of grape juice to wash the cookie dust down and placed the bottle on the table beside my porch rocker. "Mouse, humans say you should never look a gift horse in the mouth."

"Why not?" he asked after a thoughtful silence. "Stands

to reason that if a mortal is given a horse, he should make sure it's of sound health. Poor sod's got nothing else going for him."

Truth.

And here's another: Mouse needed to go to school, where he could learn about humans, and gift horses, and PlayStation, and hockey. I'll head over to St. Hubert's on Monday and get him registered. Maybe I'll talk with the headmistress about tweaking the curriculum so that lupine pride is merged with some Fae recognition.

Trowbridge broke away from a group of Weres to walk toward the porch. As he passed a small clutch of women, they visibly melted—those jeans cupped the swell of his ass almost as neatly as my two hands—and this time I didn't feel like tearing their collective hearts out.

I don't live in jealousy anymore.

He's mine.

Another fact, this one without a shred of myth to it.

My One True Thing leaned down to plant a kiss on my temple. "Everybody's got food. I'm suddenly sleepy. Want another nap?"

I grinned.

He stepped back so that I could uncoil my legs, and as he did his gaze casually roamed over our pack and, from there, beyond. Suddenly he went as still as a pointer spotting a pheasant.

Trouble? I pivoted to see what had raised his interest.

A car.

Even from this distance, I could see that the old red Subaru was filthy. Bug guts coated the glass where the wipers couldn't reach. A tall woman sat behind the wheel. Beside her, a slighter silhouette. The driver turned the dusty sedan into the long driveway.

"Oh."

My hand traveled to cover my trembling mouth.

"Mouse," said Trowbridge quietly. "Go get Lexi."

The driver braked—her head swiveled to take in all the vehicles, and the people, and the general carnival air—then she touched the gas again and let the old car motor up the drive, and as she got closer I could see her red hair and her big hands on the wheel and the final knot inside me loosened.

Ten days.

I'd missed her so.

My Cordelia was a woman who took her word very seriously. I'd asked her to take Lexi's daughter, Anu, away from the dangers of this life, and she'd done so. Right after placing that collect call to Petra, she'd headed for the West Coast. She'd driven straight through, leaving without her clothing, makeup, and, most important, cell phone.

She'd motored through four provinces and 4,921 kilometers without knowing if I was alive or dead.

There'd been no way of reaching her.

Best I could do was make sure a message waited for her in Prince Rupert. We knew that she read it because Trowbridge's friend called to say that he'd watched her unfold the paper. According to him, she'd sat for a couple of minutes staring blankly ahead. Then, she'd refolded the paper on which the e-mail had been printed, said something to the teenage girl sitting in the passenger seat, and driven away.

It takes five days to reach British Columbia and an equal number to drive back. *Ten freakin' days.* She could have called collect to ease my mind. She didn't.

I guess in her mind that was fair. It was my turn to fret.

The Subaru drove right past the Raha'ells' pig feast, right past the beer table, all the way up to the burning bush that anchors the northeast corner of the Trowbridge house.

She turned off the car, then snapped the visor down to check herself in the mirror.

People stopped talking.

Lexi came around the side of the house. He wore mortal clothing: a pair of jeans and a shirt that hadn't been tucked in. Today, he bears little physical resemblance to the Black Mage's Shadow. Gone is the long sheaf of blond; his hair has been shorn to a half-inch stubble. If possible, he looks harder and tougher. I have to work not to stare at the paw print inked over his ear.

The jury's out on my twin's future.

I don't know how much magic he retained from those two days in Merenwyn. If he has some, he hasn't demonstrated it. If he has none, he hasn't complained about it.

But that's my twin.

And only he can make peace with his wolf. He goes down to the pond most nights to sit on my pirate rock, to stare up at the moon or perhaps the air above the pond. I can't tell which. A few nights ago, I joined him. We didn't talk about anything important—he asked me a few questions about iTunes and its cloud, which I couldn't really answer (who the hell knows what the iCloud is?), and eventually our conversation died out. We sat quietly on our old pirate rock, at rest with each other. When the cold got to me, I started shifting toward the spot where I could wedge my foot for an ungainly dismount.

He leaped to the ground with effortless lupine grace. He held up his arms and took my weight. Then, he stood there, not letting me go, but not really holding me. I'd said, "We'll face the moon together."

His hug had bruised my ribs.

So, I think there's hope.

Cordelia opened her door and slid out of her seat as if she were wearing a pair of Jimmy Choos and a beaded gown, not a pair of flats and a crinkled skirt. Her red wig needed a wash and restyle. She rested an elegant arm on the top of the car.

Arctic blue eyes studied me, then softened. "So. You're not dead."

"I'm not dead."

Strange. As my mouth started quivering in earnest, hers clamped down. Forever, the ying and the yang. Over the Subaru's roof, she gave Trowbridge a tight smile and he gave her the old Robbie Trowbridge grin, and life was almost perfect, though Anu hadn't opened her car door yet.

My niece sat, clutching her pet ferret in a death grip, staring at my brother through her window.

Lexi cast me a helpless look.

There was a lot of crap I could have said and questions I could have asked. But this isn't Camelot. This is simply my new life, with my family once more almost intact, and friends, and cookies, and the smell of grilling meat.

I opened my arms wide. "Welcome home, Cordelia."

Acknowledgments

I'd like to thank my editor, Holly Ingraham, for buying my first novel; for leading me through the highs and lows a novice writer is sure to experience; and for giving me consistently strong advice. But mostly, I'd like to thank her for being who she is: Holly Ingraham, St. Martin's best damn editor *evah*.

Next, I'd like to mention my amazing agent, Deidre Knight. I had a manuscript in deep need of burnishing. Deidre showed me how to improve my writing, and then springboarded that debut novel into a four-book contract. Along the way, we've gone from freak-outs to laughter, from contracts to conventions, from agent-client to dearest friends. She is the best agent you could ask for.

Additional thanks to the lovely Bella Pagan, my UK editor, and the fabulous art design team at Pan Macmillan.

Last, here's to the people who helped me cross the finish line: Julie Butcher, Suzanne McLeod, Rebecca Melson, Janice Pia, Kerry Schafer, Tricia "Pickyme" Schmitt, Amanda Seebeck, Susan Seebeck, and Lynsey Taylor.

extracts reading groups
competitions books new
discounts extracts
competitions
books new
events books
extracts
new titles reading groups
interviews
events extracts
discounts
new books events
events new
discounts extracts discounts

www.panmacmillan.com

extracts events reading groups
competitions books extracts new

reading groups

events

books